The Diomedeia

Printed by KDP

ISBN: (pbk) 978-1-7782977-2-4
(hb) 978-1-7782977-0-0
eBook: 978-1-7782977-1-7

DokNyx Publications

The Diomedeia

Diomedes, the Peoples of the Sea, and the Fall of the Hittite Empire

Sello del rey Suppiluliuma y de la reina Tawananna hallado en Ugarit

Royal Seal of Suppiluliuma II

Gregory Michael Nixon

Dedication

For Gurby, who never believed in me,
thus inspiring me to finish.

CONTENTS

Appendices:

I. Invasion & Migration Routes of the Peoples of the Sea:

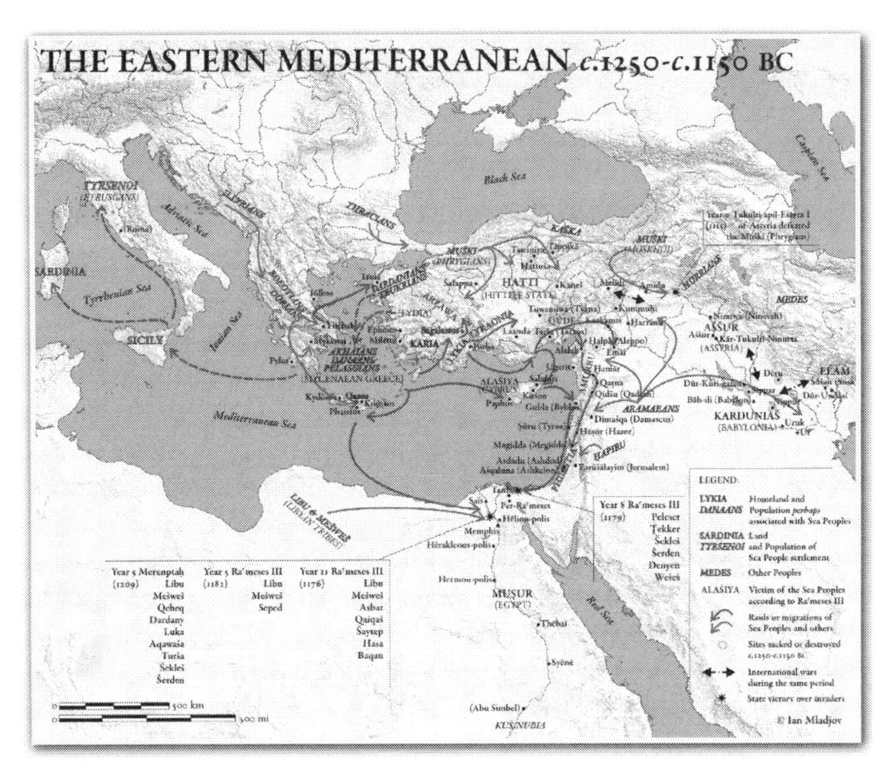

Note: The best map of the Hittite Empire and its dependencies about 1260 BCE is on Ian Mladjov's Maps page. It's too colourful, dense, & detailed to post here, but everything in the book is on there. Plus it's so huge, you can zoom in: *https://drive.google.com/file/d/1rtFuyZcdw5wR7f65hIqcsY5m66onF07a/view*

—A "3D tour of Hattusa, the Hittite Capital" can be found here: *https://www.youtube.com/watch?v=CgH4CxQrgRc*

II. Anatolia & the Hittite Empire, ca. 1250 BCE

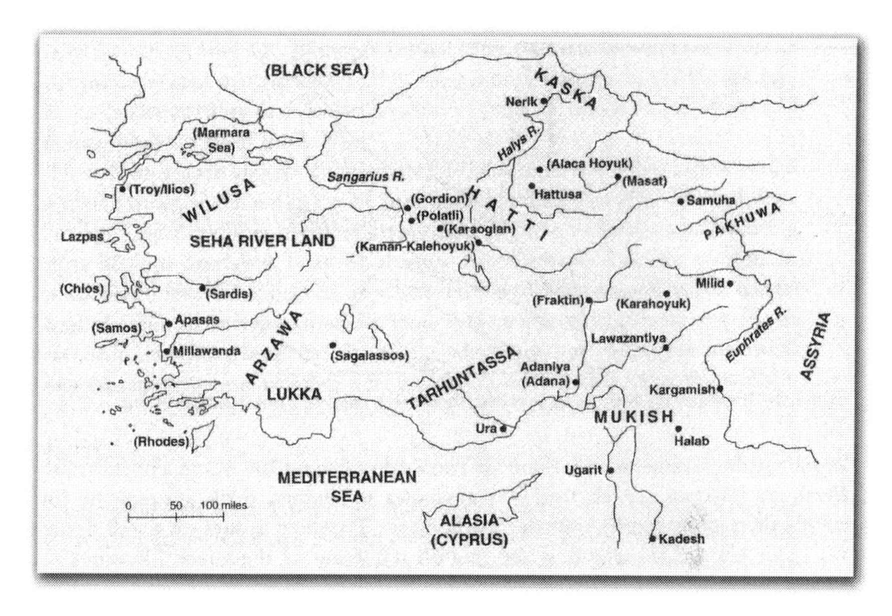

(names in parentheses are mostly modern):

III. Hattusa:

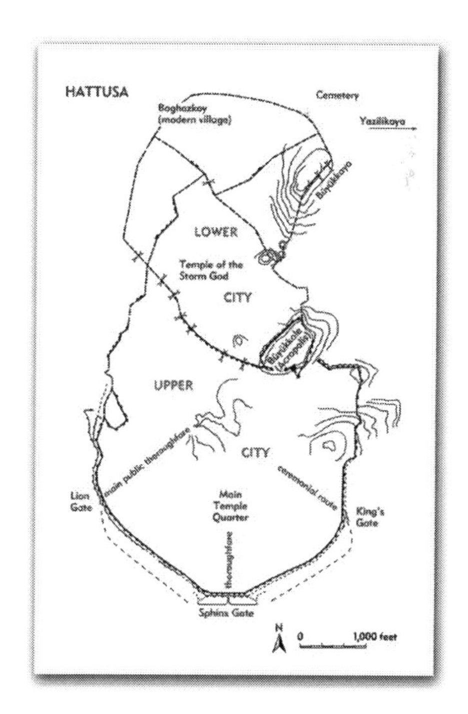

Acknowledgements: I owe a special debt to well-known historian of Hittitology, Trevor Bryce of Australia, author of a number of well-received books on the Hittites and Middle East in general. Despite his busy schedule he took the time to answer my prolonged email questions and to discuss controversial issues with me (such as the actual events at Troy, the population of Hattusa, the question of sacrifice in the endless Hatti rituals, and the ultimate fate of Suppiluliuma II). Though I owe him much for the degree of historical veracity I attained, he would no doubt disagree with some of my more extreme interpretations and mythical-archetypal explorations. Alicia Gradson I thank you for some early proofreading. Dr. Fred Mensch must be given a special tribute for his scholarly advice on literary matters and, even more, for his meticulous proofreading. I had missed so much! Special thanks must go to Rubina Akter in Bangladesh for her notable artistic contributions to the cover – love that snake!

Note to the Reader

The *Diomedeia* is to Diomedes as the *Odyssey* is to Odysseus or the *Iliad* is to Ilios. It indicates "the tale [or song] of Diomedes". Diomedes is most famous as one of the major Akhaian (Achaean) heroes in Homer's *Iliad*, but the trajectory of his mythic life goes well beyond Homer, from the Argolid to Ilios (Troy) to southern Italy. But I was most drawn to the fact that his tale indicates a major transformation of character over his lifetime, rare in mythology but a fine opportunity for a novel.

In what follows, I adhere to what is known from the historical records and to the stronger positions in historical interpretation, though on occasion I found myself siding with minority viewpoints. Myth and legend were also indirect sources, but in all cases I tried to deal with them realistically and avoid catering to popular depictions. This is historical fiction but not fantasy. However, I take seriously the myth & ritual studies of J. G. Frazer, Jane Ellen Harrison, Mircea Eliade, and Marija Gimbutas, as well as the psychological work on the universal image of the Great Mother from Erich Newman – while contemporary historians, archeologists, and ancient linguists do not. The gods are felt presences. I can claim that little occurs in the book that is beyond historical or even rational possibility.

A number of my characters actually existed, notably all the kings and two queens, Puduhepa and Anniwiyanni, but also Shipibaal the Ugaritic envoy and Penti-Sharruma, the Kings's scribe. Others are derived from myth or legend but are put into an historical context within the novel. Gods are mythical yet experienced as real, but only one may literally enter the tale. Other characters are entirely fictional.

Some understanding of the era and locale is necessary to really grasp the immensity of what is going in this story, especially to do with the epoch-ending *Bronze Age Collapse*. Its various natural causes (e.g., drought, earthquakes) led to the loss of international commerce, uprisings of the lower classes, and the attacks of the legendary Peoples of the Sea. It was these that brought an end to many great Bronze Age empires and associated kingdoms, including that of the Mycenaeans, Trojans, and Hittites. Only the Egyptians endured in a much-weakened state, and the Assyrians shrank to a small inland kingdom. All trade broke down, so bronze could no longer be made in quantity and most writing systems disappeared. The Dark Age of Iron sets in after this for many years. But it does seem many small city-states flourished in Anatolia, once again under the embrace of the Great Earth Goddess instead of warrior kings or sky gods.

There are many fine academic sources to consult, but if pressed for time an online encyclopaedia will do, including Wikipedia, and there are numerous entertaining videos on these topics on YouTube.

I strove for both authenticity and otherness in my use of names for places and people by attempting in most cases to use the names the ancients would have used. To avoid confusion, I *strongly advise* the reader to make liberal use of my ***Glossary of Names*** that I appended following the main text.

To add to the solemnity of sacred ritual and because no one can say things more authentically than the mythic mind of the ancients themselves, I have paraphrased or quoted from actual ancient texts (often clay tablets) in English translation throughout. Most times I do so, the paragraph is block-indented. I reference it by its page number and link it to the original text in the appendix ***Citations of Ancient Sources***. If you are reading an e-text, I encourage you to copy and search for individual names or the first phrases of block-indents or other paraphrases, which will take you to the appendices.

Epigraphs

> *When your messenger arrived promising help, the army was already humiliated and the city sacked. Our food on the threshing floors was burnt and the vineyards were also destroyed. Our city is sacked. May you know it! May you know it!*

—clay tablet found in the ruins of Ugarit; it was never sent... (source p. 406)

> *And I shall destroy everything I created. Earth will again appear as primordial ocean, as endlessness as in the beginning. I then am everything that remains – after I have turned myself back into a snake that no man knows.*

—Khemenu City, ancient Egypt: the ouroboric snake of the primordial ocean speaks. (source p. 415)

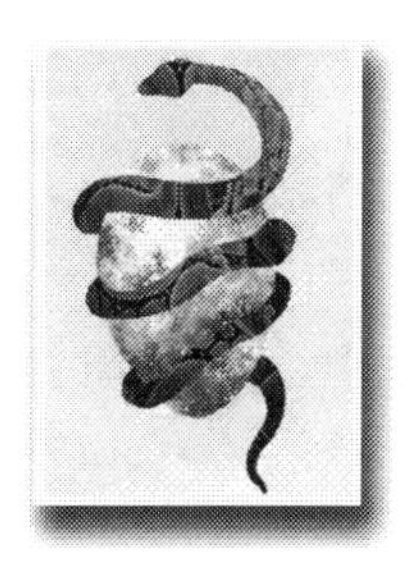

Sing, O Muse, the song of Diomedes, the greatest warrior at Ilios who strove with gods. Sing of how he abandoned the siege before its end to wreak havoc with his bronze blade in the vast lands of the Hatti.

Book I: The Fall of the Hittite Empire

The Gathering of the Invaders

Chaos is the fount of creation, the man pacing on the hill considered to himself. Civilization and order become rigid and barren, as he had seen so many corpses stiffen soon after death. Death returns life to its origins: it is the mother of beauty.

The dry wind blew steady across the barren rocky hillsides as it had always done. Below on the eastern slopes and in the valleys, the wind lessened but there was still no sign of rain. The heat blasted and the drought continued, so most fields were fallow. In the few still planted with thin stalks of barley, emmer wheat, or lentils, only women or the very old appeared occasionally to tend to the parched crops since all the men of fighting age had long since been absorbed into the Hittite military. Herd animals had largely disappeared. He was not surprised.

Over the rough hills ahead as far as the Sardinian could see, there was no sign of life at all beyond a few crows and circling kites. Somewhere out there, he thought to himself, the ancient city of Hattusa lay. Its once massive population had shrunk considerably in recent decades as the result of drought, plague, war, and declining trade, but now it likely had far more than its usual twenty thousand souls in and around it, for all the countryside will have gathered there to escape the impending storm of destruction, the storm of destruction that he, the Sardinian, was planning to coordinate.

He knew what he and the others must do, yet it puzzled him, this strange eternal empire of the Hittites. What was the source of its power? Surely only the protection of the gods could have allowed such a vast kingdom to endure so very long on such poor soil. Not only that, but it was mostly land-locked! It had no ports in the north so no direct access to any of the great seas around it, though centuries ago the empire was said to have included the port cities of Ura and Ugarit in the south, which remained vassal-states, so it had indirect access to the Mesogeios Sea. But links with these had weakened in recent times and they were far away. Strangely, the Hittites had seaports on neither what the Hellenes call the Aegean Sea, nor on the Pontos Axeinos (Black Sea). Recently Ugaritic ships had landed Hatti troops on Alasiya to secure the copper trade, but Hattusa itself had no port city. If it had, the peoples accompanying him who embraced the sea as a second home would have attacked it before the great city itself.

He shook his head, mulling over the fantastic tales he had learned from other warriors and sailors who were neighbours or allies of the Hatti. He made a point of sending out spies, getting information from the local tribespeople, and interrogating prisoners. Their compact capital city, Hattusa, itself, was located on a naturally defensible rolling hilltop within a bend of the Delice tributary of the great Marassantiya River where its turbulent mountain waters smoothed out onto a shallow plain. There were some imposing bluffs and mountains in the vicinity, but the builders did not choose to make direct use of these natural defences. What they did do, however, was build defensive walls like no city he knew of had ever done. The city's giant fortification walls surround its two square kilometres. It could easily contain numerous Troys, yet it was said to have few permanent residences within its upper city walls for commoners; only priests, attendants, military leaders, and guardians dwelt there. The extended royal family lived in the great palace itself, which was on the rocky akropolis of the lower city so high that it looked down upon the upper city. The city of the gods engaged in commerce but discretely. It was not a centre of commerce. External caravan trade was in the hands of the rulers not competing merchants. Within the city walls, there were no open marketplaces with vendors displaying their wares and shouting out their bargains. Hattusa was a sacred city, a centre of power, and its purpose was to maintain close ties with the all-powerful *1000 gods of the Hatti* who alone determined destinies.

In fact, though the Hittites called themselves the Hatti, the Hatti were a different people with a different language and different gods who in ancient times were conquered and absorbed by a warrior tribe from the north of Europa who called themselves the *Nesa*, but who now took the name Hatti for themselves. In fact, some said the Kaska who were coming to parley were remnants of the early Hatti. Outsiders combined their names to refer to the *Hittites*. This amalgamated Hittite people were not strict on keeping their gods to themselves and they were no spiritual seekers, but they were avid copiers and syncretists. The Hittites so freely integrated the gods and customs of other kingdoms that the reference to their 1000 gods was not an exaggeration.

The will of all these gods was realized in the person of the *Tabarna* or Great King (also the High Priest) whose dictates are carried out by the nobility and the massive standing army. Its enormous gates are in walls so thick a space is left in them where city activity is carried on. They have over a hundred tall guard towers along the ramparts so no one can approach unseen. Hattusa had never been conquered since the building of its great walls began in the time of the first Hittite Great Kings, though the royals had been forced to move their capital twice because of the threat of Kaska invaders. The mighty walls had never been breached; since their construction the city had never been desecrated and plundered – as the Sardinian and his allies were determined to do.

The Sardinian turned away to face west, from where he had ascended the hill. Filling the meandering valley along the broad but shallow arm of the Sangarios River below and extending onto the hillsides beyond was the vast but varied army of eight thousand warriors he and the other leaders had brought together for this boldest of adventures. Amidst and behind them were their horses, chariots, and chariot transport carts, as many as could be gathered in such a short time, and following that were their families, households, and the usual camp followers swelling the total number by a half. The clatter of cookware, the whinny of horses, the bray of asses, and the noise of human voices speaking too many different languages to count rose to his ears as a familiar dissonant chorus. The sights and smells of the encampment rose up in his senses. The colourful array of the disparate peoples each in its unique clothing with their own style of billeting, their own tents, shelters, and banners, and their own take on eating and sleeping procedures, would have confused the mind of many an observer, but the Sardinian had been observing such aggregate gatherings for many years now, more on the sea than on land, and he had a discerning eye. He reflected that despite the departure from their diverse homelands, voluntary or forced, or maybe because of it, they seemed to cling proudly to their local customs, raiments, and speech. Uniting them in single cause had not been easy.

He knew the pirates and warriors gathered below were indeed ferocious marauders. Earlier, they had been still gathering on the east of the island of Lazpas or the coast of the Seha River Lands south of Wilusa when they learned a quickly gathered force from the Hittite vassal kingdoms of Pitassa and Hapalla joined by Wilusan refugees still loyal to the Hatti had gathered to drive them back into the sea. However, their new conglomerate army of southern exiles and seafarers pulled together quickly and moved out, attacking the inlanders within the week on the plains of the Seha River Land. There was no battle plan. Each language group organized its own bowmen, chariots, and infantry block formations. They fought mostly in separate blocks for there had been no time to coordinate but still with such fury that the Hittite allies were crushed, left for dead, or dispersed within hours. The various groups tried to outdo each other, which only added to their fervour. Now they knew their power.

Though most of the original nations of this mixed group were more from local regions gathered from western

Anatolia – the Lukka, Mirans, Maionians, Akhaians from Miletos (called Milawata by the Hatti), and, from the north coast, mercenaries from Taruisa – there were still many like himself from further afield (though he had family in Sardis nearby). Among them were included some groups whose origins were unknown to any but themselves. People with white skin, light hair, and blue tattoos from unknown northwestern regions and a few others with skin like mahogany from beyond the Great Desert in Africa. These lean Nubian warriors with shining ebony skin from the land of Kush stood over most others and were made even taller with their multicoloured feathered headdresses. From north Africa came the scarified Libu. All were one in cause, yet each group mostly stuck to its self-identity, obviously in modes of attire and battle armour, but also in mannerisms, habits of relationship, and attitude. Each worshipped different gods and had its own customs of appeal and appeasement, but it was notable how such rituals were performed without fervour, their focus on immediate survival, unlike former days when animal or human sacrifice was common. Their tribal or national deities were thought to be particular manifestations of the same generic gods – how else could it be with immortals who must be everywhere? – so there was rarely any conflict over religion. Perhaps the fact that no specialists of the sacred – no priests or priestesses – were included in their numbers made it easier to assimilate beliefs. The various peoples differentiated themselves more by way of their singers of tales, their bards, who in the evenings around communal campfires filled the air with the sounds of plucked lyres or tambourines while reciting plaintive chants in numerous languages all telling of the glory achieved by their heroic ancestors, most often warriors and always men. The singers were also fighters, so had no sacred status beyond their talents.

Of course, the most distinguishing feature of each tribe or nation was its language, and these differed greatly in sound. Few had any written form, but those that did had a higher status so contributed most to the common pidgin speak. These included Akhaian Hellenic, Luwian, Arzawan,

Babylonian-Akkadian, Misriwi (Aigyptioi), Hurrian, and Hittite. But in this polyglot army, Luwian had come to predominate as a second language, as it had throughout Asia Minor. The Luwian, Lukkan, Hittite, and Hellenic seemed to share common features, making it easier for those most valued of people, the interpreters and translators, to work out shared meanings. Without interpreters who spoke more than one language, the entire expedition had no chance at all.

The Sardinian had never been to his distant ancestral island. He had been born at sea during some early migration away from Sardinia and had spent most of his childhood in the town of Sardis, many leagues to the SW of where he was now, a city founded by his ancestors as indicated by its name. So he spoke both the ancient Sardinian dialect that all Sherden speak, learned from his parents, but also the more widespread Luwian, along with a smattering of Hittite and Akhaian from Miletos. His clothing and weapons identified him as Sherden (the name given by the Misriwi Nile peoples to his wandering tribe). He was armed with a three-hand long heavy bronze dagger, a trophy from the conquest of Mykenai, with an exquisite gold etching of spearmen in a lion hunt on the dark metal strip down the sides of the blade.

He was about to begin his descent to the masses in the valley when he saw the dust cloud indicating the Kaska leaders were approaching. Kaska messengers had already arrived and demanded that the Kaska be a part of this expedition against their hated traditional enemies, the Hittites, but messengers had no power to make alliances. Within moments, scouts appeared, confirming what he was seeing. They would be riding in four-wheeled carts pulled by the small horses of the region. Horses were faster than oxen but the quicker ride could not have been pleasant. He descended to join the other leaders of the invading army to meet the war-loving Kaska.

As the soldiers set up an open tent with a long table for a meeting place, the Sardinian went to put on the rest of his military attire. One has to make one's identity known and status declared, after all. As he burnished his bronze helmet and heavy gold-embossed sword, he considered the situation. His first instinct was to attack immediately, so the Hittites had less time to prepare. Suppiluliuma II, their Great King, would have been alerted to their presence by now so must already be arming his citizens, calling up allies, and fortifying the defences of the giant walls around Hattusa. Why wait? He shook his head. He knew that, first, a plan of attack must be agreed upon – as much as possible with such a heterogeneous horde – and that, second, coordination with the Kaska, who occupied the mountainous terrain just north of Hattusa right to the coast of the Pontos, must be achieved, for they were in a position to determine the outcome of the battle to come. The fact that the vast Hittite Empire had never been able to entirely subjugate their northern enemy and link to a port on the sea testified to the ferocity of the Kaska warriors and to the rugged mountains in which they dwelt.

His trusted colleague, Payava the Lukkan, approached. Though the confederation of regional peoples and those from over the sea had no single leader, the Lukkan was widely accepted in that role due to his local knowledge, fair treatment of all factions, presence at the failed defence of Taruisa, and, most importantly, his notable oratory before crowds. The strands of grey in his beard and hair testified that he was a veteran warrior. He was in full regalia, wearing shining bronze plated armour including greaves, a patterned purple cape with a fringe, and a bronze helm topped with an upstanding multicoloured reed headdress nearly two hands tall. He did not carry the famous Lukkan shield but he brought a long ashwood spear with an impressive gold-engraved bronze head ending in a perfect point.

"Greetings, friend," The Sardinian announced so others could hear, but with a nod of recognition and eye contact for the more personal bond they shared. "You look ready to become the King of the Hatti."

“Perhaps I will have that chance,” he smiled and walked to the head of the table, “if we can hold our army together and agree to work with our new acquaintances. We will need all your battle savvy,” he winked. “Any word yet?”

“The Kaska have arrived. They are currently washing off the dust from their long journey and are being served some sustenance, so they won’t engorge themselves while we negotiate.” The men smiled at the reference to their presumed savagery. “It’s a small troop of about ten men, but it seems that only one is in charge.”

“Why would they travel across this war-torn land with so few warriors?” Payava asked. “Have they no fear of Hittites or mountain brigands?”

“The Kaska control the northern mountains and foothills, but getting here must have put them in some danger. It seems they know of hidden passes. That could be very useful to us.”

Other war leaders of the conglomerate forces arrived. All in full regalia, looking more ready for battle than to parley. They were a colourful yet fearsome group. Each tribe or nationality had chosen its own leader most often by acclamation (though often this had been determined in advance), the loudest clamour meaning he was chosen. Much the same process continued with various regions or alliances choosing leaders from the group leaders, and so on, narrowing it down to this council. The attack on Hattusa had ultimately settled on the shoulders of the five men gathered here now. None was commander-in-chief, but the Lukkan usually had the last word. The Sardinian led more from behind the scenes, his words most often chosen for counsel rather than harangue.

They greeted each with harsh cheer, striking each other’s shoulders with the laughing bravado of seasoned warriors. Wine was served in large copper goblets, premixed with water.

“Do we wait for the Kaska?” asked Leukos of Kriti indicating his cup.

"No need," said Payava, and the men all laughed, one or two downing the entire goblet in one glug.

The Kaska were announced by the guards, and soon three of them entered with the obvious leader in front. He was short, broad, and with a rough full beard, wearing leather armour and carrying a pointed copper-plated leather helmet in his arm. The Lukkan spoke a greeting in Luwian, but it was not enough. The leader waited while the man on his right translated the words into Kaskian. The leader spoke and the translator replied in Luwian, "Greetings to you and your gods. I am called Kaskaili, man of the Kaska. I am here to speak for all Kaska peoples."

"You and your gods are welcome here," said the Lukkan. "Please be seated." He signalled and a cup of wine was brought to Kaskaili but not to the guard or interpreter. Kaskaili sat and, looking warily about, tasted the wine. He smiled broadly, indicating he liked the raw vintage. The men of the council then also sat, leaving only Payava standing. He was the first to identify himself. He was bearded and of medium height though he appeared taller in his colourful upright reed-topped helmet, which he removed before he began to speak in the common Luwian.

"I am called Payava. The Hittites call my people the Lukka, the Akhaians call us Maionians, but we refer to ourselves as the Termilai. Once we lived on Megalonisi, the big island of Kriti. My mother was called Poulxeria, and she could trace her lineage back to the goddess Amitirita, whom the Argives call Amphitrite." He heard the mumble and looked up to the confused faces of the Kaska. "In my land, we trace our lineage through our mothers, but men and women rule equally. I speak for many tribes and nations from southwest Anatolia and more from out in the Aegean. The Lukka Lands are our homeland, but we have expanded our boundaries out onto the broad seas and found adventure on many shores." He waited while this was translated and he continued by listing some of those adventures. "Though my people have never been conquered by the Hatti, we once fought for them in the greatest battle of all time against Ramses II and the Misriwi at Kadesh, and we helped them prevail. But in return the Hatti turned on us and attempted to annex our lands, so we have been their enemy ever since. We are here to avenge the recent attacks against our borders by the Hittite Great King, the second Suppiluliuma, who has even brought war ships from Ugarit to our waters. It is we, along with our neighbours the Arzawa, who first set out to destroy Hattusa to protect ourselves," he paused, "and because it is time. As you can see, we have called upon the raiders from the sea to share in our glory. After the seaborne marauders attacked our lands, we saw that the old gods had departed and without their guidance our leaders could no longer defend us, so to protect our families we fighters joined the wandering warriors. Since that time years ago, many are the ports I have raided and plundered. I already had family, thirteen suns ago, when I took part in the great raid on Misri from the western desert and along the coast led by the Libu but the gods determined the old Pharaoh Merneptah was to repel us. Many Libu died and many others were captured, but I escaped, finally returning to my homeland, but my family was gone. Not long ago, I led many Lukkan warriors in defence of high-walled Taruisa, which the Akhaians call Ilios or Troy. On the windy plain, I sent many Argives and other sea warriors to dark Hades, though now we are friends and allies," he said with a nod and a grim smile to Leukos the Tjekker-Peleset and the Danaan, red-haired Eruthros. With the mention of Ilios, he had the full attention of the Kaska. Kaskaili did not speak until the Lukkan was finished.

His translated question was, "You fought at the defence of Taruisa?" Payava nodded. "A terrible catastrophe. It fell only four suns ago," Kaskaili continued. "The citadel of Ilios was said to be impregnable. All was destroyed in the flames?" Again Payava nodded. "You are most fortunate to have survived a siege that is said to have lasted many years and ended in utter destruction. How was that possible?" The Kaska leader looked both skeptical and suspicious.

Payava smiled, "The siege in fact lasted two years, off and on, and certainly seemed like many more. No doubt its length will grow as the bards sing the tale. Most of the time, the Trojans were kept contained in the city, fighting from the walls. We were not in the city but in the hills beyond from where we could harass and attack the Akhaians, Peleset, Danaans, and their seaborne allies. When the walls of Ilios were finally breached, the destruction began. The people were slaughtered. The city was ravished, and finally torched and there was nothing we could do, so we left." His words were simple facts to him, neither a complaint nor an excuse, just the truth.

In the silence, the Sardinian arose. He left his bronze Sherden war helm with bull's horns and silver sun disk before him on the table, yet he was nearly as tall as the Lukkan would be in his reed tiara. As was his people's custom, his beard was so trimmed as to be hardly visible. His great bronze sword nine hands long was in its engraved leather sheath across the armoured plates on his chest. Speaking in Luwian, he intoned, "I am called the Sardinian for I am of the Shardana-of-the-Sea peoples from the great island of Ichnussa, which the Hellenes call Sardinia. It lies beyond the island of the Sikeloi (whom the Misriwi call the Shekelesh) in the western sea of the Great Green. I have never been there and met my ancestral gods, nor have I seen our famous *nuraghes*, holy well temples, or the giants' tombs, for I was born at sea and grew up in Sardis-Hyde at the foot of Mount Tmolus in what the Greeks call Maionia and the Hittites the Seha River Land, southwest of here. The city was founded long ago by one of our people, a queen named Sardo. I left Sardis very young, joining with the sea raiders even before my first beard. In fact, so many of our people have left the land and become raiders that the kingdom is quite undone. Our Sardinian language is Sassarese but I speak Arzawa, Luwian, and some of the Hittite and Akhaian tongues. I am a learned man: I read the Hittite cuneiform and the Luwian glyphs. My name in Sassarese is *Al-la-an-se-ri-da-ni*, which others seem unable to pronounce." He paused to let the chuckles subside. "If you need a name, you can call me Sarpedon as others do, the name of my stepfather's Maionian ancestor in Sardis-Hyde who fought in the first war at Wilusa. My people have ridden the waves for many generations, freebooting as pirates and selling our skills as warriors to the highest bidders. They, too, were at Kadesh, but they fought *with* the Misriwi and many were in the Pharaoh Ramses' royal guard. It was there we learned to attach the sun-disk of Ra to our horned bronze war helms." He indicated his own impressive example, its polished bronze and silver glinting in the evening sun. "But, up until now, our loyalties have been only to ourselves, for, like the Lukka, we fought against old Pharaoh Merneptah with the Libu even while other contingents of our people were fighting for him. We gave no quarter even against our own kind. It was there I shared delight of battle with Payava the Lukkan but have not seen him again for these many long years. It is good to share a war again." They grinned fiercely at one another. They meant it. Sarpedon sat.

Leukos rose in turn and placed his feathered leather helmet before him. He was short and sinewy with the bow legs inveterate sailors so often have. Holding the hilt of the short stabbing sword slung across his hip and speaking in a Hellenic dialect, he was the first who identified his home as primarily the sea itself. He puffed himself up with pride and spoke long, yet kept himself just this side of garrulous. Leukos told the story of how his people of the northeastern side of the island of Kriti or Megalonisi, known to some as Caphtor, deserted their homeland devastated by drought, earthquakes, and sea raiders to become sea raiders themselves. He said some of his people still struggled to work the land in the valleys around Phaistos, but others had now migrated to Canaan where they were called Peleset or Philistines. They now also dwelled on the island of copper, Kyprios, known as Alasiya in Luwian and Hittite, where they were called the Ekwesh. The Misriwi called them the Peleset. He and his seaborne troops had also participated in the initial attack on Ilios, but they had left for better rewards after the outlying city was pillaged and the survivors went behind the great inner walls for the long stalemate. But he thought better of mentioning this to the

Kaska, as they seemed sympathetic to the fall of Taruisa. "Not long ago, the Great King of the Hatti ordered the ships of his vassal state of Ugarit and other cities along the Syrian coast to take on Hittite troops and attack Alasiya. They took most of the island, burning some of our ships and killing many Cypriots and many of our families too. Suppiluliuma has listened to demon gods. We seek to wreak terrible vengeance on the Great King of Hattusa and on Ugarit. Be it noted that Ugarit is currently without its navy, which is still ferrying soldiers of the Hatti in the Lukka Lands and on Alasiya..."

Even before the words were translated to Kaskian, the man of Kaska shifted impatiently. Once translated, Kaskaili sneered without rising: "No doubt you are all redoubtable warriors and your credentials are worthy. However, you have too many names for us to remember who you are or where you dwell. Unlike the Kaska who have held the same homeland since before the Hittites came, you seem mostly to be nomads and vagabonds who have deserted your homes. So why don't we just get on with it and decide exactly when we, the Kaska, will lead your troops to finally crush Hattusa out of existence?" He slammed down his empty wine goblet, gesturing for more. His guard tensed up straight, gripped his spear tightly, and eyed the other leaders warily. The words were translated. Leukos glanced at the Lukkan and took his seat. The allied leaders were taken aback at this breach of warrior protocol. What point is glory if your name is not known?

The Lukkan rose and spoke low but his tone was not without implied threat. "We have come to take down the Hittite Empire. We were not invited by the Kaska who have never been able to do more than defend their own territory from the Hatti. You asked to join us, but we will proceed with or without you. If you wish to join us, it is the custom of noble warriors to identify themselves to each other. You will have your chance, too. If you cannot bear to wait, I invite you to leave and go attack Hattusa on your own, as you have attempted so many times before." He paused and looked directly at the Kaska leader. "Are you willing to join us on our terms – or are you leaving?"

Kaskaili slurped some wine and grunted looking down, glancing sideways. Then he looked up, smiling through wine-stained brown teeth and said in feigned cheer, "Proceed, by all means, proceed."

"We must proceed, and quickly," continued Payava. "The Great King, Suppiluliuma, has sent word he wants to negotiate. He wants to send us a delegation, no doubt to bide for time but also to attempt to buy us out. He knows our numbers and our strength. And we both know," he looked at Kaskaili, "that the gods of the Hittites have deserted them. They have sent this long drought and have repeatedly shaken the earth, destroying allied cities and granaries. People from the towns are crowding into the city and surely starvation threatens. We know the Great King has sent messages to bring his armies home, so we must act before they get here. The ancient city is vulnerable and ready to be brought down, but it is still Hattusa, the most impregnable fortress the world has known. What we are undertaking makes the fall of Mykenai look like a skirmish and the fall of Troy but a single, pitched battle."

Point made and purpose proven, Payava glanced at the Miran commander and sat down. An older man with battle scars and grey in his beard arose. He wore only a simple, much-abused leather cuirass over his linen tunic and no helmet on his balding head. "I am Uhhaziti and I speak for all Arzawa, though it is now a dispersed land. My own region is known as Mira. Like the Lukka and the Kaska, we have been enemies of the land-stealing Hittites since time immemorial. We had hoped the Great King of the Hatti, the second Suppiluliuma, would allow us to move back onto our ancient lands, but when we tried he turned on us with his vast armies, taking even more Arzawa territory. War is upon us, so we must strike now. I still live on the land of my ancestors as do most of my people and we have not joined the sea marauders in any numbers, but I will ignore the insults of the Kaska that we are vagabonds. Arzawa land was once as great in size as the Hittite kingdom, but the Hatti broke us into pieces. Both the Lukkan and the Sardinian from Sardis dwell on lands that were once within Arzawa land. Our kingdom is no more, but the gods have given us undeniable signs that our ancestral homeland is about to be returned to us. Our day of vengeance is at hand. So I agree we must proceed like hungry wolves upon the flock of sheep before they realize what we are doing."

All nodded in agreement though the issue of who would lead the charge remained unsettled. The largest man of the group stood up, his archaic boar's tusk war helm before him. He had long, reddish-bronze coloured locks with a black silver-studded headband and a full beard partially concealing a long scar. His massive shoulders and chest were encased in a thick black leather corslet with bronze stars embedded in it; a large, curved sickle-like sword hung at his hip. His thickly muscled arms were left bare. He held a sturdy spear upright in his left hand and spoke, "Too much talk. I will not detain this meeting long. I am Eruthros, king of the Danaans of Aitolia. Don't know or care what the Aigyptoi or Hittites call us. We fought first for, then against Mykenai, burning it to the ground. We fought at Ilios and burned it to the ground, killing everyone," he looked at the Kaska with a malevolent smile. "And we are here to do the same to Hattusa or to anyone else that gets in our way." He paused then sat down again to his wine. The three Kaska shifted uneasily.

Understanding reached, Kaskaili stood, placing his pointed Assyrian-style war helm before him, and repeated he was speaking for all Kaska and that he and his followers had been waging guerrilla war against the Hittites all his life, just as the Kaska had always done to those who take their lands. He regaled everyone with the tale that in ancient days before the Hatti had become the Hittites and built an empire, they, the Kaska, had burnt the forerunner of Hattusa to the ground, and, further, after the Hittite Empire had been established, attacks of their ancestors had twice driven Great Kings to move their capital elsewhere.

“But, even with the Great King elsewhere, you were unable to take Hattusa itself. Is that not so?” asked Uhhaziti the Arzawan.

“That is so,” admitted Kaskaili. “Still, I have come to lead the Kaska in the first charge against the greatest city in the world. We are willing to attack the Lion Gate itself,” he stated, for the moment forgetting its famous high thick walls and postern passageways for sorties of Hatti defenders. “We will bring down the great Lion Gods who defend the gate and then open the way for your warriors from many homes. Or you can attack the Sphinx Gate after we have broken through.”

Everyone was aware that these were empty boasts – no one could break through the aggressive defences of the famous Lion Gate, the main entry point of the city – but the allied leaders also understood what the Kaska chief had in mind: vengeance, glory, and being the first to plunder the unimaginable treasures inside the city.

“You will follow our plan,” the Lukkan spoke in a low hiss. “Our numbers and siege weapons give us the power that is necessary to attack several gates at once, but you would be welcome to storm the Lion Gate with all your forces once we have the rest of the city engaged.”

“Or you can stay home with your women,” gruffly added flame-haired Eruthros. “But if you interfere with us in any way, we will turn our attention to your lands and your people next, from both land and sea.”

That ended it. It was agreed that the allied forces of the free Anatolians and the sea peoples would move out in a week. They should be in position for a full attack on the city in two weeks, so the Kaska could gather their forces in the mountains north of Hattusa at that time. The siege was likely to last a long time in any case. There were no reports of Hatti armies returning to defend the city since all were elsewhere engaged. In the southwest they were defending the recently extended borders against the Arzawa and Lukka, and in the south on the Great Green they were backing the navy of Ugarit. In the east they were holding back the attempted incursions of the Assyrians. The approaching army of vagabond warriors was unexpected and Hattusa had only what forces were in the city. It was time for war whether the 1000 gods of the Hittites agreed or not.

Kaskaili accepted the terms; he and his squadron left the same day. It changed nothing when only two days later, another Kaska squad arrived for parley. They met only the Sardinian and the Lukkan with their leader declaring, "I am Kaskaili. I speak for all Kaska. Not this one." He opened the straw basket he was carrying and unceremoniously dumped the gory head of the former Kaskaili on the ground. He insisted the Kaska would lead the charge against the Lion Gate but was quickly made to understand he had no choice in this, just as the first Kaskaili had learned. He was duly instructed on the plan, no discussion permitted. The Kaska would arrive later as backup forces. He and his troop were given sustenance and sent packing back to from where they had come. It was clear the Kaska were not a united people but one still caught up in tribal conflicts. "No matter," said Payava, watching the dust of their departure.

2. Suppiluliuma II

The Great King lay prostrate, his arms spread wide, on the marble floor of his meditation chapel before the painted gold statuette of the Storm-God, which impassively glowered down at him. He felt the room shift as the god entered the image. The human king's heavy, pointed, jewel-studded crown was placed beside his head. Golden Tarhunta forever held the thunderbolt trident raised in his left hand and in his right a double-headed hatchet was held aloft. On his head was the horned crown that proved his godhead. The pointed top came to a bauble from which a long gold tassel fell.

Both the Great King and the Storm-God had long, braided black hair and non-moustachioed beards coiffed in carefully formed plaits and ringlets, though only the hair of the Great King was perfumed and oiled while the god's was rigid stone. A bearded king went against all tradition, for male nobles of the Hatti had always been clean-shaven.

However, Suppiluliuma wished to strengthen his sense of identity with the immortal Storm-God as his own mortality currently felt fearfully in jeopardy. Besides, after meeting with Ashur-nadin-apli, the Assyrian Great King, for territorial settlements, he had been impressed by the mighty black beard of the ruler from Assur; finally, it made him look more ferocious than his father.

Suppiluliuma finished up the long list of titles of praise and got to his supplications more quickly than usual. He was managing to ignore the irony of praying to the Storm-God when there had been no storms – or rain – for many months and not much more since he had become king only twelve years before.

> "All the lands of the Hatti are dying, so that no one prepares the sacrificial loaf and libation for you, O God. What god or demon has decreed this wasteland? Has thy son, the god Telipinu who brings vegetation, wandered off again and forgotten his duties? The ploughmen who used to work the fields of the gods have died, so that no one works or reaps the fields of the gods any longer. The miller-women who used to prepare sacrificial loaves of the gods have died, so that they no longer make the sacrificial loaves. As for the corral and the sheepfold from which one used to cull the offerings of sheep and cattle – the cowherds and shepherds have died, and the corral and sheepfold are empty. So it happens that the sacrificial loaves, libations, and animal sacrifices are cut off. And you come to us, O Gods, and hold us culpable in this matter! I beseech you mighty Teshub, all-powerful Tarhunta, to relieve my land of its woes. Turn the plague, the hostility, the famine against my enemies. The crops have dried up and my people are starving. How can we worship you? *Bring us rain*!"

The King's last three words were boldly asserted. Suppiluliuma's gold earrings clattered on the marble floor as he looked up nervously, realizing his temerity, as though he might be struck.

In fact, the land had begun the severe drought near the end of the twenty-eight-year reign of his father Tudhaliya IV and it continued during the single year his strange older brother, Arnuwanda, had held the throne of the empire. Did he hear the Storm-God whisper "*pollution*"? If so, he knew the god did not mean the pestilence that first accompanied the drought and lingered still, but the lack of attention the people were paying to their gods. Rituals were no longer being strictly followed, as the 1000 gods of the Hatti demanded."How can the gods be properly worshipped when so many people have deserted them, leaving the holy city? But I, Sun of the Hatti, have done my duty, Holy Ruler," the Great King whispered, and indeed had he not spent the entire morning circulating from temple to temple to lead in the prescribed ritual activities, just as he had done every other morning? "*The land is impure...*" Suppiluliuma heard the god's whisper like the sigh of a low breeze in his own mind.

Could he himself be the impurity? "It's true that I, My Majesty, had Kurunta killed, he who had been appointed by my grandfather the Great King Hattusili to be vassal-King of Tarhuntassa. But in sacrilege during the short reign of my weak brother he declared himself Great King and had it so inscribed in sacred hieroglyphs. There cannot be two Great Kings of the Hatti! What right had he...?" He trailed off. Was it his own thoughts or did he hear Tarhunta whisper, "*His brother Urhi-Teshub was Great King. Kurunta was his heir, but since he sided with your grandfather, he was rewarded the local kingship in Tarhuntassa...*" "But he wanted more," said Suppiluliuma to the voice within him. "*Fear not, O King, it was your destiny,*" the inner voice replied. The Great King added even lower, "I killed my brother after he was anointed Great King. I strangled him with my own hands using a garrotte," he hissed, "but Arnuwanda was ... *unnatural* and not fit to be ruler. He would not marry even to make an heir..." "*All is well, be at ease,*" breathed the voice of the Storm-God. "*It was all planned by the immortal gods. If it has happened, it was destined. There is no avoiding this logic. Your Majesty is not the pollution.*"

“Then why have you allowed a foreign army into the land of the Hatti?” Suppiluliuma hissed, his outrage showing, his golden earring again clattering on the marble. *Silence*. “My Majesty has received reports that a gathering of forces from many lands has taken place to the west in the Seha River Land, likely led by the same men of Lukka and Arzawa I only recently thrashed into their place. They have already crushed a force from my vassal kingdoms to the west, strengthened by loyal Wilusans who survived the destruction of their city. If the Ahhiyawa are among them, these may be the same rebel sea peoples who burnt Taruisa to the ground! Is Hattusa next? Why, Great God Tarhunta, have you allowed this to happen?” “...” “Yes, yes I know, they are not your people. They do not make sacrifice or send sweet burnt offerings up to you. Perhaps, Storm-God, you do not venture to their territories or have power there.” “...” “But,” Suppiluliuma actually rolled to support himself on one elbow and face the sky, “we are your people who offer you gifts. And My Majesty is your chief priest and Great King. We supplicate you, mighty Storm-God, deliver us from this approaching evil. My Majesty, the Sun of his people, must not die!” *Silence.*

Later in the day, the Great King withdrew to his quarters and had a trusted bearer sequester his tall golden crown whose weight he would not miss. His high priest robes were removed and he was dressed more parochially in the kingly robes of administration. He sent a servant for warmed honey-barley broth and sat in a comfortable but still kingly chair. He had his beard and long hair combed out and he covered his head with a woollen shepherd’s cap. Now prepared, he called for Mahhuzzi, his chief advisor and his cousin, and for his scribe, Penti-Sharruma, to attend to him. They briskly arrived, the fleshy scribe seating himself cross-legged on the floor while the vizier remained standing, his narrow, clean-shaven face alert.

Suppiluliuma had a noisy sip from the drink that arrived and got right to the point, not his usual custom, speaking in the direction of Mahhuzzi: “We have had little assistance from our sacred gods in the matter of this drought or these recent earthquakes..."

"My King, my prayers and sacrifices are going on ceaselessly. Only today—"

"Stop," the Great King ordered with a wave of his hand. "Our more immediate problem is the approaching army who have already destroyed the army I sent against them from Hapalla and Pitassa. Where are our friends and allies? This is not the time to be tending to their own gardens when the Great King of the Hittites is threatened! It is an offence to the gods to so threaten My Majesty!"

"They will never be able to take Hattusa, Great King. It is protected by the Storm-God, Tarhunta himself! Some of the people who migrated away in such vast numbers have now returned to seek shelter from the approaching army, so we have more defenders." In a quieter voice, he added, "Still our armies are mostly far afield so it may be wise to seek their return and other reinforcements."

"The Storm-God seems to be too preoccupied trying to share the sky with the Sun Goddess to end this drought. Who can we call upon? It seems there is trouble everywhere – sea pirates, revolts, trade routes falling into disuse, people leaving the sacred city in droves but now returning again to huddle at the Lion Gate in fear. Dare we approach the Kaska?"

"It is no use, Great King. They have proven their hostility to us again and again. We are already fighting the Assyrians in the east. We must look to the south, but we have an army engaged in fighting in Tarhuntassa, too."

"The south, yes. The Sun of the Hatti must call upon the great states of Amurru and Ugarit. They have soldiers and a mighty navy,"

"Yes, my Lord, but you yourself ordered their navy and warriors down to the Lukka Lands to fight incursions of the sea pirates in those waters and you had the Ugarit navy carry Hatti soldiers to attack the alien ships around the copper island of Alasiya, which they are still doing."

Suppiluliuma sat up, shaking his head in growing frustration. "All this is no matter! I am the Great King of the Hatti, chosen by Tarhunta-Teshub the Storm-God. Our will cannot be blocked. What we decree happens! Penti-Sharruma, attend to me. I command that an urgent message be sent in dried clay to Ammurapi, the underling I have allowed to be King of Ugarit. Take note of these words." Penti-Sharruma had his stylus ready for the quick copy. "I am not going to bother with the usual praises and pathetic grovelling. No, don't record that. Start here:

> 'To Ammurapi who rules Ugarit at my mercy. From My Majesty, your Lord. With My Majesty, all is well, but My Majesty is distressed that King Ammurapi did not come to his court as ordered for his required obeisance. However, My Majesty notes we are all troubled by the drought and the unknown invaders in our lands, so My Majesty is grateful that Ammurapi has sent food and supplies to the Hittites at great privation to himself. Still, the unknown enemy advances against us in numbers beyond count. My troops are far afield and our numbers are few. I demand your military assistance. Send whatever is available. Look to it and send it to me now!'

Form these worlds into a strong clay tablet and have it sent to Ugarit with fast riders immediately."

Suppiluliuma the Second dismissed his advisor and his scribe. Penti-Sharruma left to prepare a carefully-inscribed clay tablet in both Akkadian cuneiform and Luwian hieroglyphs, adding another thin clay layer as an envelope with his scribal seal imprinted on it, and baking both to dry them more quickly. He had it sent forthwith with trusted swift couriers to Ugarit. The Great King had himself changed into garments that identified him as the war leader. He prepared to lead his retinue to view the further work on the colossal holy sanctuary and festival complex known simply as the Mountain Temple of the Gods within the towering cliffs just northeast the city. He reflected that the massive restoration project begun by his father Tudhaliya IV and nearly completed by himself was itself proof of his piety. Tudhaliya had wanted to build a grand memorial to himself in the fashion of Misri, but he, Suppiluliuma, would dedicate it to all the gods, and they would favour him. In fact, it had been truly begun by his grandfather, Hattusili, known as the third, but it was he himself who was chosen by the gods to complete it.

His absolute devotion to the Storm-God and all the gods was beyond question and the giant rock images of so many gods were the proof of that. If there was a pollution in the land it had to be because the people themselves were not tending to their ritual duties, not practicing the respect and obeisance the gods have demanded since time immemorial. The earthquakes and drought must surely be punishment for *their* sacrilege, but such divine retribution was also related to the way the trade routes had fallen into decline and the borderlands of the empire had grown restless and begun to revolt. During the plague that came to the sacred city toward the end of his father's reign, finally carrying off Tudhaliya himself, people lost faith in both gods and kings to protect them and departed the city in droves, often to join rebellious kingdoms on the borders. So he, the Great King, had been forced to expand the ranks of his armies, which of course meant hiring foreigners and taking young men from working the fields causing more hunger and destitution, but that was not his fault. Because of the breakdown in international commerce, grain could no longer be imported in the necessary amounts. Famine in the countryside became a reality, as did the disease that inevitably followed it. As a result, more and more of the common people were moving next to or even inside the city walls and were so desperate to feed themselves they often ignored their sacred duties or forgot the thank their deities for their gifts. Sacrificial animals were becoming hard to find as they were being surreptitiously eaten with no ceremony. The ways of the gods are mysterious, he reflected, for their punishment for the people's sacrilege was also its cause. *Fate*, he nodded to himself, as though all was now explained.

The Great King in royal military garb of copper and bronze, and wearing a tall, fluted, gold-embossed diadem with a chin strap was accompanied by the ever-present twelve members of his personal bodyguard, the *Meshedi*, four before him, four after, with two on either side. Each carried a long gilded spear, a reminder of earlier times when there was a second troop of personal guards called the *Men of the Golden Spear*. They had been chosen by ruthless competition for personal bravery and skill in arms but even more so for their devotion to the Great King. They were daily conditioned into absolute loyalty to his Majesty above all else, over the Great Queen or even the gods. He mounted his chariot, a solid structure of strong wood with railings embossed with gold and bronze over the leather panels, helped up the step by a servant who was unable to avoid touching his person. Suppiluliuma shook him away in disgust and stepped between his guard and the young charioteer. After all, his royal personage had just been physically and ritually purified from head to toe, and all his body hair removed to avoid any possible defilement. The enlarged chariot with the axle across the middle of the carriage held the three of them safely if not comfortably. The guard held a sun shade over his royal person, but still his Majesty did not look forward to the journey in the heat and dust. Still, all paused while he intoned the proper ritual prayers.

The chariot of the wife of the Great King pulled up alongside in all its radiant, golden splendour. The Great Queen's personal name was Lieia-Hepa, but she was also the High Priestess and incarnation – the eternal *Tawananna* – of the Sun Goddess of Arinna, who is said to have ruled the Hatti before the first Great Kings took power. Though this status was sacred and continued even when the Great King changed, she had become High Priestess soon after Suppiluliuma had taken the office, for the high priestess at the time, formerly the senior wife of Tudhaliya IV, had suddenly been possessed by demons and had to be kept a virtual prisoner in isolation. Lieia-Hepa, fresh from her own purification, nodded imperiously to the king, who waved a hand and the lead chariots with the skyward-pointing gold-tipped spears of the Meshedi began to move, followed by the chariots of royals. Around the royals and behind them came the rest of the elite king's bodyguard, the Meshedi, other chariots that included the Great King's royal scribe, his chief advisor, and General Kil-Teshub, his uncle, military advisor and the *Gal-Meshedi*, commander of the royal bodyguard.

The entourage descended the splendid royal way into the streets below, and many people along the way dutifully cheered as they passed, but others were perplexed since they knew this was not a festival day. Suppiluliuma noticed that some looked away instead of cheering, and the cheering was done with less enthusiasm than was usual. "They are ashamed of ignoring the sacred rituals," he thought to himself. They went through the northern Gate of Processionals onto the sacred way toward the Mountain Temple. Here was a smaller copy in relief on a raised pedestal of the fully armed Warrior God Sharruma. The grander two full arm-spans tall original (that resembled his father who had ordered its construction) was at the King's Gate in the upper city. Suppiluliuma felt himself inflate at the sight of the mighty god with his tall helmet of leather and bronze, his axe of war in his right hand, and his raised fist of victory in his left. Surely anyone could see that he, the Great King Suppiluliuma, *was* this very god, or that this god was manifest in him. Without his beard, his face resembled that of his father.

They traversed the flat plains in about the time it takes to eat a comfortable lunch and arrived at the mountain limestone cliffs that had been sculpted into the shape of the Temple of the Gods. People looked up at their passing, but since this was not the time of the New Year festival of renewal or the Spring rites and since nothing was being offered to them, they soon turned back to work. They were saluted by sentries at the well-guarded portal between two narrow cliffs and entered the stone pantheon of their gods sculpted onto the cliffs around them, along with hieroglyphic symbols indicating the identities or stories of the deities. Standing high and huge above them were the mighty Storm-God and the Sun Goddess of Arinna. As always, the awesome assemblage silenced everyone.

The royals dismounted their chariots, encircled at distance by the Meshedi. Any dust was gently brushed away by servants as they were approached by the chief priest who first bowed to them all from a distance, then came before the Great King and Queen and lowered himself to his knees, hands folded as if in prayer. "Welcome, O my Priest and Priestess of the most mighty!" He gave the usual ritual salutations and incantations but then added one compliment of his own: "This is the holiest shrine in the land of the Hatti. All credit should go to the gods for choosing to appear here, but, next to them, great praise goes to our two earthly rulers for acting on the behest of the gods to bring them forth into our world!" A mumble of appreciation followed his words. This being but a royal tour and not a community festival, rituals were more perfunctory. Still, the temple chief priest had to do the blessing:

> "May the Tabarna, the king, be dear to the gods! The land belongs to the Storm-God alone. He has made the Tabarna, the King, his administrator, and has given him the entire land Land of Hatti. The Tabarna shall continue to administer the entire land with his hand. May the Storm-God destroy whoever should approach the person of the Tabarna, the King, and the borders of Hatti!"

This was followed, as always, by a reverential tour of the holy site. Above and around them in the first chamber within the roofless cliffs were carefully rendered horizontal relief sculptures of gods, kings, and heroes, some larger than life-sized. The eye was magnetically drawn to the great procession of deities, high above all the rest – a line of armed male gods (with the goddess Shaushka as a warrior of male aspect included) on the left facing a similar line of goddesses on the right (including Sharruma, her son, the Storm-God of Nerik, and Shaushka again, as love goddess). They were organized so the deities toward the centre were larger and more significant than those down the line. More

or larger horns of divinity on the conical caps of the gods indicated their greater importance. The goddesses all had tall cylindrical, fluted caps and long pleated skirts, but all deities wore shoes with significantly twisted back toes. The two largest figures in the very centre dominated the tableau. The Storm-God faces the Sun-Goddess; each is identified in Hittite hieroglyphs by its Hurrian name, Teshub and Hepat respectively, which indicated their archaic origins. Teshub stood on two mountain gods whilst Hepat stood on a panther. The overall impression left those seeing it with both a sense of divine order and symmetry, yet also with a certain tension between contraries since the ultimate power seemed to be divided. Order on earth would ensue only as long as these opposing lines remained suspended, only as long as the Great King and Great Queen were balanced and held in symmetry, as well as the chief deities behind them.

Much lower down, two bull men stood between male gods on the hieroglyphic symbol of the earth supporting the sky. The earth and sky are two aspects of the same essence, yet the earthly power is dependent on heavenly power. Strange, thought Suppiluliuma, that he felt anxiety whenever he viewed this aspect of the tableau.

It was his father who had commissioned much of the work in the great first chamber, and no doubt Tudhaliya was guided in turn by his mother, Puduhepa. She was recognized as Chief Priestess and even Goddess during his earlier reign. It is no wonder that, near ground level, Tudhaliya had ordered a twice-normal-sized replica of himself prominently displayed in the raiments of Chief Priest – close-fitting skull cap, long robes, upturned shoes, and holding a *kalmus* or shepherd's crook in his role as shepherd of his people.

The Great King and the local chief priest withdrew to the little temple near the entry where several priestly dressers removed the Great King's military attire, cleansed his body, face, and hands, and dressed him for his role as Chief Priest, very similar to the shepherd's clothes in the statue of his father, but with an even more austere robe. They emerged and poured a generous libation to all the present deities.

With only the most prestigious of the procession, they proceeded out of the narrow passage and entered into the smaller second chamber through the niche between them where winged lion-headed demons stood eternal guard. Servants and guards were not permitted. This chamber had a different feel, as many more sombre Underworld deities and former Great Kings were sculpted. It was darker with hollow tombs in the walls.

This shaded chamber was the netherworld revealed, yet it was a thing of grandeur. On a facing wall, twelve chthonic gods of the Underworld are portrayed marching purposefully with drawn sickle-bladed khopesh swords. They are running left to right toward a centre, and, directly facing them, running from right to left, another line of similar warrior-gods but in different armament and garments advances to meet them. Their overlapping legs give the impression of determined motion. At the centre, leading each line, two larger deities face one another, each superimposed over a prancing bull that adds depth to the spectacle. Even though many in the elite procession had viewed this scene before, the suspenseful sense of an impending clash of armies of netherworld gods remained overwhelming – a symmetry that indicates great tension.

Nergal, the sword God of the Underworld, was made present in stone. His fearsome head and strong shoulders in full armour with two inverted lions as legs and two more on either side of him were actually the hilt of a giant oblique stone sword whose blade was half plunged into the rock, indicating the power of the hidden Underworld. Great Kings of the past such as his grandfather Hattusili III were also portrayed, but Suppiluliuma swelled with pride at the next relief since it was he who had ordained its construction (inspired by the gods, of course). Right near the entrance, they walked reverentially by another relief carving of his late father, Tudhaliya IV, larger than all other kings, in the protective one-armed embrace of the even larger Sharruma, his patron deity, showing the appropriate humility of kings to gods. Sharruma had been the storm- and war-god as sacred bull of the Hurrians who became so revered among the Hatti that he threatened the dominance of Teshub-Tarhunta. At this confluence of deities, Tudhaliya's mother, famed Puduhepa, reported a visionary dream in which numerous imported deities became identified with the twelve major Hittite gods. Sharruma, now in human form, was revealed by her vision to be the son of Teshub and Hepat but was still held in high esteem as the Storm-God of the northern city of Nerik, so he remained the patron deity of Tudhaliya. The pantheon was at once more organized, yet it continued to grow. In the present, burnt offerings were made to the dead and Suppiluliuma intoned a prayer for protection to his father, now a god himself though his body was no longer present.

The entire smaller chamber was in fact a funeral chamber holding the remains of bygone kings. But it had been vastly upgraded to become the mausoleum of Tudhaliya, Suppiluliuma's father, and it was Tudhaliya himself who had closely directed the central, heightened placement for his body's tomb, with space for the sumptuous and valuable grave gifts that would accompany him when he awoke as a god. When he died, his son Arnuwanda, the new Great King, had his body tightly wrapped and placed in his tomb with a grand ceremony lasting days. After Arnuwanda's short reign, however,

Suppiluliuma had himself commissioned the mausoleum chamber's upgrade soon after ascending to the throne. However, on the advice of the Storm-God, which only he could discern, he decided that his father's body was not safe from evil spirits or grave robbers within the grand tomb in the cliffs, so he had the body moved within the city into an artificial mountain temple he had built with dark stairs for the chthonic descent to the tomb. Later, he had a carved likeness of himself as a warrior king placed within the temple at the entry, perhaps as guardian, but the addition of the horns of deity on the portrait while he was yet alive was something new. He found that right next to it was the perfect place to build a monument tower to record his achievements as warrior king, so he had his chief scribe design and manage just that in Anatolian cuneiform. He liked it so much, he had his exploits copied onto a much larger outcropping rock face higher up on the akropolis where even the gods could see them.

After the obsequies, the chosen few returned to the others in the larger cliff chamber. The Great King, also the chief priest, again washed his hands carefully, poured libation to the gods, and drank dark red wine from the silver goblet in the shape of the fist of the Storm-God himself, knuckles down with a sword hilt clenched in the closed fingers. This sacramental act meant he drank the power of the god into him. He raised his arms skyward, waited until everyone had fallen to their knees and loudly pronounced a long ritual prayer to all the gods. The priests and attendants of the sanctuary intoned or shouted responses, "O hear!", "kasmessa!", "missa!", "blesséd be the gods!" The Great King then turned to the relief carving largest and above all others on the cliff wall:

> "O Mighty Storm-God and all gods, pay heed! It is I, My Majesty, who addresses you. Are we not bound together as the sky is to the earth? What have you done? Why have you allowed this wretched drought and sickness into the land? Why does the earth shake so often? O gods, whatever sin you perceive, either let the Wise Women or the diviners determine

> it, or let ordinary people see it in a dream! O gods, have pity on your land of the Hatti! On the one hand, it is oppressed by the plague, on the other hand, it is oppressed by its enemies. ... Thou mighty gods above and below who see and know all, why have you allowed the gods of foreigners to enter the Land of the Hatti? Do the invading barbarians from the sea bring with them gods unknown to you? Invite their gods to feast with you, great gods, speak with them and ask what they want here. If they refuse to parley, warn them that the wrath of the Storm-God's thunderbolt will smite them all and their people too!"

He ended his prayer and stepped back. Into the space stepped Lieia-Hepa, the Great Queen, who raised her arms to heaven and pronounced the ritual praises and prayers to all the gods. But then, instead of stepping back, she looked up, as though startled. Her face became transfigured, and she stared with shining eyes as though into a distant light that no one else could see. She turned to face the Sun Goddess of Arinna on her fearsome panther and extended her arms to her:

> "Sun goddess of Arinna, my lady, queen of all lands! In the land of Hatti, you ordained your name to be the 'Sun goddess of Arinna', but also in the land of the cedar you ordained your name to be Hepat – yet all are the Great Goddess Ishtar who arose in Babylon. As is known to all but those who hide their eyes, you, Great Goddess, ruled this land before the Hatti became the Hittites. You ruled alone yet as three, and priestess-queens carried out your will on Earth. Tarhunta the Storm-God was but your love-slave."

Everyone looked at her aghast. No one was more shocked than Suppiluliuma. Was this sacrilege?

> "Long, long have you waited, O great Queen Arinniti, with your sisters of heaven and the Underworld, to cease the humiliation brought upon you by being relegated by the northern warrior gods into a mere

> consort and mother, when you are in reality the greatest warrior of all, controlling the power of love."

Suppiluliuma looked both frightened and angry and attempted to catch her attention, but she stared as if possessed and did not stop. To change the ritual is to risk the gods' wrath. To insult the Storm-God is to invite death.

> "Now your power is returning to you, fourfold in strength. As the Goddess of Earth and the Underworld, you bring down cities as you shake the ground. Your mighty rays parch the land, destroying all crops and stopping trade, as you have decreed, and the Storm-God, your love-slave once again, is helpless to bring rain or thunder. Soon all power will be yours again. Soon Hattusa and the Empire of the Hatti will fall. All must prepare for the end!"

There was a shriek from the women as she suddenly seemed to lose the force that had entered her and fell toward the ground. She was held by her handmaids and a nearby guard until the Great King got to her and lowered her to sitting position. "She was possessed by demons! You can all see that! These were not her words that were torn from her. This is to be forgotten. This speech did not happen!" He stood and waved his hand in a chopping motion. "Penti-Sharruma," he addressed the chief scribe, "no record whatsoever is to be made of the Great Queen's demon-possessed ramblings."

The return trip back was much more fearful than the trip out. Everyone knew the drought had devastated the land and, combined with the lack of trade, had led to disorder and famine. Many had heard rumours that the outlying states were in revolt, but had not the Great King just extended the borders of the empire and replaced the kings of neighbouring lands? His Majesty's prayer to the gods to stop an approaching army had been startling news to many, but when capped by the Great Queen's apparent vision of the end of the world, everyone in the entourage was deeply unsettled.

The procession returned through the same gate that led up the royal way to the akropolis of the lower city where the temple complex stood with the royal palace above it. Before entering either, the Great King's processional was dispersed. Lieia-Hepa was put into a sedan and carried to her rooms in the palace proper, for though awake she still seemed confused and likely to swoon. His Majesty decreed she was to rest there for several hours.

He sat in silence on his golden throne, alone and brooding. His queen has been possessed, and the Sun Goddess of Arinna was declaring herself a threat! This rise to the sun of the ancient goddess of the Underworld was throwing the cosmic order off-balance. It was heresy and a direct attack on the manhood of Tarhunta the Storm-God himself. If the mightiest of all, the great Storm-God, was endangered by his consort, the ancient dark Sun Goddess, then he himself, the Great King of the Hatti, was endangered by his consort, the Great Queen. This will not be! The cosmos must be put back in balance with the Storm-God and the Great King ruling over all. Then the drought and earthquakes will stop, and the rebels and invaders will disappear. He began to conceive a plan.

Lieia-Hepa, the Great Queen of the Hatti, the Tawananna or High Priestess of the Sun-Goddess, manager of the royal household, and guiding mother of the royal harem and the children born of its concubines from the Great King's seed awoke from her sleep in a state of confusion. What had just happened? Had the spirit of the Queen-Goddess Puduhepa, grandmother of the Great King, really possessed her? She found this such an amusing thought that she burst into pleased giggles. Had she wanted to say such things since she was a girl of eighteen suns from a noble family chosen to wed the younger son of Tudhaliya, who later became the second Great King named Suppiluliuma? "I don't know if the Queen-Goddess spoke through me or not, but it felt just like what I always wanted to say myself. Yes! It was her, it was also the earth Sun Goddess of Arinna – and it was me, Queen of the Hatti."

She was aware she had probably brought down the deep resentment of the Great King upon her, but she knew he was too fearful of the gods and their mysterious ways to do anything rash. He ruled the kingdom and was inspired by the greatest god, but she ruled the palace and many of the temples and she was surely inspired by the greatest goddess. He dare not threaten her in any way. In fact, the crisis may have given her more power, not less. She decided to skip the ritual purification and rose to notify the guard at the door to send for a cooling beverage of honeyed lemon water. To identify with Puduhepa is to identify with Ishtar herself, she thought to herself and had long felt to be true. A sense of power and delight rose in her. She reviewed what she knew of the woman.

Puduhepa had been discovered by Hattusili, later a Great King, when he was a combat general under the Hatti Great King, the second Muwatalli, returning from the victory against the Misriwi at Kadesh. She was the High Priestess of Ishtar, the Babylonian goddess of love and its power, in the Hurrian city of Lawazantiya east of Tarhuntassa, and, since Hattusili was a devotee of the goddess, he prayed with her father the chief priest and then was brought into the presence of Puduhepa. She was very young for such a position but she radiated dignity and divinity. As the high priest's daughter, she had long been groomed for it. Her mystical beauty was legend, and Hattusili fell under her spell from the moment he saw her. He took her with him back to Hattusa where she took the status of first wife and Great Queen, replacing another, also becoming the Tawananna of Hepat. She organized the runaway polytheism of the Hatti pantheon so there were only twelve chief deities and most of those she called by their Hurrian names. After the death of Hattusili, her power only increased. Under the reign of her son Tudhaliya IV, father of Suppiluliuma II, she was given the extraordinary title of Goddess-Queen. Some say it was by her divine guidance that Tudhaliya had so much initial success, but she eventually succumbed to old age on earth becoming one with Ishtar in the heavens. She had been replaced as high priestess by one Anniwiyanni, the first wife of Tudhaliya, but she was no longer recognized as a goddess.

"And that," thought Lieia-Hepa, "meant it was not a sin to poison her food with mind-altering plants, again and again and again, until she was a frightened, gibbering idiot, who needed to be locked away. By then Lieia-Hepa was the wife of the new Great King, Suppiluliuma, so of course, she became the rightful Tawananna. "Rightful" for whatever happens is the gods' will, and, if so, it must have been destined to be.

Young as she was, she had seen with her own eyes the weakening of Hattusa, the sinking water levels in the reservoir pools, the disappearance of the city brook, the dearth of arriving trade caravans, the decreasing grain in storage, the increasing population of the starving poor, the smaller and smaller gifts given to the gods, and, most unsettling, she had heard the recent reports of an approaching army bent on the destruction of the city. The last coupled with the fact that there were hardly any Hittite troops about made her realize the end of Hattusa was at hand. This probably meant the end of Suppiluliuma, as well, and in her heart she welcomed this. The balance of the gods and the world was being thrown off, and as the avatar of Ishtar, she hoped to bring about a return to devotion to the Great Goddess and a new way of living without being controlled by power-driven men.

The men who ruled were nearly all the same. They loved games and they loved war. But they were hypocrites about sexuality. All of them, even the priests, wanted to be able to have a woman whenever they wished, but at the same time they were puritanical in their moral strictures. The women must be seductive but always compliant and yielding, never demanding. Their role was to serve the needs of men, not to seek pleasure or power for themselves. She undressed and went to her marble basin and cleansed her body in rose water. She then sat at her mirror and prepared her features, adding red rouge to her lips and kohl to her eyelids, dressing again in her finest gown of golden sea silk, a fabric painstakingly crafted from the fine, strong fibres of the organ that attaches molluscs to a rock foundation in the intertidal zone.

Her drink arrived. She accepted it, closed the door, went to a little gold box in her cabinet and sprinkled in a pinch of the stimulant concoction infused with the dried poppy juice of the east. She did not belong to the Thunder God and would pursue the light radiating from the Sun Queen alone. Obedience and submission are not the way of Ishtar, who was goddess under the name of Inanna when time began. Men were driven mad and seduced to serve her will, and they did so willingly. They abased themselves to bring her pleasure, and often, in times of old, their blood was needed to renew the earth and fertilize its soil. She drank her special juice with relish, a drop dribbling through her red lips and down her chin.

Clearly, power was shifting among the great gods. Few clouds, no thunder, no lightning, no rain: the Storm-God had become impotent. Yet the sun beat down relentlessly in all her glory. Hepat had seduced Teshub and he had become her love-slave, and mankind would have to adjust. All the great civilizations seemed on the brink. Communications and trade had broken down. It seemed the age of great palaces and weapons of bronze was nearing the end of its cycle. The harmony of opposites was broken. The heavens were indeed unbalanced. It was time for the old ways to become the new ways again. Sacrifice must be made for the transformation to take place.

As the drug took effect, the Great Queen lay back on her pillows. She fell into a reverie thinking first of the previous short-lived reign of the Great King, Arnuwanda, and later of the Ahhiyawa who had been imprisoned. Arnuwanda was a slim and gentle man with pleasing soft eyes. As new wife of his younger brother, Suppiluliuma, she had known him, for he would often go to the harem she managed, but not for the reasons any other man might. Instead, he liked to just watch the courtesans or order refreshments and nutmeats and chat and giggle with them as though the empire would take care of itself. She saw he was possessed by Hepat in her guise as Ishtar. He was in fact a woman but he did not know it yet. She took pleasure in befriending him, and one day after a bit of wine had been poured, she led the courtesans in daring to strip him down and dress him in women's clothing. He playfully resisted but when the job was done, he glowed with delight. He was given a mirror of polished silver, and he was entranced to the point that tears of happiness welled in his eyes. After that, he came less frequently to the harem, but whispers around the palace were that he was bringing first young male slaves then manly guardsmen into his private quarters at regular intervals. He dressed in feminine styles more openly now. Lieia-Hepa was amused.

Needless to say, Suppiluliuma was enraged when the stories finally reached him, both another example of the stringent moral codes of the warrior patriarchs and an honest fear for the empire left to the brothers by their father. The fact that Arnuwanda refused to seek a bride even for appearances made it all that much worse. "What demon has done this? Such perversions do not happen amongst the warrior Hatti!" he bellowed. Suppiluliuma insisted she do something, so she brought in the so-called Old Wise Woman, the Tawananna Anniwiyanni, formerly the first wife of the late Tudhaliya.

Lieia-Hepa had a difficult time convincing the Great King Arnuwanda to consent to the ritual, but she was very loving, seductive, and motherly and told him it was what his father Tudhaliya would have wanted. That didn't do much, but she told him it might open him to a whole new realm of pleasure in which he might experience the best of both worlds. He looked at his beautiful sister-in-law adoringly and agreed.

Only the Old Wise Woman, the Great King Arnuwanda, and Lieia-Hepa herself were present, along with a pure white baby lamb. All were sworn to secrecy. After ritual prayers, the Tawananna invoked the intervention of Uliliyassis – a minor god who removes impotence – then she explained what was to happen:

> "I place a spindle and a distaff in the patient's hand, and he comes under the gates. When he steps forward through the gates, I take the spindle and distaff away from him. I give him a bow and arrows,

> and say to him all the while, 'I have just taken the femininity away from you and given you masculinity in return. You have cast off the sexual behaviour expected of women; you have taken to yourself the behaviour expected of men'. After this has been accomplished, the woman in him will enter the lamb, who shall be forthwith given to the gods."

All this was done. The Great King Arnuwanda even had himself dressed in military garb for several days, but soon he was back in the harem sharing his woes with his sympathetic lady friends, and after that he was again bringing his favourite guardsmen into his chambers. There were sounds of leather slapping flesh, but the moans of pain and pleasure that came from his chamber were not made by the guardsman.

It was not long after this that Suppiluliuma reported that the "worst had happened." While walking amongst the people dressed in a woman's cape, he was attacked by a mob. The two guards were quickly overcome, and the Great King was carried away, bloodstains were found, and he was never seen again. He had obviously been murdered by his own people and probably rendered into small pieces. "There was nothing that could be done. The gods had spoken. Though I did not want the responsibility, I had to step into the sacred obligation of becoming Great King, for there are no other candidates who qualify." Lieia-Hepa laughed grimly, for of course she believed neither Suppiluliuma's unproven tale nor that he had forgotten that the vassal-king of Tarhuntassa, Kurunta, was the brother of a Great King, Urhi-Teshub, and thus had an equal claim to the throne.

Lieia-Hepa took a long sip of her drug-enriched drink, which left her senses alert but her mind dreamy. She remembered several years before when the ten wandering Ahhiyawa mercenaries had been brought before the Great King, at his request, after having been captured trying to openly enter through the Lion Gate. They were a dangerous-looking but also ragged crew with their weapons having been taken away and their bronze-plated armour clinging to them in fragments. The helmets they carried must once have been splendid, some once had tall horsehair plumes that were now in tatters. Those of bronze were dented in several places and two helmets had sword splits. They bowed their heads but did not prostrate themselves in the eastern manner.

They brought in the young slave girl from the harem who spoke the Ahhiyawa tongue of Milawata so could translate into Luwian. Questioned by Mahhuzzi, the Great King's Lord Stewart, the warrior in front who said his name was Sthenelos admitted they had fought in the initial attack on Taruisa five years earlier, but his leader, whom he called *the Akhaian* and gave a name that the translator did not understand, had them leave the attack when the Taruisans locked themselves behind their impenetrable walls. The Great King was incensed at this news even though these Ahhiyawa weren't there for the final pillaging and burning of the important coastal city and in spite of the fact that Wilusa the Troad was no longer a vassal state. Suppiluliuma still considered the city in his territory and he had them all put under guard. Kil-Teshub whispered to his Majesty that they looked like redoubtable warriors – scarred and sinewy with the level-eyed hostility of veteran warriors – and could be useful in the military. The Great King paused a long while before agreeing to accept these outlaws into his forces, though without the special status they had expected.

The Great Queen had paid only half attention until she saw the tallest warrior on one end. He had not spoken, but he was clearly different from the rest in both his bearing and his attire. His cuirass was layered bronze plates but it also had gold and silver medallions on his chest and shoulders that had been rubbed with dirt to hide them and further hidden by the light cloak thrown over them. He looked about boldly but under his brows, which the Hatti were careful never to do. Indeed, he looked up directly at Lieia as she was looking directly at him. The moment was seared into her memory, for such shared looks were forbidden, and the man could be killed on the spot if it were noted he had even looked toward the Great Queen. She kept silent while the dangerous glance extended into long seconds and enjoyed the sensations as her blood quickened. This warrior stood straight up like a king surveying his kingdom. He had long sun-streaked chestnut hair over very pale green eyes whose pupils held an intense, pulsating glint from an inner source. Yes, beneath the scruffy beard, his sculpted features were godlike. Lieia enjoyed the warm pulsations sent by Ishtar, goddess of desire, and her heart and body moistened, but she forced herself to look away.

Unfortunately, as the Ahhiyawa were led from the palace, some of the men were seen glancing at women from the king's court whom they passed on the stairway. The Great King saw and ordered their immediate arrest. This was a fatal breach of protocol. The Great King arose from his throne and addressed them, actually walking toward them, followed by a guard and the nervous translator from the harem:

> "Do you not know that among the Hatti women are treated as respected objects? You barbarians who have sex with any woman you choose do not realize the proper way of things! For the Hittites, it is not permitted that a brother sexually take his cousin or his sister, or that you look openly upon women that do not belong to you. You can build your own harem, but you are forbidden to look upon that of another man! Do you not know the story of Mariya? And for what reason did he die?"

The Great King was waving his arms now, incensed at the insult but needing a myth of justification he told the story of Mariya.

> "Did not a lady's maid walk by and he look at her? But the father of My Majesty himself looked out of the window and caught him in the offence, saying, 'You – why did you look at her?' So he died for that reason. The man perished just for looking from afar. And now so shall you!"

At a signal from Suppiluliuma, Hittite soldiers with drawn spears closed in around them. "Take them away; they shall be executed," announced the Great King.

To the discomfort of General Kil-Teshub, whose armies were always in need of more good men, and to the dismay of the newly smitten Queen Lieia-Hepa, the men were immediately taken away to the lower level prison rooms. After his Majesty returned to his throne and whispered to Mahhuzzi, in a loud voice his chief administrator ordered their beheading two days hence (since the following day involved the sacred festival to the agriculture gods).

She did not question the judgment of the Great King; she knew the Hittite custom of treating women with abstemious respect on the one hand but on the other the nobles could choose whatever woman or girl they wished from the general population to be *honoured* by becoming a courtesan in their harems. There, they served their lord's pleasure and not their own. Lieia-Hepa did her acts of obeisance and returned to her quarters. She had to act quickly and she did. She prayed to the Sun Goddess of Arinna and to Ishtar for help, but she also sent the captain of her trusted personal guard, a tough but loyal Hurrian named Zunan-Teshub who had been with her for years, to convey to the chief guard of the jails that the tall dark-bearded man of the Ahhiyawa with the single gold earring in his left ear and the red horsehair crested bronze helm was to be separated from the other prisoners, cleaned up, and brought to a private audience with her. This was to be kept in utmost secrecy as the gods were watching all and would destroy anyone who shared the information. She felt secure in this directive for she doubted that the Great King had even made note of how many Ahhiyawa warriors there were, much less noticed their faces. She had no doubt her orders and her erotic plans were approved by Ishtar, for the goddess held dear such intrigues of love. (Back in her dreamy reverie lounging on her bed, the Great Queen twisted about and smiled at the memory of her swift actions and how successful they were.)

While Suppiluliuma was out on his endless circuit of leading routine rituals in various temples of the gods, Zunan accompanied by two other guards brought her the Ahhiyawa called the Akhaian, thoroughly bathed. His face was clean-shaven revealing a sculpted chin and a strong lip line, and his hair was trimmed, perfumed, curled and oiled in the Hittite way. His hands were tightly bound behind his back. He had lost five years in appearance and now looked less than thirty. She was delighted to see he was both more beautiful beneath the grit and full beard than she had anticipated but also apprehensive that he was much more powerful and dangerous so close up. He had no fat, and his shoulders and dark arms were harder and more vascular than she had ever seen. She sent everyone from the room but Henti, the terrified blonde girl from the harem who was needed as translator. Henti did not ask but feared she was participating in something of which the Great King would not approve, but she was not left a choice.

Lieia was dressed in her finery as chief priestess but in a much more revealing manner than was usual; her bare arms wore only golden bracelets and the golden snake curling around above her left elbow. Her silken bodice was open above her breasts, which rested on a high waistband, revealing layers of jewelled necklaces on her upper chest. Her black and golden robes extended to her ankles but were made in separate strips that readily parted. Around her head was a golden diadem set with small jewels and a rare deep red ruby set in front. She raised her face with its darkened lips and Misri-styled kohl eyes to look down at the man who had entered two steps below her and pointed her silver-handled leathern ceremonial whip to the floor before him. The Akhaian, understanding, bent to his knees and further bowed his head when the Great Queen imperiously indicated so with her staff. "You, Ahhiyawa–*Ah-kee-an*, have been brought here to me to pay obeisance to the Sun Goddess of Arinna, and through her to the Ugaritic Ashtart, both of whom are ultimately Ishtar the Queen of Heaven who rose into the world long before the ancient city of Babylon was ever imagined."

Henti translated and the Akhaian looked in surprise at the girl, surely no more than sixteen or seventeen years old with startling light blue eyes. He was rewarded with the snap of the leather whip on his shoulder. He looked up and into the dark and dangerous eyes of the earthly representative of the Queen of Heaven, smiling as she dangled the horsehide whip across his face, but he returned to his bowed head posture without a sign of emotion. Lieia made it clear that his life might be saved if he showed devotional worship to Ishtar. He spoke low, wanting to know if his actions might save his men, asking as humbly as he could. Henti translated. The Great Queen replied that it was not her decision to make but that if Ishtar is pleased by his service to her, the High Priestess of the Queen of Heaven, she would do what she could to keep the Ahhiyawa alive. He looked at her with a peculiar light in his pale green eyes and nodded. She had his agreement and knew he would submit.

Henti was permitted to leave but required to remain nearby. Communications would be done by gesture, act, and touch from here on, and Lieia-Hepa knew they would mainly come as commands from her and the goddess who possessed her. The door was sealed, and the ritual of abasement began for the Akhaian, just as the ritual of goddess power overwhelming an initiate and breaking his spirit began for the High Priestess of Ishtar. She looked at the sinewy strong man kneeling below her and licked her lips, feeling the divine power of the goddess surge through her.

She smiled down at him wickedly and directed him to the floor where he was made to put his forehead. She tore off his upper garments and ran her hands and fingernails over the ripples of his shoulders and back, singing and speaking in the ritual Hurrian tongue. She noted the scars, signs of serious wounds – spear points, sword slashes, and arrowheads – and touched them with some awe. She had never seen such scars, healed or not. The noble warriors of the Hatti fought mainly by chariot and preferred a safe distance. Still, now hissing like a serpent with little cries of effort and joy, she applied the little whip to him, starting slowly. He neither resisted nor made any sound at all, which drove her into a fury that left lacerations in the man's brown weathered flesh.

She proceeded in this manner, going through many of the ritual tortures and humiliations, mixed with caresses and kindnesses like allowing drinks of cold water, that usually led the novitiate to break and plead for mercy from the goddess and thus begin to be possessed by her. The possessed was grateful when the tortures were paused, so he loved the goddess for her tender mercies. Lieia had even heard tales of some who had become so intoxicated by the goddess in her dark aspect that they had harmed their men's parts or dressed as priestesses ever after. This man, however, clearly was not going to break, plead, or even respond, and she grew both frustrated and excited.

She went to the next level, bringing him next to her bed and forcing him to commit acts of submissive eroticism that would be unthinkable to any Hittite, directing his head up between her knees even while she splayed her legs and stood over him, so he was directly faced with the demanding power and intoxicating scent of the female mystery. (Back on the same bed where her present reverie was taking place, Ishtar aroused her senses and Lieia found herself so enthralled by her own memories that she rhythmically squeezed her thighs together in pleasure.) Recklessly, she unbound his hands, thrilled by the sense of danger but trusting that he would not harm her for both his own sake and that of his men. She lay on her back and pulled him by his hair into her personal Temple of Ishtar. She was pleased, not angry, to feel he had become fully aroused himself. Yet the queen was even more surprised that the Akhaian understood the secrets of a woman's anatomy, secrets usually assumed to be known only among women, but was unwilling and unable to stop what he was doing with his lips, tongue, and now his fingers until she lost herself in shudders of ecstasy. She was in such a state that she pulled him atop her and directed his rigid manhood into her body. It had been quite some time since

Suppiluliuma had done this deed and more room within for this man was needed, so, despite her pleasurable pain, she could not take him very deeply.

However, just as she was about to lose herself, the thought of becoming the bearer of a barbarian child brought her back to her sense of identity: before the Akhaian could spend himself, she pushed him away in confusion. She directed him to leave her bed. The Great Queen attempted to return to her sense of divine superiority, so she haughtily pointed to the marble basin for him to purify himself and prepare to leave. But feelings of pleasure still coursed through her, so she was only partially successful. She went over to the man, feeling the glow of his warm body, taking in his scent, and in the pretext of directing him where to stand to await the guards, she pressed herself against him. Did a smile play on his lips? She went to the door and signalled. Zunan, the captain of her guard, came for him and she had Henti tell him he would be called for again, in due time. Then she called for her most trusted sub-priestesses to come in and cleanse her, both physically and spiritually.

Such meetings in honour of the Queen of Heaven continued to take place at her demand about once every full moon, which seemed appropriate to her. She was fascinated by this big, powerful man who so readily worshipped the goddess through her, yet never seemed to give up the secret core of his identity. She brought in Henti and, while pacing around the prone, naked man carrying her little whip, she asked him openly, “Clearly Shaushka-Ishtar has asserted her power over you through me, and it’s obvious to see that our domination excites you,” she smiled wickedly, “yet you still do not relinquish your soul. You will explain this to me.”

Henti translated and the Akhaian looked up, “You are the goddess, are you not?” She nodded. “Since it is so, it is but pious devotion for me to fall into the ecstasy of goddess worship. The humility is real but that does not mean I will allow myself to be destroyed. If I lost myself entirely, there would be no one here to worship you, is that not so?” She nodded cautiously this time. "So I still my pride and worship the goddess by submitting with pleasurable anguish to all her demands, but I cannot give up my soul, for it is not mine to give. It is my ruling *daimonion*, my life's guide, and I am but the shadow of its dark inner light." Henti could not hide a faint smile at these words before translating. Lieia was pleased.

She managed to keep the other Akhaians alive by gently and provocatively dissuading her husband from giving the order to have them killed. She had the Akhaian leader given separate quarters in which he was watched over by guards but had decent meals brought to him by resentful servants and was allowed a space in which to take exercise and carry on weapon practice. Hittite soldiers gladly volunteered for the chance to spar with this foreign warrior for he had much to teach them. Not one, or even two or three, would have dared encounter him on an actual battlefield.

But eventually rumours did find their way to the ears of the Great King. As puritanical and hypocritical as he was, Suppiluliuma was enraged and confronted his Great Queen in privacy on this matter. She admitted that she had practiced archaic mystic rituals with one of the Ahhiyawa soldiers, not mentioning the tall one she had set aside. Knowing how religiously fearful of the gods the Great King was, she claimed she had been ordered to do so by the ancient Babylonian aspect of the Sun Goddess of Arinna. The goddess had demanded that she bend and humiliate one of the men to the domination of Ishtar, the Queen of Heaven, to prove her power over all nations. She had done nothing but ritually torture him, she claimed, and he had submissively broken, embracing her feet in gratitude, after which she had then had him killed. Her story also had the advantage of explaining the number of Ahhiyawa left together. Suppiluliuma wanted to know which one it was, but Lieia-Hepa did not know his name. The Great King had the remaining nine Ahhiyawa beheaded in secret the next day. She had not brought the Akhaian to her since then, though she had Zunan see he was kept alive. He may blame her, and, with his men dead, she no longer had power over him.

Back in the present in her room, Lieia-Hepa fell into a sleep. Such strange memories coming hard upon the realization that Hattusa itself was in grave danger and so was she, proved too much to deal with.

After refreshment and rest, Suppiluliuma chose to undergo yet another ritual and physical cleansing to avoid any possibility of defilement, especially after the Great Queen had displayed obvious demonic possession. His dressers then put on him the garb of the military commander-in-chief, including his tall, pointed crown and he was given his short spear of silver to indicate his office. He called his top general, his chief advisor, and his scribe to him, and, with the usual twelve royal bodyguards, set off to view the dual monuments to the glory of the Hatti military – but especially to himself – that were nearing completion. Going on foot, they set off down the elegant steps from the palace akropolis, into the temple complex, down a long hall with polished walls, passing by the entrances into granite sanctuaries for various gods, and out the steep ramp of shining limestone and marble that led down into the upper city, which was still below the palace on the akropolis.

They walked along an enormous viaduct until they came to the great outcrop of rock that held the declarations of conquest of Suppiluliuma II in large Luwian hieroglyphs for all to see in their final form where they would surely last for all eternity. He had, after all, the same name as his great forbear, Suppiluliuma I, who had expanded the Hittite Empire to its greatest extent – from Wilusa in the west into what were then the Mittani lands beyond the great Mala River to the east, and south from Amurru to the Black Sea in the north. It was important to make it known to the Hatti and to the world that he had accomplished nearly as much as his namesake even though he had been Great King for a mere twelve years and was faced with drought, desertion, and disease. He looked at the majestic hieroglyphs and felt himself inflate with his own glory. Truly, he was taller and stronger than most other men, certainly including his father, so he felt himself to be a great warrior king. Only he, guided by Teshub, could lead his people through this temporary crisis of famine, rebellion, and invasion, he told himself, and there was much more yet to be done. Exactly what and how was in the hands of the gods.

"Excellent work, Penti-Sharruma, both by you in your design and by your rock-carving craftsmen."

The chief scribe beamed gratefully and bowed low. He then raised his arms, palms up, toward the king: "I live to serve your Majesty, but the brilliance of your Sun comes from the gods alone." His eyes were moist: he meant it.

They continued on to the huge, placidly beautiful pool that served as one of the reservoirs of the city. Over the low marble wall surrounding it could be seen that the level of the waters was considerably diminished. "Once this current situation ends, the waters will rise again," said the Great King, jaw thrust forward. All around nodded and murmured agreement.

Close by was the high-domed pillar that had the original record of his Majesty's glorious conquests as the one copied onto the large outcropping rock from which they had just come but in smaller glyphs. It was built just outside the entry of the mountain-like burial chamber he had built for placement of his father's body taken from the Mountain Temple. Just inside, he was pleased as always to see the stalwart relief sculpture of himself as warrior with godlike horns guarding the passage to the "underworld", down a long series of steps right into the rock of the akropolis. Pity he had to move the likeness of his father from this tower to make room for this vital record-keeping. This pillar's writing had progressed further, however, as it was carved before the monument on the rock outcrop. This one ended with the three naval battles off the coast of Alasiya, in which Hittite infantry on the battleships of the vassal kingdoms of Ugarit and Amurru boarded Cypriot vessels and beat back a move toward independence, which seems to have begun with the migrant groups of Peleset and Danaans. The Great King wanted to hear of glorious victories again as he looked at the still beardless relief sculpture of himself in the doorway of his artificial mountain tomb, but he could not read the Luwian hieroglyphs: “Penti-Sharruma, royal scribe, read to me of my victories at sea.”

The scribe read aloud as though he were addressing a crowd, proud to speak for the king himself:

> “I mobilized and I, Suppiluliuma, the Great King, immediately crossed the sea. The ships of Alasiya met me in the sea three times for battle, and I smote them; and I seized the ships and set fire to them in the sea. But when I arrived on dry land, the enemy from Alasiya came in a multitude against me for battles...”

The soldiers of the Hatti had even temporarily occupied much of the big copper-rich island for the first time since his father Tudhaliya had landed troops there. It was an important victory and worth noting on his monument as the first naval battle. However, the troops and ships were still being kept at Alasiya, for other marauders from the sea had begun to move in to fortify those that were already there. The latest news was that the island had mostly succumbed to the invaders. At the moment the Great King and his entourage felt it best to ignore that.

“It is a fine monument and a noble record of victories,” said the chief advisor, Mahhuzzi. “The gods have decreed that you shall preserve the kingdom, even in these times of great crisis.” The Great King preened, though such flattery was expected.

“Yes, though it seems a shame the monument to the Great King Tudhaliya had to be moved to make room for it,” interjected General Kil-Teshub, who had served as a young chariot warrior under his much older brother Tudhaliya. “After all, by the grace of the gods, he expanded the borders of the kingdom on all sides and even took control of vassal states beyond them. It was he who first took Alasiya when the Cypriot king cut back our copper and blocked grain shipments. We needed food and we needed more bronze." He stiffened his hard old body and stared through the glyphs into the empty space where the old monument to Tudhaliya had been. The air seemed to stand still.

After an icy silence, Suppiluliuma pulled himself up to his considerable height. "You dare to question the judgment of your heaven-appointed ruler, O Uncle? The Great King is still right before you, and he remains your Sun," and he gestured at the life-sized relief carving of himself inside the gateway. His image stood one foot forward, broad and strong under his conical, tasselled crown, his custom-breaking godlike beard not yet begun, and with the horns of divinity sprouting from his forehead. The figure held a huge lance pointing skyward in his right hand and a long bow over his left shoulder.

The grizzled soldier turned to face his nephew the king, but he was unruffled.

"Know you not that it was the conquests of my father into foreign lands creating new borders that needed guarding and new cities to occupy that first began to empty the fields of able workers and transfer populations away from our biggest cities? Standing armies far afield became necessary. At the end of his reign, during the sickness that he could not stop, many people deserted the holy city of Hattusa, leaving the centre of the kingdom weakened."

"It is so, Great King," intoned Mahhuzzi.

"Know you not that the reason he needed to attack the island of Alasiya was that we needed its copper to make more bronze weapons? We lost the copper mines at Isuwa to the Assyrians long before, but the Assyrian Great King Tukulti-Ninurta seemed willing to trade for its copper. However, we had not much to trade any longer, so His Majesty, my father, chose to attack the Assyrians by crossing the Mala and meeting them at Nihriya. You know what the result was."

"Yes," gravely nodded General Kil-Teshub. "I was there, a chariot bowman. It was my first battle. Promised allies did not arrive. We were crushed. I lived because my commander ordered the retreat. The gods left no doubt they favoured the Assyrians."

"I love and worship my father the Great King and certainly respect his protector, the Hurrian god Sharruma, but his expansion and loss to the Assyrians cost us greatly. It is I, My Majesty, who early in my reign recrossed the Mala and took back the copper mines, which were, alas, nearly depleted. My Majesty is left to be the one to save the Hatti from what he has wrought. That is why his monument has been hidden. My Majesty, son of the Storm-God, is the last hope of the kingdom of the Hatti."

"So it is," agreed Mahhuzzi the courtier. "Just look at the truth of this beautiful monument," he waved at its splendour. "The earthquakes, drought, and famine may require the intervention of the gods, but, look! You fortified our defences along the Mala and the Assyrians have not dared to cross since. You sent allies to help protect Taruisa from the ruthless Ahhiyawa invaders. You, Great King, led the army yourself in your gilt chariot and pushed back the Arzawa and the Lukka, taking their kings as prisoners. After that, like the Storm-God who watches over you, you stormed into Tarhuntassa Land in the far south, sacking its capital, and mercifully accepted the surrender of the traitor, Kurunta, allowing him to kiss thy holy feet."

"Yes, pity the old man tried to escape," ventured General Kil-Teshub, glancing skyward. "He may have become a wise advisor."

"It was not meant to be," Suppiluliuma shot back. "He had committed sacrilege, so the gods decreed it was his time to die. I made his lowly nephew Halata into my vassal, a man who has no wish to rule." But within his heart Suppiluliuma felt a glow of pleasure as he recalled watching Kurunta, the traitor who would be king, tied to a throne-like chair be garrotted slowly to death. It was Suppiluliuma's favourite method of execution for he could observe the moment of death itself in the frozen horror on the victim's face.

"Shall I attempt to remember any of this conversation to record it later?" asked Penti-Sharruma, the chief scribe.

"Record nothing unless you are commanded to do so," Suppiluliuma snapped.

"My King, it is time to speak openly," General Kil-Teshub spoke. "Can we sit?" The four did so on marble steps, the highest one being occupied by the Great King. "I am going to speak the truth, your Majesty, and I ask your permission to do so."

Suppiluliuma scowled but nodded, pulling the oiled curls of his beard, "Proceed."

"O Great King, as you know, a famine is in the land for there is drought and a shortage of fieldworkers. Trade has all but ceased. An army of invaders approaches, so a great many of the common people have surrounded or entered the sacred city of Hattusa seeking safety and food. There is little or no food for them, nor is there the space to give them all living quarters. The troops protecting the grain supplies that the nobility need for sustenance face mobs in the day and groups of thieves at night. This cannot continue; they will break through." The Great King now looked both surprised and concerned. "Spies have made it clear a great army of nearly eight thousand warriors is near and continues to approach. The Kaska too are on the move. We have sent envoys to the invaders to ask for a parley to at least delay their advance, but though they said they would like it very much if your Majesty were to come to them, they know we don't have much to offer and they aren't going to accept a little gold when they can have it all. They could be upon us any day now. We must act."

"What are you saying?" Mahhuzzi the grand vizier broke in. "Not only are we protected by the ancient gods of the Hatti, but, as the record attests, we are led by the greatest war leader the Hittites have ever known. No army, no man can stand against him. And if those don't suffice, we are the mightiest city on earth, as grand as Babylon or Memphis on the Nile, but with even thicker, higher walls!"

"Let him speak," said Suppiluliuma with furrowed brows. "What do you suggest, my general?"

"These words will be hard to hear, O Great King. I see no way to victory, yet I do have a suggestion. What

Mahhuzzi fails to note is that all we have to defend Hattusa is your royal bodyguard of thirty-six golden-speared Meshedi, the regular city guardsmen numbering a hundred, plus one regiment of less than a thousand on leave from the field including fifty chariots and charioteers. The enemy are likely well over eight thousand experienced and determined outlanders, to which we can add another four thousand Kaska savages. The rest of the vast soldiery of the Hatti are too far away to get back to us in time for a defence. They are southwest in Lukka Land and Arzawa, straight south in Tarhuntassa, and on the island of Alasiya. They are on the eastern frontier facing the Assyrians. Your Highness, we will not be able to hold Hattusa."

"So my military General is saying that My Majesty and his royal city are doomed?"

"I am," said the general, not bothering to include any royal titles.

"But you said you have a suggestion?"

"Only one, but it is most humbly made in the name of the heroic warrior code of the Hatti. I say to you, O Great King, lead all your remaining warriors and guardsmen to battle in the field with the enemy without further delay. We will be defeated and killed, but our name will be remembered in awe until the end of time, long after you take your place in the tomb built by your father in the Mountain Temple. Your name, Great King, will never be forgotten and neither will your glorious Hittite soldiers. You will be immortal!" The old soldier knew how to appeal to his nephew the king.

"There is another choice, your Majesty," began Mahhuzzi thoughtfully, though General Kil-Teshub glared down at him. "It seems the common people of Hattusa will not be saved even if we do go to battle and sacrifice ourselves to become carrion for the kites, crows, and the dogs of war. We will rot on the field and the Great King will not reach the royal tomb and attain to his godhead." He glanced toward his king, waiting for his nod. He skillfully extended the pause. "So why don't we save ourselves by abandoning the city to preserve the sacred life of your

Majesty so your Majesty can carry on the empire of the Hatti from a new capital? It has been done before, so the gods have already approved this action by allowing precedents from the past!"

There was a long silence as the Great King ran his fingers through his carefully curled beard. He scanned the horizon. He looked at his own graven image. "Is the fearful vision of the Great Queen Lieia-Hepa already coming true?" he wondered to himself. He looked sharply at his three closest followers. "We need to mobilize immediately," and both the general and the advisor looked hopeful, but it was Mahhuzzi who was heard. "We must evacuate ourselves from Hattusa as quickly as possible."

3. Peoples of the Sea Inland

After days of preparing, the war council of the five leaders of the sea-borne invaders met to plan the imminent attack on Hattusa, but all sorts of reports brought to them by spies and hearsay needed to be discussed. The first was that their numbers were decreasing, as groups of warriors headed back to the sea they preferred. Proof of this was evident in that their council of five was now a council of four.

Uhhaziti the Arzawan spoke, "Leukos of Kriti led his troops away in the night back toward the coast. The 'Peoples of the Sea' are living up to the name given them by the Pharaoh of the Nile lands and deserting our high plains army bent on plundering Hattusa. They yearned for the big waters and wish for easier plunder. News is spreading that the ancient port city of Ugarit far to the south is less defended and ready for the taking. Most of Ugarit's fighting ships are engaged by the Hittites against other sea pirates off the coast of the Lukka Land and others, further south yet, are still ferrying Hittite troops around the copper isle of Alasiya in a losing cause. Ugarit is a worthy prize indeed."

Payava the Lukkan retorted, "Hattusa is an even bigger prize, indeed the greatest prize this horde of sea warriors has ever attempted. Yes, it is far inland and no one is yet sure taking it is even possible, but note the Hittite forces are also in the south, and they are in the east facing Assyrians too. The time is right, and the time is now."

"Let them go," added Eruthros Danaan king of Aitolia, waving his giant paw dismissively. "Hattusa is still ours for the taking, and we will now have more of the treasures of the Hatti to share among fewer of us."

"You are both right," added Sarpedon the Sardinian evenly. "Losing Leukos, the Peleset, Ekwesh, and others is no great hindrance. Locals are joining us every day too. But we have more immediate news of concern: There is great activity in Hattusa, though its purpose is not yet clear. A clamour has arisen and the chariot horses are being brought together. Maybe it's just one of their extravagant religious festivals. But why now? Something is afoot."

"You don't think they could be planning to attack us before we can approach the walls?" Old Uhhaziti asked.

"But they haven't the forces for that, at least according to all we've learned, unless one of their field armies has somehow returned or ..." Sarpedon trailed off.

"Or?"

"Or they are intending a suicide attack, an honourable death in battle in favour of being cornered like rats within their walls like the Taruisans."

"The Taruisans came out at the last. They say the sea god shook their giant ramparts apart in places. Exposed and desperate, they poured out and fought like titans for a time, pushing the Akhaians back," Payava interjected. "They couldn't have anticipated the unheard-of manoeuvre of the Thessalian horsemen who rode behind the Trojan defenders by going around them over rugged hills where chariots cannot. They rode through the broken walls and opened the gates from within. I saw the end of it though we arrived too late to be of any help."

"Who *rides* horses?" the Sardinian asked with a grim smile, shaking his head. "You can't fight from one. If they can bear your weight you've still to stay on and direct the beast."

"The Thessalians lead each other by halters and use their knees and hands, I'm told, but no one can fight from horseback. The counter-attack of the Akhaians was the end. The sea god and the horse brought the city down."

"Payava, from what we know of Suppiluliuma, does a suicide attack seem likely?"

"Not one bit, so either they've received reinforcements or they are considering doing what was done twice before – relocate their royalty."

"In any case, if you agree, we must mobilize now and head out early tomorrow. We should reach Hattusa in little more than a week. I will send a courier to notify the Kaska to stand by but stay back," concluded the Sardinian.

"Ah, the Kaska. Only this morning, my spies brought me one more very important item of information. It concerns our great friends, these Kaska," Uhhaziti swirled his watered wine and looked at the others. "They have retaken the ancient city of Nerik from the Hittites without any resistance. The Hatti there were outnumbered and hoped to avoid bloodshed. It didn't work. The city is intact, but all the Hatti in residence were slaughtered and their gods pulled down."

The horde moved out the next day leaving the families, beasts for meat, and most camp followers behind at their base on an arm of the Sangarios River, which supplied them with vital resources for their temporary home. The army of warriors and freebooters was organized well enough into four divisions, one under each commander, with the Lukkan in the lead, followed by the Arzawan, the Sardinian, with the Danaan behind. Each division, rough as it might be, was subdivided into the various subcultures, which mostly kept to their allotted places though sometimes the alignment became stretched out horizontally instead, approximating a line. Most of the fighters proudly wore their colourful military garments, though few bothered with their hot helmets or bronze greaves. These, along with their heavy swords, shields, and ashen spears, were carried by servants, women, or on donkeys, old horses or carts, or by themselves in a duffle.

The warriors were ready for action and excited by the anticipation of great plunder, so a good pace was maintained. There were few horsemen, mainly restricted to northern Hellenes on their tough ponies, but at the front nearly eighty carts, both two- and four-wheeled, rumbled along, each conveying a war chariot within it, some entire, some disassembled, some splendid, others dilapidated. With their light frames but strong mid-cart axles, these chariots were sturdy enough to carry three men on a flat battlefield but not across country. For the journey the men walked and the horses had a lesser burden. Most chariots had been gained from the men's recent victory over the Hittite allies so they lacked veteran charioteers, but there were a number of such veterans among the host and they were chosen to drive strong chariots over the bumpy ground so the leaders and commanders could mount one quickly if necessary. Standing in a bumpy chariot for any length of time was worse than walking.

On the morning of their third day, light-riding scouts on horseback galloped up to Payava the Lukkan at the head of the army. The breathless rider in front informed him that a long line of people was walking toward them and would soon meet them head-on.

"Are they warriors?" asked the Lukkan.

"Not by the look of it. We didn't approach them yet, but they're on foot and few appear to be armed. There are only about fifty, so not much danger. In fact, they look like a tired, bedraggled bunch."

"Why are they leaving the city? Could be more starving peasants," Payava considered, "or worse, exiled plague carriers."

"Unlikely, my Lord," the curly-haired scout said, the unaccustomed title causing Payava to raise an eyebrow. "Bedraggled or not, everyone was walking on his own and no one was falling behind. There is a big one with a spear who seems to be leading them."

Payava sent out messengers on horseback to bring the other three leaders to the front for immediate counsel. Then he looked back at the scout to correct his labelling.

"Scout Kabi, we who have no homelands and must make our own way overland or by sea into the homelands of others are all of the same class. We have no lords, but we have no slaves either. We are all outcasts and freebooters, so no one among us is a noble or king or queen. Unlike the Hatti, Babylonians, Misriwi, and other soul-enslaved castle-dwellers, we no longer await direction from the gods before we act. We do not waste time appointing priests or priestesses, soothsayers, wise women or augers to tell us what is the will of the gods and how best we can follow it. People can worship whatever gods they please but as for guiding our choices, those days are over. Everyone in the cities knows what we want. What we want is what they have and what we are coming to get. There is no need to read an animal's liver to know this. We practice our divination by watching the sky and the trees in the wind to foresee the weather, but even more by listening to the words of our spies." The Lukkan laughed with an evil grin, and, after a moment, the scout joined in, pleased to be alerted to his expected reaction.

The young scout named Kabi rode back to his troop; he dismounted and led their little horses to leather bags of water, which they then shared. Kabi reflected that he had never heard it said before, but Payava was right. The peoples' gods seem to have left the earth. They may be prayed to in times of need or thanked in times of plenty, but no one any longer seemed to feel their actual presence in their hearts, guiding their thinking. *They do not whisper in our heads any longer*, he thought. In fact he had largely forgotten the numerous Canaanite deities of his childhood; but when it thundered, he still heard the Sky God known only as *I Am* of his nomadic Khabiru tribe, who insisted he was the only "true" god. Kabi had been little more than a boy when the Hatti destroyed his family and sheepherding village. He found himself tied to others in a long slave train march to Tarhuntassa where he was sold to a horse trader, so he learned horses before escaping across the western Taurus mountains to the Lukka Lands. Once he learned the languages, he found he also heard the whispers and felt the presence of the Hatti and Lukkan gods. They were implied within the speech. But something *big* collapsed when the coastal cities and the palaces began to be attacked by the uprooted marauders from the sea and, soon after, by uprisings of the common people, himself included. It seems that when the palaces fell, so did the speech of the gods, perhaps the gods themselves. He had felt his head clear and had joined the rebels. But perhaps the gods departed first, for when did it begin? He didn't know but the water was refreshing.

Dust rose as two small troops of five approached at double pace, each led by a clattering chariot. The nearest and first to arrive was Uhhaziti the gruff Arzawan who had chosen to wear his brightly plated war helm, as had his guard. His chariot pulled up close to the standing Lukkan. "News, my Lord?" he asked, and Payava saw that old habits die hard.

"We have a body of men, maybe some women, approaching coming from Hattusa. Our scouts did not speak with them. When the others arrive, we four and a troop of warriors shall ride to them to discover what they are about. Hattusa itself is nearly in sight, so we don't want to be delayed too long."

"Shall we dispose of them?" asked the old warrior. "The men could use the sport."

"We shall see. They may be coming to join us!"

Soon the Sardinian arrived in a chariot studded with bronze disks driven by a young charioteer with long hair flying in the wind like the horses' manes. He descended to the group where he was alerted to the situation. He was the thinker, but no explanation for this exodus came to mind beyond the idea of vermin escaping a sinking ship. He looked behind. "Where's our big 'King of the Danuna'?"

"Eruthros prefers the Hellenic dialect, *Danaan*, over the Maionian," Payava smiled in a low voice. "He was in the back and hasn't arrived yet, but perhaps we'd best not wait." Then he raised his voice: "We can send along a few armed chariots to follow our scout back to the strangers, leaving a space to bring back one or two of our guests." He looked at the other chiefs. "One of us can go along and bring their leaders or spokesmen back to us here." The Arzawan and the Sardinian both volunteered for the task, but Payava pointed to Uhhaziti. "You go," he said. "You're the most expendable." Uhhaziti laughed along, but looked quickly away since it was probably true.

"Can I kill a few?" asked the Arzawan, not indicating whether he was joking or not. Not waiting for an answer, he quickly pointed out four other chariots to accompany his own, picking two from his own party and one from each of the others. He boarded his rough-hewn but solid chariot, and gave the scout a one-word order, "Go." Kabi did so and the Arzawan's driver had his dark horses pull the chariot behind the scout's horse with the other four quickly following.

Over hillsides and through fields they went, but in little time they sighted the approaching line of strangers coming from the direction of the great city of the Hatti. The ragged line paused as it saw them just as they paused to look down upon it. The leaders looked it over. "This certainly doesn't look like a threat," spoke the scout.

"Pity," grunted Uhhaziti, who like the other warriors lived for battle and was anxious to put his bronze spear to use. "It looks like they have a leader for he gave the signal to pause. Let's go see." And he led the troop of chariots and one rider toward the front of the line at a steady pace to avoid the appearance that they were attacking.

Starting at the front, the entire line was stilled. All eyes were upon the approaching chariots. The tall man with long chestnut-brown hair and beard put his sack of goods down and stepped forward a few steps. No one followed, including the young woman in the hooded cloak right behind him. He wore rough peasant clothes and had no spear but did wear a new-looking heavy leather sheath from which flashed a pearly off-white dagger hilt with a significant pommel of some amber-green mineral.

The curly-haired scout rode up close and looked him over, nodding to him and receiving a nod back. He greeted him in Luwian, and the stranger returned the greeting in Luwian, albeit with a strange accent. Kabi saw that beneath the rough edges he was facing a warrior the like of which he had rarely if ever encountered. He rode back to the chariots guiding his well-trained horse with vocal noises and the squeeze of his knees.

"He speaks Luwian, a little," Kabi said. Uhhaziti nodded grimly staring openly at the stranger. "But..." Kabi continued. The Arzawan looked at him, waiting. "He's not a Hittite; he's a warrior, I think, but ... unfamiliar."

"I see that," rejoined Uhhaziti and moved his chariot forward toward the big man. The others followed but at a hand signal stayed back. He stepped out of the chariot, one hand on the hilt of his sword. He left his translator behind.

"Greetings, may the gods of the land smile upon you," said the Arzawan in Luwian.

"Greetings," the stranger replied, this time in Akhaian, but he continued in rough Luwian. "No need for the sword, friend. Most of this troop is unarmed. We are all refugees from the great city of the Hatti."

"You are Ahhiyawa? The others...?"

"I am called the Akhaian, yes. Others are all former mercenaries or slaves or the poor among the Hatti, some *are* Hatti."

"You are exiles?"

"No, my Lord, we are refugees. We have escaped what remains of Hattusa. I was making my way out amidst the chaos and helped out a friend or two. Others saw a ray of hope and joined the line to follow me out."

"What *remains*... Hattusa cannot have fallen!"

"Hattusa still stands. But the Moon God has gone through more than three phases since the city was deserted by its Great King and Queen who were led out of the southern gate by the royal bodyguard. The royal household and retinue, the troops and their chariots, the temple priests and those who serve them, the nobility and those who serve them, and anyone with arms and mobility — all left the city in a long caravan with wagonloads of treasure and most of the grain that was left. They left the rest of the people to starve or form gangs to kill each other off for the remaining food that was to be found. Most have hopelessly wandered off into the countryside."

"They did it again!" Uhhaziti burst out then contained himself. "Did they know we were coming?"

"Who are you?"

"We are the horde of noble warriors about to plunder Hattusa! Who are you, and why weren't you among those who chose to run from their fate?"

"I was a prisoner, but at the end of the day of evacuation, I found the doors unlocked and the guards all gone. I gathered other prisoners and we found what weapons we could. Avoiding the mobs, we went up to the palace but it too was nearly deserted, except for one of the king's ... attendants, who out of fear for her life had hidden and stayed behind. We made our way out through the Sphinx Gate and others saw fit to join our troop, so here we are, hoping to join you."

"This news must be relayed to our warrior force," Uhhaziti said. "Will you come aboard the car and to speak with our ... *generals*?" saying the last title as though looking for the right word.

The Akhaian waved back to the group, now sitting or even lying flat out. The girl who had been behind him waved back, and others raggedly acknowledged the signal.

Though there was no longer a need, the scout led them onto the trail, up the rise and over several rocky hills right back to the impatient leaders waiting before an impatient army of warriors who yearned for pillage and even more for the glory of war itself. Kabi looked upon the diminutive young girl in the hood and saw a tuft of blonde hair fall over the most beautiful face he had ever seen.

All eyes were on the wild-looking Akhaian as he strode beside Uhhaziti to the front of the gathering. He was a head taller than the Arzawan with an erect posture and a way of walking with his head held high that spoke of noble breeding. As he got closer to the leaders, they could see the many scars on his sun-darkened, hard-muscled shoulders and arms. Beneath his dark mane of tangled hair his light green eyes flashed as he openly glanced at their faces, one by one. Payava the Lukkan stepped forward. He was about to speak when the belated chariot driven by Eruthros the Danaan rumbled up amongst them. Eruthros leapt out, leaving his spear and heavy shield, and ignoring the army walked directly toward the Akhaian. Everyone tensed, for the flame-haired Aitolian, known for his impulsivity, was broader than the stranger and almost as tall. He strode with purpose toward him with his hand on his sword hilt. An old enemy?

But his stride became a walk. His walk became hesitant steps and slowed until he paused wide-eyed directly in front of the Akhaian: "Diomedes my King!" He blurted, and the massive warrior threw himself to the ground raising dust in front of the stranger, his head to the Akhaian's feet. Others froze in astonishment.

"Eruthros, old comrade, is it really you?" the Akhaian asked. The bearlike man on the ground looked up, eyes glistening with tears. "You scoundrel, you survived Ilios!" Diomedes drew the now grinning Danaan to his feet and the two embraced like long lost brothers, laughing in the joy of mutual recognition.

The chieftains and soldiers watching were taken aback, not knowing whether to be pleased or worried. There was a stir in the front ranks and each tried to peer over those in front. Word travelled quickly that this stranger was a famous warrior, though his name was soon lost in passing. *Diomedes*: the name of the Akhaian warrior and once king in his homeland was known to every Akhaian, Danaan, Peleset, and any Wilusans who had joined this motley force. He was recognized as one of the leaders – whom the singers of tales called *heroes* – of those who had ravaged and utterly destroyed the city known to all Akhaians (both among the attackers and those who now dwelt in the city) as Ilios or Troy, called by the Hittites Taruisa. It was a famed port and channel guardian on the lower end of the Sea of Helle – or Hellespont – on the NW coast district the Hittites know as Wilusa, the Troad to the Akhaian migrants who lived there.

The leaders themselves watched wide-eyed. Neither the name nor the person was known to Uhhaziti the Arzawan or to most of the others in hearing range, yet all could see that this dirty vagabond was a warrior to be reckoned with. What was that pearly dagger? Payava the Lukkan had certainly heard the name as one of the attacking Akhaians against whom he was fighting four years ago, but he had remembered hearing that Diomedes and his Argives had left the stagnant encampment of ships on the beach before the final attack. Eruthros, an Argive only by association, certainly knew him well.

But the cunning Sardinian showed no response. He did not know *this* Diomedes, the hero at Taruisa, but years before that war he had encountered King Diomedes after his Shardana pirates came ashore to attack Pylos in the Hellenic Isles. Diomedes had dissuaded them with gold and by inviting them to join Dorian tribesmen and the noble rebels led by himself and the crown prince of Mykenai. After a long and bloody struggle, Mykenai and its allied cities fell – all but Tiryns, the kingdom of Diomedes, which had become the gathering place for the pirates, rebels, and Dorians. Agamemnon had turned against his uncle, Great King Thyestes of the Argolid and Achaia, who had begun to murder his own people en masse to stop their starved uprising against the holy order of things. Diomedes and he had met only briefly, but they were among the attackers when Mykenai was finally taken, the great palace destroyed and its royal graves pillaged. Thyestes had been cut to pieces in the royal palace by enraged farmers. Agamemnon became wanax of smoking ruins, so soon he led rebels and pirates across the sea to invade Ilios. Was Diomedes friend or foe? Could such a turncoat be trusted?

If the appearance of this Akhaian warrior caused a stir, it was nothing compared to the tumult unleashed when Uhhaziti took it upon himself to announce to the leaders in words loud enough for others to hear that Hattusa had been evacuated three weeks earlier. Shock and angry questions followed in an uproar spreading like a tidal wave across the entire gathered army: Had Hattusa been taken?

It must have been the Kaska! Did they flee in terror, leaving the fat, unpillaged city behind them? Let's get them! Meanwhile, the Sardinian talked intensely to Payava, offering direction.

Payava stepped forward onto a large rock and waved his arms. The guards banged their spears on their shields and others followed suit until the crowd was overwhelmed. This gathering of warriors and pirates was not much given to order or discipline, but they became quiet to hear what their leaders had to say. Payava was thoroughly political, as he shouted, "I am calling a Council of War for all chieftains and their seconds, in one hand span of sun shadow from a spear. We will meet on the bluff above. It is said the great citadel of Hattusa has been abandoned by its leaders!" A wail of consternation arose from the troops. Payava waved his arms again for silence. "That is all we know right now. We do not yet know what has happened or what is left. We will meet with the Akhaian who has just arrived from Hattusa. We will then report back to you and make our plans!" A strange noise arose, mixing cheers with grumbles, fear with hope.

For the moment, Diomedes was welcomed by the leaders of the polyglot army. Accompanied by Eruthros, he was taken and treated as well as a famous war leader could be treated within the confines of an army on the march in a starving land. He was given no information on his fellow escapees but was told it was forthcoming. He was allowed enough water to drink his fill and wash his body as best he could. He used the keen edge of his silvery iron dagger to trim his beard and hair. Before he ate he poured a libation of the raw local wine into the earth first to Zeus the thunderer, but he poured a little more for his patron deities Athene Areia, the warlike, and Hermes Masterios, the searcher or boundary-crosser. He was brought rough barley porridge without honey, a few olives, and some unknown meat in a white sauce (someone had found a cow or goat to milk). The meat was tough, either donkey or horse, but he wolfed it back. He was ready.

He was preparing to go meet the council in a loose himation (cloak) given him by Eruthros when there was a commotion near him. Coming out of the crowd and being harassed by those curious or daring enough to reach out and touch her was Henti, the former harem-girl of the Great King and translator across several languages. Her hood slipped back revealing a delicate, frightened face and shortened hair the colour of ripened flax. The pair of camp guards pushed the crowd back and at a signal from Diomedes allowed her through. She fell to the knees of Diomedes and begged not to be abandoned with the other refugees. Eruthros eyed her with appreciation, but Diomedes stood her up and shamelessly gave her a consoling hug. "You are useful to us here, Henti. We will not let you go. There are few women with this army but I'll see you stay with them. I will have need of your skills."

"Can't I stay with you?"

Diomedes looked around at the small campsite of Eruthros and his few retainers and told her *no*, they will be too often gone and she would be without protection. But he promised that he would keep in touch in case he needed a translator. "In fact, why don't you come with me right now as I meet the leaders of this band of bronze-clad villains? First, young speaker, have some of this food."

At that moment, Sarpedon appeared with two followers carrying armloads of goods. The guards immediately stood back. The men looked at each other with cautious recognition. "I am called Sarpedon the Sardinian, one of the appointed leaders here," the visitor said in the Maionian dialect of Luwian. "We were never introduced, but as a comrade who once fought with you before Mykenai, I bring you armour suitable for a warrior and once king." As Henti translated the words into Akhaian Hellenic without a pause, the followers placed the armour at his feet, along with a long, tapering bronze sword sheathed in leather, a copy of the one Sarpedon wore. Diomedes stood and nodded. He looked over at the Danaan. "I know broad Eruthros may have extra armour to share but who can fit his bull's attire?" Henti translated again and the three men laughed aloud. Eruthros had no extra armour. "Though leaner, I am nearer to your size, so I have brought you some attire fit for a nobleman. But no extra helm."

Diomedes spoke evenly in the rough Luwian he had picked up since being imprisoned, so Henti translated anyway. "I am in your debt, O Man of Sardinia." He picked up the sword and pulled it partially from its sheath. "I have seen grip-tongued blades like this, the entire sword from hilt to tip all one cast; but this one is finer – and longer – than most," he said, impressed. "The size and balance are perfect for a good arm, but the weight indicates it is an unusual bronze alloy."

"Yes, these swords are twins, made by a Sherden craftsman. I'm told the copper and tin for both were smelted together over a charcoal fire large enough that the bronzesmith could gather plentiful flakes of carbon to add to the molten alloy before it was poured into two identical moulds." Diomedes pulled the sword entirely from its leather scabbard, swinging it lightly left and right and hefting its balanced weight with great pleasure. Sarpedon continued, "If you look closely, you will see the blade edges have a slight boundary around them, so a little extra molten tin can be poured into them to retain their sharpness by making them harder, especially after hammering, but perhaps more breakable. The fuller part of the blade remains more flexible and less breakable with the usual twelve percent tin." Since Diomedes seemed entranced by testing the great sword, Sarpedon continued, "This tin is said to have been mined on a misty isle north of the great mountains of Europa out in encircling Okeanos. There the savages or their gods have built upstanding rock temples of such titanic size that they dwarf our Cyclopean walls." Diomedes looked at him with interest, but he went back to the sword. "I don't understand all this sword-casting wizardry, but these swords have never been broken and yours is barely chipped. Mine is not chipped at all, for I have kept the unused one for myself," Sarpedon smiled and winked.

Henti was very interested in the talk of faraway lands, but she smoothly translated the words as spoken. With the discernment of a veteran warrior, Diomedes looked with pleasure at the sculpted hilt built around the tang of the bronze blade, fitted with a riveted walnut hardwood handle then bound tightly with layers of boiled leather, the outer one being a single piece of thick ox-hide, well-fitted for a strong hand. Its point was too keenly sharp to be safely touched, and, on the other end, its pommel was a gold sphere moulded atop the bronze tang with a glittering purple amethyst embedded in it – a killing tool of extraordinary beauty. It had been a long while since he so appreciated worldly things.

"I am deeply honoured by your noble gift, O Sarpedon. You have made a friend," intoned Diomedes, putting the blade back, and the two clasped wrists. The Sardinian and his soldiers left while Sarpedon hoped his extravagant gifts would prove to be worthwhile whether the Akhaian proved to be friend or enemy.

The council of leaders stood and sat in a circle just under the bluff's summit to be protected from the constant breeze. The guards held back the masses but they refused to back up very far so they themselves became a wind barrier. The four chieftains were the inner circle and a place was made for Diomedes as he arrived, splendid now in his shining bronze-plated cuirass. He brought neither helmet nor sword, but the translator was with him.

"I see you are reborn. For anyone who does not yet know, this is Diomedes of Argos, famed among the warriors who took Ilios," began the Lukkan in Luwian.

Diomedes smiled and spoke in Akhaian. "Argos always claims credit for that which does not belong to it. In truth, I was the King of Tiryns, an Argive only in the sense of being one of the vassal-kings, a *lawagetas* of the Argolid plain near Mykenai in the land of the Akhaians." He waved off their translator who had begun, and indicated the young woman with him. Surprised, Henti looked about nervously, but then, to his pleasure, spoke his words in Luwian clear and loud enough to carry several rows back.

Eruthros stood up, interrupting, “My Lords, you have all heard of Diomedes the Akhaian king. He was my king once since his grandfather once ruled in Aitolia. He outranks all of us here. I propose he be given full leadership of this army and be declared our king, if others wish it so.” He looked around proudly as Henti interpreted his words but finding himself shouted down, he returned to sitting, satisfied.

Diomedes arose. “The age of kings has ended. Kings in palaces have become prey,” he announced loudly, looking round, “and those that are not yet prey soon will be!” The vigour was retained in the translated words. A cheer went up. “I am content to serve the army’s choice. My sword belongs to this band of free raiders.”

After the roar of approval passed, Payava continued, “Be that as it may be, we are more interested in the news from Hattusa.” Everyone rumbled agreement. “Was the city taken? Who has departed? What is left there?”

Diomedes first gave background by noting that when he arrived and was locked away, Hattusa was even more splendid and rich than he had been led to believe. On the other hand, though it had many regiments of soldiers about, most often kept outside the walls, its actual population was much lower than others had guessed, consisting mainly of the royals, nobility, priesthood, and those who serve them. It was a city of temples, home to the gods, not a market centre. “Though Ilios, Taruisa, had a much smaller citadel, before it was sacked it had about the same number of people, and the earlier Ilios that was burned generations ago had even more, for Ilios was a port city and trading centre.” Henti translated and the crowd murmured in awe: more treasure but fewer defenders? This sounded good.

“However, during my captivity, it seems the military forces were sent to deal with troubles elsewhere, and the continuing drought, famine, and fear drove many from the villages and countryside to demand entry into the sacred city. They pushed in beyond the Lion Gate where they crowded into the upper city before the main temple quarter to share their suffering together, but at least they had access to water from the underground springs of the southern ponds. Even then the population was but half of what we had been told."

Diomedes summed up the end of the tale as well as he knew it, mainly learned from others once he had emerged from the unlocked room. The vanguard left three weeks ago headed by the Great King's bodyguard, the royal family and retinue, the priests, and the entire single regiment of defenders that had been present in the city. Before the soldiers came the wagonloads of most of the remaining grain from the great silos within the city walls, all remaining livestock, and several water wagons. Within the armed troop were numerous wagonloads of royal treasure, precious metals, and of course image after image of the gods, major and minor, many of them sparkling with jewels. Anyone who could mobilize and take along enough food to survive was allowed to tag along. Left behind was the starving throng, most of whom had come in from the surrounding towns and fields, but many of the servant class were left too. Now that all hope for help was gone but some grain remained in storage, those still strong enough joined warring gangs and fought to the death to break into the granaries for the rotting wheat, barley, or lentils that remained. Seeing the turmoil, Diomedes made his escape, taking with him many prisoners who had been fighters. Others, seeing a choice other than mutual slaughter, simply followed along.

"This girl who speaks many tongues was part of the royal retinue. I found her at the palace; she hid behind because she feared her life was in danger from the Great Queen, for whom she had translated private messages," added Diomedes, carefully choosing which information to include. All looked at her as she translated. "She took me to the Great King's quarters where she found this silver dagger in its hiding place." No one asked how she knew about the king's private bedroom, much less how she knew about the dagger.

"Can't be all silver," interrupted the Sardinian. "Be too soft to be of use."

"No, it is not. It is made from *iron*, the 'metal of the heavens', because most of it is found within chunks of stars that have fallen from the sky to the earth." He drew out the long royal dagger and showed it to the others. The blade was smooth, a mirrorlike silvery-grey, sharp and hard. The hilt was mother-of-pearl, an iridescent yellow-tinted cream colour, harmoniously topped by a pommel of startling dark yellow amber. "Such weapons are similar to good bronze in weight yet stronger, but it takes smithy earth magic to heat it enough to forge. These rare blades are found only among the noble Hatti who gift them to other great kings and pharaohs."

"Is there treasure left anywhere in Hattusa?" an impatient voice called out from the crowd.

"I don't know," stated Diomedes. "They apparently took everything they could carry, but Hattusa is a city of great treasure, probably some of it too much or too big to carry. But the people left there want food, not treasure, and they could not fight a troop of housemaids, so where's the sport? We could take what we want and leave them." Henti repeated in Luwian and some laughter rippled through the crowd, thinking Diomedes was making a joke. These rebels and sea pirates generally killed whoever got in their way without question.

The Lukkan looked at the others. "We have come this far. My gods tell me that we must complete our journey and see for ourselves. We can decide what action to take when we get there. The Kaska must be near, so we must advance quickly."

"There is also the question of where the Great King and his vanguard have gone. They have a significant lead, but might it not be worth sending out well-armed chariots to pursue them?" Sarpedon asked. "Any treasure and supplies will be with them."

"Yes, but they have with them the Hittite soldiers that were guarding the city and a regiment of a thousand that were on leave. Plus they include the redoubtable Meshedi, the Great King's personal bodyguard," Diomedes ventured. "It is what we would have faced in attacking the entire city, so we would need most of our whole force. They wouldn't have gone north toward the Kaska or west toward us, so that leaves south or east. East is the vassal kingdom of Isuwa and south is a long journey to friendly cities over rough terrain."

"We do not know what is ahead," interrupted the Lukkan. "We must continue to Hattusa or any other prizes we see first. We will make our plans from there."

All in council agreed, but the men themselves put up such a roar that the leaders knew their hunger for action must be sated and soon. Their only battle had been glorious but they had gained few prizes. Such a long march so far from the sea over dry land that often shook unexpectedly had been hard on them. Eruthros rose and drew out his own bronze dagger and tapped his hand with the flat side, speaking in response to the din. "There is no glory in peace, like a rusting blade not shining in use. Warriors must war. We cannot hold them back for long. We advance tomorrow!"

Just before noon, the royal caravan at last departed. General Kil-Teshub talked steadily with the Great King Suppiluliuma as they rode together in the chariot just behind the first half of the Meshedi. From her shaded four-wheeled wagon, the Great Queen watched the proceedings. Sometimes they had the driver pause and Mahhuzzi would join them on the ground. Something was afoot but for once the general and the grand vizier seemed to be agreeing about it, as they nodded together while the Great King talked. She saw nothing to be concerned about but did consider that it was time for Hepat to take control of Tarhunta – time for the Sun Goddess to use her erotic persuasion to have the Storm-God submit to her and release his rain. The king had not spoken to her in private since her divine seizure in the Mountain Temple of the Gods, for divine it must have been even if she added dramatic emphasis. She was not about to be ignored. If he was fearful, it was time to clear the air and bring him home to bow to his goddess. She looked out. It seemed to her they were going slightly toward the sun, but more north than west, but that was not her concern. As the cart rolled along she made plans and began to attend to her mission.

Since the Great Queen was in charge of the harem, following her came the well-guarded troop of the Great King's ten children by his concubines, along with the two daughters she had birthed herself. After the second, Suppiluliuma began to come to her bed more rarely feeling it unnecessary. Five of the ten harem children were sons, so he had named the oldest, not yet in his teens, his *tuhkanti* or heir. Besides, he was not comfortable with the queen's wantonness or occasional aggression. He told her she must follow the sacred protocol ordained by the gods. She told herself that's exactly what she was doing, though it was ordained by the ancient Goddess instead. After he grew his beard, she grew less enthusiastic than ever, so he turned to his harem instead.

The caravan halted toward late afternoon. Kil-Teshub looked around. As expected, they were just in sight of a significant town. Smoke hung in the air over the distant buildings. As others set up camp, Kil-Teshub the Gal-Meshedi called forth twenty chariots and charioteers. He made his way among the Great King's bodyguard choosing twenty trusted spearmen to follow him. Another twenty loyal soldiers from the infantry were collected. Kil-Teshub conferred with and gave them his orders. He also had them given the supplies they would need, including sealed containers of oil. They mounted the chariots with three men each in the Hittite manner, one chariot driver and two fighting men, one Meshedi and one regular. No shield bearers were included. Finding a road headed straight toward the city, they set out leaving a dust cloud behind.

The first evening dinner on the road for the royal couple was prepared and served in the well-appointed royal tents by devoted servants who spent the day getting everything ready. Even though they were now exiles from their palace and their city, cleanliness was still the Hittite rule, cleanliness being equal to morality which is equal to royalty. Everything in the tent was triple-cleaned and purified. In spite of the current need to conserve water, the royal couple themselves were bathed and examined for possible pollution before dining. But nothing compared to the scrupulous checks on what was given to the royal couple to eat and drink. Those who brought them water were required to strain it several times before placing it before them. A lyre player entered and began a low-key tune. Soon elegant silver goblets of imported sweet wine and flatbread *ninda purpura* were placed before them. The King and Queen each intoned thanks to their chosen deity and, when the King nodded, they sipped the wine looking upward rather than at one another. This was followed by servants bringing in steaming bowls of a lamb and lentil stew with cumin and raisins, and after that sweets, nutmeats, and fruit, carefully cleansed, were put before them. They ate with pleasure but in silence.

Then at last the Great King spoke with unusual directness: "Lieia-Hepa, you have not yet spoken of the sacrilege you committed in the name of the Sun-Goddess of Arinna before the Altar of the Gods in the Mountain Temple and before all our people."

Taken aback by the informal address of her real name, she replied in kind, "Husband, you must know I myself have no memory of the incident. Whatever occurred was an aberration in the holy order of things. Surely some demon possessed me!"

"Could the demon have been Arinniti herself? Could the Sun-Goddess really be seeking to overthrow the rule of the mighty Storm-God?"

She knew she could not deny it and pretend she recalled nothing at the same time. So she boldly went on to state the obvious. "I am only the vessel of Hepat, but, Husband, it is clear that all rain, all storms have ceased, yet the sun rises from the Underworld each day and never hides. The land is parched and little grows. Who is in ascendance these past many years, the Storm-God or the Sun-Goddess? And what does that tell us?"

"It tells us the Sun-Goddess is trying to unbalance the cosmos! She has somehow weakened the will of her consort Tarhunta and has used you to weaken the will of your Great King. The land dies from too much sun — especially since that sun rises from the dark of your Underworld each morning. Does Arinniti wish to bring darkness back to the world?" He rose to his feet, pointing and shouting, "Do you wish to destroy the manhood of the Great King of the Hatti?"

Cornered now, she fell back on the devices she knew best, "O no, Mighty Ruler, my husband. It is you who have the power on Earth, no one can deny that. But you cannot rule alone. Since the beginning of the ages, it is the Sun Goddess who has always allowed the Storm-God his time in the skies. It was she who allowed your rule to happen. Sweet husband, can you not see the joy you have been permitted?" She opened her royal robe to reveal her significant breasts with rouge-tinted nipples. She licked her lips, throwing her head back and with bright eyes swayed seductively toward Suppiluliuma, and the Great King slapped her face so hard she was knocked from her feet over the cushions.

"Woman, I am a Hatti warrior – your rebellion is over! The cosmos must be realigned. This drought will only end when the Storm-God ascends to be the sole power over the land once again! You and your dark Sun-Goddess are banned from the order of things, at least until the order finds its balance once again."

"My king," Lieia-Hepa moaned in confusion from the floor, "this is a great evil."

"It is not my doing," the Great King spoke, raising himself to his significant full height and looking upward. "I am but a slave of the will of Tarhunta, the Storm-God. He has decided the Sun Goddess of Arinna must be brought down in order to save the Hittite lands from total destruction. I have heard this command and followed it. Already I have sent troops north to the city of Alaca that you know as Arinna to burn the temples of the dark Sun-Goddess. If she is really the 'Mother of the land' or the 'Sun of Earth' then this will return her to it." He ordered picked soldiers of the Meshedi he had kept nearby to take the queen under guard and keep her isolated until he called for her. They stood her up but, somewhat uncertain or in awe, let her walk out with them under her own power.

4. –*Interlude: Kolkhis*

Eruthros and his former king Diomedes found their way back to their campsite with Henti following closely along. Diomedes turned to her, "Well done, O wise one!"

"Clever girl, looks like a nymph-goddess, too. Guard her well," he whispered to Diomedes.

While the men removed their armour and put it into the tent of Eruthros, Diomedes asked the Danaan, "So, Eruthros, did you really mean to anoint me king, after all we have been through these past years with kings and fools?"

"I did and did not," the red-haired warrior replied, "but I knew how you would respond. You endeared yourself to the king-hating rabble, did you not?"

"It seems so; apparently I am in your debt."

Eruthros asked his attendant freeman to bring them wine. "It's all words, ain't it? *Lawagetas* and *wanax*, kings and great kings, lords and overlords, slaves and their wives. Past time to do away with all that."

"Yes, the age of royal fortresses, great palaces for the few, is coming to an end. The gods have ceased their support."

The men sat down around the fire as the afternoon waned, and Henti was given a robe. "What I want to know," asked Eruthros, "is why you took your Argive warriors from before Ilios when you did and what has happened to you since. Where are your stalwart comrades, Sthenelos and Eurylos, two other Argive kings?"

Diomedes smiled ruefully. "We fully intended to come back," he paused as earthenware bowls of wine arrived for each of them with a jar of water for mixing. "It's too long and woeful a tale to tell. I decided my men needed some action and some plunder. It was getting stale staring at the walls of Ilios every day, as you yourself know. Within the walls, it was grim, I'm sure, but they had access to underground sources of water and people from the countryside kept sneaking in food. Whereas amongst our ships on the beach, the trading vessels had ceased arriving and we were always hungry. After more than a year, the countryside had been thoroughly foraged and nearby towns already sacked. We had water from the Skamandros and the muddy Simoeis but little else. My men needed some adventure and so did I, and it didn't look like Ilios was going to capitulate any time soon. We boarded two ships and headed north."

"My lord, is that the only reason you left, or were you avoiding the final destruction of Ilios? Don't look at me that way, Diomede. Not even the gods would dare question your courage – certainly not me who has stood with you in the ruthless fray. Not even legendary Akhilleus himself could have stood up to your man-killing assault. And I know conditions of the sea-borne allies among the beached ships were getting desperate, but Priam's city could only have been worse. Our patrols stopped most attempts to sneak in supplies. But I have heard men speak amongst themselves and I have myself noted that when we lay waste to coastal towns the Lord Diomedes is not seen leading the looting, killing, or the despoiling of wives and maidens."

"Or grannies? Why leave them out?" Diomedes raised an eyebrow and smiled, and the tension subsided as Eruthros laughed. "Yes, Akhilleus of Phthia achieved glory though he was dead before the Ilios of many generations ago fell to our ancestors. They say he was killed by the arrows of the Trojan King Alexandros, so what kind of glory is that? The greatest Ilios fell a hundred suns ago and its people were killed or enslaved."

"All you say may have happened but it was far, far worse when our Ilios was finally taken. The warriors were enraged after suffering for so long. Not a babe or child or beast was left alive," the Danaan spoke ruefully, "...as far as we know."

"I know whereof you speak," said Diomedes looking at the horizon. "First in Aitolia then in the Argolid, we were involved in cattle raids and man-killing before I had finished growing. It was the way of all Akhaians and good sport it was, is it not so? We did not attack families or rape wives. Most of us anyway. But after many of our fathers were killed in the attempt to take Thebai and then were left to lie unburied in the dirt where they fell for crows and kites to tear asunder, their souls not given the chance to cross the Styx, we Argive princes grew crazed for revenge. Zeus, it was said, had decreed that their attack was destined to fail, but the decision to leave the bodies unburied was that of the Thebans alone. I did not yet have a worthy beard when we, the Epigonoi, the sons of the Seven, laid waste to Thebai. You know the tale, I'm sure. What you may not know is what we did inside it – probably the same as you did to Priam's holy city only four suns ago. Theban babes and children were speared or sliced and only a few innocent royals and the sage, Teiresias, were allowed their lives while the city was razed to embers. All I know is that, in a mad rage of revenge for my lost father, I burst into a room where a mother guarded her pair of still budding daughters. She begged me to take her and leave her girls alone. I tore the robes from her and savaged her quickly but was not yet sated. My memory is unclear at that point, but I know when I left that room three victims were flailing on the ground and other bloodthirsty Argives were already entering the room. They had no chance and I did nothing to stop it. Half a lifetime ago yet the events are ever present..." He paused, dead cold on the surface while his soul twisted in Hades. "So your intuition is correct, my friend. I have no need for more gold or treasure than I can carry or more slaves to wait on me. I have lost all taste for the ravishing or murder of the helpless, though good horses and women for comfort remain essential. And, as you will surely see, I still drink delight of battle with my peers on the windy plain or foamy sea."

Eruthros looked down. Further back Henti gaped wide-eyed but silent.

"Because it is you, my lord." Diomedes looked disapproving, "uh, my *friend*." Diomedes nodded and Eruthros continued, "I accept your path, though it is strange to me. The gods long ago decreed that we warriors are to live for battle, beyond all else, and our booty and fame reveal our greatness to the world. Some are destined for great glory while others fall into the dust early with brains or guts spilling forth. Some, like Akhilleus of old, achieve both early death and fame. When we take a city, it is our sacred duty to leave our mark or it will be as though we had never *been*. We all end up as shades in the dark Underworld so it is only here on earth that we must become known so we can live on in the awe of others. Mercy, to me, is a quality meant for mothers or shepherds, but now I see it can even exist in the mightiest of warriors."

Diomedes swallowed the rest of his watered wine and waved for more. "So. I will not play the bard but instead merely report how I got to Hattusa. Our two ships went north, and since both the winds and the current come from the north it was slow rowing with occasional billowing sails tacking across the oncoming breeze, but all the towns along the Hellespont had already been taken or were supporting us. Finally, passing between Sestos and Perkote, on into the more open Propontis we went.

"We came to the fine harbour of Kyzikos, which we found settled by people speaking Milesian Hellenic like the Trojans. They had sent troops to fight for Ilios so weren't about to welcome us. Our fifty men threatened to burn the town, but a noble-looking old priest of Drimios, son of Zeus, came to the ramparts and made us an offer. If we agreed not to enter the city, they would reward us by bringing extravagant gifts of forged gold, silver, and bronze, intricate jewellery, and marble sculpture, and feast us like kings with delicacies served by their daughters. The men gave a roar and agreed. The gifts were brought and stacked up in a grove of trees, a ways from the shore, but our hosts gaily invited us to dine and play first then gather the treasures later. They feted us in the grove with unwatered Pramnian wine, dark, sweet, and strong, and included musicians who played wild terpsichorean music on lyre, flutes, and some hollow instrument on which a steady beat was drummed out, exciting the blood. Thinly dressed maidens and a few pretty cupbearing boys pranced about keeping kylikes full with the heady sweet wine. Soon the men were up dancing like fools with the women, thinking they had entered paradise. Couples were disappearing into the foliage or letting it happen right there and then. The men gave themselves over to the moment.

"It wasn't hard to see which way the wind was blowing, but few would listen to my warnings. They were no longer my subjects, after all. I sent Sthenelos and Eurylos to try and get the men back to the ships while I mounted a hillock to look for the inevitable troops approaching in quiet march. I saw them coming from both sides within minutes. I ran shouting down to the men that we were under attack. A few gathered their senses and their clothes and headed for the ships. Normally, we would have readily overwhelmed their fighters, but the men were drunk, so many lingered confused until the Kyzikosians were upon them, killing anyone within reach. Then their minds awoke and they ran for their arms and the protection of the ships. My childhood friend, Eurylos, once lawagetas of Asine in the Argolid, took spears and his great body-length, oxhide shield and what sensible followers he could find to meet the attackers on the left while Sthenelos, once lawagetas of Lerna, did the same on the right. Within the frenzied orgy, many of the young dancers brought out concealed daggers and began to stab my befuddled men. It was then that I swept down amongst them, joining Sthenelos on the right and killing many of the city men with wide sweeps of my bronze blade.

"We backed our way up to the ships. The 'gifts' of treasure were lost to us. Though many had fallen, we held the traitorous enemy troops back while the ships were pushed into the water. Our fighters from the left side returned but Eurylos was not among them. Only about thirty of our force managed to get away. I was told later that Eurylos had refused to back up so his men could do so safely behind his spear and shield. He was surrounded by bowmen and brought low, never to rise again. His body could not be retrieved. What fools we had been! But those of us who made it to the ships departed using oars and push poles and soon escaped to deeper water. We were too exhausted to mourn at first. A few of the men had even forced some of the bait – young women dancers and a pair of cupbearers – on board with us. Over the next few days I looked away as they were either fucked to death or used as targets by the crew as vengeance for their lost comrades. They were finally thrown over the rail into the sea. Speak to me not of my 'mercy', Eruthros."

More wine was brought, and they generously poured water into it. Tomorrow they would march, hopefully to war. "Blindly continuing north, we entered the narrow Bosporos and discovered a settlement in Europa called Byzantion, which we raided after climbing the steep ascent up to it, but the people saw us and had deserted the town, leaving us much in the way of supplies and a number of worthy trophies. Feeling the gods were smiling upon us now, no one suggested returning to grim Ilios, so we went on into the Pontos to see what further adventures and wealth could be found." Diomedes looked back at the girl and beckoned her over. "Would you like a little wine to warm you?" he asked. Eruthros looked at him with a raised eyebrow for this breach of custom. Diomedes said seriously, "We have slaves no longer, my brother-in-arms."

"Yes, no slaves. But still, a woman...?" Eruthros groaned and shook his head.

"Once we open the doors to all humanity, who knows where it will end?" grinned Diomedes. "Someday a woman may lounge at table with us."

"Ye gods, *shared humanity*," Eruthros shook his head ruefully. "Who will be left to kill?"

They laughed. An extra bowl of wine was brought and Diomedes poured water into it. Henti mumbled her thanks for her cup then retreated further back.

"So you escaped back into the salty sea with only thirty men and two ships?"

"Yes, with some fear of being pursued, we went northeast with a new current instead of returning south. We entered the rough seas of the Pontos Axeinos, which some call the *Black* because it is northern and has dark waters. We soon found that the hills rose in cliffs along the shore so beaching our ships was often impossible. When we did land, any tribes we met were hostile but refused to meet us in battle by instead trying to kill us from a distance. We found ourselves being inevitably drawn further east into the dark sea along the Anatolian coast. But when we wished to turn west and go back to Ilios, we were met by winds and sea currents going the opposite way. The sky was often cloudy so we could not see the stars to navigate. We kept expecting further towns to plunder along the shore so east seemed to beckon us. It was as though we were spellbound or led by unknown gods. We reverted to piracy to live but there was not much sea traffic and very few towns near the sea waiting for us to lay waste to them. Storms came without notice, so we would head for shore to camp but then, as often as not, unknown tribesmen would appear at night to rob us of what little we had or even to murder a sailor or two. We spent nearly a year wandering this way as though caught in a desperate dream until we were struck at sea by the frothy anger of the sea god."

"Him again," said Eruthros.

"Yes, the wild storm carried us out to sea and by morning when it cleared we could see no land. One ship had lost its mast and was so flooded it was sinking. It could not be saved, so we gathered the men onto the Sea Horse, the name given to our remaining vessel, and headed toward the rising sun. Toward evening, we were overjoyed to see the shore and soon even more excited to see a small city appearing out of the mist. We went to it. We pulled up a good distance away and attempted to hide the old ship.

"Ah, Eruthros. This tale could be an epic in itself. I will squeeze the juice into a smaller container or we will surely be here until morning. We walked toward the city and met herders who attempted to hide from us, but we brought them out. We could not share speech, but they sent for someone who spoke Milesian Hellenic."

"Those Milesians certainly ventured far afield in their colonizing ventures."

"It is so. We learned the harbour town was Phasis as was the large river it was on, and that we were in the far-famed land of the Kolkhians. Yes, my friend, legendary Kolkhis. The capital of the land was further inland and known as Aia, a noble city said to have been founded in the age of heroes by Aietes when our ancestors still walked with the gods. You of course recall the ancient tale of Jason and his Argonauts? The king today was still called Aietes, we learned, a descendant of the founder, and the land was said to have rich farmland and that it prospered in gold, iron, timber and honey. We all stirred when we heard the word *gold*.

"We decided that attacking Aia would be futile, so we marched overland to the low-walled city where we presented ourselves as mercenaries looking for employment. We must have looked more like ship-wrecked castaways at that point, so few would come near to us much less talk to us. We were at last shown to some official who spoke rough Akhaian and said he represented Aietes the King. He asked me about our experience and when I mentioned we had been fighting at Ilios, he looked at us disdainfully. 'So you come here after you have destroyed the great citadel of Troy?' We were confused. 'Know you not that the city has fallen and been utterly destroyed? Are you deserters or refugees?' he asked.

"I replied, 'No we are not. We are Akhaian warriors. Our weapons should tell you that. The gods in their wisdom took us away from the windy plains of Ilios and brought us here.' I told him the truth, but the men glared at me resentfully, clearly bitter about my leading them away from such a prize. 'We could be useful to your king,' I concluded.

"The official saw our mettle beneath the grime. 'We have a prosperous, peaceful land,' but added, 'but it's true that's only because we keep our enemies at bay beyond our borders and control the tribes in conflict within them. Follow this man who will take you to a barracks to clean yourselves in case the Lord of the City wishes to view you, and so the rest of us can avoid the smell.'

"And that was the beginning of our two-year stay in the fabled land of Kolkhis. It was a land of plenty but its peace was based on dominating nearby nations and keeping its tribes from each other's throats. Plus our informant did not tell us the Dark Goddess had many temples in Aia and that witchcraft was common, as we should have known by the legend of the first Aietes whose sister was Circe and daughter Medea. A number of my men became bewitched, it seems, and chose to serve the local incarnation of Hekate instead of the king or their former comrades. But this was later. We never met the king and some of my warriors asked to be separated from me for leading them from the riches and glory of Trojan plunder. The Kolkhians readily agreed so as to weaken our combined force. Indeed we were posted in distinct groups mostly to borderlands on the edge of high mountains or along the river Phasis. Sthenelos and I were sent out furthermost away along the boundary of the river Korax. In time, we proved ourselves in combat and requested a chariot, which we were given. Days of glory again, like early in the Trojan War. I had my charioteer back and whether I cast javelins from the car or descended to use my sword, no one could stand in our way. We became highly regarded for our prowess on the field of battle."

"Yes, all who were there on the ringing plains of Ilios will testify to that. It was said that not even Ares withstood your relentless charge. Were there not tales that in your war madness you wounded the fearsome god of war?" Eruthros laughed. "I trust that is not sacrilege, this far from home."

"Things continued that way until the borders were secured. We found ourselves with more time. During our forays I had noted well-guarded trains of donkeys being led up a mountain pass and returning heavily laden. I was ordered to pay no mind to such activity, which alerted my interest. I took Sthenelos and on foot we trailed one of the little caravans going up a steep trail into the mountains by sticking to the forest. We followed it all day and the next until they decamped near a steep mountainside glistening wet with fast-running rivulets or brooks. From the trees we watched as they brought forth rich sheep fleeces of all colours, each hide made porous to act as a sieve. They set them upright on wooden frames submerged into the streams so the water ran through them, and with enough bracing they were not pushed over. The hides caught larger floating debris like pebbles while the fleece itself acted as a fine strainer for gravel and sand. We slept in the trees and the next morning the miners hung many of the fleeces from trees to dry and took dry ones down from which they shook the sediment and pebbles onto large copper pans and there it was spread out and examined. And what do you think we could clearly see in those pans from where we were?"

"It must have been gold," guessed Eruthros, "for surely you are telling me the true meaning of the tale of Kolkhis and Jason's Golden Fleece!"

"Ah, my friend, you are much wiser than you look. Yes, it was gold so pure that it shone in the morning sun so that even we, hidden a distance away, could see it flash. A plan began to form in my mind."

"How did you kill the guardian dragon?"

"Alas, we saw neither dragons nor Argonauts, but we did have to outwit the guardians," he smiled.

"It took about a year before we were trusted to lead resupply expeditions into the city. Sthenelos and I sought out our old comrades-in-arms, but, to my disappointment, a few of them had become devotees in the temples of the chthonic witch goddess, and more had married local women and were now field workers or merchants. Others had simply settled into life as paid mercenaries and did not want to get dragged out to sea or into new adventures again. Eventually, we gathered about twenty of them and met them in out-of-the-way wine holes to scheme of ways to get our hands on the gold being shipped back from the rich mountain streams and also to become masters of our ship again. The Sea Horse had by now been found, dried out and refitted by Kolkhian shipwrights in the port of Phasis, but reports were that, like most ships in that safe harbour, it was left almost unguarded.

"Eventually, at our request and to the regret of our fellow border guards, we were posted to Aia from where our plans were solidified. Looking back, I wonder what god drove me on. For surely we were well situated in that prosperous land. Sthenelos enjoyed the raucous tavernas and I admit I enjoyed the dangers of venturing into the precincts of the ancient goddess to linger in pleasure with her well-trained priestesses. But the idea of escaping with the Golden Fleece had come to possess me. Perhaps it was put there by the Dark Goddess in vengeance for my incomplete service! In any case, the day came when we put our plans into motion.

"I'll skip the details, but the group of us Akhaians managed to get hold of a two-wheeled cart pulled by a mule and we deserted our posts to position ourselves near the returning caravan of gold miners and their guards. When we broke from the woods and attacked with a great uproar, most gave up without a struggle. Some brave guards formed a wall but once two were speared where they stood, the rest threw down their arms. We transferred two heavy goatskin bags of gold dust and nuggets with a number of larger lumps into our cart and made off. It was a long hard journey, but we passed around Aia and headed across country, travelling through the night to make it to the harbour. Those we sent ahead had found the reborn Sea Horse and there was little resistance when we boarded it. We were exhausted but excited, for the gods had permitted our adventure a smooth unfolding.

"However, smooth sailing did not await us as we drew on the bank of long oars and made from the harbour. Sleek Kolkhian vessels finally roused themselves and came in pursuit. They caught up with us easily enough but my Akhaians fought like they were defending their families. Grappling hooks were thrown but their ropes were cut, and I myself stood at the bow destroying any who sought to board. We lost several good men to arrows but the Kolkhians were unable to block us or board us, so we headed out to sea with our treasure intact.

"Many long days sailing later we arrived at the coast of Anatolia again though we did not know where. We pulled up in a harbour at night and, storing our leathern sacks of gold in the hold of the ship with a few guards, went seeking others who could assist us. We thought the best track was to head back towards lands occupied by Akhaians, which now included Ilios, or at least lands free of kings. Kyprios was likely to be occupied by bands of the peoples of the sea, some wanting to settle, so it would be a good place to bring our gold. But none of this was to be. We were seen by the local people tending to their herds and working the dry soil of their land. When we approached, they ran, so we simply headed inland. Soon troops were seen coming our way, the front squadron in chariots, and my remaining fourteen men soon found themselves surrounded. These warriors were in war armour much like Assyrians but with an obvious Hittite influence. There were three men to a chariot like the Hatti, and they were not happy to see us.

"They sent an envoy and we discovered to our dismay that we were in the land the Hatti called Hayasa-Azzi, to the east of Hatti lands near to the mountainous headwaters of the Euphrates River, called the Mala by the Hatti. With the drought and chaos on the borders, the confederation of peoples called the Hayasa and the Azzi had joined forces and defended themselves both from the Hittites and the Assyrians. They were not welcoming to strangers in armour arriving by land or sea. In short, they attacked and we fought. Though we were outnumbered, we stood our ground at first but soon were overwhelmed. It was bloody hand-to-hand battle until I managed to commandeer their leader's chariot and lead our remaining men away from the battlefield toward the west and Hatti lands. Others gathered horses or chariots but most just ran in full retreat. Our path to the loyal Sea Horse was blocked and we saw their troops heading towards it, so we headed inland down a narrow gorge and formed a barrier at its opening. We soon realized we had left enough of an impression that we were being left alone to our fate. Sthenelos was present but we had only eleven men left. We had lost the others to battle. We had lost our ship. And on that ship, we had left our fabulous treasure of the fleeces of gold."

"Excuse me, your lordship," Eruthros interrupted with a quizzical smile, "but are you sure you're telling the story right? I mean we sing our tales of glory, of attaining riches and fame, but what you are saying sounds like just the opposite. You were defeated in battle and lost your treasure? Isn't this where you meant to add that Pallas Athene or Hermes intervened to save your gold? What kind of *mythos* is this?"

"Athene would not bother with men's gold," Diomedes replied, "and Hermes helped me steal it though not to preserve it. It is not a tale meant to exalt my glory, old friend, it is my shameless recollection of the way things unfortunately happened. It's the simple truth."

"The truth? I thought the truth is what is told. What will true memory get you?"

"I'm not sure, Red Beard, but surely the truth will lead to the true and the good. The real is my actual life experience, which is always more than the treasures that will be buried with me in my tomb or depicted on my death stele."

"That's a novel way of thinking. Treasures in themselves mean nothing except to show the world our victories, to give witness to our glory, which can only live on in our fame as we are remembered in tales, songs, offspring, and, yes, monuments."

"Yes, Eruthros, but my daimonion within wants to be set free, so it directs me towards it from ahead, a *telos* or distant light toward which I can only strive. Glory in the eyes of others or wealth on earth is only temporary. There may be no final truth, but for me the true path is always beckoning from my hidden soul. *Soulmaking* is to bring the world to it."

"Strange words! I have to admit, your truth, though unsettling, makes for a good tale. What happened next, since it doesn't appear you and those left were all killed?"

"Some also disappeared in passage. Two phases of the moon later, ten of us arrived – bedraggled, exhausted, and hungry – at the Lion Gate of Hattusa. We had little time to wonder at its resemblance to the narrower Lion Gate of Mykenai for we were immediately arrested and our weapons taken away. No one spoke Akhaian, but gesturing and spearpoints moved us along into the great city. To our confusion we were paraded directly across the city and up the akropolis into the palace and brought before the Great King and his court. Sthenelos, inspired I know not by which god, insisted I move to the back of the group and look inconspicuous. This I tried to do. This translating girl was brought from the king's harem so we could communicate. Sthenelos did most of the talking. We were soon being taken away when suddenly the Great King who is named Suppiluliuma ran towards us haranguing us loudly in his officious voice. Spears were pointed toward us and we were taken to locked rooms at lower levels. Strangely, I was soon removed from the others and put into a cell of my own. I was thoroughly scrubbed and my hair was cut. They fed me well. I know not why." Diomedes looked over at Henti who smiled down into her wine bowl.

"Perhaps you were recognized," ventured Eruthros. "Your fame is widespread."

"I think not," said Diomedes. "But I was allowed physical training of various sorts, even instructing Hittite soldiers by sparring with them. Members of the Meshedi, the king's elite bodyguard, came to watch and eventually a few chose to engage me in swordplay until one was injured. They were good but not Akhaian warriors. This continued for some time then abruptly stopped though my isolation continued. I later learned that the other nine men had been unceremoniously killed, beheaded by direct order of the Great King Suppiluliuma. Sthenelos, my childhood friend, the former king of Lerna, and the best charioteer to have ever walked the earth was among them."

"Ah, I see," said Eruthros, "this war is a personal war. Honour is involved. Why were you allowed to live?" He tossed back his bowl of wine.

"Perhaps Athene was protecting me. I do not believe the Great King knew of me."

Food was brought and to the discomfort of Eruthros the Danaan, Diomedes had Henti sit with them to eat. Evening was coming on so they ate more of the barley porridge with olive oil floating atop but this time with raw onions on the side instead of olives; and the meat seemed to be roasted goat ribs, though it was difficult for them to be sure. Dates were brought afterward with a handful of pistachios. "Fit for kings, eh?" smiled Eruthros at the irony. Soon more bowls of wine were brought and the water was refreshed.

5. Five Cities Burn

–Interlude: Fall of Ilios (Troy)

"My friend, the speaker's staff is in your hands now. Tell me of the fall of Ilios. What is there to this story some are telling about a horse that brought the city down?"

"Alas, I am much further from being a singer of tales than even you. I cannot readily sew the gods into my story since it is not the way my mind works."

"Yes, it is happening everywhere. Without the kings, the gods seem to have gone into hiding. They reveal their presence less readily. They indicate by signs but do not speak in our heads. Tell it in your voice, in your own words, Aitolian."

"And I won't do epithets!" Now they laughed and even Henti joined in, for in the king's court she had heard the hyperbole of singers of tales. "We understand each other. I will tell what I saw without burnish or blame. I will try to approach this *truth* of which you speak, but I am but one viewpoint, so it will only be my truth. Tell me, Diomede, how was it we could speak with many of the Trojans so readily?"

"Because, Eruthros, there was an earlier Trojan War. Another, bigger Ilios with greater walls was brought down only a few generations ago. Those great walls were shattered by Poseidon Earthshaker, and it was then destroyed by Tyrsenoi warriors. The city was rebuilt into the polyglot seaport we attacked and among those who moved into it were the conquering Tyrsenoi, who speak a language unknown to us, who speak a language unknown to us, but Akhaians and Aeolians from Smyrna also came as migrants. The most mighty god of the Ilios that we destroyed was Hyperborean *Apulunas*, God of Gates, who was brought from Miletos. He failed them at the last."

"So we were able to speak Hellenic dialects with a few but most spoke only Trojan or, as you called it, Tyrsenoi. Okay, but my king, how dare you call our Ilios a *small city*!"

"Our Ilios was a minor city compared to the one many years earlier when the region was under Hittite domination and called Wilusa by them, as I have learned from others nearby on my travels. Mainly Maionians lived in the earlier Troy when it was the Hittite city of Taruisa. But its king Alexandros was an Akhaian loyal to the Hittites who called him Alaksandu. The broken-walled city fell to the Tyrsenoi who were aided by mainland Akhaians and Danaans led by the first Atreus of Mykenai, whom the Hittites know as the Great King Attarissiya, ruler of the Ahhiyawa empire."

"How strange you talk," Eruthros broke in, "as though time did not repeat itself in the eternal return. But there must have been many Troys. Is it not said that our great hero, Herakles, once destroyed the Ilios of some king named Laomedon?"

"But Herakles is so ancient, he may have existed before we became mariners. His very name means *glory to Hera*, the death goddess, so in reality he is unlikely to have ever left the Peloponnese. Akhilleus and Hektor may have had their final duel before the great walls of the big Ilios I mention or even earlier before the cities of mainland Hellas were united into one great kingdom. The truth of time seems to rest in the telling of the tale, which at best has a beginning and an end, not a return. Things change. The Ilios of Alexandros was brought down, it is said, by Poseidon the Earthshaker, but in our time the Trojans made sacrifice to him as one of the gods supporting them."

"Is this so?" asked Eruthros. "For surely Poseidon must have suddenly recalled an old wrong committed by Laomedon or some other king. You do not know about the horses of Ilios already becoming legend, for you had already left. Do you not know that Poseidon's horses are both his waves and the power that shakes the land?"

"I see that in spite of your words, you include the gods," Diomedes smiled.

"I must, for he enters the events. The Akhaians on the beach said Poseidon sent his rampaging horses – once again! – beneath the Trojan plain. At first the earth shook so badly we feared for ourselves, but then the walls crumbled and fell apart in places. We saw our opportunity and Agamemnon urged us into our chariots and battle order. We went on the attack, but the Trojans had the same idea and came pouring out of their gates and through the fissures in their walls. We attacked and they attacked but more of Poseidon's horses came ashore as great waves swamped our ships. Many ships were lost and we became desperate. With our greatest heroes all gone, it looked bad for us." He glanced at Diomedes. "But something stirred in the foothills and the Thessalian corps of horsemen came out at full gallop and encircled the battlefield. These were not the seacoast Myrmidons of Thessaly but the inland riders of the plains. Chariots could not have ridden over the rough terrain they traversed, but they managed to enter sacred Ilios with few losses and from thence threw open the gates. Our troops awoke in maddened fury and we overcame the last Trojan resistance, entering the city to begin a savage rapine and slaughter like no other."

"I suspect you had a glorious time," Diomedes ventured. "But I am confused. Which accounts for the Trojan Horse tale, the earthquake or the cavalry charge?"

"Who is to say?" smiled Eruthros. "Those who tell our story will no doubt bring in the gods or the Moirai to make sense of it all, which is no sense at all. This is what happened. I was there. And you are correct that I went mad in destructive *ekstasos* within the city, as did the other attackers. King Priam was beheaded in the throne room; Queen Hekabe killed herself before being raped. I myself saw their youngest son, a mere babe, thrown from the battlements. All the nobles were killed, but many of the women, including the priestesses and royal princesses, were raped and enslaved. Another prince called Aineias is said to have escaped by leaving the doomed city before the final attack, so terrified was he of you, Diomede, since you had nearly killed him in battle and made him run like a rabbit for the city. No escape for the rest of the royal family. Princess Kassandra was taken by Wanax Agamemnon and some other young princess noted for her beauty named... I don't remember... was taken by Menelaos of Lakonia, his brother. Other priestesses were raped and murdered. I left nothing alive before me and I regret nothing. I was bathed in blood and my lust was bottomless. The less detail the better. This is how death is defeated. I was invincible. We left the city in ashes. It will never rise again."

At nightfall, others gathered round to sleep nearer the fire. Nothing was said about Henti sleeping with the women servants. A soldier brought her two rough woollen blankets – a luxury, one to sleep on and one to cover, and she lay herself down next to Diomedes in his open tent. He did not protest. Sleep came quickly; he was exhausted.

6. The Plunder of Arinna

The army with no homeland was mobilized at sunrise. Within the hour they moved out in the same order as before but headed north to approach Hattusa, Diomedes marching in the rear troop with Eruthros, and made their way into the more highly populated countryside in which some of the fields seemed to have crops. At mid-morning, Kabi with two other scouts returned at a steady pace but not a gallop from his reconnoitring the land ahead. He skillfully rode his mount directly up to the Lukkan striding in front of the rabble surrounded by his two personal guards.

"We are approaching a city, my ... leader." Kabi smoothly dismounted, still holding the halter.

"Yes, there is a number about as we get closer to Hattusa itself. Has it walls or fortifications, temples or palaces?"

"It is surrounded by a rampart, not impenetrable. There seems to be a palace over the city, but the curious thing is that it looks like three of its larger buildings, temples perhaps, have recently been destroyed, burnt to the ground. Their pillars and some walls still rise from ash. It is a large settlement, with fresh water from a dam nearby, yet I saw no sign of any other defences and no guards on the perimeter."

Payava wondered how to hold back the battle-craving warriors who followed him, at least until he could discern a course of direction. He called for the other four leaders, Diomedes among them. When they arrived they agreed to proceed immediately but that it would be prudent to determine what happened there before attacking.

"The Kaska have already been here," blurted big Eruthros. "They must be coming back to finish what they started. Our time is *now*. We will not be held back for long. We are city-takers and there lies a city that sleeps to wake. Even better, it is Hittite." Payava nodded, but he knew the Kaska would not have stopped with three temples.

The entire army of eight thousand *barbaroi* and pirates, Akhaian and Lukkan, Arzawan and Cypriot, Sardinian, Aethiop, Rodian and more appeared before the city led by a long row of chariots with two men in each, unlike the Hittite practice. Three of them pulled to the front and went directly toward what appeared to be the main gate. It was surrounded by a pair of intricately carved female sphinxes on either side, one of the pair looking outward and the other inward toward the city. Payava knew from hearsay that a similar gate was one of the entrances to Hattusa but this was not Hattusa. He felt he knew where he was and told this to the Sardinian as they pulled up to the gate.

"You think this is the sacred city of the Hatti Sun-Goddess?" asked Sarpedon.

"Yes, the Sun Goddess of Arinna, known as Hepat to the Hurrians. This city must be Arinna, but what happened to the three great temples?"

At the gate, the three chariots paused and waited to be greeted or attacked. Two other chariots arrived. People from the city did gather around the gate waiting and watching from inside. The chieftains and others came forward and looked more closely at the relief carvings on the gate and wall. Most had no idea what they were seeing, but Sarpedon, Payava, and Uhhaziti, who appeared out of nowhere, seemed to comprehend from stories they had heard of the Hatti religion. Diomedes, too, was able to understand. A king and queen were depicted before an altar of the Storm-God as a bull. Next to that, slightly larger, was seated the Sun Goddess of Arinna before a procession of cult officials, animals for sacrifice, acrobats, and even a sword swallower, accompanied by players on lutes and some sort of windbag instrument. The Sardinian read some of the Luwian hieroglyphs aloud, "Dedicated to the Sun Goddess of Arinna by Tudhaliya the Great King," though which Tudhaliya was impossible to know. To the Hittites, this was a holy city.

Diomedes with Henti aboard rode first through the gates, heedless of any danger. Two more chariots with the Lukkan in one and the Sardinian aboard the other followed. Looking at the skyline and the statuary in the distance, Diomedes remarked what a beautiful city it was. Curious townsfolk stepped out from the crowd, staring agog at the unfamiliar armour and especially at the bronze-plated helmets topped with colourful horsehair plumes, upright reeds, or unreadable symbols. They found themselves becoming spokespersons. With Henti translating, the three leaders quickly learned some important facts. The city did have leaders – priests and priestesses – but they were not facing an army and had hidden in smaller temples higher up. And, incredibly, the temples of the Sun Goddess had been destroyed nearly three moon phases (weeks) previously by a squadron of the Hittite army led by the king's bodyguard as it fled Hattusa going south. They had announced the destruction was on the orders of the Great King Suppiluliuma, so they met with no resistance. The people were shocked and confused, and now so were the leaders of the polyglot army.

"It might be the Great King is acting to curb the power of the Great Queen," Diomedes suggested. "In these times of drought and destruction, the Sun Goddess may have been in the ascendant. After all, in her aspect as Shaushka, she is Goddess of the dark Sun of Earth and the Underworld too, and as the Dark Goddess she welcomes death and chaos. If the gods strive for power against each other in the heavens, their royal avatars on earth will do so too. All power is sacred power."

The leaders realized the main body of warriors had not managed to stop. Pressure from behind had moved them steadily forward and they had now arrived at the gates. "If you wish to save your lives," the Sardinian proclaimed to the assembled crowd, "hide yourselves now and do not fight back. Your city is about to be sacked!"

He had hardly finished his words when the line of chariots separated and the plunder-starved masses of infantry poured through. The discipline of the palace-era military was long forgotten. Most ignored the Sphinx Gate since all gates were unguarded, but others set up ladders and easily ascended the low walls of the sacred city. The invaders flowed inexorably toward the city like a dark flood.

"Glory awaits!" roared wild-eyed Eruthros coming through the Sphinx Gate pushing others aside. "Diomede, come taste battle!" he beckoned as he ran on with his scythe-like sword drawn, his Danaans attempting to keep up behind him. Diomedes saw little chance of glory or actual battle ahead, but gave instruction to some guards to take Henti back behind the lines, and poising his spear he made toward the city. The other chieftains did likewise but moved out to be amongst their own brigades first.

What ensued was plundering indeed, but there was so little resistance the bloodlust did not grasp the hearts of many of the warriors. People ran or hid or simply fell to their knees. Wanton slaughter did occur as well as a number of rapes and the theft of women to be slaves, but mostly it was a search for treasure or supplies. One tall granary silo of four was discovered to be half full of emmer wheat grain, which meant bread again and relief from barley. However, as Eruthros ascended the hill over the town and approached the palace, a Hittite corps of guards in surprising numbers emerged in pointed bronze helms and full battle gear and descended toward them. He saw Diomedes coming up behind his warriors, and shouted one word back to him: "Battle!"

The guards charged down upon the invaders. They appeared to be older soldiers perhaps on a retirement posting, but they put up a good fight, at first. Eruthros in his boar's tusk headgear and, using his large heavy shield as a battering ram, roared through them. As a farmer cuts down his grain field with wide sweeps of his scythe, he swung his heavy khopesh from side to side with such force it mowed down the guards like so many stalks of grain. His strength was more than any had encountered before. Skulls were split and chests were cleaved open with each slash of his curved over-sized blade. A bigger guard bore down upon him with his spear before him. Eruthros actually paused to let him get closer as he pushed his way through other Danaans. Soon he faced Eruthros and pulled back his spear to deliver it into the stomach of the Aitolian, but Eruthros simply parried it with his shield and with his right arm brought down the curved blade with such might onto where neck meets shoulder above the armour that it clove a bloody ditch through the cuirass right to the heart. The guard's head wobbled unnaturally sideways on its untethered neck as he collapsed heavily, already dead.

Diomedes came up, blood-spattered himself, but saw his red-haired friend was lost in battle fury. He had cast aside his spear or left it in someone and was now experimenting with the perfectly pointed, gold-adorned bronze sword given to him by the Sardinian. He deflected a few attacking Hittites with his light shield and went methodically to work, raising his bronze slashing-thrusting sword over his head and unleashing his fierce battle cry. Like an artist in man-killing, he noted the perfect balance of the big weapon as he slashed through armour, helmets, shields, and flesh. It proved to be exquisitely sharp and seemingly impervious to impact. When the guards repositioned themselves in anticipation of his deadly slashes, he turned the tapered blade's sharp point outward and stabbed his way through the defences of the soldiers, who now began to back away to avoid him. Soon all opposition collapsed in front of both Eruthros and Diomedes, and the Hittite guard retreated, stumbling over the corpses or groaning wounded of their comrades. The whole guard soon turned in full rout. Eruthros still lost in his fury pursued them until he was called back by Diomedes.

"Is it not sweet?" Eruthros laughed from his blood-spattered face, putting his gory khopesh-scythe back in his belt. He approached Diomedes who looked only a little less grim and happily slapped him with open hands on his shoulders. "Are we not great warriors?" he proclaimed. The Danaans all round gave a boisterous cheer, for their leaders and for themselves.

"Let's go see who rules here," Diomedes indicated the modest palace atop the hill ahead. The free warriors of sea and plain followed the two leaders to it.

The remaining guards had deserted and the few servants about seemed to be huddled together and weeping, not even trying to escape. Curious, thought Diomedes, but this was explained as he entered the main altar space and saw the two figures lying on their backs, hands clasped together, with the pallor of death in their placid faces. Their robes would have been pure white but for the blood from their slashed wrists and forearms. A man and woman of mature years, apparently the chief priest and the chief priestess of the Sun Goddess of Arinna, had chosen to exit this world by their own hand rather than allow invaders the sacrilege of doing it for them. Even after such a battle, it was a striking sight. Here, even in death, the presence of the sacred was palpable.

"Kill or kidnap no one else in the palace," ordered Diomedes to the gathering men behind him. "Leave them here in their sorrow."

"But do seek out anything of value and take it. They no longer need it," announced Eruthros indicating the dead couple. To Diomedes, he whispered, "Leave even the women?" Diomedes nodded, and Eruthros strode away to plunder. Diomedes looked at the noble corpses but considered them already well-placed for what would follow. He waved his sword to indicate the servants should flee the palace, and they did so. Getting assistance from other warriors, he built a funeral pyre of anything of wood or flammable materials, like the curtains and drapery, in the room. On it, the dead couple were carefully laid, and, getting fire and oil from one of the various lamps about, they were set aflame.

They later left the palace mostly in ruins with the fire spreading. There was surprisingly little in the way of treasure, though a number of figurines of various deities encrusted with jewels were taken. Silver mirrors had been found along with bronze and golden icons of a sacred nature likely used in rituals and processions. No rape or murder had occurred in the building. Diomedes looked back at the ruin and reckoned the whole structure had too much stone to burn to the ground. For some reason, this pleased him. As they passed one of several palace pools, he splashed water over himself to cleanse the blood from his face, and others followed suit.

On their return path through the city, they merged with the mixed contingent of the Sardinian, coming back from exploring the furthest area, which appeared to have only low buildings and a number of mounds with stelae or monuments atop them. They had two wagonloads of exotic wonders, most now wrapped in oilcloth. Sarpedon called to him, "Diomedes, forget your scratchings, come see what we've discovered." The Akhaian came over. "Some recent earthquake had opened a rent in the ground and one of the mounds had caved in, spread nicely by the splitting earth. We could see timber planks constructed in careful order about four full arm spans below."

"You're not telling me you found a royal tomb? Was it a shaft grave?"

"Oh yes, and very ancient too. The locals who would talk to us said it was dug when the real Hatti still ruled here before the invading Nesa people built the Hittite Empire. The timbers turned out to be a roof, and below it the rectangular mausoleum has firm walls on four sides and a floor paved with pebbles. Two rotting carts were within with shining metalwork. We opened the central sarcophagus – not without some trembling among the others, I could see – and inside were the bones and clothing remnants of two people, a royal couple as it seemed, curled up like babes and made to face the south. We left them there but gathered the grave goods from their remains. Come see."

Diomedes looked into a wagon a saw a shimmering pile with gold fibulae, broaches, diadems, and belt buckles along with chased and repoussé gold-leaf figures. Beside them were items from the rotting cart next to the queen – extraordinary jewellery, jewelled containers for cosmetics, bronze and copper mirrors, silver combs, gold necklaces, pins, bracelets, ear pendants and diadems. From the king's cart were taken copper, bronze, and silver tools and weapons, and a pointed golden crown. The wagon also included domestic utensils and vessels, long-stemmed gold goblets with glittering jewels in the stem, gold jugs, gold fruit stands, and ritual implements, all to accompany their dining in the afterlife. The following wagon contained larger metalwork sculptures.

"These standards were once part of the ancient carts, held aloft on wooden poles or attached to the carts in front. Some were carried by mourners, no doubt in the funerary procession." Some were shaped as disks or arcs. Each incorporated a stylized bull or stags with massive antlers, bronze inlaid with silver or gold. "It is indeed a king's treasure".

Diomedes looked over at Sarpedon and spoke to him privately, "What of the other mounds?"

"Ah, you are keen," the Sardinian replied in a lowered tone. "I blocked any attempt toward such thoughts. They all have stelae on them so are likely to be royal graves of the ancients, but do the men need more treasure to fight over before we even arrive at Hattusa? Perhaps they would want to return to the coast after weeks of pillaging these graves. And then there's the matter of delicacy."

"Delicacy?"

"These deep shafts are royal graves, very similar to those I saw near Mykenai and heard were in Sardinia." Diomedes suddenly recalled seeing Sarpedon at the Battle for Mykenai. "Could these people's gods be related to ours? I don't know, but robbing a royal grave gave me unease, so I would prefer to avoid doing more of the same."

The horde camped right outside the sacred city, celebrating their victory. Only a few of their vanguard had been killed or wounded, but Uhhaziti was among the latter, having a head wound from tiles thrown or fallen from a roof. Many of the inhabitants of Arinna were allowed to live as they were no threat to anyone and had no wealth in any case, but some of the men did bring back women for the evening celebrations. They weren't considered slaves, yet they were given no choice.

Seeing Eruthros return carrying a skin of wine and hauling two women by a single tether, Diomedes and his translator gathered what they had to camp further away. "What a fine battle we had, eh, my Lord!"

"Yes," replied Diomedes evenly. "It was a dangerous *hour*." He smiled sarcastically.

Eruthros laughed and pointed for his captives to sit down. The dishevelled women squatted down without expression, accepting their lot. Diomedes noted they were at least mature and appeared unafraid. "Okay, I admit it was perhaps less of a desperate struggle than enduring a day-long tumult against a Hektor or even a Memnon but agreeable nonetheless. Did you not experience the joy of Ares at least for moments?"

"I saw your brief battle fury," my friend, "but Ares keeps his distance from me. Did you not know this? Athene Areia is my war goddess and she is *controlled* fury."

It was a long, raucous night in the light of the burning city, but there was fresh baked bread available for many in the morning. Surprisingly, the flames in Arinna had mostly burnt themselves out by late morning when the assembly of warriors mobilized to continue their journey toward the final conquest of Hattusa, just out of sight over a few hillsides. The men were temporarily sated with feasting and wine and other delights of the flesh. Some were pleased with the plunder that had been distributed to them, but most ended up with little or none, so they were ready to take another city before finding a homeland. The smoke rose from the burning of Arinna as the mixed group of warriors moved out, but it had not been utterly destroyed and most were left alive.

7. The End of Hattusa

General Kil-Teshub rode his strong stallion, adorned with drapery identifying his station as military commander, up to the sturdy wagon near the front of the caravan where the Great King's chief minister Mahhuzzi sat uncomfortably behind his driver. "Come aboard, uncle and noble colleague," he spoke. "We have matters to discuss." No sooner had Kil-Teshub manoeuvred his substantial frame next to the Great King's chief advisor than Mahhuzzi continued. "Any sign we are being followed by either of our enemies?"

"No sign at all," spoke the general. "We have sent scouts back but ... nothing. We have travelled far these several weeks. We approach yet another holy city on this river called the Samura. This one is mountainous Kummiya, chief city of Kizzuwatna kingdom." Kil-Teshub pointed ahead downstream to a cliff face on the west bank of the fast river. "The city is right under those cliffs. Can you see the figures carved on them?"

Mahhuzzi squinted and saw two giants on the cliff face. “These are Great Kings become gods?”

“Yes, my friend. One is Muwatalli II, the destroyer of the Pharaoh’s army at Kadesh, made to look like Estan, god of the day sun who sees all evil. The other is his bastard son, the short-lived Mursili III, whose semblance has been damaged by the troops of Hattusili, your grandfather, my father, who righteously took the gold throne from him.”

The giant figures grew in size as they approached and the chief steward felt tendrils of awe rise up his spine. As he looked, the sky darkened and distant lightning flashed.

“Teshub Storm-God’s bull is near. Hear the distant thunder? See the dark clouds gather? We are beyond pursuit,” the general confirmed.

“We seem to be in a new land, a land that rains.” Mahhuzzi then looked over at the old soldier. "I have spoken with the Great King. He seems to think Tarhuntassa is our destination, but he is awaiting a sign from the gods. What does Kil-Teshub think?”

“It has the seaport of Ura, so it’s valuable territory, and it is not long since we returned from that land after taking it back from old Kurunta. So Suppiluliuma may feel he is still in charge. However, my spies have told me that the new vassal-king he appointed, the nephew of Kurunta named Halata, is not as loyal to his Majesty as he swore he would be. He is aware of the precarious situation of Hattusa and is preparing to declare himself Great King. We may not have the strength to take the city back since we are not sure of the loyalty of the larger forces stationed there.”

“And the other choices are...?”

“Karkemish or Lawazantiya. Karkemish is a powerful city that holds the best ford across the Mala River and it declares itself as loyal to the Hatti.”

“Ah.”

“But again it has more powerful forces than we have, so we would have to be sure it would welcome the Great King himself. Talmi-Teshub is its ruler; he has been on friendly terms with Suppiluliuma, but whether he wishes to be the Great King himself is unknown. Their patron goddess is Kubaba, a dignified matron in the pantheon and mother goddess, unlike dark, hungry Shaushka-Ishtar, so it is unlikely the Great Queen Lieia-Hepa would be put in a place of power."

"She is currently without power or place amongst us right now," Mahhuzzi whispered. "Ever since the righteous attack you led on Hepat's temples in Arinna, the Great King has had her under guard in isolation. She has been a ... threat to the order."

Kil-Teshub took off his sky-pointing war-helm. "It is not a comfortable situation. There are a great many among the people who hold the Sun Goddess of Arinna supreme in the heavens and the Underworld and agree that her influence has become predominant on the land. There is already a stir and talk among them, even among the Meshedi. They feel the Sun Goddess needs to be placated, not locked away. The cosmos is indeed out of balance. But what can be done? The Great King has made his choices!"

"It may not be too late. We know the Great Queen favours Lawazantiya, the Hurrian home of Puduhepa, the home of the sun-of-the-earth goddess Shaushka-Ishtar. Lieia-Hepa is her priestess." He looked at General Kil-Teshub. "It could be no bad thing if we were to please her Majesty even though Suppiluliuma thinks she is no longer a factor. The city is not large and does not have a strong military, but it is a sacred city and has good walls for strong defences once we're inside. And it is the nearest to us. If we tell his Majesty that in this city he will be safer from his enemies and more likely to retain power, it may be we could sway his choice in that direction."

Kil-Teshub smiled, "You mean sway the scales of destiny among the gods."

"Yes, of course," Mahhuzzi smiled too. "That is exactly what I meant."

The road toward the Hittite capital was well-worn and the invading army made good time. The sun was moving inexorably toward the horizon when Hattusa suddenly appeared as they rounded a bend in the mountains. Though coming from the west, they had inadvertently gone north to Arinna first. Hattusa was south but they had to go downstream further south and around the city to ford the Delice River, after which the army now went north again to approach the southern Sphinx Gate. The city's white stone and concrete shone brightly with the reflected yellow light of the early evening sun rays, though there were pillars of smoke rising from within. At first there was a notable stir of excitement among the multitude of warriors but this soon settled into something like hushed wonder. Across the shallow waters of the river stretched the Great Rampart leading up to the Sphinx Gate and into the sacred Hittite capital. There was no attack for scouts had reported the state of the city. The invaders forded the river and some moved west toward the unguarded main Lion Gate further along. Most followed the chieftains as they ascended the shining limestone of the Great Rampart. Others yet veered off and chose to enter the city through the unguarded postern gate, which was a large tunnel going right through beneath the Great Rampart, braced with the same sort of corbelled arches of hewn stone blocks Diomedes would have known from Tiryns. However, he and Eruthros joined the other two leaders at the front, Uhhaziti wounded and not present, and ascended the 250 inclined great spans to the top of the city wall some thirty great spans high (a span being both arms open from fingertip to fingertip). It was an impressive entry to one of the great cities of the world, and nearly every man felt some sense of awe, so unlike their usual screaming destructive fervour.

However, at the summit on the wall, Hattusa lay revealed before them, and the glory of the many temples and the palatial akropolis in the distance was dampened by the sense of hopeless doom that overlay the mostly deserted buildings. Desultory fires burned everywhere with milling groups near them. The city's reservoirs were all but empty. There were more people than expected, but nowhere was an animal to be seen, beyond the crows circling above or perched about. Though the lower city was not clearly visible there seemed to be huddled masses around the grain silos though it was soon learned they were empty to the last seed. A smell arose that was unlike the battlefield stench of death and more akin to that of old rot. Most people were gathered just within the Lion Gate and right below them in makeshift hovels. When they saw the warriors appear at each of the other main gates, most were too far gone to do anything. No one ran but some approached with wails and begged desperately for food.

"I see a couple of thousand starving Hittites," said Payava, "and a city likely bereft of anything worth plundering. What shall we do?"

"We could still attack," Eruthros spoke, stretching his big arms. "Hope of loot and the sport of slaughter binds the men together."

"There is no sport in slaughtering the helpless," Diomedes looked at him sharply. Eruthros winked back, indicating he may not have been serious.

"We need to get away from here and make plans before the Kaska appear, if they are not watching us already," Sarpedon intervened. "What they will do not even the gods can guess. In the meantime, I suggest we send out patrols to check for anything of value left behind. What kind of leader deserts his own people, leaving them to starve? The question is, do we pursue the villainous Great King of the Hatti south into the rugged heartland or do we return to the coast empty-handed."

"Yes, I'll arrange to send out well-armed patrols immediately," said Payava. "But, Sarpedon, the men will go no further inland, that I do not doubt. Their hearts cry out for the sea and we do not even know where Suppiluliuma has taken his kingdom."

"Send the patrols then we shall talk," the commanding voice of Diomedes cut through the air. "I suggest we give them each a bushel of the wheat we just captured to give to the dying souls we see below."

"What? There are too many. It won't save them for long," the Lukkan asserted.

"It may help them enough so many survive this disaster and begin new lives."

"I am in favour," spoke the Sardinian. "They are dying and no danger to anyone."

Payava looked at him astonished, "These are Hittites!"

"Kingdoms are dead or dying. A new age awaits. These are starving people," Sarpedon concluded. "We need to send out those patrols now!"

Surprisingly Eruthros agreed, so Payava gave way though he was clearly disgruntled at being overruled. The orders were given, and quickly passed down into the irregular ranks, going right back to commanders and sub-commanders to patrol leaders to the full supply wagons still near to the river. Five patrols of size and armament to keep desperate attackers away set out, each with a cart with one bushel of emmer wheat. It took a while but they entered through the grand Lion Gate to the west. Once inside the first patrols forced their way quickly to the lower city, already being pursued. There was no question of orderly distribution. The patrols simply dumped their cargo on the ground when they reached a clearing and backed quickly away to explore the fine marble or limestone temples while others searched through the palace. The two patrols near the gates did likewise and were astonished as the ravenous crowds stormed in grabbing what containers they could to scoop up the life-giving grain. The men in the patrols faded quickly backwards drawing their weapons, but they were no longer of interest to the desperate masses.

The chieftains called for watered wine, pouring some to the earth in cautious libation, and sat in a circle, respectfully waiting for Payava to speak. He did, "So we retreat with what we have, perhaps taking what cities we come across on the return journey to our encampment?" The other leaders looked at each other.

"We must send envoys to speak with the Kaska and warn them off. They won't be happy about being left out though they don't yet realize there is nothing left here worth bothering with."

"Yes," said the Lukkan. "But should I not go myself to speak to the Kaska men, so they know we are dead serious?"

"I think envoys are the way to go," repeated Sarpedon, glancing meaningfully at his friend to make him aware of the danger of being an envoy to the Kaska.

He understood. "Let us pick some bold warriors and find a translator who speaks Kaskian, as well as a guide who will lead them into the mountains and find the nearby Kaskan forces under an envoy banner. They will be directed to warn the Kaska to go home to their mountain fastnesses or to their new home at Nerik, for if they advance to plunder Hattusa, we will attack them with all our force." It was agreed.

"There is another matter on which I must speak," Diomedes ventured and all eyes turned to him. "I can understand how people of the sea will refuse to go further inland after a fleeing Great King of the Hatti and his chosen nobles who are all probably doomed anyway. But I have unfinished business with him that cannot be left undone. He had my Akhaian brothers-in-arms beheaded without ceremony. I do not know what happened to their bodies, but they were neither burnt nor buried. I cannot leave this be. Even if I must go alone, I am going after them to seek my vengeance on this Suppiluliuma the Mad. I would prefer a patrol to accompany me if you can spare the volunteers. I would choose other Akhaians but Lukkans or Arzawa, I admit, would be less conspicuous and able to speak to strangers. Is this acceptable to all here?"

There was a stir. Nobody wanted to lose such a famed warrior. "I must go with you on this adventure, my king, uh, my lord, uh, my ... friend," announced Eruthros, whose uncertain labelling broke the tension.

"I admire your courage," said Sarpedon. "And I wish I could join you both, but my duties are here, getting this band back to join our major assault group. Amurru awaits, and who knows what after that?" He came over and he and Diomedes, standing at different levels, clasped wrists. "We shall arrange a small patrol to accompany you. You must take Kabi, our best scout, who knows the land. I suggest you travel at night. May your gods guide you."

"Eruthros, let us gather those who would come and leave first thing tomorrow."

Diomedes and Eruthros had only ridden horses experimentally before, but carts would be too slow and the land ahead may be too rough, so Kabi took them aside and taught them each how to squeeze his legs together to get a grip and to guide a trained horse by directionally pulling its halter to the side from the rider's seat atop it. The strongest of the little horses was chosen for the big Danaan, but Kabi warned he'd better switch mounts regularly. A squad of veteran Lukkan warriors whose native tongue was Luwian and who spoke a few other languages readily agreed to set out with him and Eruthros.

He left his own translator, Henti, under the care of Sarpedon, whom he had already come to trust. Henti repeatedly pleaded to come along but was ignored. Diomedes took her aside and put the silvery iron dagger she had found for him in the king's bedroom back into her hands. "Hide it well. It may save your life," he whispered. "I expect it back," he winked. They left the next morning, heading due south, soon fording the Delice tributary. The Hattusan caravan was assumed to have taken the longer but well-travelled road southeast.

The army of many peoples pulled back from the city, camping on the plain while Payava and Sarpedon with a few guards stayed behind for a final tour. The patrols in the city had found many valuable items but little in the way of gold or jewels. Bolts of elegant cloth had been located near what must have been the harem quarters, as well as bronze and silver jewellery with some outstanding examples made from smooth sky iron. Large carvings and statuary had been left because they could not be transported.

"There is beautiful stonework everywhere, limestone, marble, and even granite; the building looks indestructible," Payava continued while Sarpedon nodded his agreement. "But note the pillars and the structure. It's all done in *fachwerk* – halved timber framing. This whole city would burn like a dry forest."

While the city's wretched occupied themselves with making bread or wheat porridge or fighting over the limited amount of grain and disappearing fresh water, Sarpedon went with Payava to walk along the main viaduct to the massive outcrop of rock. There were carved the Luwian glyphs apparently in the Great King's own words celebrating his victories since he became ruler. The Sardinian read the words as best he could and the Lukkan shook his head in wonder.

"He began well, did he not? From the Hittite perspective I mean. He regains control of the coastal kingdoms of Amurru and Ugarit. He pushes back the Assyrians in the east as atonement for his father's defeat. In the south, he takes back Tarhuntassa. In the southwest, he brags about driving back the borders of my land and Arzawa and enslaving our kings. But who will maintain these borders now that he has fled? Alasiya that he claims to have taken with ships is already back in our hands. He posted so much of the grand Hittite army in foreign lands, he leaves the fields empty and Hattusa undefended! What is the purpose of all these inflated words of glory? Who is it for?"

"Ah, good question," said Sarpedon. "I'm sure Suppiluliuma believed the words on the giant rock open to the sky would be read by the gods. His glory is their glory. It's also a message to the people of the empire: *Have no fear. All is well. You are being protected.* Finally, no doubt, it's also to make himself feel more worthy of his namesake, the first Suppiluliuma, greatest of Hittite conquerors."

"One more question?" asked Payava, looking at his friend. Sarpedon nodded.

"How do you manage to say that name, to just roll it off your tongue – *shupillu-loomy* or some such thing?" The warrior leaders laughed and continued their tour.

The following day, the local guide into Kaskan territory who was also the translator appeared on the horizon with the two envoys trying to keep up behind him. Word spread and the three remaining chieftains gathered to meet them, including Uhhaziti the Arzawan, who was supported by two of his soldiers. "Dizziness," he explained. He had a blood-stained single cloth pinned around his head. The envoys walked into the gathering, proudly looking around, the translator-guide right behind them, feeling they had accomplished their dangerous mission.

"Back so soon, your flag of parley still with you. Did you not find the Kaska?" asked Payava.

"We did, my leader," said the shorter one. "They were not that far away. We saw the smoke from their encampment after crossing only two valleys into the third. They must know that we're here. We were taken by guards and surrounded, but their chieftain..."

"Named Kaskaili?"

"Yes, it was he," said the Maionian translator. "Old friend?" he asked with a smile.

"Anyway, their chieftain heard the pleas to parley in our Maionian's rough Kaskian, and he invited us to speak," the shorter envoy who seemed in charge continued. "In all truth, we were relieved to still be alive at that point, yet I announced that their forces were not needed since Hattusa was virtually deserted and already in our hands. But when I told them outright that by your order they were forbidden to come any closer, I fully expected we would be struck down."

"It is good to see that is not the case," smiled Sarpedon, for he and Payava had expected the same thing. "Could you discern the size of their force and did you learn where they have been? Most important, what was his reply?"

"They probably have less than half our number but are notably mobile with many horses. Kaskaili smiled and declared that they have already pillaged and destroyed a number of Hittite towns to the east of here, so they had no need to bother with a deserted Hattusa. He mocked the cowardice of the Great King. In fact he told us that they were in the process of withdrawing to their regained capital of Nerik, so they would allow us safe passage on our return journey back to the sea."

"They lie," interjected Uhhaziti. "They are the Kaska." Sarpedon looked concerned.

"Why would they?" asked Payava. "They have all they want. They have their chief city back. They have gained plunder from the Hatti. Their ancient foes have fled the land. The Gods of the Kaska must be rejoicing. Besides, they recognize we would destroy them in direct battle."

With such strong words from the most influential leader of the conglomerate of warriors, it was decided to head back to the coast immediately, perhaps veering north to take any towns still loyal to the Hittites. Since most of the horde were more seagoing pirates than land warriors, a sense of relief went through the troops. They began to head back to pack up their campsites.

"Payava," the Sardinian whispered to his ally. "I suggest most strongly that we camp in the first hidden mountain valley we come to for a day or two, far enough away to hide our smoke. Let's just see what the Kaska are up to and which way they go."

"My deity tells me there is no reason to do that, but I will agree just to be certain. Surely the enemy dare not attack us, but if they betray their word, I will throw myself on the Kaska like a shark on a school of herring. But the gods who once whispered in my head make me feel we are safe, and they are returning to their mountain fastnesses."

The Great King of the Hittites called his chief advisor to him. Suppiluliuma trusted his cunning advice though noted he sometimes did not seem to pay full respect to the vital rituals of daily life in honour of the gods who ruled all. Still who else could he seek counsel with for his choice of destination? After a ritual cleansing and a prayer, they sat in council in the king's well-appointed tent. Elegant, long-handled goblets of deep red wine liberally splashed with purified water were brought to them.

"Mahhuzzi, my seer and cousin, I trust all is well in your travel arrangements?" The Great King did not await a response. "My Majesty has not received direct guidance from the Storm-God, so perhaps he is waiting for my choice of destination, which will have been destined by Teshub of the Storm. I am thinking of returning to Tarhuntassa where my ancestor Muwatalli moved the palace of the Great King only a few generations ago. It was he who named the city Tarhuntassa after the Storm-God as Tarhunta. And we will have a seaport in Ura."

"Yes, as always your Majesty speaks with great wisdom. But perhaps Muwatalli was not guided by Tarhunta of the Storm. Did he not leave his brother and your grandfather Hattusili in control of Hattusa? Was it not destined by the gods for him to be overthrown by Hattusili, which led to Tudhaliya your father becoming Great King in succession? Perhaps Tarhuntassa, despite its name, is not blessed by Tarhunta."

"Yet it remains a safe haven for did not my forces recapture the city after the rebellion by Kurunta? And did not Halata, his nephew, swear fealty to me?"

"Yes, your Majesty, but these military matters are not clear to me. Do I have permission to bring in our great General Kil-Teshub to speak on wars?"

Permission was granted, the Great King not bothering to wonder why he was standing by outside. Kil-Teshub was given the summary and spoke, "Great King, I do not have your wisdom, but just as Kurunta had the brass to declare himself Great King in your Majesty's absence, I have received reports that his nephew Halata may be planning to do the same thing. There is no certainty as to which side the local Hatti warriors will take. It is said Halata has been very generous to them. There is a chance going there could lead to civil war. And one more thing, Ura the seaport is likely next to fall to the sea raiders as Alasiya already seems to have done."

"Ah, it is good we have my servant Ammurapi of Ugarit and his ships of war to stand as a bulwark against those pirates." Suppiluliuma stood up to his considerable height, his royal two-span gold and bronze pointed mitre making him taller yet. He paced about and pulled the coiffed ringlets of his beard. “Then perhaps the wiser choice is to go to mighty Karkemish, where my brother in royalty, my vassal-king Talmi-Teshub rules at my mercy. He will surely welcome his sovereign.”

“This is unknown, Great King,” went on Kil-Teshub. Again, he has been taking care of his subjects and is known to support a standing army by the fees collected from caravans crossing the ford in the great Mala. They will likely be loyal to the king who pays them, and his forces much outnumber our own. It may not be up to him to choose whether to relinquish power or not, but instead it will be in the hands of the city’s protecting deity. And this is where we must tread carefully, for the city’s stern mother-goddess Kubaba may not welcome the Storm-God or his proxy into her land.”

“The ways of the gods are mysterious, are they not, Great King?” Mahhuzzi spoke thoughtfully. “But, as your spiritual counsel, I must tell you that the omens of the soothsayers with regard to Karkemish have not been propitious.”

“No?”

“No, your Majesty. Only last night I looked toward Karkemish and immediately was shown a falling star. How could I think of anything but the implications for your Majesty, the bright star in the heavens of the Hatti?”

“This is not good,” said Suppiluliuma, shaking his black curls. “My advisors do not recommend either of the two likely destinations. Why do neither of you then recommend Lawazantiya even though it seems to lie before our path?” There was a pause.

Mahhuzzi spoke first, “Great King, Ruler of the Hittites, favourite of the Storm-God, we dare not lest you become storm-ridden and disturbed.”

“The disruption that has occurred between you and the Great Queen, between the Storm-God and the Sun Goddess of Arinna is known to us, your Majesty,” the more outspoken Kil-Teshub added. “Lawazantiya is the sacred city of Shaushka-Ishtar, the Sun Goddess of Earth. Though the Storm-God is unconquerable, we dared not mention this choice lest your Highness...”

“Yes?” The Great King towered over both of them, glowering down.

“Lest your Majesty feel threatened. Though the city has few warriors, we thought Lawazantiya was now beyond consideration since you must fear reprisals from the Sun Goddess in her form as Ishtar.” Kil-Teshub looked away.

“Fear? Are you mad? Have the two of you become heretics?” Suppiluliuma puffed up red-faced waving his arms in the air. “My Majesty is a scion of Tarhunta the Storm-God who rules all. He knows no fear so My Majesty knows no fear. I am Myself the greatest warrior among the Hatti! You have just given me more reason to believe that this is what the Storm-God desires – to finish this business and lower the status of the Sun Goddess so My Majesty can put the cosmos back in balance. Then and only then will this drought end and rainstorms return to this parched land. Send envoys to announce our coming. We are going to Lawazantiya!” The Great King put his hands on his hips and looked skyward proudly, feeling his destiny.

8. *–Interlude: The Palladion*

Diomedes shifted uncomfortably as his buttocks and lower back by now felt the anguish of riding his skittish but strong young mare for an entire day and part of the day before that. Of course, he never complained, just as he never complained when he was seasick on the Pontos more than anyone knew. The horse’s strong muscles meant its hard back would change shape with every step and that was wearing. He was getting better at squeezing his knees together just enough so he could raise his sore ass muscles just slightly above the riding blanket on his horse’s undulating back. Eruthros kept falling behind as he found it necessary to dismount and walk-trot alongside his beast more often than Diomedes was doing. The horse of Eruthros needed the break, too.

Kabi came riding smoothly towards them so much a part of his mount he seemed a centaur. “Alert, comrades, there are bandits ahead in the high hill passes around Tatta Lake who seek to surprise us. They are well-armed but have few steeds. They will not face us on the plain, I do not think."

Diomedes used the occasion to slide from his horse and stretch his legs, squeezing his buttocks to bring feeling back. "Are they a threat?"

"They may use bows and arrows to pick us off or they may jump anyone lagging behind."

"Let us pause to kill them," grunted Eruthros from his strong stallion.

"We don't have time to waste," countered Diomedes. "Kabi you say we're taking a shortcut through the lower mountains but the Hatti, who are moving slower, likely took the long road through valleys? So, if we continue our path, we should catch up to them at some point. But these bandits could help. If we could get our hands on one or two, we might learn from them how long ago the caravan of the Hatti passed nearby here."

"Scout, as the rest of us continue on into the pass, do you think you could lead three of us up behind these robbers, so we might drag one back with us?" asked the red-haired warrior.

"Yes, or die trying," laughed the scout, as delighted as Eruthros at the thought of action. Diomedes was sensible enough to stay to lead the troop into the pass since he knew his horsemanship skills were still a liability in a battle.

Things proceeded as anticipated. In the pass the remaining sixteen were subject to arrows and a few javelins, but they were ready and blocked them with their stout shields though one horse received a deep gash in its haunches. Above on the bluff, the noisy attack of the four riders scared most of the robbers in a false direction leaving two laggards to be captured, one by Eruthros and the other by a pair of Lukkans. They brought them back and kept them under guard while an evening camp was set up in a defensible position. The wounded horse was set free and the better of the two captured nags was given to its rider while the second one was made a pack animal.

Speaking Luwian and a patois of various languages, the two thin, dirty bandits understood all questions from Kabi, with the help of a translator from Karkisa, and were glad to offer any information they had. Most of the troop understood the words and gathered close to hear. The bandits had heard that the royal expedition had passed slowly by on a more eastern route up the valley of the Delice River and into mountain passes more than two weeks earlier. They did not know its destination but it had been heading south so any number of cities were possibilities. Kabi suggested Tarhuntassa, but no one was sure. Diomedes and his troop had taken the more direct route south and had just left the Marassantiya River valley to enter the rough hills above salty Tatta Lake. They would have to go nearly due east to follow the king's escape route.

The crude evening meal consisted of dried wheat bread, dried lentils, and a basket of figs. For meat, they cooked two thin rabbits, three grouse, and a muskrat from the marsh. Everything was shared equally among the seventeen men, for the troop saw no reason not to feed their hungry captives.

"They are no longer any use to us. Kill them?" asked the Danaan in Akhaian.

"This is not a Dolon situation," replied Diomedes looking into the flames. "There is no prize of captive horses ahead, and we are not at Ilios." Eruthros grasped the Trojan reference. "They are of no use to us, but I don't believe they're a threat either." In bad Luwian, he called to the others, "I say we keep the animals and send the bandits packing without their weapons. What say the rest of you?"

"I think you should free us with our weapons," the older bandit surprisingly spoke up, and everyone laughed at his temerity. "Sorry, me lord, but since you were asking for opinions, I thought I'd venture mine. A few victuals for the return journey would be much appreciated too." This boldness caused such merriment that it was decreed to do exactly that.

"Who are you?" the younger more nervous of the two captives asked.

The older one continued, “We see no common mode of dress, and though we hear the voices of Lukkans and Arzawans among you, your scout is maybe Assyrian, but your two leaders speak a tongue unknown to us. From what land have you come?”

Diomedes understood the gist of the question, but Eruthros did not, so various men who spoke Milesian Hellenic came forward. Eruthros nodded to one named Saddirme the Karkisan, a seasoned front liner, who translated the question for him. Diomedes replied in Akhaian with the tales he had learned from the Sardinian while the nimble-minded Karkisan translated into Luwian: “We come from no land and many lands, from near and far. Many of us take the great sea as our home. We are much like you, bandits and freebooters, for we too have been forced from homes by drought, famine, plague, and war, but even more by the collapse of those who ruled us and the withdrawal of the gods who once ruled them. We are not merely bandits, however, for elsewhere others have brought families with them to seek new homelands in which to settle, the richest and most fertile land that can be found. Those of us you see here are but few, but we are part of such a vast movement of uprooted peoples that no city has yet stood before us. None. We have taken Mykenai, Miletos, Smyrna, and Ilios, and now we add to that Hattusa itself. South of us, our allies now close in on Kyprios, Ugarit, Amurru, and whatever rich lands lie beyond that. And the curly black hair of our scout is not Assyrian but Canaanite, the tribe of Khabiru.”

The two bandits were agog at such ideas, not really grasping their sense, but the men of the troop were so exalted by the soaring words they broke into cheers. They felt a sense of identity and a purpose, which were not always clear to them. The bandits were given food, their weapons back, and released. The troop prepared to rest but Eruthros was now excited and wanted to talk in his native tongue.

“My Lord Diomedes, I have not heard you speak this way since you addressed the Great King Agamemnon, the

Wanax of the Argives and Akhaians, back among the ships at Ilios. He had called the meeting of the Hellene generals to announce he was going to return to Mykenai since our siege was no longer making progress. You spoke against that saying you and Sthenelos would stay to the end. Hermes guided you again tonight."

"Agamemnon conveniently forgot that Mykenai was by then a burnt-out shell and that he had barely escaped with his life when we all took to sea to escape the Dorians and the starving locals."

"You're implying he didn't really want to go home and was relying on you to rally us?" Diomedes nodded. "But did you know," Eruthros continued, "that once Ilios was in ashes and we had dried our ships out so we could tar them and make them seaworthy again that he again insisted on returning to reclaim Mykenai?"

"I did not know this. Tell me, my friend."

"We had gained a worthy collection of loot and captives from Ilios, and everybody was anxious to escape that morbid shore. But he and his brother had a terrible falling out. Menelaos had captured some wily princess of Ilios and the goddess of love confused his mind, for he wanted to take her to the land of the Nile to begin a new life together. I do not know if he meant to stay with us and conquer Aigyptos as some men dream or to simply move into the country as an alien guest. Agamemnon insisted he return to Mykenai with him to *make things right*. They went their separate ways in anger, and we watched as each took their contingent in different directions. Incredibly, Agamemnon went southwest directly island-hopping across the sea to Hellas while Menelaos went straight south toward the Levant. I do not know what became of either of them. Most of us simply continued to raid the Aegean and sometimes each other or beyond into the Levant, but others settled in valleys far from the sea with their families where things were likely to remain dangerous."

"And I deserted the plains of Ilios after all," Diomedes looked at the dark horizon.

"Yet here we are, Akhaian warriors, in the prime of our strength, in pursuit of glory again! Is this not destiny? We are where the gods have decreed. Tell me, O thief of the Golden Fleece, what is the plan for when we catch up to *Shupplu...* the Hittite king and his troop? Are we fifteen warriors just going to march up to his throne and cut his throat?"

"That is something I have not entirely faced, but Hermes Masterios, the searcher into mysteries, guides my thoughts that tell me subterfuge is better than bold attack."

"For trickery, Hermes Dolios, the crafty one, would be a better guide. Among men, a cunning scoundrel is the Sardinian who calls himself Sarpedon; he would be of help now. Or, better, going back, imagine guidance from your Ilios comrade, the wily Odysseus, with whom you stole the ancient Palladion that had safeguarded the citadel of Troy."

"Yes, my *trusted comrade.* And where is that wooden icon now?"

"The Palladion is made of wood? It must be from the olden time in the northlands. So Athene was Goddess before all goddesses!"

"Your words outstrip your thoughts as usual, my friend," smiled Diomedes. "Yes it is wood, but very hard wood with a solid weight to it, but only Athenians declare the figure is Athene. Its origin is unknown but it may predate both the Trojans and Hittites. She is a tough-looking mother with a babe at her small breast. She is naked, lean and strong, wearing a towering turban and her feet merge with the lion on which she stands, obviously a worthy protector. I have to admit she is more formidable than any of our goddess depictions." He smiled. "The Palladion, as we call it, was still in one piece when last I saw it. She had been very well cared for, regularly cleansed, oiled, repainted, presented with food and drink, and appointed with modest drapery. She is only about three spans tall, so I carried her off easily. I think she liked me."

"You and Odysseus are unlikely to have walked in the main gate and asked to be given the Palladion. Without beginning an epic song but leaving out the gods again, how did you do it? And I must ask, is there any truth to the widespread tale that Odysseus tried to steal her from you?"

"We shall sing no epics tonight, my friend. We learned from a captured spy that there were several tunnels in and out of the city used for sending out scouts and bringing in supplies and that each allowed for only one man at a time. So there was no point in trying to steal in a troop of us: the Trojans would simply have dispatched them one by one as they emerged. We dirtied ourselves up, put on worn field clothes, and looked as peasants except for hidden daggers. The spy took us to a tunnel he recommended, so I thanked him and quietly sent him to Hades. It was a long crawl but we came out in the city within a deserted hut. It was evening yet we actually found our way up the hill without too much trouble. No one accosted us until we came near the temple area. There we dispatched several unsuspecting guards and dragged their bodies into alleyways. We went deep into several temples within temples. Our steps guided by ... luck, we avoided the bald-headed priests and mantled priestesses and came to the candlelit Holy of Holies where the painted lady of the Palladion awaited us. We wrapped her in my cape and spirited her out. I carried her and Odysseus only needed to play the assassin a few more times before we emerged out of the tunnel back into the night air of the Trojan plain. It is true he drew his blade behind me but when I turned to face him, he sheepishly put it back in his belt, so I don't know what his purpose was. If that tale got out, it was he that told it."

"So, Diomede, you still have it then?"

"I thought we were going on our excursion into the Propontis for but a short while, and I did not wish to endanger the invaluable and lovely ironwood Palladion of whom I had grown so fond, so to whom do you think I entrusted her?"

"Who else but the little Ithakan who helped you steal it!"

"Yes indeed, so I have no idea where the painted lady has been taken. Do you?"

"Odysseus left with twelve ships going south toward the Syrian basin. I heard it said he was planning to return to Ithaki the longest way possible by raiding along the wild coastal regions of Africa and not going north until the land of the Sikeloi could be seen. From thence, he could head across the Ionian Sea to Ithaki, his home island."

"But such an adventure will take him many long years."

"Yes," concluded Eruthros with a grunt. "I think he was hoping for his old wife to die before he returned. He always had a taste for bewitching young nymphs."

9. Ishtar's Sacred City

As the Sardinian had expected, scouts from rearward arrived at noon on the second day after the departure of the warrior force. There was no doubt about it. They had witnessed a huge black smoke cloud rising over Hattusa, once the greatest city of the Hittite Empire but now abandoned by the gods. It was aflame. They did not get close enough to identify the attackers with certainty but many were in light carts with four wheels and a number of horses were being ridden, which pointed to the Kaska. They were screaming their war cries and making a royal din, as though there was someone to scare. The scouts saw no sign of any fleeing masses of those souls who had been starving inside.

"Maybe it's a challenge to us," Uhhaziti said from where he sat. "Just daring us to do something. This is their territory and the Pontic Mountains are their home. And we threatened them! What a fix we're in, and the reasons for it are not hard to find. It was your decision, Sardinian, to leave Hattusa untouched..."

"Not *untouched*," Payava stepped in. "We touched them with gifts. We fed their starving masses with some of the rich wheat we had liberated from Arinna, though that idea may belong to the Akhaian stranger. It seems learning mercy was a mistake." He looked bitterly at his friend the Sardinian.

“We should have either burnt the city ourselves or just turned it over to the raging Kaska. Warning them to stay away and, if they don’t, threatening them with dire consequences just drove them to attack once we were out of sight. Even they have pride!” The Arzawan’s face was growing red.

“If the Kaska have burnt old Hattusa to the ground, I say let it burn,” added Payava with a sneer. “It’s time for us to return to the Aegean Sea and join our comrades and listen no longer to those with no fight.”

“*I* have no fight?” Sarpedon rose to his full height looking down at his interrogators, but his voice remained even. “Let us see where we’re at. So you two are telling me that Kaskaili and his savages deceived our envoys? They let them leave with promises of obedience just to seize the city the moment we had left?”

“Just so!” snapped old Uhhaziti, but failed in his attempt to stand upright.

“You know that’s what they did,” added Payava.

“And you two agree it would be suicide to attack the Kaska in their mountain fastnesses.”

“Even the Hatti never succeeded for very long and they knew the passes,” Uhhaziti croaked.

“Yes, but the Hatti were in control of Nerik until recently, so they had no reason to attack it.” Sarpedon let that sink in.

“Yes, the Kaska have risen, taken Nerik while conquering everything in their path...,” Uhhaziti began.

“You Sherden devil!” Payava burst out, realizing the truth. “You planned this! You set this up. You guessed what the Kaska would do in the face of our demands, and you made sure they knew we were leaving.”

“But why...?” Uhhaziti was a little slower on the uptake.

“Because, my ungrateful friends, we now have an unabandoned city to conquer and pillage, and Nerik is more than a collection of ancient temples,” smiled Sarpedon. Even Uhhaziti’s eyes went wide and even he grasped the bigger picture now. "If they had killed our envoys as expected, that would have sufficed. I must mention that we all swore an oath to seek vengeance if the Kaska ignored our warning, for I see the two of you are all too ready to forget it."

"Nerik, of course. It sleeps to wake. But we all know the Kaska will put up a nasty fight to defend their recent reconquest. Let them deal with me!" Payava exclaimed. Uhhaziti was helped away to inform his people of the city attack that was about to take place. "Yet," Payava went on, looking down, "this city may be the last I take."

"What is in your heart, old friend?" Sarpedon asked when they were alone.

"Great warrior, we have seen much and been in many fine battles together, beginning with the attack with the Libu against Pharaoh Merneptah in which we were on opposite sides."

"Mercenaries have no *sides*," Sarpedon added smiling. "So I switched when I saw the size of your forces. Turned out to be a mistake when the Misriwi counter-attacked from the sea and brought in more chariots from the gods know where; but since I escaped with my life and met a fine comrade-in-arms – yourself – I consider it a victory."

"Yes, I came back home and fought the Hatti, again and again, and in the midst of it all, I began a new family. Then my homelands were attacked by pirates from the sea, again and again, until at last I joined them to feed my family and help my friends. I ended up defending Taruisa while you were raiding the Argive ports. It has been a blessing of the invisible gods to fight by your side again, old comrade, but I have long passed beyond my fortieth year and I feel it is time to give the family that loyally follows me a true home somewhere." Payava looked pensively into the distance.

"Perhaps such thoughts come to all of us at some point. I have no family with me as you do, but I can still understand your yearning. Many of the wandering sea peoples to whom I have spoken seem to think our journey will only end when we take the rich land of the Nile Delta, which at this point is still a beggar's wish for a horse."

"Impossible dream. I do not think I will ever see such a thing. But rumours are that Alasiya is back in our hands, which may become a safe enough place to settle. Or it may be even better to join Leukos of Kriti on the Canaan coast where his Peleset-Philistines are said to be establishing a homeland." He looked at his comrade. "I do not wish to place a burden on you, Sarpedon, but I have a request." Sarpedon nodded. "I have sworn to protect my little family of three. If I am not fated to return from this grand adventure of ours, make sure they receive my share of whatever wealth we have won and that they are dropped in a safer land, like the ones I mentioned."

Sarpedon laughed aloud, "You've been a warrior all your life and you've hardly been wounded. You're too nasty and tough to die! You will be there to take them to a settlement yourself. As to that wealth, we have a city to plunder."

"Indeed we do," smiled the Lukkan, picking up his tall helmet of multicoloured upright reeds. "Indeed we do."

The very next day the army of eight thousand returned the way it had come covering their two-day departure in one. Long before they arrived they could see remnants of black smoke still circling into the air with such an acrid odour the god of war himself would desert the city.

The Kaska had gone and nothing was moving about except for an exorbitant number of crows and kites circling and landing. As the vagabond army approached, the mighty walls appeared mostly intact but had collapsed at regular intervals where fires had broken through. Led by Payava and Sarpedon, the troop entered through the mostly destroyed Lion Gate, yet the guardian lions still stood, toothless mouths agape as though aghast at the destruction. The stink hit them before the sight. The smell of rotting bodies was known to them yet this seemed the most foul of all past experiences. The first bodies were piled up near the entrance, perhaps killed while trying to escape. They were horribly mangled. The Kaska seemed to take special pleasure in genital or facial mutilation and disembowelment. On entering further into the city, it was seen that a few jackals had appeared out of nowhere to feast. The noise of screeches, cawing, and growling as the dead flesh was rendered seemed to hang in the air. The carrion birds looked at the newcomers indifferently.

The two leaders went up on the remaining battlements to see what there was to see, but, as anticipated, all buildings were fallen except for the main palace. Most official buildings were made of wood covered with limestone paste, so they had readily burnt or were still doing so. The main palace had been fortified in its construction with granite and marble so still stood though it had gaping fissures from which smoke arose. There were human bodies everywhere in all sorts of anguished contortions. No one had been allowed to escape, the hatred of the Kaska for the Hittites ran so deeply. Clearly an effort had been made to pen the starving remnant in various areas and kill them in as brutal a manner as possible. No one was left alive – not one of the nearly two thousand souls who were neither allowed in the king's evacuation nor had made their way back to the countryside.

Breathing properly was impossible until they got out of the city walls once again. Even these hardened veterans of war and death were sickened. Yet, when the order was given to march to Nerik, a ferocious cheer went up.

Zunan-Teshub appeared beside the Great Queen, so covered as to be unrecognizable as she walked in the dust behind her well-appointed wagon. She was under guard but she herself had insisted she be allowed to walk during the day if she so chose, for she knew Ishtar demanded her priestesses stay active and lithe, and besides it seemed a less monotonous way to travel than sitting on the wagon seat all day. The Great King had not spoken to her since the day he had struck her face and put her under royal guard. She had sent him no messages. As High Priestess of the Sun Goddess of Arinna, she was still in shock at what the Great King had done. The Great King was himself the High Priest and thus protector of all the gods, all their rituals, and all their temples. Even if no one's person had been harmed in the act, the destruction of sacred temples in the land of the Hatti by a Hatti Great King was an inconceivable sacrilege. It had never been done before. Since Suppiluliuma had always been painstakingly scrupulous about following the complex Hittite rituals to the letter, his behaviour was unprecedented and inexplicable. To attempt to achieve cosmic balance by unbalancing the eternal pantheon of the Hurrian-Hatti gods was backwards. One does not achieve cosmic harmony by openly using violence to create dissonance. The Great King must be himself unbalanced. And the fact that the man, Suppiluliuma, actually struck her in the face so hard he knocked her over was a personal insult beyond all forgiveness. The throbbing of her bruised, swollen cheek kept her reminded.

Members of the king's guard walking alongside Lieia-Hepa glared at the Hurrian captain as he crossed their path to walk with the Great Queen, but they did not stop him.

"Zunan, my trusted friend, so good to see you. Walk with me."

"I came as soon as word reached me of your circumstances, my Queen. I was not included among those with whom such information was shared."

"I expect not. Whispers from above have reached me that we have already entered the kingdom of Kizzuwatna and will soon be in Lawazantiya itself, our destination."

"From above, you mean...?"

"No, I do not mean from the Goddess," Lieia said, knowing how devout Zunan was.

"I was not told."

"It was not what I expected. Why would the ... Great King burn temples of Arinniti one day then go to another of the Goddess's sacred cities on the next? Lawazantiya is not well-guarded. Does he have evil intentions there too?"

"I do not know, your Majesty. There is no sense to be made of any of this. Perhaps in his arrogance, he simply assumes he will be embraced as the Great King of that city."

Zunan noted with pleasure that Lieia did not flinch at his reference to the Great King as *arrogant.* The royal animosity was serious indeed.

"Perhaps he does, yet I do suspect evil demons have entered his mind. The worship of the Sun Goddess – Arinniti, Hepat – may be endangered for, if he is willing to destroy her temples in Arinna, might he not also do so in Lawazantiya? If he is capable of desecrating the Sun Goddess of Earth, why not the Goddess of the evening star and lower realms – Shaushka-Ishtar – who is dominant in this city? He does not know into what darkness he is wandering. Zunan, you are the only one I can trust now, and I know you are loyal both to Hepat and to me. I need you to get a message to the High Priest and Priestess of Ishtar in Lawazantiya before we arrive. They must be warned of this threat. They must be told that Suppiluliuma is possessed by the madness of the Storm-God and is planning evil actions against the Great Goddess. They have my encouragement to protect the Goddess by any means they feel are necessary. Tell them of my situation and that I will be there soon."

"Know you that when the time comes, I will not hesitate to be your right arm, Great Queen, no matter what the circumstance. I will set out tonight."

Shipibaal couldn't believe his luck, that is, he couldn't believe that Gad, the Amorite god of good fortune, had so blessed him again. First, he had risen quickly to the high estate of being a special envoy (which means also scribe and spy) of Ugarit. He was still a young man and here he was in Lawazantiya a recognized diplomat on his way to Hattusa to deliver a plea for help from Ammurapi the King of Ugarit to Suppiluliuma the Great King of the Hittite Empire. His journey would be much faster and more certain than sending messages in cuneiform on clay tablets via caravan. These were troubled times to be sure and Ugarit was in great danger, which is why Ammurapi had sent him on such a desperate mission on short notice across vast territory. Truly, there weren't other volunteers, but from the warnings of mysterious approaching invaders, he welcomed the chance to be out of the ancient city.

But then luck or destiny intervened again. Only this morning, his sources among the powerful had revealed to him that Hatti messengers had arrived at the temple of the High Priest and Priestess of Shaushka (whom his people called Ashtart) to announce that the Great King himself was nearby with a great armed legion and about to enter the holy city. Surely he and his forces would be welcomed by all for was he not the Storm-God incarnate? (He did not allow himself to consider that the Storm-God might be a secondary power in the holy goddess city of Ashtart-Ishtar.) Shipibaal could deliver his message right here in Lawazantiya, and, by Gad's good fortune or even with the guidance of Ashima, goddess of fate, he might come before the presence of the Great King himself. This was wonderful news. Perhaps he could become the saviour of Ugarit!

Shipibaal the Ugaritic envoy went to his appointed room below the temples where he put on his apron, set up his workshop table and began to crush, moisten, and knead older, unbaked clay tablets into soft clay with the smooth surface he would need to receive the imprints of his stylus. He could then inscribe the Akkadian cuneiform message that needed to be immediately sent to King Ammurapi informing him the Great King of the Hatti had come with his court and a troop of soldiers to this very city of Lawazantiya – a few days' travel from Ugarit! He knew he must see the Great King or at least one of his chief advisors. The fate of Ugarit depended on it, as did his own future as a diplomat. He went to work painstakingly inscribing the message before setting the tablet in the sunlight to dry.

Once they had crossed the central plain and were back on the main road, Kabi readily picked up the trail of the Great King's caravan. It was not hard to follow and any townspeople the troop of fifteen talked to confirmed that the cream of the Hittite Empire along with many warriors had indeed recently passed through, virtually emptying the town of its remaining foodstuffs and supplies. Within days, they had caught sight of the dust cloud over the caravan and soon the scouts had climbed the surrounding hills to confirm that the retinue of pilgrims from Hattusa was approaching the main gates of Lawazantiya. Kabi reported back to the Akhaians that there were about two thousand travellers including many horses, pulling wagons, carts, or chariots. About half the people were military, a considerable force for the dispersed times, likely to strike fear into the fewer defenders of the sacred city though no match for a trained field division.

Kabi had gotten closer for observation. "The gates were opened with great fanfare; trumpets blared their welcome as the first of the royal refugees came to the main gate," Kabi reported. "The bodyguard officers led the way through in their polished bronze armour, pointed helms, and with their shining gold-plated spears held skyward. The Great King in his gilded chariot with no shade and his retinue came next, but it was a strange thing..." Diomedes nodded while Eruthros waited for the Karkisan warrior to translate. "The Great Queen was nowhere to be seen, nor was her chariot on display as proxy."

"Odd, for this is a city sacred to the Great Goddess in one of her forms," Diomedes managed in Luwian.

"Yes," said Kabi who knew this kingdom well from his slave days delivering horses to it from Tarhuntassa. "Though not a city of the Sun-Goddess, as such, here are the holy temples of Ishtar, she who is also the ancient Goddess once known in the first kingdoms as Inanna who journeys to the Underworld and back. Ishtar rules much that is earthly and beyond – erotic love, war, mastery of animals, and the powers of darkness. Still, the avatar of the Sun-Goddess should be welcome here, so it is a great mystery that the Great Queen is hidden."

"Let us be off to our appointed hour in the city," Diomedes announced to the troop in accented Luwian. "Just follow my lead. I need a warrior who speaks Luwian, Hittite, and Hurrian to ride in front with me. You, Saddirme? Come forward, Karkisan." Saddirme had shown he also spoke acceptable Akhaian. Diomedes frowned and spoke in that tongue to Eruthros, "Something is happening with Lieia the queen." Kabi caught the name too and was surprised, for it was rare to hear the personal name of the Great Queen, especially in the informal short form. "We will look into this mystery," Diomedes said and signalled for the final ride to the gates of Lawazantiya to proceed.

The strange sense of predestination continued when the rough troop arrived at the city gates. It was a beautiful, well-appointed city with towers that appeared to be marble in the distance. The walls were solid but were comparable in size to those at Arinna, for many sacred cities considered themselves already protected by their gods. Most prominent were the polished limestone and granite temples, each topped with a prominent keystone arch and placed on the temple akropolis within the city. One was a tower, taller than the rest. Diomedes led them directly to great wooden gates, which were still open from the Great King's caravan having just passed through. Guards approached spears at ready, but looking more bemused than threatening at the troop of dusty warriors.

"Who are you then, friend or foe?" the first guard asked.

"Friend. We are the rearward scouts of the Great King of the Hatti," answered Saddirme in perfect Hittite. In Luwian he asked, "Is there a need to repeat this message?"

The guards looked at them without much interest, their wonderment and suspicion already exhausted from having just observed the massive parade of Hatti go through these gates. The Akhaian-led troop was waved through with no further questions.

Inside the ancient city there was little sign of the starvation and desperation that had been so obvious in Hattusa, but few citizens were about in spite of the recent grand arrival, unexpected by the city people. Diomedes noted the marketplace was entirely deserted and there were no wares available for sale or trade. Even though the guards had not found them of interest, Diomedes ordered his Anatolian warriors to disperse into small groups so as not to draw attention to themselves. Each had enough in silver or gold shekels and valuable iron ingots from the taking of Arinna to find lodging, and even a holy city would have wine shops or alehouses. Diomedes, Saddirme, Eruthros, and Kabi went to the lower part of the city and found an inn, which was amazingly well kept for what should be the city dregs. This was no port city or military outpost with wine shops outside the walls.

They took care of their needs with rough ale and much-appreciated simple but fresh fare. Though they were glanced at, it was assumed they were merely a lower class part of the Hatti assemblage that had just arrived, most of the soldiers being billeted just below the hill of the temples. The four realized the nobles and royalty would be on the city akropolis, the quarters of city leaders – which in this case were a high priest and priestess. The city had no king or queen but the function was much the same though more ritualized and formulaic, if such were possible.

"Will they be welcome?" Eruthros rumbled under his breath though no one could understand him anyway. "You know, not just the crowds of newcomers during a famine, but I mean their new rulers. How will the holy city leaders react to suddenly being made into servants of the Great King and the Great Queen?"

Saddirme responded and in so doing included Kabi by translating the gist of the question. "This is indeed a holy city. It may not be a matter of who is in charge here, priests or kings, but which gods are in power here. The Great King *storms* in here and expects his god to be accepted as the most powerful among the 1000 gods of the Hatti, but there is no certainty in this. Among the first cities, Inanna, the Goddess of Earth and Underworld, was already ancient when Ur was built. Enlil the Storm-God had to take power from her later, but such power is never complete and cannot be or the cosmos would lose all order." He shared his thoughts with Eruthros. "It is unknown whether Suppiluliuma the Great King is willing to share his god's power, so there may be strife in the heavens."

"Indeed there is," Diomedes added. "Know you not that the Great Queen was not visible when the Hatti caravan entered the city? She should have been next to the Great King. Is she alive? Where is the Sun Goddess of Earth, and what can we do to help her avatar the Great Queen join with the servants of Ishtar to subdue this monstrous King of the Hatti?"

There was a pause as the enormity of their undertaking sunk in. Everyone drank. "We are in the bottom of the city. Those to whom we must speak are in the top of the city and they are now well-protected by the Hatti Meshedi. Even though we are great warriors, we are not going to be able to brute our way through, no matter what gods we have to support us," Eruthros uncharacteristically said, for if anyone sought to brute their way through it would have been he. Kabi did not understand the words.

"What are we to do?" Saddirme translated for Kabi.

"I am but a scout," Kabi began, "but a scout may be what is needed to guide us into the palaces and temples." All looked at him. "Still, it goes without saying that we will need the assistance of a local who knows the byways of the city. Perhaps by using subterfuge and hidden paths we can work around or through the Great King's bodyguards and talk to those in power who detest the intrusion of the Hatti." Eruthros looked confused.

"Maybe we can sneak in," Saddirme translated to Eruthros who nodded.

"We need to get Diomedes a private audience with the High Priestess of Ishtar, or maybe even with her Majesty the Great Queen herself," Eruthros grinned at Diomedes.

"Maybe…" Saddirme translated back to Kabi.

Even with most of their number remaining at the campsite on the Sangarios River, there was still a congregation of camp followers behind the main body of fighters as they made their way up into the foothills beyond the plain where the two branches of the Marassantiya River flowing north joined into one. Henti of Miletos found herself among this assembly as it struggled to keep up with the army. The march was demanding and her feet bled. It was hot and dusty in the daytime yet a cold wind would often blow at night. The food was rough and sparse and cleanliness was out of the question. Yet she endured and did not complain.

Her father had been an Akhaian merchant who moved to Miletos from the island of Rodos. She grew up comfortably amidst her family with other Akhaians in the Aegean city, even though it was by then under Hittite domination, which is why the Milesians had to send a contingent to help defend Ilios. But her life remained unaffected. She played, worked, and learned: she was even tutored by their Luwian slave woman.

Henti was barely into her teens when she became the object of unwanted attention by males of all ages. Her long, wavy straw-coloured hair over a delicate face and the early ripening of her lean body seemed to cause admiration, longing, or jealousy in most who saw her, so her father attempted to protect her by keeping her home though he himself seldom was. But she would still fetch water and talk to the women at the well, and one day she glimpsed one of them following her home. The next time she went to the communal well, she saw two men watching her from the shadows. She tried to get home quickly but they caught up with her and, covering her mouth, they carried her off, leaving her water jar shattered. They took obscene liberties with her and forced her to do things that were revolting to her, but they made sure she remained a virgin so as not to lower her price as a slave. She had only lived through fifteen suns, but she never saw her home again. Soon she found herself sold as a slave to a Hatti trader who took her away. Seeing her obvious value, he protected his prize and brought her all the way to Hattusa, where she was privately displayed to the harem mistress, the Great Queen herself. Only stopping for a moment of pleased appreciation for the girl's beauty, she nodded and left Mahhuzzi to handle the purchase.

Life in the Great King's harem was one of strict supervision in which few of the women ever left their designated area. They were treated well, even respectfully, by those who guarded them, and they were encouraged to exercise and eat wisely. They were like well-treated pets who had no personal freedom of their own, and in private Henti would weep for her family and lost life. But when the time came and she was called to the bed of Suppiluliuma, she steeled her will and acted with all the charm the senior harem girls had taught her. It seemed more of a ritual than an act of passion as the Great King acted in conformity within the patterns decreed by the gods in time immemorial and directed her to do so too. Through the fear and pain of the first night, she showed only delight, and Suppiluliuma was himself delighted that she bled so richly. In later visits, he often disdained the ritual of intercourse but became heavily aroused by using his open hand to leave reddened handprints on her white body. His favourite game was to retrieve from a secret drawer his hidden silver dagger with the glistening pearly handle and amber pommel and run the point over her face and near her eyes and the edge across her throat. He wheezed with pleasure at her fear and humiliation. He demanded she not flinch or raise a hand when he drew the blade over her naked, hairless body though trembling was beyond her control. He used the exquisitely sharp point to just break the surface of the skin but leave no scars, even when he made point wound patterns on her small breasts or vaginal lips. Enduring such pain and fear at least saved her from the chance of becoming pregnant. He mumbled to himself and gave commands to her but otherwise there was no conversation. She only wept when she was alone later but soon suppressed that too. In nearly two years there, Henti adapted and survived, but when her language skills were discovered, she would be called forth from time to time into the halls of power.

Things might have remained that way but suddenly the harem learned they were to pack up their things and prepare for a long journey. Many of the women who had lost the Great King's favour were to be given away to members of the king's bodyguard or the soldiery; others thought to be undesirable or too old and uninfluential were simply given back to slavers to attempt to sell in the general population. If not sold, they were among those left behind when the royal caravan left the city. When the time came to leave, Henti contrived to hide, and those who knew her story kept quiet about it. She knew that Lieia-Hepa would not feel her secret was safe with the presence of the harem girl translator who had been aware of her ecstatic love rituals sacred to Ishtar with the unknown Akhaian warrior. She would have made her *disappear*, and Henti was not ready for that.

The women among the camp followers were deferential to her, thinking she was the lady or the servant of one of their leaders, but, perhaps since she never clarified her status, they also talked amongst themselves while looking at her. She saw no reason to confide in them that she and Diomedes were just companions and he was her protector.

The small army of warriors marched north, circumventing the town of Sapinuwa and going past the ruin of Arinna, within which life was already returning in a rudimentary fashion. But at this point, they ceased retracing their steps and went straight north into the forbidding Pontic Mountains. The river ran downhill into narrow canyons, yet the mountains grew upward around them. Somewhere ahead lay Nerik, once again the capital city of the Kaska and sacred home (again) to Kaskan gods. It lay spread out and ready on the approach to the mouth of the Marassantiya River where the flow was wide and deep, but they must first get there for the assault to begin.

It was late summer and the endless drought continued. Obtaining provisions for an army on the move was a desperate challenge. The only trade that continued was local so no grain imports had been seen for over a year. The whole cosmopolitan world seemed to be shrinking to local again, as it had been before there were palaces, cities, and kingdoms, back to a time when gods were village gods not decreed by kings and priests. The women's corps would try to keep up with the main body, by now mostly stretched into a file on the narrow riverside road, while searching for plant foods as they walked. The men ahead will have already harvested any wild animals that were foolish enough to come within sight. They came across recently harvested or desiccated grain fields. It was the reconnoissance troop and designated hunters who would occasionally bring back game, but more likely to be found were domesticated animals they stole, like pigs, sheep, goats, or, rarely, cattle, still not enough to feed everyone.

The scouts came back to report a town ahead down the river. This turned out to be Hurna, a Hatti village based on agriculture and herding. The reconnoissance troop rode in alone and commandeered with little resistance wagons and carts along with donkeys to pull them. There were no standing defences, so nothing could be done to stop them. More resistance came when they stole whatever food resources or other supplies they might need and put them in the carts to take back to the other warriors. Most of the people stayed out of their way or restricted themselves to shouting insults from a safe distance, but a few pelted the troops with debris. Warriors approached but allowed the pelters to shrink into the crowd. It wasn't until a group of young male villagers began to use slings that they truly caught the attention of the riders, who rode at them. But then a few more stalwart but foolhardy lads appeared with swords and axes, so a more deadly response was needed. The troopers brought their lances down and rode down the rebellious defenders, spearing some few through their chests. They dismounted, drawing their short swords, and encircled the Hatti youths, and bloodily dispatched them into darkness like slaughtered sacrificial animals. After that, no one stood in their way, and they stripped the town of the little it had. However, they did no house-to-house searches, so there would be something left for those who had managed to protect their own.

This pattern was repeated at the river towns of Kapperi and Karassuwa, which became much poorer and more desperate while the vanguard became better provisioned and less desperate. The latter town had many who were not Hatti but of an ancient kingdom whom the Hatti had long ago overthrown, so they – joined by those wise enough to see which way the wind was blowing – welcomed the foragers and called them liberators. Some fell on their knees and thanked them, praising their gods, and others yet put garlands of flowers around the necks of those who allowed it. They gave them jugs of raw barley ale and what few beasts they had left. In short, they stocked them so full of provisions that the reconnoissance troops rode back to the leaders of the expedition and announced that there was nothing left worth plundering.

"So we have found friends in the Hatti backwoods, have we?" Payava asked. "That is something of a surprise but a good thing, for at this point we can no longer travel along the direction the river takes us but must make our way up and through the mountain passes to reach our destiny at Nerik. Chariots are no help when laying siege to a city, and the chariot carts we've been dragging along will only slow us down. It will also free up more horses to carry baggage or riders. I propose we leave all the chariot carts and anything else we will not need on this primary assault right here amongst the good people of Karassuwa. This means much of our baggage train. Not long and we will return here from Nerik as conquerors with the booty we deserve, and we will take back what is ours at that time."

"And the Karassuwans?" asked Uhhaziti.

"If our goods are as we left them, they will be rewarded by being allowed their lives. And if they have betrayed their word, which they will soon give to us, Earth will be enriched with their blood."

Sarpedon spoke: "And what of our women and the other camp followers? The Kaska will be attacking us from the cliffs and will make an effort to destroy any who lag behind. Can we do without them as we cross through this wild range of crags? I think we can; they only slow us down. Plus it will make some of the men more eager to get our work done and get back here."

"I agree," said Payava, "but then we must leave a squad of our warriors to guard them. The Kaska are unlikely to come down this far from their mountain hideaways and they will be preoccupied with slowing our main force, but still one never knows. There are two villages we have just sacked that may dare to seek vengeance."

"Uhhaziti?" Sarpedon looked at the leathery old warrior. "I realize your pride and that you have longed to take a real city since we landed, but would you be willing to remain here with your personal troop of Arzawans and others? No one denies your fight, but you still often are undone by head pains and such dizzy spells you have trouble walking, not even to mention riding a horse. You are needed here and will likely be much better healed when we return bringing you wealth. Will you stay?"

Payava nodded in agreement, for Sarpedon knew his thoughts. Uhhaziti looked down, shook off inner objections, and looked back up, "It is well. Perhaps I can find a Karassuwan matron willing to nurse me back to my former glory. My guardsmen and I will stay, and the camp will be kept protected. I will send my brave old uncle to lead our troops. Choose your guides and go."

Kaska warriors in the mountains at first forbore from any attacks on the thick line of the Anatolians and allied sea peoples as they ventured into the rocky passes among cliffs and peaks, heading directly toward Nerik via a dangerous mountain pass. Kaskan observers were soon spotted looking down from viewpoints too far away to be pursued. As expected, the first attacks were on the fighters at the end of the rugged, snaking trail. The Kaska came rushing down on the warrior line from hidden clefts in the rocks, and for a time the fighting was ferocious. In the narrow passage, however, the Kaska could not bring in many of their fighters and after a brutal time they were pushed back with significant losses on both sides. After that, only occasional showers of arrows came down but were mostly deflected by shields. There were attempts to send avalanches down on the troops, but, by luck or destiny, they went over the trail and did not wreak much havoc or block their progress. The biggest losses were among the reconnoissance troop or scouts who ventured too far ahead and were picked off. The local guides were kept well back, so the direction forward was maintained. The conglomerate warrior army was too large and determined to be stopped. After several harrowing days, the Lukkan and the Sardinian allowed some relief to sweep over them as the trail steeply declined and soon the scouts ahead reported the plain of Nerik opening out before them.

As the city itself came into sight, the warriors perceived that a notable force of Kaska lay between them and their goal. But the Kaska's apparent numbers were still less than half of those of the invaders. They would have to be twice the warriors to make it an even fight. The army of freebooters spread out to make camp, setting up sentries in shifts more numerous than ever before. There may be no single code of war behaviour for warriors with dissimilar gods, but the Kaska had savage war gods that directed them to break all codes of honour ever devised. The invaders sent no envoys demanding surrender, for what would be the point? The Kaska were not about to surrender their recently recaptured sacred city.

At another sacred city, far to the south and east, Lieia-Hepa paced the floor of her chamber awaiting the return of her man, Zunan the Hurrian, from his mission to approach the high priestess and her consort the high priest about freeing her and perhaps uniting to block the power play of the Great King of the Hatti. Zunan-Teshub, her royal bodyguard and chief attendant, had at first been carefully monitored by the four palace guards, members of the Great King's Meshedi, who had been assigned as in-house gaolers for the queen, two inside her chamber doors and two outside of them. She was only allowed privacy in the inner rooms that seemingly had no other means of exit, though there was a stairway down to the servants' quarters that was sealed from the inside. Escape seemed impossible.

She feared whatever intentions darkened the mind of her husband, Suppiluliuma. If he was rash enough to actually order the burning of the sacred temples of the Sun Goddess, what would stop him from ordering the murder of the High Priestess of the Sun Goddess – or doing it himself? When she herself had felt her mind overthrown by the possession of the Great Goddess, she imagined that others must perceive the divine presence as well. All must now know of the power of Hepat! There was no doubting or questioning the reality of such exaltation, so to discover that not only the Great King but also ever-loyal Meshedi did not fear to betray and assault the Sun Goddess in herself left her deeply perplexed and anxious. Something had gone wrong in the heavens, or Suppiluliuma had gone mad. Perhaps he had no secret plan, she considered, but was only desperately lashing out as he felt his power, both kingly and divine, ebb from him.

Zunan, after the outside sentries checked him for anything he may be trying to smuggle in, exchanged respectful words with both sets of guards before and after the thick doors. His hostility to the Meshedi guards was hard to conceal, for in his mind they were committing sacrilege of the highest order, but he thought it expedient to retain the formality of duty-driven soldiers. He had his duty and they theirs, but there was nothing personal to it, or so he played it. Who knows what they really felt, if anything?

He approached the Great Queen and, against their custom, prostrated himself before her on the floor. She knew he was doing so for the guards' benefit and grandly allowed him to stand. He followed her as she walked further away from listening ears and they spoke in Hurrian to each other.

"Were you followed? Did you get an audience with the High Priestess?"

"I was not followed, your Majesty. I approached the tall temple altar where petitioners make sacrifice and pray. There I whispered to a priestess who had signalled me and asked for a private audience with the High Priestess. It was as though I were expected. I was taken immediately to a private chamber, in which the High Priestess was accompanied by her consort, the elder High Priest. No names were used. I confess I was dizzy with awe, your Highness, as these divine representatives are Hurrian as am I, and I have known of them and held them in awe all my life."

"Continue, Zunan."

"They agree that it is an offence to heaven that you are being kept a prisoner, especially here in the ancient city of your ancestors, the city of ageless Ishtar herself, before she manifested as Shaushka or Arinniti. They do not have the soldiers to protect you or to break in and steal you away, but they swear they will keep you safe if you can find a way to escape to the Temple of Ishtar. They will resist any attempt by Suppiluliuma to be declared Storm-God and Great King with power over this city."

"After all that has happened, my friend, do you feel such resistance is likely?"

"No, your Highness," he replied but felt himself flush at the familiar address.

"We will depend on the wiles of the Goddess then. Surely some unexpected factor is about to enter into this situation. I feel it, Zunan, Ishtar will not abandon me."

Shipibaal of Ugarit was further astonished by the grace his gods continued to bestow upon him. Gad, the gambler's god, had again brought unexpected luck to his unworthy person. (He did not trouble himself about logical questions concerning human luck coinciding with immortal destiny.) He had hardly sent off his recent message tablets to Ammurapi then a boyish, light-footed messenger had come to his door with word that the Great King of the Hatti "requested" to see him in person to receive Ammurapi's latest message, which Shipibaal knew to be a desperate plea for help, and to send back a reply. This could be hugely important. Perhaps he, Shipibaal, the cloth merchant's son, was about to accompany Hatti warriors back to Ugarit to save his king and his city in their moment of dire need!

He told the messenger he would be at the temple of the Storm-God to meet with the Great King as soon as he could get there, but he added he would need a guide since he was new to this city and the temple of the Storm-God was not the major temple on the akropolis. The messenger himself smirked and promised to serve him as he wished. He twirled his messenger's baton with a winged sun-circle atop it, waiting and watching while Shipibaal got into appropriate diplomatic dress, put on the pendant of an envoy from Ugarit, and covered it with a green cape. He inserted the hard tablet with the seal of Ammurapi on its envelope into his leather wallet for transport. "This will be a stroll for a dashing athlete like yourself," winked the messenger and leapt gracefully onto the path.

As they began the walk, the fantasies of Shipibaal began to fade along with his high confidence. The first part of the message is the admission of King Ammurapi's inability to send any assistance to the Great King of the Hatti. Shipibaal's heart began to fret, "This will not be well-received. But perhaps Suppiluliuma and his advisors will understand how the tables have turned and now Ugarit is in more desperate need than Hattusa. What am I saying? If the Hatti royals and nobility and so many troops and rich goods have come here, it can only mean Hattusa itself is deserted, so what help can the Great King offer when he is in exile himself? Oh great gods, am I to suffer the wrath of the Hittite Empire?"

"What are you mumbling about?" the messenger-guide asked, smiling back at the nervous envoy. "You should be pleased. The Great King has so far allowed audiences with only a very privileged few. Now take wing so we don't keep his Majesty waiting."

It was an uphill trot all the way toward the summit of the ancient city, getting steeper near the top. By the time they approached the temple palace of the Storm-God, not the tallest or most central, Shipibaal felt the strain. In response to his question, the messenger braced an arm over his shoulder and answered that the two biggest and most beautifully appointed temples, one tall and the other broad, were both dedicated to the honour of Ishtar, the most ancient goddess of love and death who allows the Sun Goddess to rise each morning and welcomes her back into the earth at night; she shows herself in the east as the morning star and in the west as the evening star. He used his arrow-shaft wand to point out each temple, “The tall tower temple with the eight-pointed star atop it and the snake-encircled lion over the main portal is the temple of the Goddesses known to the Hurrians as Shaushka and her older sister Allani, but whom the ancients know as the sisters Ishtar and the dread Ereshkigal. Therein dwells the High Priestess. The fat, stumpy temple with the wounded calf over the door is the temple of her consort Tammuz, so it is her temple too. Therein dwells the High Priest.” Shipibaal was going to ask why husband and wife did not dwell together, but he was distracted by the etching of intertwined serpents up the shaft of the messenger’s winged baton.

They walked right up to the pair of Meshedi guardsmen at the turn off the road to the broad temple pathway. Each held his spear with gold-plated heads straight up with a folded arm resting it on his shoulder protected by a scarlet cape, but they crossed the spears together to make a barrier as the young men approached. One held both spears while the other searched for weapons only on Shipibaal. They ignored the messenger who turned and faded away. They questioned Shipibaal, studied his bronze pendant, glancing curiously at the clay tablets, and allowed him to proceed, signalling the *okay* to the other guards by the entrance. Shipibaal noted two more patrolling the grounds. He went up the three steps of the perron to the entry-level where the doors were opened for him by the next pair of golden-speared Meshedi who seemed to stare right through him. Inside were two more yet who frisked him again and accompanied him into an inner antechamber where he was required to strip and cleanse himself with water brought to him in a basin. Servants dried him. Then at last he was taken into the audience room where he was brought before the Great King on a large chair approximating his throne. There was a man on either side, one fleshy and sitting, the other lean and peering right at him, with a throne guard standing behind each. The king had layers of robes on him, a gold sceptre in his hands, and a gold-flecked, layered high crown. “You may approach,” he said.

Shipibaal stepped forward and fully prostrated himself before the Great King, not daring to speak without being invited to do so. He felt the guards who brought him withdraw several steps, no doubt in response to a signal. “You may rise,” the rich, low voice of Suppiluliuma intoned. Shipibaal rose. Even sitting, the Great King seemed to be twice a normal man’s size, likely increased by Shipibaal’s awe.

“You have a message from the servant-king of Ugarit?” the standing Lord-Stewart asked.

“Yes, my Lord, it is in response to the request from the Great King of the Hatti for troops and supplies. He reached into his bag and carefully withdrew the clay tablet.

“Proceed,” Mahhuzzi ordered. Shipibaal took a breath and read the usual preamble of humble praises and professions of loyalty, then got to the message itself:

> “O Great King of the Hatti. To my bottomless regret, I am unable to send you any support in grain or troops. Ships of the enemy have been seen at sea! The enemy ships have been coming and burning my cities and doing terrible things in my country. All my troops and chariots are in the land of Hatti, and all my ships are in Lukka country. My land has been left defenceless. I beg you for military forces to help me fight back these invaders!”

There was a silence that filled the room as the tablet was given to Penti-Sharruma to be checked. He nodded his approval that the message was correctly read and kept the clay tablet. Shipibaal felt he had done his duty to the fullest and delivered the petition clearly. Surely deliverance was at hand, for, beyond the guards, he had seen numerous Hatti troops on his way up here. The Hatti army was here! The Great King waved his hand, and the grand vizier told him to adjourn himself to the next room while the matter was discussed.

He was soon called back. The Lord Steward announced that the Great King had a reply to send back to Ugarit. He looked at the scribe, who rose to his feet with some effort and, in a high-pitched voice, read his quickly made cuneiform notes, apparently dictated by the Great King. There was only a brief preamble then it was direct:

> "As for what you have written me: 'Ships of the enemy have been seen at sea!' Well, you must remain firm. Indeed for your part, where are your troops, your chariots stationed? Are they not stationed near you? No? Behind the enemy, who press upon you? Surround your towns with ramparts. Have your troops and chariots enter there, and await the enemy with great resolution!"

Shipibaal was stunned. He looked up to see the Great King of the Hatti smile with satisfaction and already begin to lose interest. He had offered nothing at all. Penti-Sharruma the scribe asked if he had the means to make the message into a more formal tablet to be sent on to Ammurapi, vassal-king of Ugarit. He had the means, he said.

"Then the audience is at an end," the chief advisor stated and nodded toward the exit. The chagrined envoy rose.

"One more question," spoke the deep voice from the throne. "Just who is this *enemy*? From where have they come? What do they seek?"

"It is unknown, your Majesty. They are from many lands or perhaps from the sea itself. They are said to speak many languages and wear different sorts of battle dress. Their leaders are unknown. They may be followed by baggage trains and settlers. What they are after appears to be our land and the destruction of our kingdoms. They are relentless and all known lands including Ahhiyawa, Knossos, Lukka, Milawata, Smyrna, Tarsa, and Wilusa have fallen before them, plus many Aegean islands including Rodos, Alasiya, and Lazpas, yet they have not ceased their onslaught."

"Of course I know." But the Great King looked seriously disturbed at the news. "Could these sea raiders be connected to the inland invaders who so recently destroyed the shining city of the Storm-God, Hattusa?"

"I do not know," said Shipibaal.

"It seems very likely, Great King," Mahhuzzi opined thoughtfully. "Their origins are also unknown, though they may have allied with the Kaska."

"If this is so, our gods have deserted us," moaned Suppiluliuma, but then he unexpectedly brightened. "The world would be at an end – if we did not have mastery of Lawazantiya and the other inland kingdoms controlled by the south Hatti."

Mahhuzzi accompanied the bewildered envoy to the door where he gave him a new talisman with a bull impressed on it to wear about his neck as notice of his diplomatic status, this one with the royal seal of the exiled Great King of the Hatti on the other side of it. It was common copper, thinner and lighter than the bronze one given him by Ammurapi.

10. The Destruction of Nerik

It was late at night when the Sardinian approached the Lukkan, each coming from different directions. "Did you complete your rounds? All commanders in agreement?" Sarpedon asked.

"All have agreed to your tactics, O General. It is good they are simple."

"We did not get to plunder the rich prize of Hattusa," Sarpedon said to Payava as they turned to walk the perimeter of their encampment. It was a dark night with no moon and few stars, but campfires lit their way. "But, unless the Kaska cave, it appears we will have the great battle we sought here at this northern city of Nerik on the morrow."

"I had never heard of it before the scouts reported it recaptured by the Kaska with all its Hatti inhabitants killed," Payava admitted.

"It is or *was* another of many holy cities of the Hittites. They have more holy cities than market centres! Yet Nerik was once a normal trade city of the original Hatti people. Conquered by the Hittites, it was devoted to the

Hurrian war-god Sharruma, whom the Hurrian Goddess-Queen Puduhepa demoted to be the son of the Storm-God and Sun Goddess. After that Nerik became the centre of yearly processions and festivals to Teshub, the Hurrian name for the Storm-God. Sharruma was made the protector god of her son, King Tudhaliya, father of Suppiluliuma. All clear?" he smiled at his friend. "Or so I learned from a Hatti elder among the refugees who arrived with Diomedes."

"Why do the gods tolerate such manipulation by humanity?"

"It is not seen that way, O Lukkan," Sarpedon added. "Whatever is decided by a mere human is already destined by the gods, so there can be no manipulation."

"The gods and those who believe in them seem to play a fixed game of knucklebone dice," Payava said thoughtfully. "Whatever bone is thrown was meant to be."

"So it is," Sarpedon added and the men laughed, the unusual sound before a battle catching glances. They paused and surveyed the landscape. It was quiet. "The gods are real, my friend, or we would be beasts. We know them by impulse and intuition, not by obedience or ritual acts. We give them many forms, but they have no form in themselves."

The silence filled the air. "Still, I regret nothing," the Lukkan said recalling the previous conversation. "This whole adventure inland was your idea and I still think it is as wise as it is bold. After Wilusa fell, we who were there scattered, burning villages on the Aegean islands and all too often fighting each other. You had been raiding the Hellenic Isles, taking ancient Mykenai. When we met for the first time since the Misriwi disaster – to our surprise and joy – our ships were moving southward down the Aegean coast and yours were marauding north. Together we plundered Akhaian Milawata and Aeolian Smyrna. After that, we were all at sea, battle-crazed with no plan and only greed and fear to guide us. We needed a new grand undertaking, and we Anatolians had good reason to despise the Hittites. You proposed the Hatti capital itself. How could we know Hattusa would be abandoned?"

"Yes, we had no destiny apportioned out for us by the invisible gods on immortal scales of justice," Sarpedon added. "We were on our own going nowhere, destroying each other in a dying world. What had the ones who joined the Akhaians gained by destroying Taruisa, an open entry through the Hellespont when trading vessels had ceased to use it?"

"Taruisa was a city rich in treasure, but I feared attacking it would bring the mighty Hittites to come down upon us all. So, instead, I joined the defenders but chose not to go into the city itself, for its end was clearly inevitable."

"Did you see this Diomedes on the battlefield before the city?" Sarpedon asked.

"Oh yes. He is one of the few whose legend is not exaggerated. He and his Argive warriors were unstoppable in the field. Whenever a Wilusan leader appeared, Diomedes had his charioteer headed straight toward him, and his doom was sealed. Like the prow of a ship separates the waters, his Argive chariots carved a path through the multitude, followed by his foot soldiers. He is a relentless and ruthless killer. However, once the Taruisans closed their great gates, stagnation set in and he left the field for further adventures. Did you not fight alongside him at Mykenai?" the Lukkan asked in turn.

"Not exactly. Loyalty is not what drives him. We met when we Sherden landed to take Pylos, but he kept us away from it. I saw him from the crowd when he was the young king of Tiryns. It was there in the citadel where we sea pirate captains met the leaders of the peasant uprising, mostly Dorians, and he agreed to attack old Thyestes, the Great King of the Akhaians who had been starving and killing his own people. The sons of the former king Atreus joined us. Pirates, Dorians, and local kings – thus was Mykenai doomed. We could have used Diomedes and Eruthros here today, but we will certainly prevail anyway.

At least we are here, old comrade, and ready once again to prove our worth. We did this!"

"That we did, Sardinian. No regrets about not following the other ships south?"

"None. After the cities of Hellas and the fall of Taruisa, there were many wayward freebooters about. We needed to be united in a great task once again, something that had not been considered before. Most wanted to go south to the rich prizes of the Levant, and so they did and are now there. But, after hearing your stories of the recent widespread frontier wars of Suppiluliuma and the devastation of the land, I looked east and realized how spread out the Hatti forces had become and how they must be suffering from the drought, earthquakes, and loss of trade – and how the people must be doubting the power of their Great King to win the favour of the gods. I saw the chance to take one of the greatest prizes in the world. But who would follow me?"

"Legendary Hattusa itself, inland amidst mountains and rivers. It seemed an impossible dream, but it was your far-seeing plan that made this journey possible," Payava smiled.

"Ah, but it was your knowledge of the Anatolians and your ability to convince them that made it happen – your harangue that brought other peoples of the sea from far away to join us. You became our unofficial leader by being the best at it. And here we are, on the verge. It may not be Hattusa, but I'd wager Nerik is a prize worth taking."

"We will soon know. I am ready for the storm, and we have two advantages."

"Indeed we do, maybe three," said Sarpedon, looking toward the city beyond the camp of the Kaska, also quiet but lit with many fires. "We have greater numbers and are more desperate than they, for they are near to home. That's two. But this time we also have a plan of battle and our men know it. If it works out few Kaska will escape alive."

"We attack at dawn. After our victory tomorrow or a few days after that, we can all go on to make new homes," the Lukkan concluded, looking hopefully away from the city toward the dark horizon.

At first light, Kaska horsemen rode right toward the already stirring encampment of the allied warriors, bellowing out a screeching cacophony of war cries and loosing arrows as soon as they got close enough. Some arrows were launched back and it was satisfying for the invaders to see a Kaska fall wounded from his mount and hear a horse cry out in agony. The warrior was picked up, the wounded horse still ridden, and they returned to their camp cheering as though they had just won a great victory.

The warrior camp drummers began a low beat. The instruments were small and primitive, but the steady sound carried like a heartbeat across the battlefield. The men ate whatever they could quickly, cold scraps of this and that, and got themselves fully armed, helping each other, sometimes joking but mostly grim. The organization that was ordered by Sarpedon was passed down through the ranks from the chieftains of each division to the commanders of each troop to the captains of each platoon to the individual squad leaders, and so to each man. For the first time, until the city was stormed, all were to obey orders and follow a plan.

A veteran Arzawan warrior even older than Uhhaziti appeared on horseback, followed by his large sector of Arzawans and allies. He was aged and scarred but looked formidable enough in his Akhaian-styled bull's hide helmet with a silver brow piece and bronze cheek-pieces hiding most of his face. This was topped by a startling crimson horsehair plume that shot straight up. He announced that Uhhaziti was his nephew and that he was leading this sector for now. He pulled away from the encampment to take the lead position on the field, riding confidently. Sarpedon noted he had wrapped a long leather strap around the belly of the beast he was on and then secured it over his thighs. Sarpedon reflected that the invention could help or hinder stability, for what if his horse went down? Many of the Arzawan were on horseback, pointless for actual combat, he thought, but good for transportation. Sarpedon signalled with an upright arm, several clarions blew, and Uhhaziti's uncle and his two thousand warriors began to advance. He had volunteered to lead, and the Sardinian was happy to agree. He knew the Kaska were fearsome fighters and the Arzawans were going right at them in lesser numbers, so he had considered that a sacrifice may be necessary.

Sarpedon had discussed it with no one, but he knew they were more like seven than eight thousand. Leukos and his Peleset had deserted but so had many others. Others yet, including homeless Wilusans and other former allies of the Hatti had joined, but they were not as many as had been lost. This was not going to be an easy battle, which is why he had taken the unusual course of directing these untrained soldiers, many more experienced as pirates, to act as coordinated units. The Arzawans were to take the brunt even though Sarpedon knew they may well be overwhelmed, but before that they would keep the Kaska occupied while two other divisions who had been held back did flanking manoeuvres around the main battle.

It happened quickly. The Kaska unleashed another volley of arrows, so most of the Arzawans dismounted shields up, sending their horses back toward the main body guided by only a few grooms. Sensing the danger, the horses galloped straight back. The Arzawan leader, bound to his horse, stayed mounted and so did his bodyguard. At his signal, repeated down the line, the warriors attacked. With a great cry, the Kaska also attacked, leaving half their numbers to guard the gates thus making the numbers on each side of the field almost equal.

Sarpedon thought to himself that only warriors know how a full battle attack turns the panicky furies of fear into the bellowing war gods of the killing frenzy. All-out attack erases all doubt. The only hope of survival is to kill those who would kill you. One who has never been in such a melee could not imagine what it is like – the gory horror and the killing fury, the smells and the tastes. The events in detail are often mercifully forgotten, yet specific moments remain frozen in time and will continue to appear as unbidden memory images throughout the rest of one's life.

The battlefield resounded to the sky with war cries as the two enraged battalions went straight at each other in a terrified, bloodthirsty fury. When the forces struck, it was as though the air froze for a moment. The fronts held vibrating in groaning tension against each other. The battle cries resumed, but now the air was also rent with the clash of bronze weapons, the screams of men and beasts, and the howls of death.

Already underway moving into place around the left toward the Marassantiya River were Sarpedon's own fighters – Shardana, Sikeloi, Tyrsenoi, and Maionians, but also included were the handful of tall ebony warriors from the distant Kingdom of Kush. Drought or not, the Marassantiya at this point could no longer be forded, so once committed there was no way out but retreat or into the city. On the right moving up into the hills were the Lukkans and allies of Payava, the largest group. Held in reserve were the Akhaians, Danaans, and others now commanded by a large, ambitious but dim-eyed captain named Klymenos, chosen by Eruthros.

Sarpedon moved left toward his battalion uncomfortably riding a well-trained mule who seemed to know what to do. As he crossed behind the battlefront, he noted that the tumult was not moving away from him, as it would be if the Kaska were retreating. If the Kaska overwhelmed the Arzawa so quickly, they could take control of the field, so he sent a courier to tell Payava to begin his side of the planned pincer movement attack from the hills on the right. With the noise of the battlefield seeming to come closer, he galumphed to his mixed force on the left and unromantically led them forward toward the river before dismounting and turning in to attack both the Kaskan troop at the gate and the side of the Kaskan warriors already engaged. Simultaneously, the Lukkans bore down from the left on the main Kaskan force already pushing back the Arzawans and sent spearmen to attack the other side of those Kaska guarding the gate.

The Arzawans and others felt like they had run into a wall, a wall that then tumbled down upon them. They were tough, experienced fighters, every man, but the Kaska fought like an explosion. They had no order whatsoever, just the sense to go forward and consume the enemy, every man for himself. The Arzawans at least stood in defensive formations so small squads could protect each other. It worked but it slowed them down, too. The Kaska fell faster but relentlessly gained ground. The Kaska continued to do so in this way as the fight went on for desperate hours.

Uhhaziti's uncle found he could scatter Kaska who were not accustomed to fighting horsemen. He was glad for other riders on his flanks so he could ride straight forward into the enemy without being caught from the side. With an axe in one hand and the other holding onto the halter he could rain down havoc on most approaching warriors. Still, the stalwart Kaska refused to retreat. Any that stepped back were shouted at and mocked by their fellows, so the Pontic warriors pushed ahead even with an increasing body count. The noise and chaos made it hard for the old warrior to concentrate, so he tried to pick his way with caution.

Suddenly the horse on his right screamed and fell away. He saw his fellow warrior roll and rise to face the enemy, only to be pierced in the shoulder by a javelin. He attempted to raise his sword arm, but, like wolves, the Kaska closed in and in seconds had opened his groin and split his face and skull. He fell into darkness forever.

The veteran Arzawan campaigner turned his mount and rode right at the three killers, cleaving one's neck with his axe and riding over another while bringing the axe down again on the skull of the last, who rent the air with his death cry. He exulted in the secure embrace of his steed's back, finding his leather harness meant he could lean away and use his weapons yet stay solidly in place. Other Kaska came charging forward so the old soldier thought it best to exit, but before he could do so, his strong pony was speared in the side and reared up in agony. He tried to leap free, but found he could not dismount because his thighs were strapped into place. When it fell, he fell too, with one leg beneath it. His head crashed on the ground, dizzying him as his prized helm with the crimson plume rolled away. The Kaska warriors hesitated not but moved in for the kill. But at that moment, upcoming Arzawan foot soldiers ran with spears outthrust to intervene. The fighting was ferocious, some wounded falling on the dying horse that flailed its legs and screamed hopelessly. Uhhaziti's uncle found his dagger and managed to cut through the leather strap with desperate efficiency while his frothing horse was pushed from his leg. Before he was extricated, he leaned forward and managed to efficiently sever its throat to spare it from further terror and pain. He was pulled to his feet and managed to raggedly stand on his badly bruised leg. Without his helm, he looked pathetically old. With bloodied hands, he replaced his dagger and found his axe, but still more raging Kaska kept coming.

The Arzawan force was being steadily crushed and pushed backwards with increasing speed. The Kaska fought like demons for either their renewed capital or just for themselves. Unlike most warriors on a battlefield, when one of their own fell from an injury or was killed, they hardly paused in their relentless attack. They stepped over the fallen fighters and continued forward. They seemed to care nothing for defence, losing warriors faster than the Arzawans who were about to break into full rout from the relentless pressure of the swarming Kaska. The Arzawan horsemen were either dead or gone from the field, and the infantry felt itself driven backwards with increasing speed, as though they were about to tumble over a cliff.

It was then that above the din, the resounding clash of bronze on bronze could be heard from the Kaska positions on the left and the right. The divisions of Payava and Sarpedon had initiated full attack. The Kaska seemed blind to the distraction at first, until their fellows were forced against the middle as they were crushed from the sides. The Kaskan troops left at the gate could do nothing, for they too were now fully engaged on both sides by other elements of the flanking manoeuvre. To complete the tactic envisioned by Sarpedon, the Danaans held in reserve now roared forward to support the retreating Arzawan and to move up the sides to further surround the attacking Kaska. What seemed to be a bloody chaos was in reality the well-crafted completion of a careful plan. The Kaska were enclosed on three sides by double their numbers. Given the momentum, the course of events soon shifted in the opposite direction and even the desperate bravery of the Kaska began to look for a way out.

Sarpedon led his division at a run down upon the Kaskan troop left to guard the main gates. Immediately, his concern about his battle plan evaporated and he lost himself to the *ekstasos* of the warrior attack. He was the first to reach the Kaska and he was not at all concerned that he stood out so clearly from the pack. Not only was he taller than most of the horde, but his bronze-plated, bull-horned helm was topped with the silver sun disk of Ra, which made him taller yet. His torso was wrapped in a cuirass of flexible horizontal bands of leather with bronze disks that were supported by a vertical shoulder harness of the leather-backed disks, leaving his muscular arms bare. Tied strips of the same bronzed leather flapped over his groin and thighs as his pace picked up, his light copper greaves not slowing him down. His left forearm went through the double brace of the round bronze-plated buckler that was held before him as he crashed into the enemy. But it was the long, tapered slashing-stabbing bronze sword in his right hand that relentlessly opened a path before him. He uttered no war cry, but his efficient killing fury soon cleared a path for those behind him, leaving the Kaska dead and dying where they fell.

The Kaska defenders at first put up a stubborn resistance and the advance of the Sherden and other warriors was slowed down. But soon they heard a furious tumult from behind them as Payava led the Lukkan and allied troops down upon them from the right. As ferocious as the Kaskan warriors were in the attack, once they panicked they became just as wild in their desperation to escape. They were surrounded and beaten on all fronts, but many broke through and escaped into the surrounding trees and hills, some even hopelessly venturing into the unforgiving turbulence of the deep Marassantiya River. The defenders of the main gate, however, were being slaughtered and had nowhere to go, so they threw open the huge portals of the main gate and poured into the city themselves, continuing to run once inside.

Now the rout began in earnest, as did the rapine and pillage. After such a parlous battle, the maddened invaders were especially greedy for the desecration of temples and their personnel, and in the holy city Nerik there was quite a number of them. The warriors from the sea and the coasts of Anatolia did not pause for self-congratulation or to make plans, they simply gave in to the primal lust for slaughter and theft, spreading out in all directions.

The Sardinian was concerned that the Kaska inside might reassemble and attempt a counterattack, but nothing could be done at this point. He was venturing forward, but he heard his name called over the clamour. From a distance away, he saw the Lukkan approaching, waving his curved bronze sword, easily identifiable by the tall rainbow-coloured reeds thrusting up and spreading out from his bronze headband. As he got closer, Sarpedon noted that his beautiful purple cape jauntily slung over his shoulder was now notably bloodstained. His shield had been lost but he looked unhurt.

“My brother!” Sarpedon called, as Payava strode up.

“We are victorious!” he replied coming closer, inserting his stained sword into his scabbard and flinging it over his back.

“Finally, a true city taken, and, unless I miss my guess, temples full of treasure. We must go secure our share, but I remain concerned about the remaining Kaska.”

“Last I saw, they were running in terror at twice the rate they attacked,” Payava laughed, but paused, “They proved to be redoubtable warriors, did they not?”

“Indeed, it was a good fight, but we are entire, so all is well,” Sarpedon sighed, looking across at the chaotic arrival of the cheering horde. He saw an old man hobbling on his spear, looking out of place, surrounded by foot soldiers holding back to attend to him. “Yo, Uhhaziti’s uncle!” he shouted, causing Payava to look over, too. The Arzawan leaning on his spear looked even older now that his wild white hair and receding pate were exposed because his dashing Akhaian helmet had been lost.

The old warrior was guided over to the leaders and smiled broadly. “We kicked their asses today, did we not? Tough bunch of barbaroi as they are! Had a bit of trouble out there, lost my horse and helm, yet I’m fine. But now it’s time for our reward!” He laughed wobbling on his spear. He refused assistance and hobbled off into the city with his followers.

“Pity about that fine helm,” Sarpedon spoke, a seaman ignoring the horse’s fate.

“How old is that guy?” Payava asked. “He’s surely seen well over sixty summers! We are hard to kill, aren’t we?”

“Yes, we’re still here, and he’s still got a lot of fight in him yet. Wonder what rewards he’s after!”

“No doubt he’s looking for a passel of virgins to take home with him,” They laughed.

“Payava, your grandfather served with the Hatti in this territory. You know these Kaska better than I. Have we defeated them? Will they be back?”

“The tribe we fought is Kaskaili’s own – the second Kaskaili, the head-cutter. They’re probably escaping the city right now and joining the others in the hills. They have been thrashed and are unlikely to bother us again but will regroup in the mountains with other tribes. Are they defeated? Not by a javelin’s throw. There are many more tribes. Once we depart and with Hattusa gone, it’s my guess the repugnant Kaska will overrun the territory and grow into a force to be reckoned with.”

The Sardinian found the idea unpleasant but unimportant. “We must get to work before all the maidens and the best of the booty have been taken,” Sarpedon said looking up at the looting already well underway. “I suspect there is greater wealth in the temples here than in the temples of the Sun-Goddess of Arinna."

"Let us walk, my friend," Payava leaned toward his comrade, in no mad rush to join the slaughter but began to pace towards it. "What you say is true. My grandfather told me tales. There should be some unimaginable treasures hidden in storehouses in the temples of the Storm-God and his stormy son Sharruma. Did you know that each year the Hatti priests headed by the chief priest, the Great King himself, performed the nearly monthlong spring Purulli festival, which went in procession from Hattusa to Nerik, stopping at each city along the way to perform the sacred ritual, but culminating here? At every stop, the ritual of the original creation of order out of the primordial evil of chaos was reenacted, and every year it was repeated so the humble Hatti could help the gods maintain balance in the cosmos. No doubt in the ritual combat sequence the Great King *is* the Storm-God. The Storm-God fights Illuyanka the monstrous dragon of darkness to make the light of order possible. The fight is long and terrible and the Storm-God is always nearly shamed and beaten, but at the last moment rises and kills the monster – so the gods stay in their heaven and the kings continue to rule on earth. At the end of each year, the dragon is born of chaos again and attempts to overthrow ordered harmony and bring destruction, death, and darkness to all once again – so, once again, the ritual of the cosmic battle must be repeated. Once victorious, the Storm-God declares, as triumphal horns are blown and sacred hymns are sung, if I can recall correctly, 'Let the land prosper and thrive, and let the land be protected'." He laughed grimly, looking at the riotous destruction all around. "So does this mean Illuyanka has at last won the final battle and utterly destroyed all order, all kings, and all hierarchy? Does it mean *we are the dragon of chaos*?"

"I'll tell you what it doesn't mean, my friend: we're not here to renew the power of the Great King or preserve his wealth." Sarpedon looked inward as he continued, "Wherever there are gods, kings, and order, there will be the dragon of destruction, awaiting its reawakening. Life/death, chaos/cosmos, sterility/fertility – are the two movements of a single dance. The dragon is eternal like gods. It suffocates in civilization and must break free to live. We are but its emissaries."

"Who knows, brother? I only know that there are temple storehouses fat with the items necessary for such a grand annual ceremony – jewels, silver, gold, iron from the skies, imported fabrics, and the very finest armour and weaponry especially crafted for this sacred ritual. They have been awaiting us for their liberation!"

They drew their swords simultaneously. "Then, by all means, let us proceed!" shouted the Sardinian as they broke into a run. They chose to join many others already pillaging the main temple, a huge structure with an archway built within impenetrable granite as its frame. As they merged with the greedy horde, they were recognized and often given the privilege of place, but not always, so they were reduced to pushing their way through the others like hogs at a trough.

Most temple keepers, from servants to priestesses, had run and hid or were begging for their lives. There were so many eye-catching valuables about – jewelled statuary with realistic relief sculptures carved into the limestone wall and portable works of fine art – that the raiders mostly ignored those pleading with them and went for the gold, iron, and precious stones. If they couldn't carry what they found, they smashed it. Still, a few women were carried off screaming, and one mature, plump priestess who had ceased all resistance suffered her garments to be torn from her. She was roughly pushed onto her back on the edge of an opulent marble fountain where she was held and ravished by several marauders at once with more waiting their turn. Payava turned away. Random murder was rare at this point, he noted, likely because most potential victims fled or simply refused to fight back, and there were better things to do, perhaps actual riches to be had.

At that moment, there was a cheer from the floors below. Payava looked at Sarpedon with the same idea. The postulated storage rooms of the Purulli festival and other sacred rituals had been found and broken into. Neither of the leaders felt the need to rush down and grab what they could, for they knew they could only carry so much, and they were usually given gifts anyway. But they were curious so they descended the broad staircase to the main floor and followed the considerable noise to a narrow stairway hidden behind some pillars in a corner and continued down into a bottom-level floor. Therein chaos reigned. Two of three great doors had been broken down and the third was about to follow. A treasure trove beyond previous imaginings had been discovered by these vagabond warrior pirates. Raiding shoreline towns had fed them and brought them many useful items and quick pleasures, but never had they seen so many glistening items of precious metals and unknown gems. That they were lodged in magnificently sculpted statues or standards for display in procession meant nothing to them. They found the jewellery of royalty – bracelets, rings, necklaces and even jewelled golden headbands, tiaras, and heavy conical crowns. They were attracted by exotic items and images made of material unknown to most like sea silk, Egyptian alabaster, onyx, ivory, pearls, or polished African ebony, but finally only the shiny things caught their attention. Conveniently, there were even hardwood, moulded leather and bronze chests to carry the smaller items back into the light.

What the men loved best was armour and weapons, and what they found here dazzled their minds. Since this armoury was used in sacred rituals that called forth the very gods to participate as they became one with the human actors, it was the most exquisitely wrought in all the land, created by the finest craftspersons that ever lived in the land of the Hatti and probably well beyond it. It was made of the purest bronze with more added gold, silver, and shining meteoric iron. Sparkling jewels of all sorts, in all shapes and colours, were added in profusion so some of the spears and swords were too heavy to be used as more than display. The pillagers gleefully grabbed them up in any case and carried them proudly forth.

“Much more than was taken in Arinna,” Sarpedon shouted to Payava from across the room. They had each chosen unique items to bring back with them – a jewelled bronze and gold slashing sword for the Lukkan and a bronze and silver-plated round shield of some unknown extravagantly thick and tough dark grey animal hide for the Sardinian. Thrusting forward from its centre was a conical bronze point. It wasn’t too heavy for brief use on the ritual stage, but most warriors would have found it unwieldy.

But matrilineal Payava also had picked out a pair of unique miniature goddesses. Both had startling eyes. The first was only a child’s foot tall. She was wearing only her smoothly curved cream-coloured skin, which was made of alabaster and topped with dark terracotta hair tied in a bun. She stood with her left hand forward either to offer or receive something. Shining gold were the heavy baubles for earrings, so large they reached her shoulders, and also gold was her choker necklace. An onyx crescent moon sat on her head like horns, but most notable were her eyes of flickering red rubies with another in her naval. The second was a lean goddess of solid gold that was almost the same height, mainly due to her tall layered cylindrical hat over what appeared to be a bald head. Wearing only a long patterned skirt, she held two long serpents, one wrapped around her upper arms and across her torso just below her tiny bare breasts, and the other rose from near her left ankle and twisted entirely around her waist with its head held in her left hand. Her eyes were wide, staring skyward, as though in trance. But there was no time for a more detailed examination.

They made their way up and outside through the main doors. Payava was surprised that nothing seemed to be torched, until he saw the flames in the distance near the rear gate of the city where it was assumed the remaining Kaska were still escaping. There was a noisy fracas underway, so clearly not all the Kaska had chosen to depart peacefully. The two chieftains gathered others to join them and signalled for more to follow. Payava brought out his bejewelled new scimitar and Sarpedon positioned his impenetrable shield, and they ran to attend to the scene, slowing as they approached. The Kaska had begun fires and were ambushing any of the warrior confederacy who approached with arrows from the rooftops or by encircling them from all sides. Bodies lay about and few were Kaska.

As they broke into a clearing where the enemy had gathered, the first thing that struck Payava was that the shouting man who appeared to be the leader of this remaining troop was wearing an Akhaian helmet with bronze cheek pieces and a long plume of crimson horsehair shooting straight up like a spray from its topmost point. He stood on the balcony with a spear in one hand and a hatchet in the other, directing the ambush of the Kaska against the victors.

"Do you see that helm?" asked Payava.

"By the gods, I do believe it was stolen from Uhhaziti's uncle and given to that guy up there. Why, he's nothing more than a thief!" Sarpedon declared wryly.

"We're taking it back!" cried Payava, and before Sarpedon could assess the situation and make a plan, the Lukkan raised his unbloodied curved sword and ran into the building and up the stairs, unheeding of events unfolding around him.

A number unquestioningly followed him, but the Sardinian noted the Kaskan archers on the rooftops and spearmen poised in doorways, hidden paths, and around buildings. He realized there were many rooms and upper floors in this building. It hit him that the man on the balcony may be the leader but he had also set himself up as bait.

"Payava, you fool, wait for the rest of the party!" he shouted hopelessly. Sarpedon quickly followed but upon crossing the threshold found himself facing three enemy. Payava had already ascended the stairs with few behind him before the Kaska guards sealed the entryway. Holding his mighty targe before him on his left forearm, Sarpedon charged ahead like a maddened bull, the bronze point of his shield boss piercing the heart through the leather breastplate of the first Kaska warrior to confront him. Now a javelin was flung at his head and a bronze khopesh came slashing towards his neck, but both were caught on the dense raised shield, the sword breaking and the javelin not penetrating but falling away. Sarpedon now viciously attacked the two who had placed themselves before the steps and sent them both backward. As one stumbled back, Sarpedon unerringly sank the tapered point of his bronze blade into his guts just below his cuirass. As Sarpedon stepped over the fallen, he felt a sharp pain in his calf and realized the other Kaska had slashed him with something. He did not pause to kill him but continued straight up the steps.

He arrived in time to see the warriors who went with Payava engaged with Kaska who had appeared from their hiding places. Payava had his jewelled sword raised and was going straight at the chieftain who had turned to confront him. As Sarpedon watched, the Lukkan was punctured in the back by arrows from surrounding bowmen. This did not bring him down, but he whirled around to face his attackers. That proved a deadly mistake. It was the moment the Kaska leader dropped his hatchet and used both hands to powerfully thrust his spear through the back of Payava's neck, just beneath his multicoloured reed headdress. It tore through and the spearhead appeared covered with blood and dragging sinew well out the front of his throat.

Sarpedon gave a blood-curdling scream of rage, and his companions soon grasped what had happened. Payava had been well-loved and held in high esteem, so the allied warriors lost all control and attacked like demons, yelling out their rage. Sarpedon signalled others to stay back from his fight as his red-veiled eyes saw only the leader splitting his beard with a laughing grin. Suddenly he recognized the face: it was Kaskaili himself. He forgot himself entirely, a rare thing, and before Kaskaili could do more than grasp his hand axe, Sarpedon ran his bloody pointed sword straight into his laughing mouth, its widening blade knocking out teeth as it went through the back of his head, bits of brain dripping. Kaskaili's laughter abruptly ceased as he found himself biting down on the broad bronze blade that had just killed him. His eyes widened but he stood shock-still as Sarpedon pulled back the gore-covered blade. Kaskaili fell with a clatter and a gurgle from his severed throat. Seeing their leader fall and fearing the wrath of the invaders, the still surviving Kaska broke into panicked terror and ran for their lives.

Sarpedon tore the crimson-crested helmet from the dead enemy and, holding it under his arm, he went to his dead comrade, avoiding slipping in the blood. He lifted up the staring head of Payava the Lukkan, careful not to let the sundered neck come apart even more. "I shall see Uhhaziti's uncle gets back his special helmet, dear friend, and I shall take your splendid helm from this fateful city as well. Your jewelled sword will go to another Lukkan leader. You will not be forgotten and your family will be protected. May the dark gods welcome a great soul."

Sarpedon carefully placed his head back down and, picking up Payava's helmet and fallen sword, quickly rose, lest his sorrow make itself visible to all. "We need to get this body back amongst us near the entry gate for last rites, once this business is done. I need three volunteers to each protect one of these war helms and the Lukkan's sword until they can get them back to me at our meeting place." Warriors stepped forward without hesitation and took care of the required business without direction. Trust was unspoken but certain.

As he made his way down the stairs, Sarpedon distantly noted that his left leg was shaking from the loss of blood, but he walked on ignoring it. Word of Payava's death spread quickly. Up to this point, there had been plunder and some sexual violation, but killing and destruction for its own sake had been felt unnecessary. With the death of the Lukkan, the sea people attackers fell into a murderous madness. Remaining Kaska tried to escape the city but those caught inside were gruesomely slaughtered. The holy city of Nerik was set aflame and the warriors did not stop until it was razed to the ground.

That evening the flames continued as the thousands of raiders gathered outside the main gate in which they had first entered. But this time it was a mammoth funeral pyre. The noble chieftain, Payava the Lukkan, had been placed on top, but surrounding him were the corpses of other fallen members of the vagabond warrior troop. Few living Kaska could be found to sacrifice, so thorough had been the slaughter, that the warriors insisted on finding innocent Nerik citizens to take their place. Sarpedon did not intervene. They had their throats slit at the base of the pyre as the flames were lit. The pyre flames went skyward and the thick, dark smoke, smelling of burnt meat, continued to fill the air until the sun rose, and the skies slowly cleared.

In spite of the wealth gained, there was no celebration. The men were more respectfully quiet than usual, but their hearts were gladdened as they loaded up their trophies to take back with them. Almost everyone had *something* to load into the cargo, and some few had treasures beyond what they had ever imagined, yet the usual quarrels over who owned what were muted and led to nothing. One of the most pleased among them was Uhhaziti the elder though he had not bothered with booty at all. His now swollen leg meant walking was too difficult, but he shone with joy when Sarpedon returned to him his gallant crimson horse-plume helmet. "Your courageous heart served us well, old comrade," the Sardinian declared, clapping him on the shoulder.

While the packing was being completed in the morning, there was discussion among the men to do with their next destination. Many had heard that the town of Zalpa had a harbour on the Pontos and that it lay nearby straight north. The old salts expressed their desire to go there and commandeer ships that could take them back through the Propontis and Hellespont to their comrades. Few agreed for the obvious reason that no one knew anything about this port, the Pontos Axeinos was forbidding, and, most of all, this was still Kaskan territory.

This argument seemed to be settled by general consensus even before the four representatives – Sarpedon,

Uhhaziti's uncle, Klymenos the heavy-browed Danaan, and a veteran stalwart Lukkan named Kuprlli who had been chosen to replace Payava – met to decide. It was unstated but understood that the Sardinian was now in command. As if to demonstrate his authority, he bequeathed Payava's never bloodied bejewelled slashing sword to Kuprlli, who was overwhelmed and of course indebted. Sarpedon suggested that anyone who wanted to go in a small contingent north into Kaska territory was welcome to do so. As expected, no one said a word. More important, he suggested, is where they go once they reach the others and the camp train back at Karassuwa.

Sarpedon noted that many would want to go immediately back to the base camp at the bend of Sangarios River for their families and other goods, and thence west, perhaps back to the remains of Smyrna on the Aegean coast where a good harbour still existed on the Hermis River. But Sarpedon shocked his listeners by noting they were likely as near to the southern Anatolian coast of the Great Green as they were to the cities on the west coast of the Aegean where they had already been. Tarsos and Ura on the south coast were by now likely in the hands of their comrade freebooters of the sea or soon to become so. "The legendary prizes of Alasiya and Ugarit are nearby and ripe for the taking. Beyond that, the rich coastal lands of Amurru and Canaan await our conquest or settlement. The Peleset may already have made a homeland there. Perhaps someday we may even make the lower lands of the Nile our own! That is where the greatest opportunity for the bold lies, and that is where I am going with those who choose to follow me. Our noble army will divide and go in separate directions at Karassuwa."

By late the next day, ox-carts, wagons, pack donkeys, and packhorses were filled with the illicit but hard-earned plunder of Nerik, and the nomadic horde headed back into the Pontic mountains to meet with their fellows at Karassuwa. As they ascended the pass, a lion was seen in the distance watching them, which the men considered a good omen. Otherwise, the trip was uneventful, the troop became less sombre as their leader was forgotten and their plunder remembered.

The reunification of forces was also a joyful relief, and the Karassuwans arranged the semblance of a feast, with local wine included though not much was left. Rough old Uhhaziti the Arzawan who had remained behind reported there had been no trouble, though it seemed a number of men had taken Karassuwan wives and were either bringing them along or they were themselves settling in the town. He was pleased at the success of the conquest though regretting he did not participate; he was indifferent to the loss of Payava and happy to see his even rougher and older uncle but perhaps a bit jealous of the glory his uncle had accumulated.

At the assembly the next day, the choice of destinations was outlined for the seven thousand warriors, heralds sending the message announced by Uhhaziti the younger (a description he was quick to embrace) to all corners. Sarpedon avoided the task for he was not given to shouting and it was agreed he might influence too many to go with him. As it turned out, most felt connected to someone in the baggage train, either family or companion, and they were more secure returning to the sea the way they had come with what they had gained rather than venturing further into remote lands and taking a chance on losing it. After much discussion amongst themselves, only about two thousand warriors felt unattached enough and ready to face more danger and possible glory in the lands of southern Anatolia, following the tracks of the Great King of the Hatti and the hero, Diomedes, as well as the admired chieftain, Eruthros. Most of those were Danaans and Akhaians temporarily led by Klymenos who ignored the chance of returning to the Aegean near their demolished homeland, but a general mix of others also declared themselves ready for the unknown. Kuprlli the Lukkan brought a contingent of his countrymen, feeling indebted for the fine jewelled sword, but both Uhhaziti the younger and the elder determined to return west though Arzawa no longer existed and was quickly becoming a land of migrants.

The Sardinian felt in his heart he had weighed matters well and made the right choice, but he was surprised at some of the others who wished to go with him. When he went to fetch Henti from among the women, hiding her youthful beauty wrapped in layers of rough garments, she insisted she could not return to her home in Milawata, for it had been destroyed by sea raiders. If anyone remained who knew of her, she was sure that, as a former Hatti concubine, she would be in danger. She claimed to sense her destiny lay ahead, deeper into the southern Hatti lands and beyond into the mysterious Kizzuwatna land. She was going with Sarpedon – nothing to discuss. He had given his word to protect her, so he had no choice but to accept her along and keep her close to hand. Sarpedon knew she was right; besides, another translator could always be of use.

Book II: The Apotheosis of Suppiluliuma II

Lawazantiya and the Sack of Ugarit

The guards now recognized the big Hurrian but still sneered at him when he again came to the doors of the imprisoned Great Queen. Zunan was met with a nod this time but was still searched for weapons or anything else he might attempt to smuggle in. Lieia-Hepa was delighted to see him. Not only was he among her rare contacts (beyond food servers and cleaners), but he was the key to her only hope of rescue. She broke palace protocol and gave him a hug, which caused the old soldier to stand frozen with embarrassment, not daring to hug back. She pulled him over to sit on low couches, gesturing to whisper. As always, her dark beauty awed him, but he refused to see it as anything other than the radiance reflected from the glory of the Sun Goddess.

"Zunan, it has been so long. I am so isolated in here and you are my only source of news. Quick, now, tell me: did you get to speak with the High Priestess and Priest of the Great Goddess?" She did not take time for polite greetings or to order refreshments.

"Oh yes, your Majesty, we conferred. The way is narrow and dangerous but, if the gods permit, we may be able to end your confinement and with the help of Ishtar allow you to achieve more glory and power than you have ever yet known."

These words warmed her heart and brought light into her mind. "What has happened? You must tell me, but be brief, for we have not much time allotted for private speech."

"Nothing has happened yet, Great Queen, but chariots are rolling, so to speak. The High Priestess herself told me the grand vizier had been to visit her twice, and she believed he was quite taken with her. He told her much."

"Cold-hearted Mahhuzzi? Interesting. What does this High Priestess look like?"

“She is an imperious near-goddess herself, strikingly beautiful.” He paused to backtrack and avoid jealousy, “but older, of course, with long silver hair. She is tall and has great nobility of bearing; power radiates from her presence. She looks into one’s heart quite readily, so I suspect she could not be easily fooled.”

“So... Mahhuzzi could become our ally?”

“This I do not know, my Queen. Suppiluliuma insisted the High Priestess and Priest come alone with no guards to what serves as his audience chamber. They did so and this is what they told me. Keeping the Meshedi out of earshot so only he and Mahhuzzi were party to the exchange, the King of the Hatti ordered the two sacred leaders of Lawazantiya to recognize him as their overlord and make it known to all that he was now Great King of the city, first in all things but second only to the Storm-God who had decreed that this must be so.”

“Sacrilege. He has no more respect for the Great Goddess than for his Great Queen!”

“In any case the High Priestess flatly refused and the High Priest agreed. She warned him that this was a city long sacred to Ishtar who would be enraged by such an affront. Moreover, her devoted people would not accept such an order. If he harmed them personally, the populace would rise in a rebellion that his one thousand soldiers could do nothing to stop, so either way Suppiluliuma was inviting disaster upon himself. They also confided in him that many of his own soldiers were confused by the disappearance of their earthly Sun-goddess and may not be willing to go to war for him until, in the person of the Great Queen, she is returned to her place in the hierarchy.”

“The last part is the good news I was hoping to hear. How did the king respond?”

“The Great King was astonished at this unexpected defiance; he was no more accustomed to such things than he was to being exiled from his palace. They said he was torn between rage and terror, but when Mahhuzzi agreed with this analysis, he broke down in tears, which none has ever seen before. He pleaded for guidance first to his gods then from the other three. Mahhuzzi spoke not, but the High Priestess informed him in her most motherly tones that he needed to face the truth that his empire was crumbling and that he himself seemed fated to soon meet his end. It was not his fault but long destined by the immortal gods. He had lost his blessing and special provenance from Teshub, God of Storms."

"The old priestess was inspired," Lieia said admiringly.

"She told him he was lost and adrift like the disappearing Hatti god, Telipinu, and that is why the land was rent with earthquakes, the sky refused rain, crops would not grow, and the herd animals failed to reproduce. But since there was no way for him to regain earthly power, he must accept subservience to a new ruler like his own vassal-kings Halata in Tarhuntassa or Talmi-Teshub of Karkemish."

Lieia laughed under her breath. "I'm guessing he did not take this well?"

"They told me he did not, alternately raving in impotent rage or sobbing in hopeless tears. It was then that Mahhuzzi spoke, saying there may be another way, a forgotten path but one well-recorded in the ancient texts of many lands. He would have to sacrifice himself as Great King and become a god. Both the High Priestess and Priest feigned shock, asking the grand vizier how dare he reveal the forbidden alternative to someone not chosen of Ishtar. Needless to say, Suppiluliuma stopped burbling immediately and paid full attention, for, as you know, my Great Queen, deification before death has always been the longing of his heart."

"Oh yes, even surrounded by his decaying kingdom, he began to believe in his own godhead, so he declared it was already assured. His godlike Babylonian beard with no moustache and further military successes would reveal the truth of his predestination to the world. Military successes have ended, but at least he still has the beard."

"And here was his trusted advisor and cousin, not to mention two revered high priests of the most ancient goddess, telling him just what he most wished to hear. I doubt Kil-Teshub would have stood for such heresy so it is good he was absent. Naturally, he wanted to begin immediately. He demanded to know how to proceed on the sacred journey that would lead to him becoming a god."

The two guards inside the door were eyeing them suspiciously, inching closer. They were enjoying their conversation way too much. "Hurry to the end," said Lieia.

"The High Priestess suggested that when Telipinu disappeared and the earth became infertile and decayed, he was really descending into the Underworld. So when he returned he was being born again, and so the fertility of Earth was renewed. She reminded him of the most ancient sacred tales from the land of the Nile in which Ra himself had to die and take on the form of Osiris during his night-sea journey aboard his little boat before, helped by the people's prayers at dawn, he could be reborn each sunrise as Ra again. And not only gods undertook this dark journey of renewal, for he surely knew of the myth first told among the ancient Akkadians of the mortal Tammuz who was captured and taken to the land of the dead until rescued by his goddess-lover Ishtar in the form of Inanna."

"Did he understand at that point?"

"Yes," replied the Hurrian. "It took a moment, but he has presided over enough rituals, like the annual rite of life renewal at the Purulli festival, to understand. 'You mean I must die first,' he stated. He understood that he must undergo ritual death and descend to the Underworld to rise again as a god, as has been demonstrated in so many of our ancient tales. Apparently, he put on a bold front, jutting out his curly-haired chin and saying the '*so be it*' words."

Lieia had to forcefully restrain herself from laughing with delight. "So it is all arranged. He wishes to submit to the ritual?"

"Well, yes, he said. But we still have a few problems that have not been solved yet. He wishes to submit to the ritual of death and resurrection, yes, but at this point he insists on the core of his personal bodyguard being present, and..."

"Yes?"

"He demands that you must die. For as a reborn god, what need will he have for a mere human consort?"

"I see. We need to get him away from the Meshedi and we need to get me out of here."

"Yes, my Queen. Much to hope for."

"In other words, we await divine intervention."

Five men walked through the well-trod back paths of Lawazantiya, trying to look inconspicuous, which was not easy as two of them were over two arm spans tall and one seemed half that span wide across his shoulders. Three were carrying spears, and the fourth with black curly hair had a bow with a quiver of a few arrows. Each of the four carried different swords – one across his back, the second across his chest, and the last two had short swords tucked into their belts. They were sensible enough to have put their helmets and shields into hidden storage, yet they still drew stares when they were seen. The fifth man in front, unarmed, scruffy, balding, and wobbling, had seen better days. He had no armour at all and his sandals were shredding.

"This is your secret passage up to the temples?" asked Saddirme in the local Hurrian dialect.

"Aye, me lord. We just have to keep going," he wheezed.

"Where did you find this one, Kabi?" Saddirme asked Kabi in Luwian.

"He was the only one in the wine shop willing. If he doesn't pass out, we continue to climb, so soon we will be making our way up the back of the akropolis."

"That's when things get complex," added Diomedes. "We can only hope the Great Queen has quarters separate from the Great King," he repeated in Akhaian to Eruthros.

"Why is that?" asked the big red-haired man.

"Because the Great King always has his Meshedi around or near to him. Great warriors as we are," he smiled wryly, "we would not be wise to take on the twelve most highly trained soldiers in the Hittite Empire. So we can hope that the Great Queen has her own quarters and fewer guards. We don't know if she's free to come and go, but we must talk to her."

"I thought our primary goal was to get a secret audience with the High Priest or Priestess," ventured Saddirme.

"Yes, of course," Diomedes responded, looking upward toward the temples, "but it's my guess we will find the High Priestess, Priest, and the Great Queen to be of similar mind: none will desire the Great King of the Hatti to be the Great King of Lawazantiya, the sacred city of Ishtar. Would that not be our best hope, a core alliance at the top? Thence, we shall find others to join our cause."

"Which is?" asked Kabi, not making a joke.

"To kill the Chief Priest and Great King of the Hatti, who thinks he is a god," Diomedes replied unsmiling.

Shipibaal was surprised to see the same lithe messenger as before appear before him. He announced that the Great King wanted to see him immediately to hear the latest news. The messenger said the Great King would be glad for news from anywhere but mostly from the south. "For," he confided, "I just brought news from the other direction." He whispered that soldier-couriers had arrived from the north to see the Great King. Perhaps some of the Meshedi did not show their usual discretion, for the rumour had been confirmed that the greatest city on earth, Hattusa, the capital of the Hittite Empire, had been utterly destroyed. No one was sure by whom, though the notoriously vengeful Kaska are the likely culprits.

Shipibaal found himself shocked to finally hear these words even though he had already expected it to happen. Since the Great King and his entire retinue, guardsmen and all the soldiers from the capital, not to mention wagons of valuables and supplies, had come here in a vast caravan to the holy city of Lawazantiya, what else could it mean? Of course, he had always been told that Suppiluliuma was the bravest and strongest leader in the world, but that did not mean he had the good sense to recognize a lost cause when he saw one. He told the young messenger that he did have a communication to share with the Great King though it was meant to be sent to the Ugaritic king. He immediately felt guilty for sharing too much with this stranger.

He changed into his most noble clothes and hung the copper talisman of the Great King's envoy around his neck. He covered that with a fine white cape with a bright blue border. He felt the arrogant messenger eyeing him closely. "Very pretty," said the messenger leering, "both the clothes and the fine athletic body they're on."

"That will be enough from you, young man," Shipibaal snapped, though he was also a young man. He felt peeved at the effrontery, but he also found himself warming with pleasure as he continued, "Just do your job. As you can see, I am ready to go."

The way became dangerous and more demanding since to avoid guards or anyone else seeing their approach the five had to climb up the steep rear side of the akropolis where there were no trails, gates, or people. As they drew closer to the summit, the broken crags became larger and more ragged and each limestone wall seemed higher. The four armed men had no problem with this and their climbing was smooth, steady, and quick. However, their guide was soon hopelessly left behind, puffing red-faced as he strove on, his breath stinking of old wine.

"Nice find, Kabi. What shall we do with him?" asked Eruthros. "We can't just wait."

"No choice," said Kabi. "He's all we have." They paused until he came up.

"Used to scramble up here in minutes when I was a lad," the guide wheezed.

"Are you going to make it, old man?" the translator Saddirme asked. "If you can't, it may be best to leave you here."

"Wot, and miss me pay? I've done this a thousand times. Just watch me." And he showed some vigour as he scrambled up the inclined face of the biggest boulder ahead. They felt some relief, until he got to the top and plummeted straight over the edge of the vertical drop on the other side. The warriors heard a squeak of fear then the whoomph and crack of a body landing. They went around the rock and found him splayed over the sharp stones, bloody and unconscious but still breathing.

They looked at each other and Eruthros spoke first in an emotionless voice, "He's done. We're going on without him. You three go ahead, and I'll tend to'm."

"But," Kabi spoke, "We can't leave you..."

"Onward," Diomedes indicated and they continued. "He's right here." Then Eruthros was among them again, wiping off the blade of his dagger on grass and then on the back of his loin chlamys. Nothing was said, and soon they crested the hilltop behind several imposing temples that suddenly appeared before them. The men paused and went between two to see the courtyard. They found they were between two smaller temples but could not see them all from their vantage point. They looked similar from there.

"Which one would be the *palace* of the Great King of the Hatti?" asked Saddirme. "It seems likely he'd be housed in the biggest one."

"Only if it's the temple of the Storm-God," Diomedes suggested. "But here in Lawazantiya, the home of Shaushka-Ishtar, sister of the snake goddess of Kriti, I think it likely the tallest temple will be hers."

"Then the next biggest," suggested Kabi, looking around, not sure of which one it would be either.

"Yes, good choice. Let's go introduce ourselves to the guards," Eruthros grinned. "But which one is the second largest..."

They walked forward since there seemed nothing else to do until they were visible between temples on the edge of the paved pathway. There were temples everywhere but only three stood out significantly and a fourth further away was mid-sized. Pairs of Hittite guards with spears paced around the sacred grounds, and four Hurrian guards from Lawazantiya stood ready at the high entrance of the tallest temple with walls of its own furtherest west. The gate was topped by an eight-pointed star above a solar disc with a stylized leopard encircled by a serpent on the keystone over the door. A ritual procession was gathering before a smaller temple lower down the hill. "We need to make a choice now," spoke Diomedes.

Saddirme observed, "The second tallest temple is the broadest, but I cannot make out the strange image on the lintel. That's a calf, is it not, being held down? Is it being neutered? But look, it has the same sort of Hurrian guards as the tall one, but only two."

"It's the third," said Diomedes. "If the sacred bull of the Storm-God over its entry doesn't give it away, the Meshedi bodyguard at the gates, around it, and probably more inside it would do so."

Kabi spoke up in a whispered hiss, "Lucky we did not come up to it. We would have been caught. That's where the Great King must be. But against six Meshedi and another six inside, what can we do?" He looked directly at Diomedes. "Who are we looking for, my leader, the Great King, the Great Queen, or the High Priestess and Priest?"

Diomedes sized up the situation and realized Kabi was right. They could not just attack the Great King. "First, we must get through to Queen Lieia-Hepa who can only be in a smaller temple below, perhaps the mid-sized one with only a few Hatti guards."

"Let's get at it," barked Eruthros, and was about to lead them from the shadows out into battle when he realized he was not sure which temple was meant. He paused and drew back with the rest as two men approached on the path talking. One was lean and young in an envoy's blue-bordered white cape, clean-shaven with short brown hair. The other, taller, was dressed as a Hittite nobleman in the long robes, curly-toed shoes and the pointed gilded hat worn by gods and the royal family.

"Mahhuzzi, the king's steward," whispered Diomedes, recognizing him.

Earlier, Shipibaal, again accompanied by the messenger, had approached the first pair of the royal guardsmen at the outside gate on the path to the Temple of the Storm-God, which housed the Great King. Shipibaal was stopped but the messenger walked beyond. The envoy was recognized, but his diplomatic copper amulet was examined anyway. After passing, Shipibaal felt bold enough to ask his guide in the local Hurrian tongue, not likely to be understood by the elite Hittite soldiers, to tell him again which god was in which temple.

"Ah," the messenger flashed a smile, "The gods I know. Things have certainly shifted around since our new *guests* from Hattusa arrived and took over." He leaned closer, breathing on Shipibaal's ear. "You know the temple of Teshub the Storm-God is before you since you were brought here earlier. So of course the Great King and his retinue are dwelling within for is he not the Storm-God, too?" he smirked. "The tallest temple with the towers across the hill facing west is reserved for Ishtar as both Sun Goddess of the heavens – see her solar disc up there? – and Ishtar of Earth and ... *lower*. Some have whispered the temple descends even deeper than it reaches upward." His voice dropped as he hissed, "There is said to be a gateway to the Underworld within." Back to normal whisper: "As I explained, the temple next to it is where the Archigallus High Priest dwells. But this temple before us is for the noisy Storm-God who has been quiet all these years, but it is also said to be occasionally occupied by the disappearing Telipinu, the god who crosses boundaries." He smiled enigmatically.

The guards ahead above the perron by the door seemed to be eyeing Shipibaal with suspicious impatience as he stood pausing between gateways, gesturing to himself. "But what everyone wants to know is *where is the Great Queen*?" Shipibaal asked his admirer, the messenger, with intense curiosity.

"Such secrets I will reveal to you only when we're alone," he whispered, leaning in closely to lightly bite Shipibaal's ear. The Ugaritic envoy pulled away with feigned disgust. This was not the time! Without saying farewell, Shipibaal marched up the three steps to the temple keystone archway door and was allowed to enter by the two Meshedi outer guards. He looked back but the swift-footed messenger was already gone. He went through but had hardly gone beyond the two inner guards when he was approached by a servant who pulled him aside for his ritual cleansing. But the servant also shook his head pointing to his ears, indicating *pay no attention to what you hear*. Shipibaal however could clearly hear the Great King raging at someone, likely his unfortunate advisors.

"We can never go back to our great capital," he moaned. "This cannot be part of what the gods have ordained. I have done my ritual cleansing, led all the required processions, and given blood sacrifice unto the gods, so why would they do this to me?" The king's low tone indicated great inner anguish. But then he began such shouting that Shipibaal could readily hear. "What are we doing here? Is Tarhunta even here in this bewitched city? It is you who advised me to come here, you and my turncoat uncle! Why did you two lead me here? Why did you betray me? You must have known I would not be welcome in a city ruled by women!"

Kil-Teshub stood silently.

"But my King, your Majesty," Mahhuzzi spoke calmly, "it would have been worse in the other cities, and they have the soldiers to keep us out. And here you have been welcomed. Just look around you. You are secure. We have more soldiers than the whole city but we don't need them as long as you are safe."

Kil-Teshub nodded.

"*Safe*? Are you mad? To stay here is to allow the God of the Storm to become second in prominence to – to what? – the ancient Babylonian goddess of obscenity and death? Can you not see this is a threat to me, the Storm-God of the Hatti?"

"...*chosen* of the Storm-God, yes," corrected General Kil-Teshub.

"No, you fool, can't you see? If I am not the Storm-God himself, I must become another! He desires me to become a god like him, with him, to keep the cosmic balance!" Suppiluliuma began to pace frenetically back and forth. "Allowing the High Priestess of Ishtar to retain power over me will not only bring back chaos and darkness to us all, it will also return the Great Queen Lieia-Hepa to her position. Do you forget how she used black magic to foresee the fall of Hattusa? And so it happened! She also predicted my destruction and that of the glorious Hittite Empire. I *am* the Empire so this must be stopped." He roared his defiance: "At this moment, she is scheming to destroy me! The Storm-God demands I act. She must be ended...*today*!"

Mahhuzzi saw an attendant's signal of the envoy's presence. Kil-Teshub nodded gravely, "Yes, my Great King, so it must be. Orders will be given forthwith."

"But first we must hear from the Ugaritic envoy who has been here twice before. He has said he brings an older message tablet purloined from another courier to keep us informed. Perhaps news from the south will be encouraging. The Hatti navy may have driven the strangers from the Levant."

With the Great King's distracted agreement, Mahhuzzi sent a message for Penti-Sharruma the royal scribe to be brought along in case there was reading or writing to do. He left the room and welcomed Shipibaal, ordering a cool beverage for his refreshment. He made idle words to allow time for Penti-Sharruma to arrive and, more important, for the Great King to compose himself. When they entered the room, the Great King was sitting in the large chair that was assumed to be his throne with Penti-Sharruma standing by. Shipibaal went into full prostration, but impatiently the Great King ordered him to rise and proceed, attempting to look in control, but Shipibaal could see his shaking hands and the whites of his eyes.

"You speak for Ammurapi, My Majesty's servant-king in Ugarit?" asked the King.

"It is so, Great Ruler."

"Good then. Tell your king, my servant, that the greatest city on earth has been utterly destroyed. Hattusa has been destroyed!"

"Darkness falls upon the land, Great King," the envoy intoned.

Suppiluliuma looked disappointed at the lack of shock at such terrible news but instead asserted, "Make haste and tell me what news you bring."

Shipibaal first had to give a bit of background. "Ugarit had been under combined attack from ships and inland invaders, who seemed to be working together. Much damage was done and the crops were ruined. King Ammurapi sent a message tablet here, which you received, and one to a certain Eshuwara, a high official on Alasiya, both pleading for help, as you know. I do not know what he said to Eshuwara, but this reply from him was intercepted, but only a section of it came into my hands. It is from the recent past. Eshuwara writes:

> 'It was the people from your country and your own ships who did this! And it was the people from your country who committed these transgressions... Truly, may you know this. Be on the alert!'"

Shipibaal passed the tablet fragment to Penti-Sharruma who read it quickly and agreed with the interpretation, "Piece of a longer message, it seems." Mahhuzzi nodded and, reaching over, took the tablet back.

"What is happening?" Suppiluliuma howled, looking terrified.

"Your Highness, if I may," the chief advisor explained. "Ugarit has been attacked by shiploads of unknown invaders, so Ammurapi has asked for help from Eshuwara in Alasiya. But Eshuwara claims the attackers came from Ugarit, which may only mean pirated Ugaritic ships. In short, there is confusion and no one is sure who the marauders are, but Ugarit is under attack, and, from what we have already heard, so is the island of Alasiya. Both are likely to fall if they have not already done so." Kil-Teshub was shocked.

The Great King of the Hatti screamed and came to his feet. He reached up and pulled his long hair so that his pointed gilt crown slipped from his head and fell to the marble floor with a clatter. He looked at the others without seeing them, and mumbled, "I must go to the altars of my gods, prayer... ritual cleansing..." and he ran from the room in a panic.

The chief advisor led Shipibaal to the door in person and Mahhuzzi asked him to wait there. He took Kil-Teshub aside and whispered, but the General shook his head, "It must be done!" he said. Mahhuzzi looked left and right but seemed cornered, so he nodded in agreement. Kil-Teshub's eyes narrowed, and he snapped an order to the captain of the guard to join him and immediately left to do what he had been commanded to do – find the men who would carry out such a rare deed, the murder of the Hatti queen.

Mahhuzzi took Shipibaal gently by the arm and left the temple but continued to walk with him outside on the sacred way amongst the temples. Shipibaal was surprised to see the self-contained royal advisor looking very upset in the deepening shade of the early evening. "You have heard things that were not meant for your ears, and you have seen things that were not meant for your eyes."

"I am a subject of the ancient city of Ugarit, my lord, but my first loyalty is to the Great King, so have no fear. The condition of your Great King has nothing to do with me," Shipibaal said but could hear the hollow timbre of his own voice.

Mahhuzzi scoffed, "You would be a terrible diplomat if you didn't share what you have learned with your king. I would expect you to do so, just as I would make sure you could not if I thought it was necessary. However, I believe Ugarit and its king are already beyond help or even destroyed, so you have no one with whom to share your knowledge. The Great King's state of mind has led to a mad, ruthless plan that is disturbing to the very gods themselves."

"And it disturbs you too?"

"Yes, it is so. I am disturbed to my very soul. My first duty is to the empire, not the Great King himself, so I am sorely troubled about which way to turn." He looked into Shipibaal's eyes. "This is my first act of disloyalty to the king, but I must tell you this."

Shipibaal was shocked to realize the wise vizier was about to confide state secrets to him, unless it was some sort of trick...

"Young man, the Great Queen is in serious danger, and now I have made myself part of it. Just before you arrived, the Great King ordered her immediate death. Though such things have been done by Hatti kings before, this goes too far. She is also the High Priestess of the Sun Goddess of Earth, so this order is sacrilege. The first duty of all Meshedi is to the Great King himself, so I do not think any of them will hesitate to carry out this brutal order, already underway. In this city of the ancient Goddess, known here as Ishtar, it would be the worst sort of folly to cause Lieia-Hepa, the Great Queen who serves the Sun Goddess of Arinna, to perish."

"How is the Sun Goddess related to Ishtar?" Shipibaal somehow felt the question to be important even in this crisis.

"Ishtar is Shaushka who seems to be distinct from Hepat the Sun Goddess, but behind all the veils and the many different names in various lands, have no doubt the Great Goddess is *one*, so I have learned from the High Priestess of Ishtar herself. She is immortal and very powerful, and it is not wise to challenge her."

Now Shipibaal was confused, but he decided to trust the king's advisor, for it seemed to be the best course of action. "What can we do, my Lord Mahhuzzi?"

"I have foolishly stepped into the horse's droppings. There is nothing *I* can do, for I am watched, and perhaps nothing you can do. But if there's a way you *must* get a message to the Great Queen, warn her that her death is even now approaching, though I know not how telling her can stop it."

"Where is she imprisoned?" Mahhuzzi indicated the mid-sized temple lower down the pathway with two Meshedi in front of it. "I don't see how I can help, unless help appears from the all-seeing gods, but I will try."

Mahhuzzi clasped his arm and looked at him imploringly. "You can approach the door and show the guards your diplomatic pendant with the Great King's mark, and then, if that doesn't do it, show them your clay tablets and say it's a message for the queen from me." When the envoy dumbly nodded, Mahhuzzi abruptly turned and went directly back to the temple of the Storm-God. This was the scene observed from the shadows by Diomedes and his crew.

Shipibaal was uncertain which way to go, back to his quarters in safety and comfort, or toward the Great Queen's temple of confinement, putting himself in great danger for a cause that was not his own. It was then he saw someone signalling him from the shadows between two temples. His size looked right. "Not now," he thought again but walked over anyway, expecting to meet the messenger.

Kabi was ready. Just as the envoy was close enough to see it was not the messenger and that there were others, Kabi stepped out and, putting his arm around his shoulder, pulled him back into the shade.

"What? Who are you?" Shipibaal pulled back and tried to break away, but Kabi held him tightly in his one-armed hug, revealing a dirk in his other hand. More armed figures emerged, all large men. "Stand back. You don't know whom you're assaulting! Can't you see my envoy's amulet with the Great King's mark? I am sacrosanct!"

The tallest figure came to him and lifting his pendant, examined it closely. "You are the Great King's envoy?" Diomedes asked in Luwian.

Shipibaal saw the twisted sinews on the warrior's scarred arm and the wisdom of fear so gripped him he ceased struggling. Still, he made himself stand straight. "I am the personal envoy of the king of ancient Ugarit, under the protection of Great King Suppiluliuma of the Hatti who is here in this city, in a nearby temple."

"What?" Eruthros had caught the royal names but was uncertain what was said.

"We have with us the envoy from the King of Ugarit," Saddirme explained in Akhaian. "See his pendant."

"What is the news? What has happened in Ugarit?" Diomedes asked urgently. He reached toward his own bronze replacement dagger to speed the answer along.

"Ugarit is under siege, or worse. I was sent here to seek assistance from the Great King." Shipibaal felt no need to obscure the facts so continued, "But Suppiluliuma is exiled here because Hattusa itself has been destroyed by unknown barbarians so can be no help."

"Unstoppable monsters everywhere," Diomedes said sarcastically. "So why were you with Mahhuzzi, the Wiseman? Tell us and hold back nothing or you die."

Shipibaal hung his head. So these men were part of the horde who had brought down the walls of Hattusa and those attacking his home city. "You are the invaders?" he asked. "You speak some Luwian but you are not Lukka."

"We are many peoples, but this city is in no danger – yet. What's going on between you and that schemer, Mahhuzzi?" Diomedes asked putting a giant hand on his free shoulder.

Shipibaal tried to think quickly. What to tell? What to avoid? "The Great King is not himself and has gone into seclusion to pray. Mahhuzzi was directing me on what to say to Ammurapi, King of Ugarit."

Diomedes heard the evasion, so he wasted no more time. "Where is the Great Queen Lieia-Hepa? Why has she not been seen amongst the Hatti? Is she alive?"

The envoy looked at the craggy, sculpted face of his captor and felt his few defences slip away. He knew his life was in danger if he lied and he could not see the truth making things worse. In fact, remembering his dangerous mission, truth might even help him. He sighed, "Loosen your grip, and I will tell you all." Diomedes dropped his hand and Kabi removed his arm but still gripped Shipibaal's forearm. He explained that the Great Queen was imprisoned in a lower temple, and yes he knew which one. He added that she was under a death sentence from the Great King to be carried out immediately once dependable assassins were found, probably amongst the Meshedi. Mahhuzzi was opposed to such an act of sacrilege and bad politics and had instructed him to use his diplomatic status to get in to warn Queen Lieia-Hepa of her danger."

"But you said her guards are also Meshedi, so they wouldn't help her. What good would a warning do? Are *you* going to fight them?" Saddirme piped in with rapid speech. "She'd still be the lamb awaiting sacrifice."

"We hoped for divine intervention..." Shipibaal said lamely.

"So there are two guards outside and two guards inside and likely one or two assassins on their way?" Shipibaal nodded as Diomedes spoke. "We are not divine, but I see no problem with intervention." When it was translated to Eruthros by Saddirme, he cackled with pleasure under his breath. "The question is, where do we take her for safe haven afterwards?"

"You are willing to help? We are on the same side?" Shipibaal flashed a relieved grin. "But..." The light of an opportunity that certainly felt like divine intervention banished other questions. Shipibaal realized he didn't need to know why. "I am Shipibaal, and there is still just enough light to see the temple from here. I do not think we can consider where we can take her, for the assassins are approaching. A plan?"

"You approach alone and show the guards your credentials. We will do the rest."

Shipibaal nodded, freed his arm, drew himself up and set off at a purposeful pace.

"How do we know..." Kabi began.

"We know nothing," hissed Diomedes as they moved along. "But this has begun."

Diomedes and Kabi stalked to the right of the sacred road and down the hill, keeping an eye on the envoy.

Saddirme and Eruthros did the same on the left. They watched Shipibaal slow as he approached the guards who crossed their spears before him.

The guards looked hostile but Shipibaal told them who he was and had them each examine his copper pendant with the mark of the Great King on it. He said he had been sent by Mahhuzzi himself to bring an important message to the Great Queen. They looked at each other and one asked what sort of message. Shipibaal reached into his wallet and drew out the fragment of clay tablet with the Akkadian cuneiform on it and carefully showed it to them as though it were fragile. Neither could read it, of course, but they studied it closely as though it had magical power. They knocked a code on the thick doors and when they were opened explained to the inner guards who was visiting and how important it was. Shipibaal entered and quickly made his way further inside.

The outside guards closed the doors and were about to step back into place when they simultaneously found they could not breathe. Each had just had his throat cut by an Akhaian and died with a drowning gurgle as blood pulsed from him. The bodies were dragged into the dark, their twisted conical helms removed and spears taken.

Back in front, Diomedes repeated the coded door tap, but when the doors were opened from the inside, the Akhaians slammed them wide. They circled around the two inner guardsmen with their swords drawn, so the guards were forced to face them with their golden spears by turning their backs toward the open doors. Before the fight could begin, however, the Meshedi were struck down from behind by Saddirme's sword slash to the neck and Kabi's dagger through the corslet and between the ribs. Neither was immediately killed, so the Akhaians had the pleasure of final dispatch with directed thrusts to the heart from the guards' own gold-plated spears.

Followed by Shipibaal, Lieia-Hepa, the High Priestess of the Sun Goddess of Arinna and Great Queen of the Hatti, ran out from her quarters with her crimson and black robes flaring behind her. She paused, stared, and lifted her hands to pull back her hair, but she made no sound at all. Shipibaal had warned her what was happening and rescue was what she had been waiting for. She looked at the dead guards and at the four warriors, then, startled, looked again, recognizing Diomedes with a shock. Her dark-lined eyes opened wide and she impulsively swept across the floor to embrace him. As in a dream, he returned the embrace, getting Meshedi blood on her, running his lips lightly across her brow. But he recalled his situation and gently pushed her back. "This is not over yet," he whispered. The others looked on without comprehension.

Saddirme and Eruthros were sent outside to wear the guardsmen's helms and hold their golden spears to make things appear in order, at least from a distance. Inside, Kabi loosely attached an arrow to his bowstring and hid himself in the crook where two walls met. Diomedes wiped his hands on some rich curtains and stood next to the queen. "Did the envoy tell you?" He glanced at Shipibaal. "Meshedi assassins have been ordered by Suppiluliuma to kill you and are on their way. Is there no other way in? Any more guards?"

"Ahhiyawa–*Ah-kee-an*, how did you...?" Her eyes shone in awe at the impossible situation.

"Not now," he said. "All will be made clear soon." Paradoxically, in the midst of such turmoil and danger, they looked anew upon each other and time paused for a beat.

"I... I think there is another way in though I've never seen it, used by priestly folk, food servers and cleaners. It would be barred from the other side. More guards...? I... I have heard men's voices from rooms below."

As if beckoned, a thumping beat arose as heavy footsteps clambered up a stone staircase. Diomedes placed himself in front of Lieia-Hepa, withdrawing his heavy bronze sword from its chest sheath, wishing he had his round shield. From a side room appeared two more Meshedi with gilded spears lowered as they made straight for him. One was impaled in the back of his neck with Kabi's bronze-tipped arrow as he passed by, but the other had his spear aimed right for the Akhaian's chest. Diomedes stood his ground and stopped the spear thrust by smashing the thick, upper blade of his Sherden sword directly against the spear's metal head with the force of both hands. With the clang of bronze on bronze, the spearhead split in two while the sword was chipped but remained intact. The spear shaft fell to the floor. Before the guardsman could pull out his hand axe, Diomedes thrust the long, tapered sword point through his breastplate and into his heart. He pulled it back while the man collapsed into death. He drew in air and looked around. Four dead inside, two outside, yet still no assassins.

There were shouts and clatter beyond the main door as the two outside warriors engaged with an unknown enemy. Diomedes and Kabi ran to help, but when Diomedes pulled the heavy portal open, Saddirme and Eruthros stumbled through the portal. They had sprouted arrows yet they managed to get themselves inside. Saddirme fell, his tall Hittite helm rolling away. An unknown warrior in Hittite armour but with no helmet to hide his braided greying hair followed them through with a bloody hand axe in one hand and a dagger in the other. Kabi was about to loose an arrow at him when Eruthros stepped in front, holding his hand up in the *stop* gesture and managed to croak, "He is a friend!"

"Zunan!" shouted Lieia with joy, then to the others, "This man is my personal attendant, my bodyguard."

Through the lighted doorway outside, Diomedes could see two bowmen shuddering in their death throes on the ground. They wore dark clothes and had sickle-swords at their sides "What has happened here?" he asked, nodding to Kabi that it was safe to approach their wounded comrades. Both were alive, but Eruthros was gasping.

Zunan, the brawny veteran soldier, nodded. "I was sent by Mahhuzzi to protect the Great Queen but I found these impious scoundrels shooting arrows into these... unusual guardsmen, so I struck the bowmen down with ... these," indicating his weapons. Your men were cornered but they wouldn't leave their posts until I had killed the godless assassins. How are you faring?" he asked of Saddirme and Eruthros.

"I'll be better when I get these godless stingers out of me," Eruthros lamely joked, reaching for the arrow in his chest, a little blood dribbling from his mouth.

"No, leave them so drawing them forth doesn't kill you." All arrows were in front. The Danaan had caught two arrows in his bull's hide chest plate, but only one had penetrated into his lung from which air whistled out with each inhalation. He was swaying dizzily. Saddirme had fallen but was in somewhat better shape with his two arrows, one in his unguarded shoulder and the second embedded in his thigh – however, it was not gushing blood which meant the femoral artery was undamaged.

"We have little time," warned Zunan, worried first about his queen.

"We must ready them for transport," hissed Diomedes. He and Kabi removed the cuirasses on both warriors, causing some anguish when they had to move. Without pause, Diomedes smoothly broke three of the arrow shafts between his fingers without jerking the points, throwing aside the feathered half and leaving the rest embedded, but he pulled out the entire length of one in the left chest of Eruthros. Eruthros looked down surprised. "I saw it did not penetrate deeply, and now we know they are not barbed," Diomedes flashed a smile. "We must get you hedgehogs to shelter. Saddirme, get up!"

Lieia looked at the men and announced, "I know where we must go. Our only choice is the Temple of Ishtar where dwell the High Priestess and Priest."

"Yes, Great Queen," added Zunan. "Mahhuzzi has already made arrangements, but we must make our way by way of a wide arc to avoid the temple of the Storm-God."

Taking little more than that which was on them or in them, Lieia-Hepa put on more solid sandals and a dark cape and led them into the night. Kabi and Diomedes helped along the weighty, confused Eruthros while Zunan supported Saddirme as he limped.

After they had departed, Shipibaal came out of hiding, picked up a short sword to stick through his belt just in case, and headed back down the hill toward his quarters. He was stopped only once by a regular guardsman who was readily impressed by his diplomat's pendant and let him pass.

Back in his room, he gulped down water, lit a candle and carefully inscribed a brief message in Amorite cuneiform to his king in Ugarit. In the intensity of the moment, he several times misphrased his words or improperly placed his wedges, throwing the moist clay across the room and starting again. Finally he got it right with these words:

> "From Shipibaal your servant. To the feet of my Lord seven times seven from afar I fall. Your servant in Lawazantiya fortified his position with the Great King, telling him of the attack on our ancient city from the unknown invaders from the sea. I pleaded for help. But, behold, the King wept, retreated, fled, and elsewhere made prayer and sacrifices. All is lost, my Lord. You must flee."

O where could he find a courier at this hour? Since he could not, he felt the urgency to find a horse or mule and begin the journey himself to deliver this vital message to Ugarit. If the Great King himself was falling into confusion and panic, it must be time to warn Ammurapi, servant-king or not, to save his life and escape his city. If Ammurapi survived and someday returned to power, he would surely remember the humble envoy who had saved him! He found the jar of warm beer he had saved from the previous night and drank it quickly while imagining his future glory. But soon the beer reached his head, reminding him of his current situation, and he instead began to fear he was marooned alone in this strange city. His heavy head nodded, and he realized the harrowing events of the last few hours had exhausted him, so he threw himself upon his mat and fell into a deep sleep.

The Sardinian was pleased he had decided to avoid Tatta Lake, a huge seepage body of stinking, stagnant water too salty and shallow to be of any use to anything. Instead, local guides led his troop up the Delice tributary south almost to its source in low mountains before going further south to ford the curve of the Marassantiya River. Coming down from the hills, he looked upon the once-fertile broad plain before him, reflecting that Tudhaliya, father of Suppiluliuma, would have brought his vast chariot brigade to meet his small force here to destroy it utterly. Even then, the drought and plague were upon the land, but the Hittites had the trade network and human resources to sustain itself. They could have put their well-trained standing army in the field within hours.

Now there were few standing armies. The land was devastated, trade was at a standstill, and the countryside was depopulated. Towns that had their own source of clean water from the remnants of rivers in their valleys managed with meagre crops and shrinking herds. As long as everyone continued to give sacrifice to the local gods, social order prevailed. The gods through their representatives on earth provided the people with the bare essentials of survival, and the hard times were accepted as god-given destiny. The authority of the priesthood and nobility was not challenged, at least not openly, and cooperation kept the cosmos in balance.

Elsewhere, others survived by attacking the order of things, for only those who took from others could continue to advance into an uncertain future. The Sardinian's troop of homeless barbarians cooperated with each other only enough to achieve their immediate ends and carry on. Their only goal was to continue. Sarpedon did not know the precise way to the Great Green, but he knew he wished to avoid Tarhuntassa or Karkemish, either of which had more Hatti forces than the Great King had with him. Those among the Lukkans and Hurrians who had knowledge of this territory had assured him that crossing through the vassal-kingdom of Kizzuwatna would take them to the sea, either by way of Ura, Adaniya, or Tarsa, after which they could join others of their kind.

So far the journey had its share of minor adventures and successes. They had taken towns along the way or accepted their desperate *hospitality* by taking all they had but their lives. None of the warriors were starving. The townspeople wanted news of Hattusa and were disheartened to have its destruction confirmed. But when they learned that the Great King of the Hatti had run from his capital to escape the evils closing in on him, their sorrow often turned either to fear that their universe was imploding upon them or to anger that the Great King and High Priest of the land was powerless to protect them or even himself. Young Hatti men often left their families and joined the warrior outcasts.

With few camp followers and only a small baggage train, they moved along quickly for a military troop. Any towns were first scouted out to make sure no disease was in them, but if such were the case, they were avoided. Anyone getting sick among his men was simply left behind. As always, Sarpedon sent out scouts and reconnoissance squads ahead of him, but he also got reports from the wings and even from behind.

The problem with Henti had been minor, at least so it seemed to him. Anyway, it was more or less resolved. He had shared a campsite each night with the young woman. They shared food and slept in the same tent, and, though he mostly tried to avoid it, he could not help but catch glimpses of her smooth pearly flesh as she rearranged her meagre garments. He had to accompany her when she went to relieve herself, for, enrobed or not, she was still a temptation for these wild warriors, and he did not trust even his own best men. When they had crossed rivers or found streams, she often wanted to quickly and discreetly wash her body. He had to check on her, of course, and she was more beautiful than anything he had ever seen. He was the only one who knew she had been in the Great King's harem, but such knowledge would only have made her more desirable to others, so he kept it to himself. At the same time, it *did* make her more desirable to him. Klymenos, the Danaan captain who would be king, asked many questions about the girl and his eyes followed her whenever she was near.

The thing with undoing social codes of behaviour is that they were all in new territory, which is no territory at all: the in-between of *no man's land*. Life happened within the shredding fabric of social breakdown, lost boundaries, warfare, and anarchy. Customs or status meant nothing any more. There were no royals and no gods watching over them or anyone to punish wrongdoers. It was might makes right, but, still, some of the uprooted horde clung to their own traditions or developed new codes of honour so trust could be shared. Sarpedon had given Diomedes his word that he would be the girl's protector, and he was doing so. But the Sardinian was not sure what that entailed. Diomedes had left no instructions. Does protecting someone mean you can't fuck them? He was not sure, but he liked the girl and was not about to force himself on her, so he did something he had not done with a woman for a very long time: he *asked* if she would share his bed. She didn't look surprised but seemed somehow disappointed.

"Do you think that just because you are protecting me, I should grant you free access to my body in exchange?"

Sarpedon thought a bit but had to admit that, yes, that's just about what he thought. "It's the way of things, an exchange: yes, *princess*." He spoke without irony. "Was that not your ... *arrangement* with the Akhaian?"

"It is not your concern," she snapped but then changed her mind. "No, the Akhaian has neither taken me nor demanded favours."

"No? But he probably didn't ask, as I am doing. It has been quite some time since I stooped to such gallantry," he smiled at himself.

"Has it now? Then know this: In all of my short life I have never before been *asked* for sexual favours. Those who wanted to use me and could, just did so. Even after I was taught various skills and enchantments in the harem and learnt to enjoy play with others of my kind, I never really had a choice – never. So, thank you for asking and for allowing me the privilege of saying, for once in my life, *όχι* – no!" Using the Hellenic word for "no" from her childhood felt like reclaiming something that had been stolen from her.

Sarpedon honoured her choice and a certain admiration crept into his feelings for her. But he saw clearly that doing away with mind-whispering gods as well as kings, queens, and priests, not to mention palaces and social hierarchy, was an opportunity for a new beginning. But allowing women to take back the power they once had before they were suppressed under male domination was going to be a long and perilous journey. They had already passed through a few isolated valleys in which pre-patriarchal deities, all aspects of the Great Goddess, had returned to ascendance and the thundering male storm or sky gods had been sidelined. These devoted townsfolk would mostly disappear into the hollow hills when they approached rather than bring out a force to fight them.

It happened one day that forward scouts galloped up to him and reported that they now knew where Suppiluliuma and his evacuated Hatti had gone. Sarpedon was surprised to hear the likely destination was the compact sacred city of Ishtar. Why would the High Priest of the Storm-God go to Lawazantiya? The only reason that made sense to him was that it was likely to have the least defences and the fewest soldiers than any other sensible choice. Perhaps the Hatti king thought he would be granted full authority with the least resistance. But would Ishtar accept the overlordship of Tarhunta the Storm-God in her own sacred city?

The city was southwest across the plain, then over another river and through the rugged Anti-Taurus mountains. The scouts reported they had been shown a negotiable pass through them, a pass they would have to cross through to get to the sea anyway. On the other side, the ancient city of Lawazantiya was said to be in a broad valley near the source of the Puruma River, so it was not yet in chaos.

A fine conquest it would be. Perhaps they could ransom the Great King. But could they take the city? He did not know how many forces were already there when the Hittites arrived. But why look for trouble with the unknown just when they were getting near to the south sea and their allies? Sarpedon thought it likely that the Akhaian warriors Diomedes and Eruthros and their squad had found their way to Ishtar's city, but it was unlikely they had achieved their objective. It would be useful to know. Spies will certainly have to be sent forward to investigate. There's no doubt their approach down the river would be reported to the Great King and his generals long before they arrive, so they would have to be prepared as they drew close.

Shipibaal was up and had washed himself and eaten some bread with sour cheese and olives. He had determined to find a mount to undertake the journey himself just when he saw the young messenger skip-jumping down the hill as he approached. At first Shipibaal was wary. Could he be trusted?

"Yo, my friend," the messenger waved. He approached and warmly patted Shipibaal's shoulder, ending with a squeeze. After greetings and some shared olives, he told the messenger that he desperately needed to find a courier to take a very important message to Ammurapi, the Ugaritic king. The messenger wanted more details, and, in spite of his native caution, Shipibaal found relief in sharing yesterday's adventures. The messenger's eyes widened in awe at the violence and powerful figures involved. "I can see you are not making this up. Such an astonishing tale – no one could! So you need to warn this King of Ugarit, who is already under attack, that no help is coming, that Ugarit is doomed, and that he should run for his life?"

"Yes, yes, that is my situation. Can you...?"

"Sit down again and take a breath, dear boy. I have big news of my own. I have contacts amongst the spies and couriers, as you may well imagine. I listen in," the messenger said, running his hands through the winglike strands of his sandy brown curls. "I viewed a copy tablet of a message that was sent to Karkemish from some official in ... where do you think?"

"Don't play games with me," Shipibaal protested. "Tell me!"

"Ugarit of course. It may well be that your king is no longer around to dictate messages to anyone."

"What are you saying?"

"I'm saying that, first, I didn't take the content of this tablet seriously," he said drawing out a clay fragment from his side pouch. "Thought someone was trying to make a profit, so I stole it instead," he laughed, waving it in the air. "At least I didn't believe it until you told me your incredible tale. But now I believe it. What I have here is a message, or a copy of a message, that is the last one that will ever be sent from Ugarit. The original tablet was not dried but baked hard, probably in the city's final fire."

Shipibaal heard the words and turned cold: "Show it to me." The tablet was carefully passed between them. Shipibaal understood the meaning before he actually read the cuneiform script, and the blood drained from his face as he read:

> "When your messenger arrived promising help, the army was already humiliated and the city sacked. Our food on the threshing floors was burnt and the vineyards were also destroyed. Our city is sacked. May you know it! May you know it!"

The shock seared his heart. Tears ran from Shipibaal's eyes. "Can this be? Everything was going... *so well*. Now my home is gone, my future is destroyed, and I am forever lost." He clasped his brow and wept freely. The messenger sympathized and then was there, hugging him in his arms. He lifted him to his feet and led him indoors.

With all his plans and hopes defeated, Shipibaal's mind was swept away too. He felt the hard body against his own, leaning into him, encountering each other intimately. The messenger's arms tightened warmly around his back stroking him, a cheek on his cheek, soft breath in his ear, and Shipibaal was awakened to a new impulse. His tears ceased but his breath quickened, and he fervently returned the embrace, pulling the messenger's firm buttocks towards him. They laughed into their kiss and fell onto the mat still wrapped around each other, squirming like ecstatic eels.

The following morning, the world around Shipibaal, the former envoy from Ugarit, did not look so hopeless after all. A soft breeze blew and the sun was bright but not yet hot. He embraced his new companion, loving the very scent of him, before they left together to seek sustenance, hoping to find an open bread shop or market. Shipibaal was not short of exchange. The young men joked and jostled like children as they made their way into the city.

Yes, King Ammurapi was dead and Ugarit had met its end – raped, plundered, and burned to the ground. But Lawazantiya still stood, its order disturbed but intact. Its gods were still in their places, whether in the sky above, the city itself, or the dark hollows beneath. Shipibaal happily reflected that perhaps after all Gad the god of chance had rolled him a winning throw of knucklebone dice.

2. The Great Queen Meets the High Priestess

The circling group of warriors and wounded led by the Great Queen herself, draped and unrecognizable but nimble as a deer on her feet, were met by a group of devotees of Ishtar before they arrived at the monumental temple. They had been sent forth for this purpose in dark robes to be less visible in the night. Diomedes guarding the rear saw them approaching, keeping low and silent, but surmised no threat from them. They surrounded Lieia-Hepa with low coos and murmurs of praise for the Great Queen and High Priestess of the Sun Goddess (no longer of Arinna alone), gently bowing and touching her clothes and feet. The wounded struggled but needed no help beyond what they already had, so the neophytes of Ishtar quickly and efficiently guided them to the darker side of a wall of the towering temple and took them into a thick grove around the back near an ancient well. There they lifted a bent bough on the ground to reveal a nearly invisible trapdoor a foot down. They each went through, the wounded bulk of Eruthros taking the longest time to negotiate his way down the wooden ladder and through a door into a hallway lit by flickering oil lamps. As Diomedes reached up for the trapdoor, he saw two dark-robed figures begin to lower it down upon him. He was glad to see everything had been carefully planned since he had no real plan at all.

The ones in front were met by a thin old man in white robes with a gold collar around his neck. Instead of a conical hat, he wore a shepherd's circular woollen cap and carried a long staff which he tapped before him when it became dark between lamps. Their path continued to descend, but they soon reached an open area and most of the wraithlike attendants disappeared. Eruthros was by now stumbling, wheezing loudly and barely conscious, so he was taken by attendants to another room for treatment. Saddirme tried to walk without Zunan, but he was caught before he fell and grudgingly accepted help going where he was told. However, he refused to be taken away, saying, "I'm okay for a bit. I may be needed here."

"Thank you, Father Priest," Lieia-Hepa said to the old man, as he led them into a side chamber where the exhausted group could at last sit. Armed guards stood by on the edge of the room. Saddirme still bristled with broken arrows, but he was brought bitter opium milk for his pain. The others were given clear water. No one spoke. Then the door opened and a tall woman of great nobility of bearing entered. Long silver-white hair that was both piled atop her head bound in a golden ribbon and also left to flow over her shoulders. Each ear lobe was adorned with some sort of raptor talon hanging from a gold chain. The diadem around her forehead was also gold but in its centre was a brightly jewelled eight-pointed star. Her smooth sepia skin indicated she was between forty and fifty years. She had an unexpected beauty of her own, a sharp elegance of light and dark contrasts. Her cold grey eyes with a bright diamond point in each large dark pupil had a depth no one dared look into for very long, and the effect was emphasized by the arched, darkened brows and kohl-edged black eyelids with dark lines beneath and beyond them. Her lips were painted a ruby red so dark it verged on black. She wore a gauzy robe over her head and down her back that flowed with the air as she walked directly to Lieia-Hepa, ignoring all others.

"Great Queen of the Hatti," she lowered herself to her knee, briefly bowing her head but no more, and, looking up, took Lieia's hand in her own. Lieia was startled since none had held her regal hand since her own mother. But she suppressed the feeling and accepted the warmth of the touch now pulsing through her. "You are the High Priestess of the Sun Goddess, as I am the High Priestess of Ishtar, I welcome you here as my sister, Noble One. Hepat, Shaushka, Ishtar, and Ashtart are sisters too. In truth so are Arinniti and Allani. You may call me Lilitu."

The room seemed to vibrate as Diomedes took in this intriguing information with only a little translation from Saddirme, who summed it up in Akhaian as "sacred talk", though Diomedes understood the Luwian well enough by now. The Karkisan translator had been helped to painfully sit down with the broken shaft of an arrow still protruding a hand-width from his right shoulder and another from his left thigh. He exchanged a glance with Kabi sharing the thought that they were hearing things forbidden to them. Zunan sat motionless, fearful of being so near Ishtar's High Priestess. Diomedes guessed the old man who had welcomed them must be the High Priest.

"You can call me Lieia," she began but emotion rose in her eyes. "Can you help us, O my sister?" Lieia put both hands around the one of Lilitu. "I have been imprisoned by Suppiluliuma since we set out from Hattusa for I foresaw the catastrophe that was coming. Then tonight, I have been attacked by those who would kill me, sent by the Great King. These men and the other one wounded saved my life. This one," she indicated Zunan, "is my own attendant. Eight of the king's men are dead. But the Meshedi will soon learn of what has happened and they will set out to find me and fulfill the ungodly command of the demon-possessed Great King."

The eyes of Lilitu flashed anger at the disclosure. "You are safe here, my lady. This is a very ancient temple, and we have chambers and pathways that have no entrance from the main upper floors. They are hidden from view and descend deep into the earth. You will not be found, and neither will your warriors unless they choose otherwise. We accept our god-given destinies, but that doesn't mean we are absolved from devising schemes to help the gods' will find its way into this world." She stood up, paced, then faced them all, speaking in ringing tones that echoed through the group. "There is cosmic danger here, beyond our mere lives. The eternal Great Goddess is under attack from many sides, and this is not permitted. But the immediate threat is Suppiluliuma, the Hatti King, who seems to have gone mad because Tarhunta the Storm-God has abandoned him, as Tarhunta-Teshub has abandoned us all and taken the rain with him. The drought and infertility destroying this land is because the Storm-God has joined Anu amongst the stars. Our only hope is to act on the wrath of the Great Goddess, who expects us to make things right."

"It is so," intoned the old priest in a quavering voice. Saddirme spoke a low paraphrase in place of a literal translation, though the listeners were too entranced by the silver-haired priestess to pay much attention to literal meaning anyway.

Could he really be her husband, wondered Diomedes? As if hearing his thoughts, Lilitu spoke to all, "There can be no lies amongst us if we are to come through. *None*." The High Priestess then turned to aim her severe eyes directly at Diomedes who stirred from their power but held himself still. "There may be those here who are planning betrayal. I have received word that a troop of unknown warriors has emerged from the mountain passes and even now approaches our city. *You*," she pointed her black fingernails at the former king of Tiryns, "and the others with you are not Hatti and only Zunan is Hurrian. Who are you and what do you know of this? And what is your purpose here? One lie and all strangers will be killed." Lieia looked surprised and concerned. The High Priestess with her feline glittering eyes was dead serious. Saddirme translated only when necessary, watching his leader for a cue. Diomedes seemed to grasp all of this.

"They saved my..." Lieia began to intervene but a sharp glance from Ishtar's High Priestess silenced her.

"I will tell what I know, High Priestess, but I will be brief and tell only the human story, for I do not speak well in the Luwian tongue so my language speaker," indicating the wounded Saddirme, "will transform my words when necessary. I will outline only my human story, for there are too many gods to consider."

"Yes," she suppressed a smile at this, "that is the way of men and kingdoms."

"High Priestess," Diomedes began, "My name is Diomedes, and I was once the king of a city called Tiryns in the land of the Akhaians, called Ahhiyawa by the Hatti."

"Ahhiyawa?" repeated Lilitu the High Priestess. "You have come a long way from your barbarian isles and rough seas. Is the approaching troop of warriors your people?"

"I am uncertain who is approaching but very likely it is either the entire horde of warriors I was with or some of them. We are a loose army that came to exist over time on the sea, yet we are composed of many different peoples. Most of us who came inland to the Hittite Lands originated from closer territories like the Lukka Land, Mira, and the Seha River Land, all formerly Arzawa, but others come from lands strange and unknown to us. We ourselves are exiles from dying lands and chaos. But we came together and took Wilusa then went inland to take Hattusa. That decaying city was evacuated before we got there, the Great King and his chosen followers escaping here, as you know. We did not stoop to pillaging the undefended city or killing its starving people. It was the Kaska who destroyed Hattusa against our wishes, so most of our army went forth to take Nerik, which the Kaska had reclaimed as their own. I don't know the results of the attack." Saddirme clarified as needed, wincing less as the narcotic began to reach him.

She looked into the man, sensing the truth of his tale. “So how big was your original uncivilized *army* that entered Hatti lands?”

“Unknown, O Lilitu, but surely seven or eight thousand warriors with camp followers behind.”

“My spies report the approaching body is less than two thousand. Can you explain that?”

“My Lady, I led a squad of riders south to follow the Great King and the Hatti, so I was not part of the attack on Nerik. I can only guess that either the Kaska destroyed most of them, which is unlikely, or the horde split, with most going back the way they had come toward the Aegean Sea. I know nothing certain here, but it’s likely some have chosen to go back to the Great Green south of here where there are many more of us – and where Alasiya and Ugarit await.” Again, Saddirme helped his words.

“You are bold, for I see no lies. You are no ordinary warrior, Ahhiyawa. You say you were once a king yourself?”

“I was, High Priestess, long ago in another land. So was my wounded oxlike friend. We were city kings, not the *Wanax* or Great King of the land, whose palace was at ... a larger citadel. We both came to this land in the attack we Akhaians – we *Ahhiyawa* – led on the Troad, what you call Wilusa, some four or five suns ago, and I have been wandering over land and sea ever since.”

“Very good. You’re doing well, warrior, avoiding an epic by getting to the point. Now tell me why you are here. Why did you leave your *horde* and go off on your own in following the cowardly Great King’s Hatti contingent? How did you get into our sacred city? How many are you and, if there’s more, where are they?”

Diomedes paused, looking into himself, but he reported it all. He described how he left Taruisa while the walls still stood with a few ships going north into the Black Sea, and how, years later after many adventures and tribulations, he landed again in north Anatolia where all that had been gained was lost. He and a handful of remaining fighters, among them his boyhood friend, a brother-king, then showed up at the Lion Gate of Hattusa, thinking to become mercenary soldiers for the Hatti. "Alas, the *Moirai* had other plans," he concluded. With Saddirme's help the Three Fates were explained, but Lilitu recognized them immediately as familiar to Ishtar as the *Gul Ses*, Hutena and Hutellura, with Ishtar herself as the third. Diomedes recounted his brief meeting before the king and his court, and told how his men were secretly beheaded and their bodies disposed of without ceremony. He related how he himself was imprisoned and did not escape until after Suppiluliuma and his elite followers had left the city, which soon turned to starvation, savagery, and chaos.

"You alone were not killed. Why?" The High Priestess asked the obvious question.

"This I do not know," the Akhaian stated. He and Lieia both glanced down.

"This is the first time you have hidden something," Lilitu intervened. "I think you do know but you may have your reasons to disguise the truth. You will continue."

He narrated how he led others from the city until they encountered the approaching army of pirates and warriors, which he then joined and led back to the city, which they left intact, even leaving grain and warning off the Kaska. They later learned the Kaska had betrayed them and slaughtered the people and burned the abandoned city. So they set off into the northern mountains to take vengeance on the Kaska by destroying Nerik. He and fifteen volunteers went south to catch up with the fleeing Hatti, for it was his intention to find a way to kill the Great King for his personal vendetta of honour. They caught up with the caravan as it was completing its entry into this city, and they simply followed it through.

"You had no plan?" The old High Priest asked incredulously.

"No, we depended on the Moirai and ... luck. Our group split up in the lower levels, but we four climbed to the temple mount, where we knew the king must be, by way of the unguarded steep and rocky side of the akropolis. Which temple? The surrounding Meshedi guardsmen made it obvious – but we saw we would need more than the Fates to break in there. Hermes – luck – intervened: we ran into a wandering envoy who was convinced to tell us the Great Queen Lieia-Hepa was about to be assassinated and where she was imprisoned. He took us to her and a great death struggle ensued, which may have turned out badly had not this intrepid soldier," he indicated Zunan, "Lieia-Hepa's personal bodyguard, appeared out of nowhere to turn things our way."

The High Priestess smiled, "Know you not that we had a highly-placed personage come to our side to inform us of these evil doings?" Lieia's mouth opened slightly and she looked at her sister high priestess in anticipation. "Yes, the Great King's chief advisor, Mahhuzzi, saw that Suppiluliuma was crumbling in confusion and terror, so he feared for the Great Queen and for the empire. He came to us in the night and we shared our concerns. I gave him a glimpse of Ishtar, our Great Goddess of Babylon, and I believe he suddenly saw the world in a new light. It was he who immediately sent forth this loyal soldier to protect Lieia-Hepa. And so it came to pass."

"Ishtar must be very powerful indeed to so overwhelm Mahhuzzi. He is truly a Wiseman, yet not one who has been fervent in his priestly duties," intervened Lieia-Hepa. "Such conversions are not unknown among the Hatti royalty. The Great King Hattusili, grandfather of Suppiluliuma, was devoted to Shaushka who is also Ishtar, so as a victorious general returning from the victory at Kadesh against the Pharaoh, he stopped in this very city to make sacrifice to her. Instead, he was possessed by love for her chief priestess, Puduhepa, who I'm sure is remembered here, and took her back to the then Hatti capital of Tarhuntassa. Under her guidance and the help of Shaushka, he reclaimed Hattusa, and later, as all the world knows, became Great King."

"Ah, you are my sister indeed," the High Priestess beamed at Lieia. "So, what are we to do, my friends? Mahhuzzi has confirmed that Suppiluliuma in his desperate quest for glory as his empire falls around him has agreed to allow himself to undergo apotheosis." Kabi and Diomedes looked confused. "...to undergo the ritual that will transform him into a god, a perilous quest indeed," Lilitu explained. "Before he agreed, he demanded the death of his Great Queen but instead has lost eight of his Meshedi, and she is here safe among us. He further demanded that his bodyguard attend the ritual, but such is forbidden. We must have him alone, willing and compliant. We have a small Hittite regiment occupying our city, and the Great King himself is always surrounded by a dozen of his suicidally devoted Meshedi. Ahhiyawa, where is this envoy now and what is to be done?"

Without hesitation, Diomedes replied that the envoy had escaped in terror and that he knew neither his name nor his homeland. He knew better than to lie. "As to what we can do, we have a few resources of our own, my Lady, do we not?" She nodded gravely, anticipating his words. With help from Kabi, he explained. "First, we have Mahhuzzi who can coordinate our efforts from within the Storm-God's temple. Second, we have Suppiluliuma himself who wishes to escape from the burden of his life and office. Surely we can spirit him away to this mysterious temple if we can only provide a distraction."

"And for a distraction...?"

"We not only have ourselves and eleven other warriors ready to *distract* whomever I direct them to distract right here within the city, but we also seem to have two thousand experienced warriors coming our way who are, I trust, still friends of mine. In terms of what happens within this temple, I believe two high priestesses, one high priest, and the Goddess have the wisdom and experience to manage that."

"And to that you have no objection?" She smiled darkly, "You accept our *management*?"

"There are some ventures for which I am..."

"...entirely unsuited?" Kabi finished for him, surprising himself with his eloquence.

Diomedes nodded. "Perhaps I can go to the oncoming troop and ask them to camp just outside the city but dissuade them from attacking it. They are not likely to disagree, for they don't know of the defences in here. We will sweeten the offer by sending out food and wine. All we need of them is to either bring out the Hatti troops, which would be destroyed, or to convince the Hatti they are desperately needed in, say, Karkemish. My comrades, I suspect, wish to get to the sea which is ... not that far from here?"

"I think I should deliver your message," Kabi ventured. "I can get to the coming troop faster and you, I believe, will be needed here."

"Yes, Kabi is our *hipponoüs*. He is a better horseman than anyone I've seen. I will remain and lead our local troop up to the temples to keep back the Meshedi once your Highnesses," he nodded to all three, "can get Mahhuzzi to bring the Great King here."

"Ah, what a schemer you are," commended the High Priestess of Ishtar. "But then you were once a king, you say, so that is to be expected. Are you devoted to your storm-god or a war-god? I should know this."

"I am guided and protected by the goddess we call Athene."

"Ah, it is pleasing to know we do not have an enemy of the Goddess in our midst," Lilitu smiled her ironic curled lip smile, flashing white teeth behind her darkened lips. She continued, "We're not sure how far your approaching troop is away, so I suggest we find a strong horse and send your hipponoüs on his way at dawn," she graced Kabi with her hypnotic smile. "The rest of this plan may take time. While he is gone, we shall put it into action. We must know the state of the Great King and find a way to bring him to us without his bodyguard or his general. I will have an audience with the grand vizier, for he will know what to do. Half the Meshedi will by now be about frantically searching for their lost captive, but, though they may force the main doors, they will not come to these hidden lower floors. So you must leave your wounded, Man of Ahhiyawa, and you will need to go back into the lower town to collect your dozen or so warriors, but I suggest for this night you stay right here, and we shall take care of you." She gave her raptor's smile again, clicking her taloned earring. She had never called him by name.

"Diomedes is dining with me tonight," the Great Queen Lieia-Hepa spoke up, asserting her royal privilege. "We have much to discuss." The matter was closed.

Kil-Teshub, the proud Hittite general, strode purposefully just ahead of his two Meshedi bodyguards on the stone path to the grand doors of the Temple of the Storm-God. The first two roadway guardsmen had stepped abruptly aside when they saw him approach, but his speed allowed him to catch up to Mahhuzzi, walking alone toward the same destination.

"Vizier, you have been called before the Great King as well?" The General asked aloud in his deep voice, but then sidled up to the thinner man in the tall royal Wiseman's headdress. "Mahhuzzi, did you betray me? Did you betray the Great King? If so, you are a dead man," he hissed down into Mahhuzzi's ear.

"What nonsense are you spewing?" Mahhuzzi replied sharply. "How dare you accuse the Great King's trusted cousin and chief advisor of endangering his Majesty with such treachery? What has happened?" He slowed but did not stop. The two walked through the grand doors of the temple thrown open without question by the guardsmen there. There were two more inside guards that were also brushed past. The General's personal guards marched along behind.

The two walked far enough to continue their intense, whispered conversation. "What has happened? O you sly one! As if I am to believe that anything could happen among the Great King's retinue without you knowing about it. You know very well what has happened: the Great Queen has disappeared!"

"But isn't that exactly what you had planned, exactly what your orders were?"

Now Kil-Teshub was confused. He had been sure that somehow Mahhuzzi was behind all this mystery, that he had sent troops or warned the queen. “My orders from the *God-King*,” he spat the words out, “were, as you know, to send Queen Lieia-Hepa to her home with her gods,” he whispered harshly, as if emphasizing the king’s self-declared divinity would make it ethical. “I instructed the Meshedi captain to find two willing volunteers. Shockingly, in spite of their oaths to serve the Great King as first in all things, many demurred. This time I let the men themselves choose. The Meshedi guards at Lieia’s... at the Queen’s temple were alerted to give the assassins entry – but nobody else. I had placed six good men there – two on each side of the door, and two on standby below. As far as anyone knows, the Queen was alone.”

“So, Uncle, what happened and where is the Great Queen now?”

“You be straight with me first, Chief Steward! What do you know about this?”

“You’re right, Old Comrade,” said Mahhuzzi, causing Kil-Teshub to shift from his unfriendly tone, but he put his hand on his sword hilt to emphasize he was dead serious. “Voices reached me that must have begun within your own people. How else? I was told that there was a commotion at the temple-prison of our Great Queen, Lieia-Hepa. When more of your special guards were roused to rush there and check, they could not find her... and a few of your best men had been... injured or worse. My guess is that Lieia-Hepa has been killed and dragged away.”

“But by whom? This tale has no centre – it’s about what is missing! At this point, all I know is what was found at the temple that housed the Great Queen. There was no Great Queen there. She is missing! Maybe dead, maybe not. None of her bloody garments. The two assassins are dead for sure, apparently hacked and stabbed down from behind. Stranger yet, all six of the Meshedi guardsmen are dead, not wounded, killed dead! All we found was that one of the hidden guardsman had an arrow through his neck from behind, an arrow that was not Hatti. The two Meshedi who were in front had throats deeply slashed, one to the bone. The other three inside were killed face to face. Even if you had warned her, this is impossible. Who could do this? It would take a troop of professional soldiers to succeed! But we found no one: they're missing too!"

After a pause, the King's Counsellor added, "Noble General, you must bear in mind that you yourself, in your pious faith, once said to me that whatever happens must be destined by the gods. It may be well to bear that in mind in the coming days. More such *destiny* is on the way, I fear to add. You know of the approaching troop of warriors? I thought so. They are either the same who came from the west to pillage what we left in Hattusa or they're the ruthless Kaska on our trail. They are not many but even so they are double our number, so meeting them in the field or attempting a defence behind these low walls is likely to have the same result. Perhaps we can bribe them? Or...?"

"We can also flee again," hissed Kil-Teshub. "The Hatti are not welcome here. But Suppiluliuma now has other plans. The Great King has decided now is the time to become a living god, so we had best confer with him before he flies away skyward and can no longer hear us until we sacrifice a bleating sheep." Mahhuzzi smiled at the old general's mockery, but they each took a breath as they straightened and prepared to enter the King's chamber. Kil-Teshub's guards opened the doors, remaining outside, and the two royal advisors walked in together, showing none of the stress between them. Kil-Teshub was aware the chief advisor knew more than he was saying, but who else could he turn to in this crisis?

They knew the way to the king's private chamber along the carpeted path and where they had to go first, so they waved off the servant coming to guide them. The Meshedi guards kept their distance, too. When the king was not praying, making sacrifice, or purifying his body with smoke or sacred ablutions often before his favourite shrine with the miniature manifestation of the Storm-God – brought from Hattusa and established in a convenient side room – he was in his large sleeping room, most often pacing, staring at the ceiling, or doing more praying. As far as Mahhuzzi knew, the only visitors he had requested were specialists of the sacred whose expertise was in magical spells, incantations, or potions. The vizier had not been apprised of their purpose or success. The High Priestess of Ishtar and her consort had not been asked to return.

Stopping in the shrine room for ritual cleansing, the men could smell the odour of burnt herbs with the sweeter smell of rose water. Mahhuzzi noticed a smaller idol next to Tarhunta. Was it Shaushka? Most curious, he thought, as he dried his face and hands. Perhaps Suppiluliuma was following in the footsteps of his grandfather.

As they approached the royal chamber, they heard girlish giggles coming from within and were taken aback to realize he had called upon members of his harem to entertain him. With the loss of his city and his empire and personal prestige crumbling, plus the Great Queen's apparent betrayal, they had expected him to be either in a tantrum or a stupor, not indulging in sensual pleasure.

"Ah, welcome good sirs," Suppiluliuma said, looking up from his position on the floor amidst what appeared to be about six of his youngest harem girls. All were fully dressed as was the king himself, and none were within his reach. Though there had been some suppressed giggling, Mahhuzzi could see these young women were ill at ease but trying to please their king. "These noble girls were just telling me the stories they remembered hearing as children, those tales told by mothers or nurses of the world's creation and of death, what becomes of us when our bodies die..." The two advisors stood in place. "It is fascinating to hear what ignorance is conjured by the simple and primitive to explain what only a god can know." He rose, and the harem girls did too. "Go, back to your games now," the Great King instructed, waving his hand to send them out. A matron guided them on their way and then they were gone leaving a light haze of perfume behind them. "From so many lands have they come to serve their Great King, yet it is curious how similar their folktales are. They need a new god. I intend to come back to enlighten them..."

The general and the steward looked at each other, both thinking such a scene would have been expected when his older brother was king.

"Ah, my loyal advisors. Refreshments for each of you? So what news have you?"

Now they did full bows as obeisance, for no more was required of them. "Your Royal Majesty, surely you have heard of recent events?"

"My Majesty has kept his mind on purer thoughts, my brethren, but, yes, two rumours have reached me. One is that a troop of vagabond warriors approaches, but I know you can deal with that, my General. We have our own soldiers and the Hurrians of Lawazantiya too! But I have also been told that the Great Queen has unfortunately died and her body spirited away. Some of our warriors met their end in the process. Can either of you explain how this is possible?" Despite his seeming conviviality, his face was tightening and beginning to redden.

"Wine, for both of us," said Kil-Teshub to the nearby servant. "Your Majesty?"

"Yes, fine. Who will tell me who was killed and how?" he smiled without humour.

Mahhuzzi looked about evading the king's look, which finally settled on his uncle, the Commander of the Meshedi. Kil-Teshub leaned forward to speak more quietly, "Your Majesty, the Great Queen was surely killed by the assassins we sent, but then something unexpected occurred. There seems to have been a further conflict and the guards turned on the killers. They ...ah... killed each other, unless another arrived who added to the mess. It is possible an unexpected stranger appeared and it was he who carried off the Great Queen's body."

"But who would dare...?" Suppiluliuma asked.

"In other words, you have no way of knowing what happened," Mahhuzzi intervened to Kil-Teshub. "There may have been other 'unexpected strangers', especially since it is difficult to explain how six royal guardsmen killed two assassins, also Meshedi themselves, who killed them back at the same time," he paused. "And what of the envoy from Ugarit who was here?" Mahhuzzi asked with feigned innocence.

"He is just a foolish boy without a home," dismissed Kil-Teshub. "He knows nothing about the plan I put into action."

At last the pressure reached the Great King. His voice croaked: "I ordered one simple thing be done, one act that would change everything, bring order back among the gods and fertility to the land. It was not possible to fail! This was your plan, General. What went wrong? Who intervened? If you did not like my orders, why did you not speak up? You had no hesitation in recommending we desert the holy city of Hattusa!"

"But..." Kil-Teshub began.

"O Wiseman," the king turned to his grand vizier, "I ask you who can kill Meshedi in man-to-man fighting?" Mahhuzzi was speechless. "You know the answer – only other Meshedi! And who is the commander of the Meshedi?" Again Mahhuzzi stayed silent.

"Next to your royal Majesty, I am the Commander of the Meshedi," Kil-Teshub said through a clenched jaw.

"So only Meshedi can kill Meshedi and the Meshedi obey your orders. General Kil-Teshub you have betrayed me. You gave the order for the queen's death but then you followed it with other orders to save her! You chose her over me. I have the eyes of a god. I see the hidden truth!"

"Great King, you are inventing a fiction. I have served you honourably just as I served your brother and your father before you."

"You lie, old man. Where is the Great Queen or her body? Your life and position are at stake here. If I were not about to undergo the rite of godhead, I might tend to ending your time myself."

"Great King – nephew – why would I turn on you now? I have lived sixty suns and only wish peace and order as do you. I suggest we begin to search for the Great Queen nearby at the Temple of Ishtar. We can still save the kingdom if you will only listen. We are outnumbered by the approaching troop of barbarians. We are hated here. We need only abandon this city and go on to Karkemish where you will be the Great King once again, and the Hatti will continue to rule an empire!" His hands pleaded.

"But it was you who counselled me to come here!" Mahhuzzi looked away. "You are the senior advisor. But you insisted on this city of a foreign goddess! You were wrong then and you are lying now. Mahhuzzi is my *sukkal* so his life is bound to me in sacred trust. It's unthinkable that he would betray me. You alone planned all of this. It is you who wishes to bring me down. Why? Do you wish to be Great King and marry Lieia-Hepa, if she still lives? That must be it: you love the Great Queen!"

"You are wrong!" Kil-Teshub burst out, the anger finally rising.

"I cannot be wrong: I am a god or soon will become one!" Suppiluliuma's eyes glittered as he raised his arms skyward.

"You are no god!" the tough old general thundered. "You are not even a worthy king! You are a madman who has lost his way and is now about to lose the Kingdom of the Hatti built by your ancestors!"

At that, Suppiluliuma turned white and reached for the general's throat. Kil-Teshub pushed the king back but did not reach for his dagger. Too late, the damage was done; he had violated the Great King's person. For the hand-picked Meshedi, the Great King is already a god. The nearest pair of the royal bodyguard ran toward their commander and one stuck his golden spearpoint between his ribs while the other positioned himself in front of the general to do the same. They would have speared him to death had not the Great King raised a hand and shouted to desist – but it was not an act of mercy. "Take him away and keep him alive. I will deal with him tomorrow in my own way."

As the moon rose, Lilitu the High Priestess sat alone at last with her official consort, the High Priest. "Things are moving quickly, Old One. The gods have fermented a potent brew, and they must decide amongst themselves how events will turn out here on the earthly plain. In the human present, we must do what we can to influence them to go our way, to save Lawazantiya, and to protect the Goddess."

"Clearly, ancient Ishtar is with us. Look, she brought these formidable barbarians right to us, just when we need outside agents unknown to anyone else."

"Yes, her hand is in this. We knew not how to free the Great Queen, even though the grand vizier dared to speak his own thoughts to us and not those of his role as an emissary for the Great King. He disclosed her location and the threat to her life to Zunan, her bodyguard, with whom we have met here on several occasions. But what could he have done alone? Is it not a miracle, loyal consort? In a divine intervention, rarely seen on the surface, these men appear from nowhere, somehow find the Great Queen's prison temple, kill everyone in sight..."

"Eight Meshedi!" the High Priest expostulated.

"...and break her free. Suppiluliuma knows not of these strangers. Mahhuzzi either observed the events or had spies report to him, for the message we got from him led to our sending out our young acolytes to meet the fleeing group, and their arrival here was most propitious. The Triple Goddess is indeed with us."

"Time is the tool used by the gods to work their wonders," the old priest intoned.

"We still need more miracles to get the King of the Hatti to come to our netherworld descent, so his transformation can be accomplished."

"It is as you say, High Priestess, things are flowing in the right direction. You will confer with the Wiseman again. But, if I dare ask, should I be concerned that the stated wishes of the formidable Ahhiyawa warrior to kill Suppiluliuma seem to be in conflict with ritually transforming him into a god?"

"How alert you are, father. But it seems the entrancing Queen Lieia, who has gone to take off her bloodstained garments, has begun to work Ishtar's magic upon the stranger. Unless such captivation has already been done during his time in Hattusa... We shall see what his intentions are in the morning."

After wounds were tended to the best as could be done, the three warriors were left alone and given a rare clear, residue-free wine to drink in small translucent goblets. They were expected to clean and purify themselves in the Hatti manner, but before that they were given a few minutes to rest still wearing their bloody clothes from the recent battle. The blood around his wounds had stopped flowing and, magically, his pain though still present seemed far away, so Saddirme waved away the priestly attendants who approached to take him to the healing room. He wanted a few words first, and the wine was a delicious way to wash away the bitter taste of his medicine, so good in fact he asked for refills.

"What is this, Zunan?" Diomedes asked indicating the purified wine.

Saddirme repeated in Hurrian and dared add, "He asks is it poisoned or drugged."

Zunan shrugged. "I have seen such wine drunk by royalty, nobles, and a few honoured guests. It has been filtered many times. No ill effects but smiles is all that I noticed. But in any case we have come this far, we are cornered, and we clearly share a cause with these people. We need to trust each other, so I see no reason why anyone would want to poison or drug us. I believe they would want us fully functional in good health," Zunan smiled at Diomedes and sipped, and in that moment Diomedes realized Zunan was the only other person in this city who knew about his past relations with the Great Queen. The other one who knew is with Sarpedon, but he knew not where. He felt no shame, but he did not wish to be judged for surviving when his comrades did not.

"May I ask a question?" At that moment, Kabi could no longer contain his curiosity, so Diomedes nodded. "Back in the temple where Lieia-Hepa was a prisoner, she ran to you and kissed you, and you ... *looked at each other.*

Tonight she has commanded that you dine with her, alone it seems. Could it be possible that somehow you know each other from Hattusa? Or is this territory Kabi should not be scouting?"

All eyes turned to Diomedes. "This is of no matter at the moment..." he began, but immediately realized the truth could affect everyone. He sighed, "I did not seek it, but Lieia... the Great Queen, did put me under her secret protection. She also promised to do what she could to protect my men. In exchange, if I can put it that way since one does not bargain with the Queen of the Hatti when one is a prisoner, I was required to ...participate in certain ancient rituals in honour of Ishtar. It seems she considers the Sun Goddess of Arinna to be a ... younger sister of Ishtar. They are in essence, one."

Everyone was intensely interested, so Saddirme translated quickly but found himself adding suggestive dramatic gestures to his echoed narrative. He wiggled his eyebrows lasciviously as he translated "certain ancient rituals", and licked his lips as he asked for clarification, "*Rituals in honour of Ishtar*?"

"Yes, my porcupine, just that and all that you will imagine such entails. Is this not the case, Zunan?"

"Indeed, it was my duty to escort the prisoner to and from *his* duties. If I may say so, the sacred rituals seemed to go on for quite some time and were *not* in silence." Kabi was too awestruck to see the irony. Sex with the Great Queen and High Priestess was beyond his imagination. Saddirme, however, sniggered like an adolescent.

"This private interaction ended when Suppiluliuma abruptly ordered my men beheaded. I will never know what brought that on. I don't know why, but I have not spoken with Queen Lieia-Hepa since then, but, considering how their conflict – no doubt reflecting the heavenly conflict between the Goddess of the earthly Sun and the Storm-God Teshub – has revealed itself by her imprisonment, I suspect she knew nothing about it or was unable to stop it."

"Perhaps that's why she wants to speak with you alone!" Kabi proposed, "to explain..."

"That must be it," chuckled Saddirme snapping his fingers and winking broadly while forgetting to translate.

Zunan smiled through his short steely beard. "O Ahhiyawa, I see we need to get your quill-bearing translator into the healing room while we can still move him. And, for the rest of us, it is time for our cleansing and purification ceremonies. They have attendants waiting. Afterwards, perhaps you will wish to see how Comrade Bear is faring before you attend to ... your royal duties. Kabi, you and I will rest."

3. Congress of Diomedes and Lieia-Hepa

Diomedes's cleansing was helped by a pair of brown-skinned acolytes, one male and one female, neither taller than his shoulder, who stripped down to basics, loincloths, to accommodate the process. He noted the boy was branded with a small eight-pointed star on the left side of his neck while the girl had the same brand on her left shoulder. They paused for prayer, so he stood silent. He refused the smoke purifying but enjoyed the lightly perfumed warm water wash followed by a quick four-handed oil rub. They were young but seemed to know their business, but both kept staring at him and allowing their touches to linger. He guessed it was his scars that attracted their attention until he noticed the youth stirring through his covering. He had them quickly pat him dry yet in the process the doe-eyed girl somehow managed to place herself on her knees before him, looking up at him and licking her lips while she attended to drying his genitals. He stepped away and allowed the two to dress him in fresh white priestly garments with patterned hems, giggling while doing so. Amused, he dismissed the two.

Guided by yet another priestess-to-be through labyrinthine passageways on the same underground floor, he went to check on the wounded, finding Kabi and Zunan being guided to the same place. Saying they had also been refreshed, he whispered that being renewed in the Temple of Ishtar gets very *personal*, but they only looked at him perplexed, obviously not sharing his experience.

Inside the doors, both men were found to be sleeping soundly, drugged into peace. All arrow shafts had been removed and wounds had been tightly bound; bloodstains seeped through the bindings of the wounds on Saddirme but the wounds on the chest of Eruthros were unstained. Incense burned on several shelves. Using gestures and words, Diomedes asked the older priestess in charge here if "the big one", Eruthros, was still alive, for he feared the lack of bloodstains might mean his heart had stopped from the lung wound, which he knew to be very deep. She explained with a little help from Zunan, whose native tongue was Hurrian, that the left arrow had been only a flesh wound, but to staunch the blood and seal the torn tissue from the arrowhead in the right lung required stuffing it with a special paste created by Kamrusepa, goddess of healing magic, which, she informed them, was made with appropriate spells and spiders' webs.

"A great many of them," said the healer, referring to the webs. "Luckily the bowmen used leaf-shaped arrowheads, or we may not have been able to seal it at all."

They soon left, each led by yet other followers of Ishtar. Diomedes was guided toward his destination by a pretty boy with flowers in his hair, but Zunan and Kabi were instead guided by a voluptuous and more mature lower-level priestess. Zunan whispered as they separated, "Diomedes, stay alert, not from Lieia, but from others."

As his beflowered guide took him to the door of his destination, the doyenne of the temple complex appeared from the other direction, followed by her shorter, aged consort and, as always, a group of temple servants. There must be another shorter passage from the main floor to this lower level, Diomedes concluded. "Man of Ahhiyawa, I will not question you. I honour the Great Queen's demand and realize you and she are known to each other. This could be good for Ishtar and for us. You are safe in this temple underworld for the time being, but I must warn you that when the Meshedi come to search for Lieia-Hepa, as this very night they surely will, a cord going through your room with light bells on it will be pulled as an alarm. At that moment, all lights down here must be extinguished and silence will reign. But I have come to make a demand of my own." Diomedes looked down into her black-lined luminescent grey eyes and nodded. "No matter what you hear when the royal bodyguards arrive, *you must not leave your hiding place for any of your heroics until we come for you.* The fate of the Great Queen and of Ishtar's temple itself depends on this. I have your word on this sanctified by your stern Athene. Is this not so, noble warrior?"

"It shall be as you say, High Priestess," he replied with a curt nod, admiring her natural authority. She flashed one of those smiles the lips have forgotten before they reach the eyes, and they left as abruptly as they had appeared, his pretty guide following. Suddenly, he was alone at the door. Diomedes rapped twice then simply pushed aside the thick door and walked in to face Lieia-Hepa, the Great Queen of the Hittites, the High Priestess of the Sun Goddess, and the most rapturously beautiful woman in the land.

He closed the door and bowed, but then they made eye contact. It held until they both attempted to speak at the same moment in two different languages. Flustered, the moment passed, and Lieia gestured for the warrior to sit at the low stand near to her. "How very different you look now..." she said in Luwian, reaching out to feel the finely spun wool of his white novitiate robes. "So you are becoming a priest of Ishtar?"

"So it may appear," he spoke slowly and carefully and was suddenly reminded of how rarely he had been allowed to speak in their previous encounters. "May I say, without false flattery, that you look and sound and move exactly as Mneme, Goddess Memory, has held you in my soul. You do, however, wear a different scent, though it doesn't hide the woman I remember. You remain ... enchanting even today."

Lieia now looked startled but pleased. She poured the light clear wine into a shared silver bowl with prominent curling handles and added hardly any water. They took turns sipping looking at each other over the edge. His deep, clear voice was new to her. Had he memorized this pretty speech? "How well you choose words, *Ah-kee-an*, both in your commonspeak Luwian and in what you say. So, there is no animosity between us? You may speak freely, *Di-oh-MEE-deez*, which I have learned is your name." She pronounced his name with strange inflections and the wrong emphasis, but it sounded good coming from her lips in any case. He was recognized as a person.

"My lady, my honesty about your beauty does not indicate I will be dishonest about everything else. *Animosity*? Let's investigate. I am no threat to you, Great Queen," he paused, "for we find ourselves facing the same enemy, but I am not your subject either. I am a warrior without a homeland who belongs to no one, so I now choose to speak freely. I owe loyalty to no one but to my beheaded comrades, and that is why Suppiluliuma must die."

She found herself tensing and beginning to worry, for this expressive, direct, and perhaps even ruthless side of him was new to her. What was he going to do? She sought to mollify him by assuring him that she knew nothing of the killing until it was done. Suppiluliuma had been informed she had been having at least one or maybe more of the Ahhiyawa prisoners brought to her in private. She had assured him that they were used in sacrificial rites to appease the demands of the Sun Goddess of Earth. Some blood flowed until they were broken, begged for mercy, and gladly worshipped the Goddess, but that was all. "He knew of my ancient rituals and he fears the dark goddess, so he asked no more and seemed to accept my explanation. But soon after that, my attendant Zunan brought me the news of the executions..."

"Beheadings without ritual or burial are not *executions*, Lieia, they are murders!"

"Yes, you are right. The king had it done this way to dishonour them, thinking he was dishonouring you." Few ever called her by her given name, but it felt good. She let the intimacy of its use seep into her. "I... I feared you after that for my control over you was gone. I dared not take any more chances with your life or with mine, so I never sent for you again. I did have Zunan and his trusted allies make sure you were kept alive and well-treated, and, as we departed, I had him open your prison door. You were well-treated, were you not?"

"Well enough, my lady. Your story is believed. If you were behind the murders, you would surely have had me beheaded, as well. And now I am here with you again. What now?" He looked at her and she at him and again an intimate knowledge was shared between them. But the recent talk had brought tension. She did not know this forceful man and she realized he was no longer hers to command, so an awkwardness set in.

"What now?" she arched a brow. "I suggest we have the temple servants bring us our dinner..."

Diomedes looked at her from head to toe, at her mysterious dark eyes, her purple lips, the curve of her long neck, her bare shoulders, her half-revealed bosom rising and falling with each breath. He remembered submitting to her whipping. He rose to his feet, dropping his priestly robe, and stated, "I think not."

This was new to Lieia, but she found herself thrilled, especially when the man walked over to her and embraced her tightly, pressing himself against her thin layers of cloth with their jewelled embellishments. Still, part of her resisted the implied effrontery. "What are you doing?" she snapped, and put her hands on his arms as though to push him away.

"*Lieia...*" Diomedes said and lifted her chin to look into her eyes. There were only the two of them, no gods, no obligations, no observers. Her resistance evaporated as their eyes flowed into each other like two rivers merging to become one, their mouths also meeting and merging. Such sudden and complete immersion in each other had never happened before, yet it felt so familiar, as though it were the discovery of a long-lost treasure they had nearly forgotten.

They kissed fully, inside each other yet again, and he began to work at her complex clasps, broaches, and wrappings. Instead he ceased and spoke, "Come, show me," he said. He whisked her from her feet and carried her to the bed. She did not resist.

He sat down and gazed with adoration at the tantalizing vision of the Great Queen of the Hittites carefully unlatching and unclasping her fine wool outer garments, which she let fall to the floor. She caught and held his eyes, recognizing once again her seductive powers and their obvious effects on the naked man observing her. Last, she unveiled the transparent filaments of even finer yellow sea silk from her light brown body, leaving her other jewellery intact, including the bracelets and the golden chain around her waist.

"I have you," she whispered, and beguilingly put one knee on the bed between his legs, wrapping her arms with their coiled snakes around his neck and pulling him smoothly but firmly against her red-tipped breasts. He did not resist but instead leapt into her offering, smothering his smooth face on the still-firm orbs, licking them and her armpits with a hungry tongue. Such crude bestial passion was never part of the sexual rituals she had learned, but she too was swept away by it. When he returned to her breasts, pushing them together and biting both her rouged nipples at once, she succumbed. He looked up into her eyes as the painful pleasure ran through her, as though giving notice that in their dance of love no one was in command.

They fell onto the bed wrapping around each other like the vipers of the Medusa's hair. They wrestled and each one won. Their bodies played games of control, taking turns in conquest and submission. She took his hair and pulled his head down to her belly, so he could touch her sex with his hands. Then lifting her knees she forcefully directed his head to her dripping lower lips. Diomedes did not hesitate but prolonged his approach before again tasting her excited moisture. He circled then suckled on her pleasure nub and while he teased it with his tongue, he entered her smoothly with his digits and she experienced preliminary shudders. Lost in pleasure, she wrapped her thighs around his head and turned them both over, somehow emerging astride his face and ruthlessly thrusting her hips back and forth lost in sensation. When she paused, he lifted her body into the air and onto her back, so he could return to her breasts. She laughed with delight at the joy of being handled so easily. While he squeezed and bit her nipples, she raked her nails across his back, drawing blood. The crown of his member teased open her flooded lower lips, but he entered no further. The gale was unleashed and both joyfully submitted to being storm-tossed and beyond control. All ritual performances were forgotten as ancient instincts released themselves, yet it was a power struggle in which both were the defeated and the victors.

Lieia half-expected he would seek to show her that he was not a pet of Ishtar to willingly submit to her enchantments and punishments, but as she rose back up and pulled his head back to bite his neck, he gratefully accepted the gift. As she raked him again, he closed his eyes but it was not in pain. The Akhaian savoured the sensations indiscriminately. The joy of power rose up in her and she grinned like a leopard, but just as she was wondering what she might use as a whip she found herself being effortlessly lifted again and gently placed over the man's naked thighs. The dance had shifted, and she was now exposed and at his mercy. A deep lower pleasure at being in someone else's power rose like a memory as he held her in place with one big hand. He ran his other hand up and down her legs, at first softly then more firmly, caressing her white buttocks and inner thighs, the caress becoming a grip. He squeezed and slapped the white mounds and she gasped in shock at the humiliation. The shame of such indignity to her royal behind was about to drive her to end the dance in protest, but she heard her voice cry out in pleasure and realized her helpless descent. She gasped when he at last slid two thick fingers into the centre of the wet throbbing heat between her legs then withdrew and spread the natural lubricant around. She bucked smoothly up and down as he inserted his thumb into her wet second orifice and two fingers back into the wetter one beyond. She moaned, feeling his hardened excitement pushing into her belly.

She found herself sliding to the floor on her knees. The queen looked up at the vascular man, sweating and breathing deeply in the flickering shadows of the candle. She opened her mouth in awe just as she realized he was pulling her head between his thighs. Her opened mouth took in the head of his phallus. She was unable to pull away for he had his hand behind her head that instead pulled her forward. Her mouth was engulfed but she avoided panic by breathing through her nose. She had never done this unsanctioned act, certainly the ultra-clean and puritanical Hittites never portrayed it or talked of it, though she had heard harem girls of eastern origin whisper or giggle of it. She felt obscenely conquered and was thrilled to experience it. She felt his throbbing member grow in size within her mouth and her sense of herself as queen and priestess deserted her entirely. She looked at him in adoration, but then the leopard in her acted.

She leapt back onto the bed and threw him on his back with feral strength and mounted him in a kind of frenzied assault. She slid him into her but found that, despite her gushing excitement, she could only take the head of his rigid organ into her. Slowly she tried to work its way deeper, but its size was not what she was accustomed to, and her vaginal portal tightened with anxiety. In that moment, he rolled her over and pinned her arms, and she was grateful for choice being taken from her. Ishtar's shameless eroticism possessed her and she opened to the man. A flood of moisture and desire decided the issue, and Lieia grasped the man's hard buttocks with her talons and pulled him suddenly, smoothly, in an ecstasy of pain, deeply into her.

"I am in you," he gasped in joy, and she knew he meant more than carnally. She knew his daimonion and welcomed it to merge with her soul.

She had never permitted herself to submit in spirit to anyone in her life, though she had acted that way in the ritual performances with her royal husband. Otherwise, as an aspect of the Goddess, she had found great pleasure in getting men, boys, and girls to submit to her, to perform for her, to suffer the ritual abasement, even to bleed in sacred sacrifice to Ishtar. Being taken was as yet unimagined, and she found herself giving in to the demands of the man like a loving servant submitting in joy to her master's desire. Yet there was no indignity to it, for beneath it all, they were immersed together, lost within each other in the wild rhythm of an ancient dance. With full abandon and perfect trust, they were savage beasts on the hunt and each was the willing victim. They were entangled beyond self-awareness in a dynamic pulse of mystical participation, tearing each other to pieces to become one.

The dance of the beast with two backs began. At last, she wrapped her legs about him and, face to face, they found a rhythmic drumbeat and followed it, slowing or speeding, for a long while in the shadowy room. She felt a familiar sensation arising in her but it only pretended to reach a peak. Instead it would pause and keep rising again, more intense than she had ever known. She was beyond realizing that what she felt was not hers alone. He felt her rising excitement as his own and together they fell into a prolonged abyss of throbbing climactic waves of ecstasy.

"Ah me, I die," she moaned in bliss, and the man moaned in full release, as well.

All was dark and quiet. Nothing existed. They breathed. Then at last they sighed and hugged each other. Lieia found herself sobbing, yet she had never felt happier. She felt she had rediscovered the perfect jewel of life, though she had no memory of ever knowing it in this lifetime. He exhaled and they fell into blissful contentment.

He whispered, "What god possessed us? Or are we savages?"

She sighed back, "Savagery is beautiful." Then they embraced without thoughts lost in the cosmic flow.

After a bit, Diomedes arose and poured out a draught of the lively wine into their shared chalice and brought it to the bed. They each drank a thirsty swallow in turn, but then their eyes caught each other and they spontaneously drank together at the same moment, each holding one of the extended handles and lightly bumping foreheads in doing so. A mutual giggle of pure joy arose in them. He put down the kylix (as his people called it), and they shared a look as though seeing one another in each other for the first time. He pulled her to him and they began the ancient ritual of love all over again, this time more slowly and tenderly.

At last they fell into blissful peace, exhausted and apart then coming together when she lay her head on his chest and shoulder, wrapping her limbs like coils around him. Nothing was said, but both knew something significant had happened. Like ripples around two thrown stones in a pond, their boundaries no longer deflected each other but overlapped and merged while keeping their individual forms. Their passion had led them beyond mere animal lust but also beyond the rituals of humanity. Their worlds had collided but merged, their trajectories becoming entangled in a way that is known, it seemed, only to lovers in mythic tales. A keen sense of mutual destiny pervaded the air around them, along with the musky scent of sex.

At that moment, a light tinkling of bells was heard. It seemed to suit the moment, so at first neither caught its meaning. The bells grew more insistent and pervasive until they understood and went silent. The Akhaian bestirred himself to look for his sword or a spear when he realized he had none with him. Lieia leapt from the bed, smothered the torch and blew out the candles. In the sudden blackness, she led him back to bed. A loud banging on the main temple doors above could be clearly heard even from where they were, two floors below. Members of the royal bodyguard and other troops had arrived and were demanding entry to search for the Great Queen of the Hatti, their spear butts battering the wooden portals.

Diomedes tried to rise but Lieia reminded him of the urgent instructions of Lilitu the High Priestess and pulled him back to her. He realized she was right, so they held each other in total darkness and alertly listened.

Loud voices were heard indicating entry had been gained. They could just hear the muffled voices. The Meshedi in charge barked out orders and loud footsteps spread out in all directions. Then the voice of the silver-haired High Priestess rang out, demanding further explanation. Indistinct words were exchanged, growing louder, a barked warning from the chief intruder. Then there was a bump and a surprised scream as a body fell to the floor. It was Lilitu, but the imperious tone she used to the captain of the guard meant she had risen again. Parts of her enraged sentences could be heard. Then the angry voice of an old man, likely the High Priest, shouted out demonic curses – curses on anyone who would assault his wife the High Priestess, curses upon Teshub the Storm-God, and curses upon Suppiluliuma the Great King. It was the last that must have enraged the Meshedi captain, for it was followed by a thump, a cry, a thud on floor, and then silence. A cultivated, rational voice could be heard through the ventilation channels commiserating with the guardsman. "...no need for such violence..." Lieia recognized it as that of Mahhuzzi the chief steward.

The thumping and banging spread out from the centre to all around the great temple as the searchers went from room to room. There was the occasional scream as guardsmen pushed or otherwise touched an acolyte or priestess. Lieia could imagine them going up the circular stone staircase into the tower where lay many ancient treasures, but they would not find her there. They did find the bolted door to what seemed to them the only lower floor. In actulity, this was the floor above the lovers, but they found nothing there but kitchens, servants' quarters, and storage rooms. There was no sign of lower floors and the door they had come through was the only one.

It became louder then quieter. There remained occasional voices and the sound of movement. They knew they had been told to do nothing and stay out of sight. The others had almost certainly received the same admonition. Then all noise ceased, but who knew how many guardsmen remained about? They would be fetched when it became safe for them to rise to the surface and strike back.

The tension above could not overcome the wonder each felt over the unexpected miracle that had just occurred between them. They were two very different individuals from conflicting worlds so far apart they could barely speak to one another, yet they had discovered the depths of soul as one. As time passed, they dissolved into the ultimate blackness and began to haltingly speak of what it all meant and how it all began. Diomedes recited one version of the Hellenic creation myth in which all was *non-existence* as Primal Khaos, the timeless void. Eros appeared within it, thus Khaos gave birth to the triplets of being: Ouranos, the vault of the heavens, Gaia, the earth, and Tartarus, the grim underworld below. At this Lieia giggled. "Once Khaos is divided, it becomes the Triple Goddess – so ... *organized*!"

"Yes, but now I finally understand how love – Eros – can appear out of nowhere," and they smiled unseen. "Have you a better tale of creation?"

"Indeed I have," she whispered intently, "listen..." nuzzling close to his ear:

> "Alalus was king in heaven, but Anus became more powerful. He served as Alalus's cupbearer for nine years and then defeated him, dispatching him to under the earth. He took his seat on the throne and made Kumarbis his cupbearer. Likewise, after nine years Kumarbis rebelled. He chased Anus and bit off and swallowed his phallus, which joined the previously swallowed Storm-God within Kumarbis. However, Anus had revenge by impregnating Kumarbis with the swallowed member. The rest of Anus hid himself in heaven, from where he advised the Storm-God, Teshub, on how to exit Kumarbis, that is, via his butt hole. After causing the monster Kumarbis much pain, the Storm-God slid through the lower channel in a messy and painful birth. Together, Storm-God (after considerable ritual cleansing) and Anus plotted to destroy Kumarbis and, with other gods, apparently succeeded."

Diomedes could no longer bear it and succumbed to muffled laughter. She put a hand over his lips to stifle the sound. Lieia knew the old tale was absurd but mockery seemed scandalous. "The ways of the gods are not meant for our understanding."

"Surely the gods can laugh too. Perhaps they laugh at our myths about them! " He explained how many of the names she used translated into Akhaian. She understood, and the two tried to suppress their mirth by holding each other's mouth shut.

The lovers stretched out in the perfect dark and held each other as one, with the head of the man finally at rest, facing Lieia's breast, its crown nestled in her armpit, and her arm wrapped around it. They fell into a deep shared sleep only awakening before dawn to make love once again. Somehow, even in this extreme crisis, the world seemed far away from what was happening between them.

A tap came to their door. Diomedes draped a sheet over him and answered. The same pair of bright-eyed youths who had bathed him earlier brought them fresh water and a lit candle, announcing it was morning, which could not be seen here, two floors down. The High Priestess has called a meeting, they said. Yes, finding nothing, the guardsmen had departed. Lieia rose naked and taking the candle from one of the visitors lit the central candle and others. The visitors closed the door but waited outside.

The two looked at one another with both surprise and pleasure. *Surprise* because they had never seen each other in the light with the changed perspectives they now had. It was like awakening from an intense, vivid dream to find the dream was real. Neither spoke. Diomedes poured them each water to drink and cleansed himself at the water basin. He dragged the queen's comb through his messy waves of hair. While she washed, he pulled on the white robes of the candidate priest and prepared to leave. Lieia the Queen of the Hatti demanded to come too, but he reminded her that she was the object of the guardsmen's search and the fewer who knew she was here the safer she would be.

"I will be disguised," she laughed and took up the hooded priestess robe that had been left for her. "Now, warrior, accompany your queen to the meeting place."

He smiled, accepting that she would not be thwarted, and they left together. The two who came to them guided them through twisting corridors, already being lit again by torches. They followed them through a narrow passage, then beyond a false front door. There, by candlelight alone, the two youths led the lovers up the bronze ladder attached to what looked like the walls of an abandoned well to where they emerged through the same trapdoor in the hidden grove outside, now lit by the morning sun. They entered the servants' ground-level floor with a secret knock and they were inside the upper temple once again. Thence they were brought to the private chambers of the High Priestess where she was intently conferring toe to toe with Mahhuzzi.

Their guides disappeared and, after perfunctory greetings, Diomedes and Lieia were told that the guardsmen had found no sign of their prey and had left. Mahhuzzi had led them to the Temple of Ishtar, but they were not under his control. He stayed when they left.

"Great Queen," said the vizier who fell onto both knees. He rose without command.

"It is good to see the Great Queen of the Hatti is safe, and you too, Ahhiyawa," stated Lilitu with only a nod.

"I am here," Lieia affirmed, chin up.

"We are well," Diomedes spoke. "But now it is time to strike back."

Mahhuzzi glanced at the couple, dressed in similar simple robes, standing close with arms pressed against each other, and understood the situation. "Though there has been death and serious injury, we have survived this so far, but this is not the time to act rashly. As the gods know, timing is everything and the thoughtful mind will win the day over the strongest arm. The High Priestess and I have agreed that a version of the plan you outlined will surely win the approval of the gods, so it is there we can begin."

"Mahhuzzi, O Wiseman, so you really are with us?" Diomedes asked suspiciously.

Mahhuzzi studied him with equal caution but also with curiosity. "You are clearly no priest. You are neither Hatti nor Hurrian, yet you do look familiar."

"I am Diomedes, once a king among the Ahhiyawa. I remember you well. You may have known of me as the imprisoned warrior in Hattusa who sparred with guards."

"Ah! You were the one who was kept separately and escaped the Great King's order of execution, or so my sources told me. So the Ahhiyawa warrior amongst us is you. Yes, I am on the side of the Great Queen, too. It is a mystery how you kept your head," he ventured, "but your appearance with Lieia-Hepa explains a great many things."

"*Diomeedes*," Lilitu spoke his personal name for the first time, mispronouncing the syllabic emphasis in the same way Leia had, "it *is* time to strike back. Fetch your fellow warriors and then all return here. Yes?"

"We have little time," Mahhuzzi spoke up, "but if we are to undertake this daring venture, might I suggest that bringing his warriors here will lead to drawing unnecessary attention to us and take away the element of surprise from attacking the temple of the Storm-God. Even if it is only a feint, you'll have to use all your strength and skills to survive the Meshedi's golden spears in battle formation, so I suggest you go directly there instead, just after the sun's zenith. But the weak point of our wild plan lay in the future. Say, by some divine miracle, we do get Suppiluliuma away from his bodyguards and bring him here. What next? With the Great King disappeared, it may be possible to convince General Kil-Teshub, if he still lives, to take the Hittite regiment that's here to some other place where they will be gratefully received as support troops under a new Great King, but all this would take a divine miracle. And what then? Who will protect us from the approaching troop of warriors?"

"Divine miracles are my province," said Lilitu without humour. "If the Hatti soldiers remain, there will be battle, and, no matter who wins, Lawazantiya will lose. If the uninvited Hatti leave, *approaching warriors* will always be our problem, as they were before. Anyone can see our world is crumbling; it has been doing so for years. Bands of brigands control the roads, so trade has all but ceased. Cities everywhere have become victims of rapine and ruin.

We hear of another one falling each day. It was hoped these Hittite soldiers would help fortify us but instead they attempted to take over, putting Teshub in power over Shaushka. Yet if they leave, who will face those invaders who come? I pray they are headed for the sea and so leave us alone."

"I think it quite likely they are my own ... people," Diomedes added. "If so, I know I can talk to them, offer a third choice and try to negotiate with them to pass us by in exchange for gifts."

"Ishtar has sent another idea to me," the High Priestess spoke, drawing back her silvery locks over her smooth bare shoulders. "There may be a fourth choice..."

Diomedes was guided back along the serpentine pathway – down and out and in and around – to the secret floor below. He paid close attention to remember the way but remained uncertain he had done so. The attendant banged on a door and stood back. The door was opened by Zunan who gave the man in the priestly robes a double glance before recognizing him with a greeting and pulling him inside to greet Kabi. "All is well with the queen?" Lieia-Hepa's bodyguard asked what was foremost in his mind.

"All is well. We stayed hidden all night, as directed, as did you, it appears."

"Yes," said Kabi with some excitement, "but we heard big trouble above. We are going to see? Remember, I have a mission to ride west to meet the oncoming troop!"

"Yes, we have been called by the Great Queen, the High Priestess, and the Great King's loyal Wiseman, Mahhuzzi, who seems to have wisely switched his loyalty to the Great Queen." Diomedes explained what he knew as they prepared.

Both men were dressed in their former attire, which had been cleaned overnight, Kabi tying on his leather headband and letting the tail thongs hang down his back. Kabi also showed the Akhaian his own renewed clothing, which he was relieved to wear again. The three put on their armour and arms, helping each other with straps and latches for breastplates and greaves. Zunan thrust his war hatchet and dirk into his belt and picked up his spear. Kabi had only a leather corslet with no bronze plating over his tunic and no greaves but took up his long dagger, a quiver of arrows, and strung the bow across his chest. Diomedes found his mighty Sherden sword in its leather sheath and strapped it over his shoulder and across his chest. No one had a helmet or shield.

"Plans are being furthered above by three cunning minds. We must go back into the light to learn of our damaged friends and play our part in what unfolds. I think we are about to strike back. Zunan," Diomedes spoke to the veteran soldier, "I hope with the Great Queen safe that you continue fighting with us." Zunan smiled and nodded.

On return, the High Priestess informed them that the other two were recovering well but should remain here for now. She described how the Meshedi and other soldiers had torn through the upper rooms but found nothing, but a great sacrilege had been committed by the captain of the guardsmen who had pushed the High Priestess from her feet and then, worse, struck the High Priest between the eyes with the butt of his spear so hard it left him bloody and unconscious.

"Will your consort survive?" Zunan asked.

"Zunan, my Hurrian friend," she nodded to him, "my *consort* – my father and formally my son and husband – remains dead to the world. His ears are dripping blood, but we pray he will come round and return to us. He is being tended to."

Kabi looked confused, so Lilitu quickly explained, "By blood, he is my father but gave up his fathering ability when he became High Priest of Ishtar. It is by the ritual order of the Goddess that he is now honoured also in the roles of my son and husband."

"No matter," interrupted Diomedes impatiently. "Now is the time to get to the Great King while most of the royal guardsmen are likely to remain away from the Temple of the Storm-God. I will be dishonoured until vengeance is taken upon him for his cowardly murder of my helpless comrades. Right now, he may yet be asleep!"

"That will only get you killed. Do you not recall the scheme you yourself first laid out that has been conveyed to me by Lilitu the Priestess?" Mahhuzzi looked up at the man no longer in white priestly robes but truly a warrior once again. "If you act with only two men – since the scout will be gone – as mighty as you are, you will be killed. You need to follow our plan, so I can get to the king and spirit him away. You must not kill him on sight, even if you get the chance."

"Now we are known to each other and have sworn trust, so we can act as one. Ishtar watches and waits." Lilitu took charge and swiftly issued directives. All listened intently. "Diomedes, you will take Zunan and gather your men from the lower town and lead an assault, a distraction, on the temple of the Storm-God. Setting this up will take all morning. You will begin your attack one hour after the Sun Goddess reachers her apogee. Do you understand? If you kill Suppiluliuma merely for your personal vengeance, disaster will follow. Lawazantiya will be destroyed and, though you may not care, the devotions to Ishtar will be lost. More important for you is that you will lose Queen Lieia in the chaos. This I foresee. Best for all is that Suppiluliuma complete his journey to the Underworld. He will then either become one with a god and rise again into the heavens, if he is worthy, or he will be utterly destroyed, as will his soul and his ancestry. The line of Hittite Great Kings that have oppressed all others since time immemorial will be ended."

"This shall be done," Diomedes concurred. But if he got his hands on the Great King he was not certain what he would do.

"*Di-OM-eh-deez,*" Mahhuzzi hesitated on the name but said it correctly. "I have reasons to rush too. Suppiluliuma plans to have my rival and friend, General Kil-Teshub, executed for treachery he did not commit. It is I who has turned against the king, so the general is dying in my stead. I wish to intervene, if possible. The Great King does holy rituals of purification and supplication all the morning through, but I suspect that just after the sun's apex, he will be eager to torture his second-in-command."

"What matter if the Hittite royal family kills each other?" Lilitu snapped. "As long as we can keep the unholy king alive until we bring him here." She looked at Diomedes.

"While the lawless warriors are being collected, you, O Wiseman, must go back to the Temple of the Storm-God and, following the king's morning rituals, undertake a most arduous mission. This should begin just after the heavenly Sun Goddess reaches her height. So you have an hour to succeed before the fighters of Diomedes arrive and bring the chaos that should allow you to slip away with the king and bring him alone here. You must get him alone to convince him that his taking the time to destroy his uncle the general is a distraction from the much greater task of seeking the liberation of his soul and the return of life to the lands of the Hatti. Soiling his hands with murder may endanger his metamorphosis into a god. You will remind the mad king that his glorious apotheosis awaits, but you must bring him alone and he must submit fully to the ritual. Perhaps that will give your general a reprieve. I shall make preparations for the future god's arrival and the ritual of descent." There was a pause.

"The king plans to execute our noble and brave war leader and commander of the Meshedi?" Zunan, once a Meshedi himself, was shocked. "General Kil-Teshub has always been loyal to the Great King. This is twisted. Will the Meshedi allow this?"

"Ah, our Great Queen's protector," Mahhuzzi smiled at the man and changed the topic. "So far, our little resistance movement has shown surprising results. The queen is here and safe, and we have unexpectedly gained a number of formidable allies. Maybe more, maybe not. So far the gods are with us. What lay ahead is unknown, but we too must be noble and brave so the gods will choose to weigh the scales of destiny in our favour by finding us worthy." Everyone was in agreement and had jobs to do, so the circle disintegrated.

The three warriors were shown the way to the ladder up the empty well where the attendant left them to their own devices. They emerged in the grove and made their way behind the temples once again. They readily scrambled down the cliff in spite of the steep incline and sharp rocks. Kabi noticed crows still gathered below the large boulder where they had left their former guide. Once at the base, it was Kabi who remembered the way back to their lower town haunts. Near the marketplace they encountered a run-down stable where their silver shekels or iron ingots would come into play.

Diomedes spoke to Kabi. "We will find you a fast steed. If you discover the approaching troops are strangers but still inland sea peoples, you must play the envoy and try to parley with them, exaggerate our numbers, and get them to agree to come here and accept gifts in exchange for peace before they continue to the Great Green. If they are unknown hostiles who attack you, ride back as fast as your horse will carry you to warn us. But the odds are that the troop will be a breakaway part of our Aegean comrades heading for the sea who will know you on sight. If so, it will be led by Sarpedon or Payava or both, so I now give you words to share with them, a civilized offer from Lilitu the High Priestess, for them all, but it can only come into effect once we have rid ourselves of the Hittite forces, if the gods so will. Since the future is not known to us, I would keep this secret, but if they wish to share the offer with the others, so it will be. Hopefully, you can return here before they do with their answer, but if they are already too close, all will be revealed when you arrive together. Clear so far?" It was clear and the secret offer was memorized. Onwards they went to buy or, if necessary, steal a horse for the scout, even though it was not likely to be a racer.

4. *–Prelude: The Triple Goddess*

The High Priestess of Ishtar sat with Lieia-Hepa to tell her of Ishtar and the source of all gods in the timeless vessel of the Mother of Gods herself. "Not all can be revealed, for ancient mysteries are not to be spoken of, especially in the light of day, as you yourself know. We high priestesses are to lead Suppiluliuma past the gatekeeper and into the mouth of Irkalla, and hence to take him through the seven gates on the ritual Descent of Inanna to the Underworld. Have you led this yourself, Lieia-Hepa?"

"The Descent of Inanna is well-known to every priestess or priest of the Great Goddess, for it is the founding revelation of the godhead. But, I, like most, only know of the sacred myth, recited in temples in secret ceremonies. I have led such sacred recitations and in our hearts we re-experienced the fearful descent and blessèd return to the light, but, no, I have never bodily entered the forbidden Underworld of death below the dark Earth. The rituals which I led were always in honour of the Sun Goddess of Earth whom we know as Arinniti and you as Shaushka, but similar rituals of death and possible rebirth were also done in honour of Pirinkir and even Telipinu, who some say may act as a guide for the lost souls descending into the land of no return. We did not use the title of Ishtar in Hattusa."

"Great Queen Lieia, these goddesses are helpful illusions for they are all paradoxical aspects of the Great Goddess herself who cannot be named, for she is neither a person nor a god. She is *not a being* within the world but she is both the wet clay bowl and the ever-spinning cosmic potter's wheel that keeps it in motion. She is the wheel of time forever keeping the clay bowl in the process of reshaping herself. She is the vessel within which all beings are born and die, ever-changing but always herself.

"No matter how diverse the gods seem to be, they all exist as but reflections of her divine essence as distorted through the mirrors of our minds. The Great Mother does not *rule,* for she is both order and chaos, love and hate, creation and destruction, life and death, leaving nothing to *rule over*. Ishtar and sometimes Inanna manifest their presence in this temple, but she herself is neither man nor woman but both and she encompasses the sky and the heavens beyond, as well as the earth and the netherworld below that. The world is but one aspect of her being, but she is also non-being. The Great Goddess can only exist as many changing, often paradoxical manifestations. She is herself the eternal shapeshifting clay of change, but she is also the dynamic dance that renders being into nonbeing."

Lilitu sniffed in the rising fumes from a strange powder in a copper bowl heated by candle flame and breathed in deeply. Her pupils enlarged and she stared into vistas unseen by others.

"For eons humanity had experienced itself, like all animals, as part of the *great round*, the self-nurturing, self-consuming ouroboros of nature. In this wheel of light and darkness, life spontaneously emerges from within Earth, and thence it grows and reproduces itself as each form, beast, or plant struggles to maintain its existence. Though each life inevitably ends in death, dissolving back into Earth, the cosmic game is itself eternal. For meaning-seeking humanity, the continuation of this endless cycle depends on the guidance by the gods of the upper realms on earth and in the heavens beyond; it necessitates the deathly yet deathless existence of chthonic deities of the dark realm below the earth where forms of life are dissolved, and souls may be held forever or returned to life again in new forms.

"The eternal return, the dance of existence back into non-existence with new existence ever emerging, is a mystery beyond comprehension but was almost universally experienced as the Great Mother who inexplicably gives life and just as mysteriously takes back again. She is imagined as a woman but in herself is beyond all women. She is the creatrix as hermetic vessel of transformation, but she did not create the vessel – she *is* the vessel; she herself *is* the great round. In all times and places, humanity has given expression to the pre-self experience of this image of the apperceived cycle of birth, life, and death – the Triple Goddess – hope, suffering, and horror. Since before time was known, the Great Goddess has inspired numerous artistic or symbolic representations though she herself is beyond all images, all concepts, all opposites, and thus even beyond all gods. She is beyond good and evil just as this blind paradox manifests as nature itself.

"Within her, are the many gods, spirits, and demons that haunt the world and the spaces in between, once real because they were experienced as felt presences. Every animal is a spirit and every plant, too, as well as natural phenomena like the wind. Each cavern or tunnel is a gateway to the Underworld, just as every mountain and treetop leads to the firmament of stars, sun, and moon where rain is made. Though often hidden, the gods inhabit the world among us and the realms above, below, and within us too. We are made in their image on earth, so our actions reciprocally affect them too. We must propitiate them in ritual and adoration, and submit ourselves to their power to keep life going. We must support the natural order lest it dissolve forever back into its original chaos of disorder and self-annihilation. We must renew the gods in order for them to renew the world. Since rulers keep their power by the will of the gods, they position themselves as intermediaries between humanity and divinity, so the people need them just as we need the many gods.

"However, the Triple Goddess herself precedes and will succeed humanity so needs no devotees, though women are her natural manifestation. Women were seen as the avatars of the mystery of parthenogenetic creation. Before our first ancestors from the dawn time within nature learned to plant grain and herd animals, the precise paternity of newborns was unknown. Women alone brought forth new life, so, though not rulers, they were likely to be cultural arbiters since they manifested the great mystery of creation. This may have left ambitious men feeling themselves as outsiders in the miraculous great round, perhaps even as mere drones. Once fatherhood was discovered, patriarchal ownership soon followed. Animals were owned and bred, just as marriage was invented and women became owned by men. Rule by power and authority began. Before then, there was no *matriarchy*, for there was no *-archy* of political rule and social enforcement. The Great Goddess *is* the ever-present, ever-recurring cycle of time, the ouroboros: she has no need to rule, she just *is*. Tribes lived in the sacred anarchy of nature's eternal return guided by animal spirits and shamanic visionaries both male and female. Her rituals to continue life with the sacrificial blood of death were not based in domination or conquest but felt necessity. Death brings life just as life brings death.

"It was men who first turned the tools of the hunt on each other. With weapons, they first began to rule by force. Rule, along with organized warfare, was the invention of competing alliances among the men, who soon were competing against other tribes for territory and women. It should be no surprise that at this moment, time and territory began to be measured. Male hero gods declared they had vanquished the primal woman monster and were now the rulers of the heavens. The sacred time of eternal recurrence could not be abolished any more than men could abolish death, but such time was relegated to annual rituals and festivals. Now, fallen, profane time was organized and measured, and worship of the Great Earth Mother was suppressed in favour of thundering sky gods and *heroic* violent warrior priest-kings who changed the past by replacing matrilineal with patrilineal ancestry and controlled the future by class hierarchy and force. Warrior-kings dreamed of overcoming death by gaining such glory and wealth their fame would be immortal.

"The Great Mother as time's relentless cycle cannot be destroyed, of course, but her life-transcendent mystery has become fragmented into many divergent goddesses – her paradoxical aspects dispersed, her uncanny essence diminished into many gods. Priests or scribes see only the parts while shamans and artists see the whole. The Triple Goddess is present in all gods, perhaps especially where single gods have gained prominence, but she identifies with none, for she is the paradoxical whole, not a part, even when she is later named as the first goddess. She is neither the transcendent creator nor among the created, but *is* herself the immanent ongoing dance of creation and destruction, the death within life and the life within death.

"On the human plane of being, only the most privileged of humanity can read the wishes or needs of the immortal gods and serve their demands. Only the kings and priests, originally the same thing, inherit the divine inspiration to lead the mass of people in such vital rituals and sacrifices and to accept their gifts on behalf of the immortals. They and the other nobles use those gifts and their sacred status to build temples as earthly homes for the gods and palaces within walled cities for themselves. They spread their largesse to support artists and artisans, builders who construct icons, symbolic representations, sculpted images, or idols so the gods can enter them and be among us for a time. All benefitted from the sacred order of things."

She held the bowl over the candle until it melted and began to bubble and again breathed deeply of the divine fumes.

"It was in this way that power on earth was achieved when great cities were built by the most successful local tribes, and those cities controlled ever larger territories by defeating or absorbing other such cities. Soon these became kingdoms with glorious palaces that warred against other such kingdoms until the victor led an ever-expanding empire with central authority that, like the pillars of heaven, supported the realms of the gods, which unsurprisingly supported the palace kingdoms in return. The establishment, over time, of such vast empires soon led to rivalries with other such centralized empires and war has become a way of life, not only among the empires but also among the smaller kingdoms within them or caught between them.

War has proved to be very costly for such empires, many human resources have been lost, and losing their kingdoms and their lives was always a possibility for the kings. Most unsettling is that in war, the order of things – religious, political, economic – is shaken. Trade flourishes when war does not, so when in the ancient Land of Two

Rivers and that of the Nile and even in those around our Great Green Sea, writing in hieroglyphics or cuneiform made record-keeping and communications possible among such empires. Diplomacy and at least the pretence of mutual respect revealed a more beneficial manner of supporting the continuity of their cosmic organization. If the empires could communicate, intermarry, and advance trade, everyone benefitted. The order of things seemed to become universal. Many regional kingdoms have appeared and disappeared, but only a few Great Kingdoms or true empires have arisen, and they are an elite group. I have a copy of a communication that one of the Great Kings of the Hittites wrote to a vassal-king instructing him on what is expected of him in terms of other Great Kings:

> 'If the King of Egypt is My Majesty's friend, he shall be your friend. But if he is My Majesty's enemy, he shall be your enemy. And the Kings who are my equals in rank are the King of Egypt, the King of Babylonia, the King of Assyria and the King of the Ahhiyawa.'

"But the Great Goddess is ultimately subdued neither by human power nor the many gods we believe control us. Nature has its own cycles which we humans can at worst exacerbate and at best ameliorate. When natural catastrophes occur, whether prolonged or sudden, we poor humans don't know where to turn for deliverance or who to blame if such deliverance is not forthcoming. Whether it's the more gradually appearing extremes of the weather gods like drought or more sudden occurrences like vulcanism, earthquakes, tidal waves, or floods, it's beyond human control and thus the gods themselves seem unable to help."

Once again, the High Priestess, her face reddening as she received and reported her visions, breathed deeply of the fumes from the bowl. "The people speak," she sighed.

"As we can clearly see these last years, it must be concluded that the gods have ceased to support the order of things that favour life and well-being. And if the gods are withdrawing their good will, who are we to blame but those kings and priests who have always claimed to have the special privilege and power to intercede on our behalf with these immortal beings? As a direct result of such natural trauma, we poor souls are likely to find ourselves dealing with plague, famine, or homelessness. When the kings and queens and priests and priestesses, and all the horse-owning or landowning or ship-owning nobility are unable to do anything for us no matter how extreme their rituals get, the social breakdown we see everywhere becomes inevitable. Starving, frightened people will turn on each other in desperation until they realize the lords and ladies have the water and grain, so, despite the fact that they most often have the weapons as well, eventually there will be an uprising against them, or an invasion from other lands, or both. The palatial kingdoms are being overthrown, pillaged, and destroyed. Such dispersion and displacement have led to bands of marauders terrorizing the countryside until the more adventurous folk join the marauders to terrorize the sea and any other land that has continued to prosper or at least survive.

"In this situation, the order of empire succumbs to the disorder of catastrophe. The gods become silent. Written communication is lost, and international trade ceases. Without such trade in copper and tin, bronze can no longer be made. Do you see? If the natural trauma continues, a spreading war of migration and conquest becomes the only possible way of life until, out of self-protection, people become bound only by tribal loyalty once again. The arts of civilization even now are being forgotten, except for those related to the craft of war. Without bronze, what will follow? Just as the Age of Stone gave way to that of Copper, so the Age of Bronze becomes, well, who knows? However, if we can imagine the perspective of the Triple Goddess, none of this means anything, for the ouroboric round of life and death continues as always. As vitally concerned as we are about our human destiny in a chaotic world, she is as absolutely indifferent to it."

5. Battle Before the Temple

In the temple of the Storm-God, his morning rituals completed, Suppiluliuma excitedly prepared for the execution of his uncle, General Kil-Teshub. He would interrogate him, of course, but whether he discovered treachery or not was of no consequence. "My Majesty cannot be misguided," he thought to himself, "for I am guided by immortal destiny." He was going to be rid of this man no matter what he said or how he pleaded; he felt divine power surge through him in anticipation of feeding off his suffering. Kil-Teshub even resembled his father, Tudhaliya, which made him all the more hateful. He had always felt the Gal-Meshedi and field general of the Hatti troops was over-respected. He had such vanity that he secretly looked down on his superiors. "He forgot that his nephew is first his Sun, the Sun of the Hatti, already becoming an immortal." He might even do the garrotting himself, but only after he amused himself by observing the breaking and humiliation of the proud old man. He would act in the middle of the day, for the gods may wish to view his glorious victory. No need for the Sun Goddess if this ritual of balance helps return Tarhunta to power.

He finished his late breakfast with a little extra Hurrian wine and called on his body servants to help him become purified from head to foot. His magnificent beard was curled and oiled and his long hair was combed out, plaited, and tied down between his shoulder blades as if he were going to battle. His heart was made ready in prayer and sacrifice, but, in truth, his mind kept wandering to the deed ahead that he was certain the Storm-God demanded of him – though before this Tarhunta had only asked for grain, sheep, or a bull in sacrifice. He had himself dressed in more close-fitting garments than usual to avoid contamination lest blood be spilled. With his gilded crown, a tall layered cone like those worn to sacrifices, he motioned for his personal guards to follow and went down a circular staircase to where his wounded prisoner was being kept to meet his divinely appointed fate.

The old general was bound in a chair with armrests to which his own arms were snugly fastened. His feet were tied together against the chair legs. His eyes were covered by a scarf wrapped round his head that disconsolately hung over his chest, his black and grey hair cropped short. He wore the dignified kilt of the Hittite nobility but his upper body was stripped bare. Though nearly sixty suns on Earth, his arms, shoulders, and chest were visibly strong from continual exercise with weaponry, though Suppiluliuma observed that he didn't have the dignity to keep his body shaven. The deep spear wound in his back just below his left shoulder blade was still seeping dark blood through the white cloth tied in place around his stomach.

Suppiluliuma walked alone over to the low table on which a few items that would aid the interrogation were laid out. He recognized the quartzite-knobbed, short pointed iron dirk that was sharp as a razor and the ash-handled bronze hatchet that he knew made swift work of fingers. He had his torturers avoid the use of fire, for he did not like the unpleasant odour of burnt meat nor the fact that it sometimes loosened the bowels of those so tormented. On edge of the table was a strong cord with handles at each end. To deliver the act of death to someone who had defied the ancient order in this manner was expected of royalty, a sacred act approved by the gods.

Not that he was going to use most such instruments himself though he had always been curious about how it might feel, especially when the victim screamed and begged. He liked the image and considered doing it himself, but, no, it was just too impure and dirty and thus beneath him. It was a job for an underling who would act as his hands in any case. When the time came for the final dispatch with his favourite tool, it was he who would deliver it. He was at peace with watching for now.

The two Meshedi guardsmen who accompanied him and the two already in attendance were dressed in full regalia, colours flying, a red cape draped on each. They stood two on each side wearing pointed, smooth leather helmets with burnished copper insignia and golden embroidery in their headbands declaring their rank. Their gold-plated spears were rigidly held straight upward and the guards just as rigidly stared straight ahead. They had been chosen and daily drilled to offer total loyalty only to the Great King, before any state or any god; in fact, they had been drilled to regard him as a god, inviolate and all-powerful, the source of ethics so not subject to them. What was being done in this room was therefore part of the sacred order of things. The guards' rugged, long-serving Gal-Meshedi, who had always been stern in his standards but noble and fair in his personal dealings, was understood to be merely a replaceable servant of the Great King. Though the general had supervised their training and actually led them into battle, he too was subject to the whims of their god-king. The guardsmen seemed indifferent to the fact that their god was about to torture their commander.

Mahhuzzi had a brief respite. Diomedes had headed down to the lower town to find Kabi a horse and to gather the rest of his band and return, which would take most of the morning. To arrive as planned to distract the Hittite soldiers at the Temple of the Storm-God an hour after the zenith of the Sun Goddess, they will need to take the direct public road up the temple akropolis. They will be lucky if they are not stopped sooner, thought the vizier. Hopefully, Suppiluliuma was not planning to act before evening against Kil-Teshub, for whom he was concerned more than he preferred to admit to himself. Though Kil-Teshub had been appointed Gal-Meshedi by Arnuwanda, he and the general had served together for the entire reign of the current king, often as rivals but more recently as accomplices or even friends. He did not comprehend why the Great King had turned on Kil-Teshub but not on him, but perhaps it was simply a matter of jealous hatred toward his popular general who often did not show the deference or flattery the Great King expected. The royal advisor was preparing to use all his cunning rhetoric to convince Suppiluliuma to come alone with him to this Temple of

Ishtar, which must be done before the warrior troop arrived. But if they took too long to intervene and Suppiluliuma grew suspicious or unexpectedly enraged, he might well find himself in the same position as the general. No one could really be sure what the unbalanced Suppiluliuma would do next.

The elegant High Priestess Lilitu approached with drinks of warm goose broth and of course fresh bread. She was like nobody he had ever seen before, including the Great Queen, whom he revered. Wisdom seemed to glow from her and gave her a presence to match her bewildering beauty that was sensuous yet icy cold at once. She was about his age, yet she seemed in some sense beyond time, youthful yet ancient. He was deeply drawn to her.

"So, Mahhuzzi, is there any prospect of your wicked plans getting us through all this?"

"High Priestess, I suspect my vague plans may be far less wicked than others that have been set in motion. Why would you call my desperate manoeuvres *wicked*?"

"Because you are the grand vizier who has the ear of the Great King of the Hatti!" she laughed parting wide her dark lips over white pointed teeth. "Further, you are cunning, lean, and unmarried. You are the standard character in our tales that is always evil, who serves only himself, and that is it!" She laughed into his eyes and her penetrating gaze held them. To his surprise he felt the wizard's serpent stir. Perhaps there *was* something like evil in him. But it was disturbing: *was he self-serving*?

"To this point, have you seen anything in my actions or character to indicate I am not worthy of your trust? Or do you jest at my turning against the Great King?"

"No, O Wiseman. Hittite kings have a long history of sedition, of other family members turning on them to take the golden throne, and it is that much more likely if the family member is already the chief royal advisor." Again, she flashed her twisted smile, which so suited her. "Still, beneath it all, you do not seem selfish enough to be the turncoat type. You served Suppiluliuma and his Lord Teshub or Tarhunta or whatever the Storm-God is being called today long and well. Even amidst a crumbling empire, I suspect you made him feel he was on his way to saving the land by fighting off intruders and influencing the gods to intervene. Considering how rare a rain storm has been these past years, I can only guess the Storm-God did not receive the sacrifices or hear his prayers. So you could see for yourself how ineffectual Suppiluliuma had become." She sipped and so he did too.

"I can only imagine your turn away from him took a great deal of anguished soul-searching, and I do mean *soul*, for to betray the Great King is also to betray the male war and sky gods with whom he so identifies. That took courage. In the scales of your mind, the balance shifted away from blind loyalty to disintegration and toward the cosmic harmony of your soul's integrity, which clearly seems to me to have been influenced by a more ancient and more profound deity. I refer to the Mother of Gods who brought you here, to her sacred *omphalos* within this temple, to me." She paused to make sure Mahhuzzi was suitably entranced. "Though she is known by many names, the Great Goddess is herself the labyrinth of the cosmic dance of birth, life, and death. She has always been here as earth and night sky, long before there were Hittites, Babylonians, or Misriwi, before cities and before time was measured. I say you were led to serve her divine wisdom by protecting the Great Queen and preserving the Hatti people from a demon-haunted king."

Mahhuzzi looked down, humbled and deeply moved. The High Priestess had just removed any doubts remaining within him. He knew he was not acting with personal ambition, but he had never been read so accurately before. He felt himself overwhelmed by the realization that the source of his decision to change sides may have been a gift from the Goddess Mother of all. He looked at Lilitu with gratitude and awe. "My Lady..." he began, but an unfamiliar emotion rose in him closing his throat.

She put her taloned hand softly on his. "No need to speak, dear friend. There is no evil in you. You are one with us now."

Suppiluliuma was growing very frustrated. He had ordered General Kil-Teshub to confess to his crimes, to admit to his treachery and name every name that was part of his plot. The general just sat silent breathing slowly and deeply. “Have you been in contact with Lieia-Hepa? Where is she located? ... Speak O General!”

He did not, so Suppiluliuma directed his henchman, himself a lower ranked Meshedi, to use the pointed iron dirk to search inside the spear wound. The torturer, in a rough wool tunic but shaved hairless for reasons of purity and cleanliness, was scarred and twisted from badly healed broken bones so no longer useful on the battlefield. He bent and ripped off the bandage and inserted the fine point of the exquisitely beautiful dagger almost gently into the wound without a response from Kil-Teshub, but then he began to twist it into a slow widening circle and edging deeper until new flesh was being cut and fresh blood appeared. Kil-Teshub did not even look up but sweat appeared on his brow. “Open another mouth on the other side,” Suppiluliuma pointed, and the torturer withdrew the dagger from the left side and very slowly pressed it into the general’s flesh beneath his right shoulder blade. “General, I want to know how deeply Mahhuzzi was involved in this revolt against the order of heaven. Speak!” Still, Kil-Teshub only breathed, his head bent forward. Suppiluliuma rose, his frustration running over, and ran to him in anger, tearing the mask from his face so he could see. “Speak, you now have three open mouths, so speak! Or face a long, slow death! What is your purpose? Was Ishtar or her High Priestess part of this? Who is working with you?”

The Gal-Meshedi looked up but beyond the Great King. He stared far away and said nothing. This was not right. Tarhunta of the Storm needed screams and tears on which to feed. “You will see. I will not give you the gift of death so easily.” He looked at the torture-master and pointed to the hatchet: “You pick out two toes,” he commanded and turned to Kil-Teshub. “If that does not get you speaking, we shall do two more, but after that we shall turn to your eyes…" A guardsman blinked.

Accompanied by two lightly armed soldiers from the towering Temple of Ishtar on the western edge of the akropolis, Mahhuzzi made his way back downhill to the broad temple of the Storm-God in the centre of the complex. He didn't know what had happened to Kil-Teshub after his sudden and still inexplicable arrest. He didn't know if the Great King was in the right state of mind to hear his carefully crafted appeal to his vanity as to why he must go alone to the Temple of Ishtar to be transformed into a deity, "…if he's actually transformed into anything at all," the rational, more skeptical side of Mahhuzzi's mind whispered. But that was not his concern. He must convince the Great King to come with him, and the small troop of warriors from the lower city must arrive at just the right moment to distract the guardsmen, so the Great King can be spirited away – *if he is willing.* If the Goddess did not guide, it was all too much chance. Of course, he expected the highly trained Meshedi to fight off the homeless warriors quickly, but then again, was it not only yesterday that four of them along with Zunan the Hurrian had killed – *killed*, not even wounded! – eight Meshedi? So many unknowns – it was like street gambling!

The royal guardsmen at the gate glanced at each other when they saw the grand vizier approach. They had been told to let no one pass, but, with the Great Queen missing and General Kil-Teshub in chains, Mahhuzzi was the second most powerful person in the Hittite Empire. They crossed their golden spears to block his entry, but only for a moment. All it took was the Wiseman's baleful stare and they pulled back their spears and opened the doors for him. He entered the receiving chamber and was met by servants who looked very nervous. He went to the ritual stone basin to cleanse hands and face. As he dried himself, he told them he was here to consult with the Great King.

The attendants looked at each other and the man replied, "Were you expected, O Wiseman? His Great

Majesty is in ... conference." Their nerves and his alert intuition told him all he had to know, but he dared not reveal what he knew to be true.

"Please, Sun Goddess, do not let me be too late," he silently prayed. Aloud he said, "This is not a request. This is an order in the name of the Great King: you are required to get a message to the Great King on his own authority." The servants nodded in bewilderment. "Announce to his Majesty that his grand vizier is here to see him about matters of the greatest urgency. I am sure he will pause in his devotions for this. Go now," he snapped, and he watched as they moved quickly into a nearby pillared hallway and down a circular, marble stair.

He heard voices in the distance then the Great King's bellow: "I told you I was not to be disturbed!" Low murmurs. "Ah, Mahhuzzi," as he learned who had arrived. After a bit the two attendants returned walking on either side of the Great King of the Hatti who towered over them. Suppiluliuma was actually smiling over his beard though his forehead was moist and his pupils were gleaming and tiny. He was excited.

"Your Highness, a thousand apologies for arriving without an appointment, but time passes, an army approaches, and the end of our kingdom may be near."

"That's what you've come to tell me?" Without waiting for a servant or asking Mahhuzzi, the Great King reached over to a nearby tray and took up the rest of the goblet of wine he had earlier begun. He signalled to the servants to bring one for the vizier too. "Tell me truly, O Mahhuzzi, did you have anything to do with the plot against My Majesty led by General Kil-Teshub?"

"Plot? I swear on the wrath of Tarhunta himself that I know nothing of any plot. In truth, I still do not. If I may, Great King, I would like to speak on behalf of General Kil-Teshub..."

"Do so only at your great peril. I have just come from the chamber where Kil-Teshub has been undergoing interrogation. Because of his royal bloodline, he has stood up well under torture and has not revealed the location of the Great Queen."

"Great King, might she not be out of the city by now?"

"This is not known. Nor did he implicate you, so far, but he has indicated that the Great Queen's personal bodyguard participated in her escape..."

"Captain Zunan?" Mahhuzzi knew this was a lie. It was known Zunan had not been seen since Lieia-Hepa disappeared, so this was a ploy by Suppiluliuma to pretend he knew more than he did. "That's not a surprise. He was always loyal to her."

The royal advisor's goblet arrived with a small pitcher of the local vintage. "My Lord, time is short, and I'm sure you wish to return to your interrogation, but today, now, is the time for you to escape the burdens of your high office. The fall of the Hatti kingdom is nigh, and I was informed the High Priestess Lilitu is prepared to assist you on your journey through the Underworld where you will be cleansed of your humanity to awaken as a god."

"Ah, she has decided to agree to my terms, so I am bringing a Meshedi troop with me."

"No, Great King. Their presence is not permitted in the Temple of Ishtar. Besides, my highest Majesty, they do not have your sacred royal blood. They are not worthy of such an honour. They would turn to dust in the descent to the Underworld. To the point, it is time for you to decide, here and now, whether you will soon be a dead king or a living god. A god has no need of bodyguards, for a god may take any form or appear anywhere he chooses."

Suppiluliuma gazed into the distance, obviously liking the prospect. "Yes, you are right. I am already a god on earth, but I must complete the ancient ritual to become immortal. However, Grand Vizier, I must finish what I have started below. Kil-Teshub is now One-Eye Kil-Teshub," he chuckled obscenely. "The torturer seemed unable to do the deed, so I did it myself. You would not believe how much force it took to use that little dagger to pry out his eyeball, but then it came out – pop! – all at once, hanging by its nerves, which I cut. What a mess." The Wiseman froze white with horror. “But even after that, he would not reveal any information,” the Great King shook his head in wonder, “or it may be he has none to reveal. It is no matter. I must return to end his suffering once and finally. Then I will purify and go with you to the Tower of Ishtar.” He rose.

“But...” a totally shocked Mahhuzzi tried to intervene.

“You wait here. I’ll be right back once I tend to this *twist* of fate.” The king sniggered at his own witticism and drank back his wine. Then he abruptly left to return and tighten the garrotte around the throat of his long-suffering uncle, Kil-Teshub, Commander of the Meshedi.

Mahhuzzi was in turmoil. He knew he must act to save what was left of his friend, but he could think of nothing to do that would not end in his own sudden death. He fell into a state of confusion in which he heard voices and shouts in his head. But then he realized they were not in his head at all but outside the grand entry to this temple. It was Diomedes and his barbarians, thankfully arriving early.

Attempting to announce their presence, the small pack of warriors from other lands let loose whatever war cries, curses, or bellows were known to them. Those who had managed to obtain shields were fiercely banging on them with swords or spears. Their leader, Diomedes, had arrived with all his troop but two who could not be found, instructing them to make a clamour. With them was their new accomplice, Captain Zunan of the Hittite military. They were told to expect the fight of their lives and, after the long wait in this quiet city, were like starving lions set free from their cage. Who would dare face these beasts?

The two outside guards had seen them coming before they unleashed their battle howls. One had struck his gold-coated spear butt against the door several time to alert the other Meshedi inside to what was afoot. The two outside did not abandon their posts but following their training snapped into the spears-forward, shields ready warning posture used to keep back attackers. They had guessed these were townspeople rioting, but it was a bad guess. The warriors did not pause but came forward at full trot, striking the spearheads aside. The guardsmen were quickly overwhelmed and speared and hacked to the ground but only after crying out a warning to those inside. Their golden spears were quickly grabbed and also purloined were their light leathern shields with bronze medallions hasped into them. Somewhere within there was a blast from a *sawetra* – a resonant bugle shaped like a bull's horn. A warrior in front pulled the heavy door and gave a cheer when it readily opened. Zunan, the former Meshedi, cried out a warning, but it was too late.

Meshedi in full armour came pouring out the door and up the side steps, coming together and suddenly marching in perfect order, their gilded conical helms making them seem taller than the attackers; their light knot-shaped shields were held before them always facing the enemy, though none could stop a direct spear thrust. With this shield wall and the bristling spears held above them, they faced the enemy. The warriors were startled and paused when they should have attacked, so the royal bodyguard marched steadily forward, driving the warriors back. They faced each other, the warriors three men deep and centralized and the royal guardsmen two men deep but in order, making their line wider.

There were ten Meshedi since two of the standard twelve active detail of royal bodyguards had already fallen. Diomedes' original fifteen men were now reduced to equal in number since two lay wounded in the Temple of Ishtar, two could not be located, and their scout was on horseback somewhere north of here. The addition of Zunan gave them eleven. Diomedes had anticipated leaving the men to fight it out while he barged into the temple to seek out Suppiluliuma, but something in the disciplined way the Meshedi immediately snapped into formation as one unit told him he would be needed here. The warriors may have killed eight Meshedi in the chaos of individual fighting, but the highly trained Meshedi in coordinated battle formation was another beast entirely, the many as one.

"They will attempt to hold their front while their strongest fighters move forward on each flank to surround us," Zunan the former Meshedi hissed to Diomedes.

"Spread out, only two men deep!" he roared to his men who scrambled to obey in confusion. Pointing the spear he had found, he turned to Zunan, "You and I will take the wings!" But by then the Hittites had begun their drilled advance.

They met with a clash and more howled war cries and threats burst from the throats of the freebooting warriors, but the mix of marauders and pirates had never before faced such a well-coordinated unit. The royal bodyguards marched as one well-drilled team without hesitation, their gold-plated spearheads before them, their shields below that. The warriors were primed and ready but there seemed to be no place to strike. The Meshedi spears were longer and their one-two chant brought them relentlessly forward upon the invaders, who did not flag in spirit. They poked their shorter spears, threw a few javelins aimlessly, thrust their swords, and hacked with their axes but could not push the Meshedi line backwards. It held while their golden spearpoints found warrior blood again and again. One man amongst the front Hittite line screamed and fell as a spear found his lower thigh just below his shield, but the line immediately closed and the wounded man was quickly dragged behind.

Diomedes knew he had been instructed to only cause a distraction, so Mahhuzzi could spirit the Great King away, but there had been no sign of either one and it was beginning to become evident that his loyal troop was in serious danger. The strongest royal guardsmen on each flank were indeed making headway against his untrained barbarians. They would soon be encircled and destroyed. As Zunan worked his way to the left wing shouting encouragement and forcing himself to the front, the Akhaian pushed himself to the right. As he assumed his position before all others, his eyes widened in hate as he looked upon the Hittite soldiers who had killed his comrades and kept him imprisoned so long. These were no half-retired guardsmen on temple duty as at Arinna. These were the Meshedi! He felt the familiar war rage awaken as Athene Areia surged through him and gave him power from Earth. Diomedes of the loud war-cry raised his spear to the heavens and released such a blood-curdling bellow of threat that some felt the god of war must surely have entered the fray.

He led the counterattack on the right by directly overpowering the Hittites coming forward, using his enormous strength and shield to physically push them backwards. His opponents thrown off-balance, he drove his spear with deadly aim into body after body. He rarely bothered with feints, for his war-maddened vigour drove the point right through any shield held before him and into whatever flesh lay behind. When the spear finally became lodged deeply in the chest of an unfortunate victim, he simply took the man's gilded spear to use instead. When it happened a second time, this time entangled in a brain pan, he left the spear and drew the unique bronze sword gifted him by the Sardinian and went to work in an ecstasy of bloodlust, lost to himself. The chaos rippling out from his destructive advance disrupted the drilled-in order of the mighty Meshedi guardsmen.

On the left flank, Zunan and others not only stopped the advance, but he yelled to the Meshedi in Hittite alternating with the similar Luwian in a loud and clear voice amidst the grind of battle. "Right now, inside this building, Suppiluliuma is torturing Gal-Meshedi Kil-Teshub to death. Did you know that?" "Did you know Suppiluliuma has killed the Great Queen and High Priestess of the Hatti?" "Suppiluliuma is possessed by demons! We must stop him!" "The gods have deserted the King. We must save the Hatti!" It was a bad time for conversation, but his deep voice carried and the Meshedi were already aware of the missing queen. But torturing Kil-Teshub? The Meshedi had been thoroughly conditioned to protect only the Great King and not to dare to think any other way, even if he was deserted by the gods, but their venerable and noble leader being tortured? The words were heard even if they had no immediate effect beyond a lessened determination among the attacking royal guard in that vicinity.

Against all odds, with chaos on one side and doubt on the other, the remaining Meshedi were being pushed backward on the wings. Diomedes alone was like a storm shredding a helpless village. Yet the royal protectors were not about to flee. They dutifully fought back until it began to look like a slaughter would be necessary.

But then somewhere from within the temple the sawetra bugle sounded again. Having emerged from a second doorway hidden around the side, another dozen Meshedi who had been off-duty charged into view, arms poised for battle. As if planned, they appeared at the main portal directly behind the invading warrior troop, who now found themselves outnumbered with Meshedi both before and behind them.

Suppiluliuma abruptly shifted moods as he left the Wiseman sitting alone with his wine and went back to finish the vital work he had begun to rid the land of any threats to his power and to regenerate its life-force by himself becoming the Storm-God or another. His concerns about the final process alone melted away as he re-entered the little room that he had designated as his torture chamber.

Kil-Teshub slumped pathetically, his head hanging, still managing to breathe slowly and deeply. He neither whimpered nor spoke but a slight gurgle was evident in each exhale. Blood ran from either foot onto the cold stone where the two smallest toes on each foot had been chopped off, the torturer apparently showing some mercy. His back on each side below the shoulder blades gaped open in torn angry wounds, running blood. But the blackest blood ran down his left cheek as it was mixed with bits of gore from the horrible gaping hollow where the eye had been.

The four guards stared at him, which was not permitted. They seemed agitated, even their golden spears were no longer perfectly aligned. The hairless broken torturer had sat down with his head hung low and seemed in a state of shock, if such a thing were conceivable. And what was that confounding clamour from outside like some kind of enraged mob? Then he heard the sawetra horn, and the four guards looked up, suddenly fully alert. It was the call to battle. The tumult grew.

Without a word, Suppiluliuma walked over and took up the garrotte, stretching it out into its full length appreciatively. He took it and held it before the remaining eye of Kil-Teshub, which blinked. "You keep breathing so deep and hard, Uncle, as though you are casting a spell to keep yourself from crying out. Recognize this weapon, O General? It is the final god-power and I am the god that holds it. It is about to put an end to both your breathing and your life." He ran the cord twice around the general's neck and slowly pulled it tight, using his knee on the general's back to brace himself. "You are about to see your final darkness rise. Watch closely, O Gal-Meshedi!"

The last words, calling him by his grandest title, the honoured commander of the ancient royal bodyguard, seemed to break the spell that held the guards back. The nearest one moved into action first but the other three were right with him. Against the training that had lasted most of their lives, two dropped their spears and put their strong hands on the heretofore sacrosanct body of the Great King of the Hatti, ripping his hands free of the garrotte's handles while the other two took the cord from around Kil-Teshub's neck. The hairless torturer rose with a black-toothed grin and gratefully took the garrotte from a guardsman's hand. The Meshedi kept a grip on the king as they were passed their sacred spears.

By now Suppiluliuma was raving and weeping in a frustrated rage. Nothing like this had ever happened to him before, though it may have to his ancestors. "You dare not! I am the King of all the Hatti! I am the great Storm-God! You will be smitten into dust!" A guard hit him with his gold-plated spear butt hard on the back of his head while the other slapped his big hand over the Great King's mouth and each pulled one of his arms behind his back. His golden crown toppled to the floor with a clatter. The other two guards put down their spears and loosened the bonds of General Kil-Teshub, trying desperately to get him to his feet on which he could not stand. Outside the battle raged. The highest-ranking royal bodyguards looked at each other in bewildered rage over what they had seen and done. What had possessed them and what to do now?

At that moment, the door was pushed open by Mahhuzzi who took in the situation in an instant. “To save your leader – to save us all! – we must bring both of these men to the main door, dragging them if you must. We have a battle to stop!”

It was done with great difficulty, but with a desperate will that would not be denied both men were brought forth, one limp, one struggling. The main door three steps above the battle was thrown open and Mahhuzzi the Grand Vizier stepped out before warriors hotly engaged in a fight to the finish. Some looked up at the Great King’s advisor but no one dared to stop fighting. Mahhuzzi lifted his colourfully robed arms and announced in his loudest voice, “O my brothers, look upon what evil has been wrought in this land!” Two Meshedi first dragged out the mangled Kil-Teshub whom they held up for all to see. The ghastly abuse done to the deeply respected, vastly admired Gal-Meshedi froze the Hittite royal guard where they stood. Many of the surrounded invading troop also paused to look up. Zunan raised his hand shouting to desist, while on the other end Diomedes came to his senses, looked at the dead or wounded bodies around him, and raised his hand as well.

But the shock was total among all warriors, soldiers or barbarians, when the second man was dragged outside, his mouth held shut and his eyes rolling. The Great King held in bondage – *unthinkable!* – the Great King never allowed himself to be touched! He wore no gold embroidered mitre over his long bedraggled hair, which now hung over his wild eyes. For a second, utter silence filled the air. But slow understanding rose in the Meshedi. It was his most trusted bodyguards, high-ranking Meshedi, who pinned his arms and held his mouth shut while one carried his conical crown in his hand. Clearly, if the High Priest of all the Hatti had been abandoned by the gods, he was no longer Great King. Since the Great Queen seemed to be gone, the other two men on the stoop, Kil-Teshub and Mahhuzzi, both royal family, were now the rulers of the kingdom.

"Brothers, cease your battle. There is no longer anything to fight over." Mahhuzzi understood he was called upon to make things clear. "The Great King is possessed by Illuyanka, the dragon of chaos. Your king is the cause of all that has ailed this land so long. He broke the ancient truce among the gods. He has attempted to murder his own Great Queen to bring down the Sun Goddess of Arinna. And just now he has nearly tortured to death his loyal General of the Army, our beloved Kil-Teshub, the new leader of the Hatti! Trust me as you always have and all shall be revealed to you."

"Kill him now!" a few voices cried out from among the Meshedi. "No hear him out," Zunan bellowed. "The whole tale must be known!"

"The outlanders have come here to defend your Great Queen," Mahhuzzi continued. "Look who fights with them: Zunan, the Great Queen's personal bodyguard." Zunan removed his helmet and saluted so he could be seen. "They too were acting honourably and will not be harmed. But we must immediately take General Kil-Teshub to the house of healing in hopes his life may be saved. Zunan the Hurrian, choose some guardsmen you trust and find a way to carry Kil-Teshub to the Tower of Ishtar. The High Priestess now knows you." Zunan came forward with five quickly chosen Meshedi and made a stretcher by tying together several of their red capes. They carefully loaded on the burly old general, whose one eye rolled unseeing as he still was somewhere far away in his mind. As they were departing, Kil-Teshub finally moaned aloud, which confirmed to the Meshedi the good news that he was yet alive.

As they departed, Mahhuzzi continued addressing both troops who stood as if time had stopped. His ringing voice carried and held them, and they needed something on which to hold. "Next, the fallen king Suppiluliuma is going to go on a journey where he will undergo the ancient rite of Descent into the Underworld so the dark gods there may judge his soul and determine his virtue." A murmur of shocked wonder went through the fighters. Few dared even to think of the Underworld much less speak of it aloud. "Diomedes, Mighty Warrior of the Ahhiyawa," he called out to the tall, battle ravaged warrior surrounded by bodies, "will you come up here to join these brave Meshedi and take Suppiluliuma to the Tower of Ishtar to meet his destiny? You know the way. I trust you will protect him?" Diomedes, blood on his face and dripping from the massive bronze blade he still swung in his hand, strode forward. The crowd readily separated before the fearsome sight and he mounted the three steps where he joined the four guardsmen. As he nodded a greeting to them, he wiped the gore from his sword blade onto Suppiluliuma's fine wool kilt before sheathing it. He led the way as they followed in the same western direction as the first group. His mouth still sealed and his arms pinned behind him, Suppiluliuma found himself forced to stumble along.

Mahhuzzi the Wiseman using a voice both loud yet intimate instructed the warriors to accept the peace, tend to their wounded and dead, but then to return here to the base of the perron to share speech and camaraderie. "All will be made clear and questions will be answered. You barbaroi are now among friends. This little war has ended. I shall send for jars of beer. We will speak of her Majesty, the Great Queen Lieia-Hepa, who still lives." A great cheer went up among the guardsmen as the good news spread. "And we shall discuss what lay ahead for the Hatti people and maybe also for you freebooting warriors from the north and the others like you who even now approach. Then you Meshedi must go out into the city and spread the news to the Hatti regiment there. I see a grand confluence ahead in which destinies may be altered and new fates may be forged. Now go tend to your fellows and yourselves and quickly return. We shall discover what pieces in this game the gods have put into play!" Then, as they turned to help the wounded and the dead, he spoke to himself, "But perhaps the gods themselves are but pieces being played."

6. Sarpedon's Warriors Approach (Kabi Meets Henti)

The Sardinian looked down with pleasure on the descending road into a rich river valley. If it truly was fertile, this would be a welcome respite from the long overland journey. The troop was hungry, thirsty, dirty, and tired. A warm breeze blew up from the valley over what appeared to be flourishing fields on either side of the river. For the first time since leaving the north Anatolian plateau of the capital behind, he felt something like hope though the emotion had become rare since the chaos descended. After too much time spent down amongst insect-ridden swamps and salty lakes on the other side of the mountain source of the Marassantiya River then returning to the barren south plateau among its wretched villages of poverty and disease, it had been a relief to climb into the windy passes of the inland Anti-Taurus Mountains. But there had been few villages to feed them here and none worth plundering. Water was plentiful but game was rare. The road was made from sharp rocks that destroyed most footwear and the nights had been frigid.

Local guides had shown them the way to the wild headwaters of the Puruma River and indicated that following it would take them to the sacred city of Lawazantiya on a plain where its flow smoothed out. The guide had warned him to avoid the left fork of the river that splits away ahead and plunges into a cavern in the rocks where it surely descends into the accursed Underworld, for it is not known to emerge again. Sarpedon had heard of such underground rivers in limestone-karst mountains, but had no time to explore any such side tracks. Beyond the city, the Puruma River passed by a few other towns until it finally entered the Great Green within sight of Alasiya, which was said to have become the staging ground for the warriors from the sea, but it had been a long time since any news from the larger world had reached him.

With freshwater nearby and their destination ahead, Sarpedon sent out more hunting parties in hopes of fresh meat and awaited reports from his scouts to plan a camp for the night. A conference of leaders would be needed, for with Lawazantiya within a day's journey but the welcoming sea only a few days after that, decisions would have to be made. He still had heard nothing from Diomedes and his band of would-be assassins, but local informants indicated that rumours had reached these mountains that a sizeable caravan of Hittites had entered the city below with much fanfare only about a moon phase earlier. If that were true, it was certain to be where the Great King Suppiluliuma had gone and where the Hattusa treasures had been taken. It was unknown how many regiments of soldiers were included and that might prove to be the deciding factor whether to attack the city of Ishtar, negotiate a bypass, or simply avoid it. To his satisfaction, things had been well-managed under his singular helmsmanship, but he was not the headstrong type who makes important decisions without consultation. That would be bad politics, too, and Sarpedon was a clever man.

As he enjoyed the scent of fresh water and verdant growth, he saw dust rising and riders approaching more quickly than they would if they were merely returning from routine scouting; however, it was not an emergency gallop. He called a halt and his guards gathered about him more closely. The three approaching horses fell into a trot. He recognized the two Lukkan scouts on either side by their baggy, colourful swept-back linen caps held in place with bronze fillets. He did not at first recognize the horseman between them, but he felt a certain sense of familiarity at seeing the adroit manner in which the rider handled his mount. Soon he recognized the flowing black hair of their Canaanite scout as it curled around his leather headband. Kabi, he realized, so the Diomedian squad lives,

After dismounting, before the Lukkan scouts could speak, Sarpedon called out Kabi's name and he in turn addressed the Sardinian for the first time ever by his chosen name, "Sarpedon!" They embraced with dusty pats.

They shared only the briefest of information as the Lukkans left leading away Kabi's gelding. Yes, Nerik had fallen and much treasure had been taken but at the terrible price of losing Payava. At this, Kabi was saddened, Payava had been good to him, but he was by now war-hardened enough to put it quickly behind him. Yes, the others had gone back toward the Aegean, some to try again to build a home but most to continue marauding the sea heading south. In return, Kabi assured him that the Great King had indeed come to Lawazantiya and that the Great Queen was there held as a prisoner. Kabi knew nothing of treasure but he did know that the remarkable High Priestess of Ishtar did not accept Suppiluliuma's higher authority, that a revolt was underway, and that he himself had been with Diomedes and Eruthros when the Great Queen had been set free and eight Meshedi killed.

"*That* we will hear more of later over wine in the evening!" Sarpedon laughed.

Kabi added that Eruthros the bear was wounded but should recover, and that the queen was now under the protection of the High Priestess, who was like a goddess herself. He added that Diomedes had developed a *very close* relationship with Queen Lieia-Hepa, and further that a diversionary attack had been about to take place against the famed Meshedi, the royal bodyguard of the Great King, when he had left to come here. The goal was for an inside agent to lead the king away on his own, but it seemed a long bowshot and was probably a suicide mission for Diomedes and his small squad. They would soon know. In answer to Sarpedon's question, he replied, glancing away, that he guessed there were three-thousand Hatti soldiers occupying Lawazantiya.

"By the gods, what an incredible week you have had!" Sarpedon expostulated. "Come and refresh yourself, dine on our finest camp slop, and we shall have a conference of our leaders to determine what to do next. You will speak to them. I'm sure you will have suggestions."

I will, Kabi thought, but I have already sent my most important message.

Sarpedon directed the two Lukkan scouts to find a worthy troop billet nearer the frothy waters of the upper Puruma River. Once there, he picked out his own campsite on a hillock from where he could set his tent and see the whole valley open before him. While he enjoyed the view and did some thinking, he left his personal attendants to set it up according to established preference. As always, the enwrapped Henti appeared to help out, make her space and prepare some food. "There will be one more," Sarpedon had told her as he appeared with the sinewy young scout she recognized from earlier days. They greeted each other with a distant nod. Though partially veiled, her light blue eyes were soft and Kabi felt he saw the face of an innocent beautiful child.

At the main fire where the council was being held, Sarpedon had wine and water brought. He set his heavy bronze and silver circular shield beside his sitting rock to signify his status. Big Klymenos the new Danaan leader arrived in the remains of his boar's tusk helmet, looking like Eruthros but with flat brown stringy hair, strong-armed but without the bearlike breadth. A bodyguard followed him but stood back as he sat down, nodding to Sarpedon but otherwise greeting no one. The commander introduced him to Kabi the Canaanite, and he asked without a smile where Canaan was. "Later," Sarpedon replied. He then welcomed Kuprlli, who had replaced Payava as leader of the Lukkans in this troop. He wore a tall helmet made of multicoloured upstanding reeds held in place with a leather headband, similar to that of Payava. He was middle-aged and war-worn, but his eyes were bright and he carried himself with a certain dignity. He proudly carried the amazing bejewelled bronze and gold curved slashing sword through a sash around his waist, making sure the shining hilt was visible above the leather scabbard.

"This scout has just arrived from Lawazantiya, which should be in sight tomorrow. Perhaps you remember him among us as we came from the sea, burning cities and pillaging the treasures of Arinna? He left with Diomedes, Eruthros and their small platoon in pursuit of

Suppiluliuma, the Great King of the Hittites, who had abandoned his capital city as we approached." The men laughed scornfully as did the gathered crowd. It was no use attempting to keep command secrets within such a close-knit gathering of vagabond warriors.

Kabi paid close attention to all that was being said, but even as he looked and listened, the image of the unexpected harem girl Diomedes had brought with him from Hattusa kept flickering through his mind. She was covered head to toe in modest robes in the same way as had the priestesses he knew from childhood who disdained marriage to instead devote their lives to the Khabiru singular father god. Yet he had seen her body move beneath the layers of cloth. He needed to show her who he was.

"I am Kabi," he rose and found himself loudly addressing the masses in perfect Luwian. "I am known to many here. I was born in Canaan Lands beyond Amurru before I was enslaved by the Hatti. I grew up among horses in Tarhuntassa from where I escaped on my own to the Lukka Lands to make war my occupation amongst the free peoples of the sea. I have just now come from the sacred city of Ishtar, Lawazantiya, with news of our comrades led by Eruthros and Diomedes, who are there, and to plan with you what next to do." Henti, standing beyond the group in greyish blue robes, head shawl, and veil, translated for the Akhaians who had not yet mastered the lingua franca of Anatolia. She spoke loud enough for the first rows of men to hear her but in a low enough voice not to be a distraction. Kabi outlined events as he knew them, avoiding sharing any information that might make the city seem too rich or too weak. He told them he did not know if the Great King Suppiluliuma still held power, but that in any case, his power was limited by the High Priestess and High Priest of Ishtar who would not submit to him. The Hittite forces probably had the power to subdue the city, but it would be dangerous, messy, and prolonged since the city had its own Hurrian troops and the people were fanatically devoted to the Great Goddess.

"So, Eruthros is badly wounded?" Klymenos asked, "but the Argive, as always, escaped without a cut?" A murmur went through the Akhaians. "Diomedes fought well at Ilios before he deserted us to seek his own fortune, but he never seemed to get injured, so either he gets more protection from some god than anyone else, or he knows how to stand behind others in times of danger." This time a protest erupted from among the Akhaians who were not pleased to hear one of their heroes mocked this way. "Was Eruthros protecting him?" he asked Kabi directly.

"He was on guard duty outside, yes," Kabi began, so, feeling affirmed, Klymenos and his circle chortled, "but, if I were you, I would be careful about what I said about Diomedes," Kabi interrupted, "for word could get back to him." He looked levelly at Klymenos who was about to say something but turned away instead. "Eruthros took two arrows in the chest, one into his lung, but when I last saw him his wounds were sealed and he was sleeping soundly."

"Let's not waste time," interrupted Sarpedon. "Good to know such information. Kabi tells me that the Hittite regiment in the city outnumbers our troop and that there are Hurrian soldiers, as well. The city is suffering like all others but to this point still has plenty of fresh water, and food, though limited in kind, is still available. The sickness seems to have gone on its way. As a sacred city of the gods, they don't have much in the way of taverns or whores, but as a city of many temples, they likely have treasures and supplies, as do the Hatti. Their walls are low. But all this is complicated by the knowledge that fifteen of our men, including two of our leaders, are already in that city. What do they want? Kabi has come here to speak for them. We have three choices, men. We either bypass the city and head for the sea which is near, we attack the city and hope our men inside will join us, or we negotiate for food, drink, gold, and carnal pleasures and do not attack. Kabi, what have you come here to say?"

Kabi glimpsed two large, bright azure eyes watching him over her veil. "There may be a fourth choice, O noble warriors."

"We don't need it," Klymenos interrupted, pouring himself more of the murky wine, spilling a bit over the edge of his cup. "We are indeed 'noble warriors'," he growled, "so we attack Lawazantiya on sight. Our comrades inside will soon get the drift and join us or maybe they won't. No matter. There's a city below and it has what we want. We take it, gut the temples as we did at Arinna, and kill anyone who gets in our way and many who don't. Who needs whores when we can rape the whole city?" He guffawed and many laughed with him, enjoying the burst of energy. Others, more circumspect, did not. Everyone seemed to understand the intent of the words, if not the precise meaning, so Henti remained silent.

"Arinna had only a small corps of veteran guards," Sarpedon spoke low but glared at Klymenos under his brows. "Here we will be faced not only with Hurrian and Hittite regular soldiers but with the entire company of specialist Meshedi. You do want to walk in sea water again, don't you, Klymenos?" Klymenos looked about uncertain. "There's a reason why you are not in command here, O Danaan. We might be all dead by now if you were." Now the crowd laughed while Klymenos reddened. "Speak, young scout, what is our fourth choice?"

Kabi rose to his feet. "The fourth choice is to stay, to make a home here." People looked at each other in confusion. "It is not certain yet, but I have been sent to bring word from the highest authorities that the Hittite regiment is likely to be moving on to another city where they will be more welcome, with or without their Great King. Yes, this means the City of Ishtar will become easier to conquer, but – and these are the words of Diomedes, the destroyer of Wilusa – *what is it you are looking for*? You have come to a city with food and water from which the disease has passed. Most of the young men were forced to leave long ago to join the Hittite army and protect its distant borders, so there are many unmarried women and widows about. Look down into this valley: irrigated crops still grow! There are even some sheep and cattle. You would have employment as the new city guardians. The only requirement is that you respect Ishtar the Great Goddess, make sacrifice, and attend her festivals, just as in any civilized city. And, if ever you change your mind, you are near to the Great Green." He felt the disbelief rise from his listeners. "You do not even need to act as one. If Sarpedon and the other leaders agree, each one of you can freely choose whether to make a home here or continue on to further adventures and further suffering as peoples of the sea." He sat.

It was an idea no one had before considered. Sarpedon's trim-bearded jaw dropped open. Individual choice was bad enough, but... "You mean cease warring?" he asked incredulously. He had been a warrior since before his beard had begun, so the nearly unthinkable thought was as strange to him as a hole opening up in the sky. "But, we live for war, do we not? War and glory is all we know. Glory is all!"

Kuprlli looked up and about, taking in the crowd of weary, tattered warriors crowding in about him. He stood and waved his arm toward the emaciated rabble and loudly asked, "Is this *glory*?"

There was a long pause during which Henti translated the proposals of the bold scout into Hellenic, but most were already talking excitedly amongst themselves. The rabble were no longer sure which god to follow, if any, but the thought of *home* and maybe a family did sound sweet to many an ear. However, not everyone found this idea palatable.

"There is no individual choice amongst my warriors!" Klymenos rose to his feet shouting. "We follow our leaders just as we once followed our kings, and our kings led us into glorious battle. A warrior on his own is a dead warrior. I lead the Danaans and Akhaians here, so I am like their king, and their loyalty is owed to me. Either we burn the city of Ishtar to the ground, or I will take my men straight to the sea to join the others in the conquest of the rich southern lands of the Levant. A warrior wants glory in battle, not a quiet life. There is no such thing as home or peace for a warrior!" Klymenos raised his thick arms to encourage a supportive response. Nearby cheers from his followers were surrounded by a sea of stillness, for in their weary hearts many silently yearned for freedom from the will of gods, kings, or commanders to simply have a place of their own. Klymenos sat, well satisfied that he had ended such talk.

The outburst left agreement impossible. The cheers subsided and the gathering seemed ready to disperse until interrupted by a strong voice: "You've heard of the Battle of Kadesh?" Kuprlli stood and spoke up. "Many of our forefathers fought at Kadesh between the Hatti and the Misriwi, the greatest clash of chariots, bowmen, and infantry ever known. Many thousands were killed; both sides claimed victory. Yet once it was over and everyone went home and thought about it a while, a grand and lasting peace was declared between Ramses and Muwatalli, inscribed on a sacred silver tablet. For many years after that, both empires prospered and its people also lived in peace. My friends," he looked around, "there is nothing dishonourable in peace and prosperity." This was faithfully translated by Henti so the Akhaians could grasp the meaning.

There was a moment of silence while the horde took in this statement. Some were moved but others were moved to anger. Voices rose in disagreement and there seemed a division between the Akhaians and Anatolians. "Warriors! We will not decide at this moment!" Sarpedon stood on a rock and in a booming voice silenced the crowd. "We leaders will commune with our gods and decide among the alternatives tomorrow evening. We will also consider if it would be best to allow individual choice in this matter, though an attack without a united full force seems out of the question. We can't enforce unity. Go back to your campsites now, rest and pray, and allow your gods to tell you if you are free persons or not." He smiled to himself at the irony.

Klymenos rose to leave, but as he did so, he hissed to Sarpedon, "Sardinian, the gods won't tell them; *I* tell them. And I said there is to be no breaking ranks among warriors, at least *my* warriors. You have gravely insulted my honour, and such insults will not go unavenged." He stormed away.

Back at the spot chosen for the leader's campsite, Kabi hastened to take Sarpedon aside and tell him the true story of the situation and the offer of Diomedes. It seemed acceptable that Henti was in earshot. "If it turned out you or Payava were leading this group, as he suspected, Diomedes encouraged me to exaggerate the numbers of the Hatti forces, but he wished me to tell you – and Payava if he were here – that he holds you in too high esteem to break faith with lies. He did so because he believes the talk of treasure could blind your troop, but saving the city could benefit all of us." He explained the offer to make a home in Ishtar's city was sincere and originated from the High Priestess of Ishtar who rules the city. Mahhuzzi the Hatti grand vizier and Diomedes supported it, and it was approved by the Great Queen herself. Kabi did not understand all that afoot, but he had learned that Suppiluliuma seems to have become possessed of the idea that he could escape his hopeless station as the Great King of a fallen empire by undergoing the rite of deification. "We must encourage the Hatti regiment to leave."

Sarpedon took all this in. "You stay here with Henti, who did such an excellent job at the meeting, knowing just when to translate perfectly and when to blur the message," he said smiling at her. "Something seems to be afoot right here, as well. I would speak on these matters and what you have just told me to Kuprlli, whom I trust. Must we leave the treasure of Hattusa?" Two guards followed and he left.

Left alone with the girl, Kabi suddenly felt uncomfortable. She was very young, but he wasn't all that much older. And he wasn't shy, just respectful and somewhat in awe. He looked up wordlessly as though he was part of the fallen tree on which he sat. Henti rose and went to the flat board that served as a table pouring wine into a bowl and mixing in water, with which she filled two clay goblets and came to sit next to him, throwing back her shawl and removing the fabric that served as a veil.

"You were inspired today," she smiled. The sun shone upon him.

"Yes?" he asked. "It's something I've never done before, stood in a council of leaders and expressed my thoughts. Yet it's strange. Once I began, all I could think of was my message and purpose. I forgot myself." He smiled back looking right at her and almost regretted it, such was the impact of her natural beauty.

"I remember you from before, the valiant scout who rides like a centaur. Whenever you galloped in, black curls flying, we all knew to expect important news."

"Yes, everyone knew of you, too. I wish we had spoken earlier, but even now, as the gods already know, I feel beyond my place. For most of my life, I was just a boy goat herder and then a slave, and now I am a vagabond warrior still with no home. You lived in a royal palace for years and are linked to our finest leaders..."

"Kabi," she laughed, touching his cheek with her soft hand, "you forget. I am or was a slave too – at least for the two sun-cycles I have been in the royal palace. There is no choice and no nobility in being one of the Great King's harem girls. I'd rather be a farm wife with two ugly children and a third on the way while toiling with my toothless old husband to grow lentils in our own patch of dry dirt than to be a slave in the royal palace of Hattusa."

Kabi's jaw dropped, as much over her colourful metaphor as its meaning.

"And I have been fortunate to be under the protection of two of your leaders, but I don't belong to them. Most of the time they are not around, and even though I stay robed and keep to myself men do stare at me and have attempted to grope my body. I don't leave the campsite at night."

"Yes, it must be frightening, my lady. I'm told these are difficult times, but it's the only times I've known since being taken from my desert home, which in truth was not all that peaceful either since my tribe did much sheep-stealing and land-grabbing." He paused. "Some days I find myself wondering about that, too, what it would be like – an uneventful life spent in the town of one's birth, working hard, marrying as my father directed, and raising a healthy family…" They looked at each other with understanding.

"I have had such thoughts, brave scout, but it is apparent that neither your fates nor mine have attached us to an *uneventful life*." They smiled and nodded together.

"And we're still young. What grim adventures yet await us!" Kabi open his eyes in feigned horror, and this struck them as so funny they nearly fell from their tree bench in the release of laughter. They reached to each other for balance, so eye to eye, holding each other's shoulders, they recovered, but something had passed between them.

"Tell me your story, young Kabi," asked Henti with an inviting smile.

"We will share," he said shyly.

When Sarpedon returned to the site the sun had gone down and the moon had not yet risen, but the evening star shone with a bright, silvery light. The fire was burning low and steady, and he was surprised to see Kabi curled up with Henti on a blanket, both fully clothed, speaking in low, intense voices with such engagement they didn't notice him arrive at first. When they realized he was watching them, they stopped and made as if to rise.

"Stay where you are," Sarpedon smiled, and they paused.

"My Lord…" Kabi began.

"I'm not your *lord*," the Sardinian replied with an ironic smile. "As I say, stay where you are. You two certainly look comfortable enough and that's rare enough on a march. Keep doing what you were doing and ignore me. I have a few things to think over, so I'll just move my mat to the other side of the fire."

"We're just talking…" Henti started.

"That I can hear. I'm very glad to see you two making friends. Friends are good. Now please continue," and he waved his hand in a wheel-like circle to encourage continuation. He poured himself a bowl of wine and added only a little water. Strangely, he felt pleased at seeing the two young people connect so well. He had been worried about Henti especially since earlier Klymenos had approached and offered to trade a fine horse for her. When Sarpedon declined saying he had promised to protect her, Klymenos had become insistent, upping his offer to include a golden chalice he had somewhere stolen. When he again said no, Klymenos lowered his request to one night only, but by then Sarpedon was walking away. Now, only hours ago, Klymenos claimed Sarpedon had insulted him and declared he would seek vengeance, so Sarpedon determined he would deal with that directly at the meeting tomorrow evening.

His thoughts were pleasantly interrupted by the now whispered chatter between the two across the fire, sometimes giggling and other times he was sure he heard muffled sobs. Sharing tales from their youthful lives, Sarpedon guessed smiling. How long it had been since he had enjoyed such intimacy!

The next morning emerging from his tent into the light, Sarpedon thought better of such public confrontation with Klymenos. It would likely lead to violence, which suited him fine since the man was a bully and braggart whom he had come to despise, but such a fight would likely have negative reverberations among the troops. He knew a choice had to be made as a unit, even if the choice was to no longer act as a unit. It would be best if he sought out the Danaan this morning and attempted at least to come to a procedural agreement if not an agreement on whether to attack or pass by.

He heated some warm lentil broth and barley cakes and regretfully went to wake the still sleeping pair under their open oilcloth. They were still fully clothed but their clothing was entangled like one garment, so closely had they wrapped themselves around each other. They were purring peacefully like cats before a fire on a winter night. He gently woke them, feeling a bit foolish for he had rarely acted so fatherly before, yet it felt right for the moment.

"I must leave our campsite soon, so I have made some morning victuals. We may be leaving camp to approach the city as early as tomorrow morning, so I suggest you, young warrior, accompany this maiden to her cleansing rituals. The river is near but its current is strong. I have heard there is a small cataract over the boulders further downstream that has a pool beneath it in which you each might find refreshment and renewal. Take your arms along, Kabi, and for extra protection take two of my guards."

As soon as Sarpedon had left and the pair had breakfasted, Kabi the scout and Henti the translator excitedly set about their preparation for their jaunt. Kabi put on his dagger belt and took up his bow, along with a few extra arrows in his quiver in case game was sighted. Henti took a shoulder bag to carry fresher undergarments , dried meat, and other items that Kabi did not observe. Sarpedon's campsite was near the front of the troop, so they easily slipped away without having to traverse the pathways of too many others. They were delighted both at their unforeseen friendship and the turn of events that was allowing them time to themselves amidst the rare natural beauty around them.

They resisted holding hands until they were far enough into the surrounding trees and rocky slopes to no longer be seen. Then they simultaneously reached for each other and held hands as they ran amongst the trees like young deer. The bedrock became steeper as they neared the roaring river, so they had to let go of hands to guide themselves through it. It had been a very long time for both of them since they had seen a mountain rapid like this, so they paused to stare at the foamy crests. From the water stains higher up on the shore, it could be seen the river had once run with much more volume though it still had plenty of force. They tried to talk but found they could not be heard, so they laughed instead, until they caught each other's eyes and fell into a passionate soul kiss. The river roared on but time stopped during the embrace. Then they were off again, following the current downstream, heads gloriously thoughtless but hearts running over with unexpected feelings of delight and discovery.

It took longer than anticipated, but they came to a lesser fork that flowed off to the right, which led them to the edge of a small cliff over which the water surged in a steaming cascade into a plunge pool below. They found an animal path and made their way down to it. It was not until they got to the circling pool and Henti was storing her sack of items on the soft moss under a burgeoning oak that she looked at him with her azure eyes and asked, “Did we forget to bring the other guards on purpose?”

“What?” Kabi asked, then realized he had ignored Sarpedon’s order. He looked at her as she approached the cold water in her no longer delicate bare feet realizing what he had done. On purpose? What did that mean? She began to loosen her garments, but Kabi found himself paralyzed by conflicting emotions. One was naked desire for the most charming, most alluring woman he had ever met. But the other one was guilt: what if they had been followed? What if he had left his arms on the shore and the worst thing that could happen did so? “Henti, I must not. At least not yet.” He knew if Henti dropped her robes, he would lose all caution, all sense of duty. Nothing else would matter. “Please, stay dressed while I check our surroundings.”

Henti loosened her garment so her shoulders were revealed then, disobeying him, insouciantly dropped off her loose robe entirely, tossing it upon the dry rocks. She walked two steps into the waters and looked up at him, pulling back her long golden hair. The wind itself seemed to hold its breath. Her graceful form was lean yet athletically strong. Her body was white as a lily, with flashes of darker gold hair in her armpits and between her thighs. Every move was undulant. He was lost. He had never seen such beauty – not in this life, not in godlike images, and not even in his dreams. His weapons didn’t matter. Their lives didn’t matter. He *must* strip and get in the pool with her *now*. He reached to pull off the bow. She realized the effect she was having and she was also deeply excited, but she heard a faraway presentiment and it spoke aloud through her, saying, “Kabi, we must keep our word. I will carefully wade here alone while you go do your search. Once you see nothing, come back and join me in this clear pool."

He remembered himself, and, though it seemed it was impossible for anyone else to find this little paradise that surely was theirs alone, he dutifully trudged away to find higher ground and look for intruders of any sort. If anything happened after he had ignored his orders, his newfound bliss would be shattered in shame and death.

"Ay, it's cold!" he heard Henti cry as she stepped into the water, but he refused to look back.

He went up and around the cascade and circled in the opposite direction from which they had approached, further from the Puruma and in the upstream direction. He noted the sun's placement in the sky, aligned himself with distant viewpoints, and marked his path in his mind. As a scout, he was well practiced in finding his way and not getting lost. He went through a thickened forest and back over a field of boulders. When he saw the river again he knew he had completed his circle and so made his way downstream again. He felt some anxiety, for he realized he had been so excited running toward the river with his new love that he had not done his usual scouting procedures of trail erasure and back or side checks for anyone tracking him.

As he gratefully arrived above the falls again and began to descend, he heard the scream. His greatest dread realized, he ran down the steep path, and when he came out by the plunge pool he saw two men had dragged the naked Henti out of the water to the moss near the oak tree. They were attempting to pin her down, but she was fighting like a she-demon, kicking, spitting, scratching, and cursing. The big one laughed and struck her forehead with his fist, the blow landing so hard her knees buckled.

"Enough!" Kabi yelled. "Step away now or die!" He drew the feather guides of the arrow back to his ear. The bow was fully taut and ready though he was very near.

"You!" The one who had hit her turned, and Kabi somehow knew it would be Klymenos. "This is even better than I had hoped. I was only told the girl had left with another child."

"Step back. In the next second, you die!"

The other man, a lean, brown-skinned warrior from somewhere inland, laughed with broken teeth and mockingly asked, "You going to kill both of us with one arrow?" He drew his khopesh and ran at the scout. Kabi had no choice and in the next moment the air was split with a hiss and the darker warrior had an arrow deep in the centre of his breast, tearing through his heart. He dropped his sickle-sword and stared perplexed at the arrow in him as he died and fell face forward.

Klymenos threw the girl down and drew his sword leaving Kabi no time to reload. He instead drew his dagger and ran directly at the big Danaan. Klymenos was much stronger and with a larger weapon, but Kabi was faster than anyone could have guessed. He ducked under the swung blade and slashed the thigh of the big man. But Klymenos raised his knee and sent Kabi sprawling. Henti scrambled away on all fours from beneath their feet nearer to her shoulder bag. Kabi came at the swordsman again, who raised his sword to fake a strike but stabbed instead. Kabi wasn't fooled, and dodged beside the thrust, leaping up to slash across the big man's nose and over one eye. In a rage, Klymenos went at him with wide sweeps of his bronze blade. Kabi stepped back and saw that with such a rage, Klymenos had forgotten defence and was no longer guarding his throat. Kabi waited for the sword sweep to pass by and lunged in for the kill, but, alas for Kabi, this time Klymenos was ready. He used the bronze butt end of the sword that had just swung by to slam Kabi hard on his upper forehead. Dazed, Kabi dropped onto his knees, his dagger clattering aside. Klymenos turned his bronze blade straight downward and raised it high to plunge it through Kabi's defenceless body.

But instead he froze in position, the sword poised, and then roared like a bull being disembowelled. Kabi rolled away to see Henti looking up between the thick legs of Klymenos, thrusting her iron dagger again and yet again up into his uncovered crotch. He wasn't disembowelled, but other parts fell in bloody pieces to the earth or onto her. The girl screeched like a fury and found the extra strength to drive the blade deep into him, twisting it with both hands like a washerwoman twisting water from a sheet. Klymenos stopped roaring, blankly dropped his sword, and stared into nothingness. When he fell backward to the ground like a thunderstruck tree, Kabi found his senses and his own blade and quickly moved to cut his throat.

"No," Henti said coldly. "He is already a dead man. Let's give him time to realize it." The iron blade fell. She had never killed anything before, not even an animal, but the dark goddess was singing wild hymns in her mind. She rose, her unclothed body and face now splashed with blood and organ gore, but it never stopped a relieved Kabi from dropping his weapon and embracing her, beating heart to beating heart. A ruthless ecstasy she had never known pulsed through her, as though she had been a sleeping beast her whole life. She pushed him back and began tearing at his clothes. He soon got the idea, and, once stripped, they ran together, naked as newborns, into the icy pool.

They dived beneath the water, washing clean the ways of the world. When they rose, Kabi exclaimed in wonder, "It *has* ended in shame and death, but thank the immortal gods, not for us!"

With one dead man on the shore and another soon to fall into the same state, they kissed each other madly with a feral passion neither had ever known before. Though neither was a virgin, they had no comparable experience. They had begun the previous night with spontaneous trust and open affection, but when that natural yearning was coupled with the bestial exuberance of defeating a threat to their lives, their joy in each other knew no bounds. They ran their hands over every inch of one another's body as though taking permanent possession, as though they themselves were possessed. They pulled and wrestled themselves to shore, not stopping their lovemaking along the way. They dropped to the soft moss beneath the oak tree where they attacked one another with such shameless love the gods drew clouds over the sky in embarrassment. The light rain, rare as it had become, did not register. An hour went by until their passion was sated and transformed into bliss. They held each other, eyes toward the sky, she on his shoulder, and their tears mingled in gratitude and astonishment as the wind hissed through the treetops and the dead grew cold on the rocks.

"We must get back," finally said Kabi. "There is the meeting soon."

Henti stirred, "Yes, back. I suppose we must. But the meeting will be missing one of the major players."

They realized that now things must be put back together, though one alternative was simply leaving the situation as it is. "Make it seem they killed each other and we know nothing of it?" Kabi ventured.

"Yes, Klymenos used the bow and arrow he disdains to carry? And while he did so, the one with an arrow in his heart managed to tear out his groin from below?" Henti shook her head, but both had to smile at her lurid sarcasm. "Besides, Klymenos mentioned to someone he saw us together as we departed."

"Maybe we should just go back and report what really happened, taking back all the weapons as soldiers do. We did nothing wrong. We were attacked. Let the kites feed on the corpses."

"Yes, Sarpedon and others would know we spoke the truth though they may find it hard to believe ... as do I. But what of the Danaans or at least those who are his cronies? Without Eruthros or Diomedes to stop them, they will demand blood vengeance."

"The gods protected us," Kabi said thoughtfully. "I say we sacrifice our trophies back to them and return in all innocence, forgetting what happened here. The bodies will soon be found, so we must act."

"Burn them as sacrifice, how?" Henti asked.

"No, Henti, much simpler. We just drag them into the wild river that will soon rejoin its source as thanks to the mighty Puruma for giving us this day. Only the gods will know the truth, but we must tell Sarpedon, of course."

And so it was done. They did not realize they both had serious headaches until they walked out of the forest looking like naked primitives to pull the smaller would-be rapist into the waters. Kabi tried to retrieve his arrow but during withdrawal the barbed point broke off catching on a rib, so he took the shaft to the waters as well. Klymenos was much harder to move, and as they dragged him by arms he left a bloody trail with gory detritus behind him they tried to avoid seeing. Henti ran back for his ragged boar's tusk helmet and for some reason put it on his head before they pulled him deep enough to let go yet still avoid being dragged away by the swift current themselves.

On the return, Kabi retrieved the weapons left by the two attackers and threw them into the waters too. They rinsed in the waterfall pool and dressed to return. They had just begun to go toward the path up beside the falls when Kabi casually asked Henti, "Forgetting anything?" She looked surprised for a second until she realized she had pushed all thoughts of the iron dagger with the mother-of-pearl handle from her mind. She ran back to it, rinsing it in the water longer than was necessary. Returning, she at last began to sob and shake in shock. Kabi came to hold her and, consoled, she pulled herself back together. She had on a stalwart smile when they set off.

Sarpedon stared nonplussed as the two young people told him their tale, far enough away from listening ears or prying eyes. They had been stared at as they made their way back amongst the vagabond warriors to Sarpedon's tent but no one had talked to them or even risen to their feet. Henti let Kabi do the talking and Kabi was surprised at what he had to say as he told it. He lied about nothing, but he did skip entirely over all to do with their lovemaking.

"I can't believe I didn't detect their presence somewhere behind us on the way there or when I did my circuit to be sure! It's my own fault things went as far as they did." Kabi exclaimed.

"Gods be praised you were victorious in such an uneven match," Sarpedon said evenly. "Klymenos is one of our most ferocious warriors, or *was*. Hard to believe!"

"Even so," Kabi reposed, "this is how it happened. Our harem girl translator turns out to be a she-demon when it comes to battle. Surely, you know that all I say is the truth. Our lives may depend on it."

To their surprise, Sarpedon lifted his head and laughed like a horse, stopped, and chuckled again. "I said that this is hard to believe, but of course I believe it. The proof is right before me on each of your foreheads!" The two raised their hands simultaneously, Henti feeling the painful swelling over her left eye that also left a black ring around it and Kabi touching the significant purple and black mound near his hairline. "Of course, we must keep this to ourselves. Who knows what it might provoke? Two warriors disappear. Who can say what happened? The gods work in mysterious ways. Of course, I will be the chief suspect, but that may work in my favour. His gang of supporters may show me a little more respect. But even better for all of us is the fact that now no one stands in the way of working with Diomedes and his plan for Lawazantiya. I will urge that the men themselves decide to stay or to go, but that none must attack the city. We must bring Kuprlli into this now, before we meet, and we need to know in more detail what is happening in the City of Ishtar. We will have to send you ahead, scout, where you can implant information to encourage the Hatti exit."

The three of them made their way across the encampment with Kabi accepting the pain of wearing his light leather cap over the swollen egg above his brows. Henti wore her shawl across her eye and bruised forehead but left off her veil. When she chose to come along, neither man protested. She had proven she was more than extra baggage needing protection. The day was lengthening and the traditional gathering time was after an early supper so most would not be hungry and quarrelsome.

The sounds of human speech changed their patterns as they entered the Lukkan area. The territory was no cleaner than anywhere else but it seemed so because of the profusion of bright colour with which the Lukka, both men and women, liked to adorn themselves. The warriors' headgear especially was multicoloured with purple and red being most common for the leaders. It varied from the tall hats made of upright reeds and some of actual feathers that had become tattered by now to the floppy linen or felt caps often brightly coloured in variegated stripes. They kept their bronze-plated armour well burnished. The Lukka were said to have long ago migrated to the Anatolian mainland from Kriti, so that might explain their penchant for bright purple robes and capes, but they also liked scarlet kilts.

They found Kuprlli cleaning his armour and Sarpedon greeted him. "One never knows, eh?" Kuprlli said referring to his preparation. "I am honoured to be visited by this noble assembly," he said, glancing at the girl in the drab robes, "though I do not think we need a translator. You are here before the sun wanes and we meet the others, so this must be important. Please take up jewelled thrones in Kuprlli's palace!"

Kuprlli's dry sarcasm was appreciated and they sat. Sarpedon wasted no time in getting to the point. "Klymenos and one other are dead. This morning they attacked Henti our translator by the river, wishing to do her evil. This young man, Kabi, whom you recognize, was there to protect her and, by the will of the gods, the ignoble warriors were overcome and destroyed."

Kuprlli looked at the two young people and blinked in disbelief. Henti raised her shawl to reveal her swollen forehead and black eye and Kabi pulled back his cap to show his significant purple swelling. "Where are the bodies, still there?" he asked bewildered.

"These good people acted to save their honour and their lives and are blameless, but the people of Klymenos may not agree and could cause enough of a disturbance that we are unable to act on the opportunity before us. It is best for now to play the hidden hart rather than the attacking lion. The bodies and their weapons were dragged into the waters and are not likely to appear again in the near future. As a known antagonist of Klymenos, I will be blamed, but if nothing is certain what can be done?"

"It's the work of the gods, is it?" Kuprlli smiled. "This is most unexpected, but surely you see that this is likely to work in our favour. There's no arrogant bully trying to tell everyone else how to think and act. We can proceed to make our decision with the approval of the masses."

"And what *is* our decision?" Kabi intervened. "Bearing in mind both the request and the offer of my Lord Diomedes, do we attack, join, or bypass the city?"

"An important decision indeed," continued Kuprlli. Another one is, *do we go with majority acclamation or do we allow each group or even each individual to decide*, which would not work for an attack? I might add that this decision is based on other events that are out of our hands. I thank you and Sarpedon for sharing the actual numbers of Hittite soldiery present in the city, but there are still enough to make an attack a costly venture; plus there is the fact that some of our own are already inside the city asking us not to do so, for what seems to be very good reasons. Also, if we choose to stay and become the guardians of Lawazantiya, the Great King Suppiluliuma and his Hittite soldiers would not stand for it. War again. So we have no choice but to negotiate for gifts and to pass by – unless the Hittites miraculously choose to depart! This is what is missing, Kabi."

"I am not clear on these dealings either, Kabi," ventured Sarpedon, only your bizarre story of a plan to capture Suppiluliuma and the expectation that the Hittites will leave."

"What *is* happening there, Kabi?" Henti asked boldly, surprising Kuprlli, and she reached out and touched Kabi's shoulder, which did not surprise Kuprlli.

"What has happened since my absence is unknown to me, but it is vital for us to find out before we act. With permission, I must return immediately and see for myself. Perhaps the gods have granted that the bold scheme has borne fruit or it may have turned out that all my friends are dead and the Great Queen recaptured. Let me tell you all I know." Kabi reported the behind-the-scenes intrigues of Mahhuzzi, Suppiluliuma, Lieia-Hepa, and Lilitu the High Priestess as well as he understood them. The special relationship between Diomedes and Queen Lieia-Hepa was revealed. General Kil-Teshub was being held prisoner or worse, though Kabi did not know why, but the General could be a key player in all this. How he had helped Diomedes, Eruthros, and others save the Great Queen from being murdered by assassins of the Great King and moved her into hiding was summarized. Kuprlli was again astonished. Kabi told of the planned attack by his comrades led by Diomedes against the Meshedi at the Temple of the Storm-God that was said to be some sort of distraction, from what he was uncertain. He ventured that perhaps the High Priestess was trying to get the king away from his bodyguards to help him join the gods. It felt sinful even to say such an incredible thing, and he admitted that the ancient ways frightened him. But he knew that Ishtar-Ereshkigal had great power in the dark Underworld of death, so that could greatly affect events above. How this would lead to the departure of the Hatti he also knew not, but he suggested that if they succeeded in luring the Great King to the Underworld of Ishtar in her temple, there would be no one to lead them but the Great Queen or Mahhuzzi, and both of them were now allied with the High Priestess and her consort the High Priest. He was sure things were happening as quickly there as they had been happening here, but he also wondered if creating some terror in the Hittite regiment might well speed along their prospective departure.

Kuprlli leaned forward. "This is an incredible tale but also wise counsel, especially from one so young. Yes, I agree you should head back and bring us news as quickly as possible. We will attend the gathering this evening ourselves, both to share the tragic news about the disappearance of our great friend Klymenos and to postpone further decisions until you return. Is this in accord with you, Sarpedon?"

"It is, but one more thing. I suggest we give mobilization notice to our troops to move out in the morning. No, Kabi, not to attack the city, at least not yet, but to perch ourselves on the steep hillside over it where we can be clearly seen. We will thin out our lines and move everyone forward, so it appears our numbers are greater than they are. Extra campfires overnight tomorrow will not hurt that impression. When the thousand Hatti soldiers see us, it may speed up their decision to move on. We will be able to see them leave for ourselves. But here's the thing, Kabi. You need to spread the word that our *massive* army means to feed on the blood of the Hatti men in the city, unless they depart and leave behind most of the supplies and treasure they brought with them from Hattusa. If they do not, every Hittite soldier will be slaughtered and left to rot, which won't frighten the Meshedi but it will the regiment. So, if we do not hear from you for three days, we will assume the Great King still rules and that you and your noble squad of heroes are dead or captured, so we will move to take the city as originally intended."

Kabi understood and once they got back to Sarpedon's site near the front, he began to immediately gather his things. Henti approached and gave him a prolonged, deep hug, but then she added, "I am coming with you."

Kabi smiled, "That's what would happen if this were a folktale, my beloved, but it's not going to happen here on the earthly world."

"Oh, you've never called me that before. You are my beloved too," she blushed at such a word. "But why, Kabi? I *must* be with you!"

"I need to be with you, too, Henti, but can you ride a horse?"

"I... No," she admitted.

Sarpedon appeared with a fine roan mare he said was named Pirwa. Kabi accepted the halter and went in front to share breath with it, nuzzling it, whispering to it, calming it. He fed it a handful of raw oats, a special treat. He tied his few belongings to it as best he could in leather and linen saddle sacks, including his unstrung bow and quiver. He went to Henti for a farewell kiss but was surprised when she handed him the formidable iron dagger of Diomedes in its sheath. "I promised to return it to him," she said then kissed him deeply. He secured it to himself and turned and mounted the horse with a smooth leap, his hands on its back as he scissored his right leg over. Pirwa pawed the ground and shuddered but stayed still.

To Sarpedon, "So, including travel time for you tomorrow, I have four days before you sack the city. You will hear from me in two. Take good care of my warrior lady. May the gods guide us!" He galloped away with a wave.

The High Priestess was at the open door of the Temple of Ishtar, a Hurrian guard on either side of her, as the six men approached carrying a large body streaked with dark blood on six red capes well tied together. She allowed them all entry, nodding to Zunan, but once within asked them to place the old general on his stretcher of capes upon the marble temple floor. "You may have saved a noble life, O Meshedi, and we will use all our power to make it so. But, please understand, Hittite soldiers are not permitted beyond this point. The Goddess has been violated once by such an intrusion, but it must not happen again." They looked to Zunan who nodded, and the wreckage of the unconscious Kil-Teshub was gently lowered as requested. Lilitu called for her temple guards to come forward and carry the victim to a specified "room of healing". This was done as the Meshedi departed, still confused over the fall of Suppiluliuma but proud of having saved their unfortunate commander. They also were anxious to get back to the beer promised at the Temple of the Storm-God, so they did not linger. Zunan stayed.

"Do you know all that has happened, High Priestess?" he asked.

"I believe so, but not clearly. I anticipate our next visitor will be the Great Sun of the Hatti. Is this not so?"

"The Great Sun may well have set, High Priestess. And your guess is right, but I do not understand how you could know this."

"I do not *know*, Zunan. It is just the Goddess whispering... If I am right, events fatefully unfold, as they should."

He studied her with admiration and a little fear. "You have taken much upon yourself, High Priestess, at such a crucial time. And all alone too. How is your unfortunate husband, the High Priest?"

She looked at him with her cold grey eyes. "He is on the verge of passing over into the netherworld, if he has not already done so."

There was a banging at the double door. With a nod from Lilitu to her temple guards, it was unlatched. She was greeted by the Akhaian warrior, still hyper-alert from the recent battle, his white teeth smiling through his blood-spattered face. "I bring you Suppiluliuma, the Great King of the Hatti and High Priest of the Storm-God."

Still held firmly with a guard on each arm but with his salivating mouth now uncovered, Suppiluliuma's eyes glanced about as though he were watching fireflies in the air about him. She noted his tall gold-ribboned crown being carried in the hand of a third guard while the fourth stood back, his spear upright. She was startled to see blood down the front of the royal kilt. She wondered if he had been unmanned. Indicating the blood, she asked, "Did you...?"

"No, he is intact," said Diomedes, but after looking back at the wild visage of the Great King, he added, smiling again, "In a matter of speaking. The blood is there because I wiped my sword on his royal skirt."

Lilitu raised an eyebrow, "It is important he is intact. I thank you, man of Ahhiyawa, for withholding your personal vengeance, for all things from here on in must happen according to Ishtar." She turned to the guardsmen and spoke in a voice of brass, "O Noble Meshedi, you have shown more courage than all the Hatti warriors in your ancient tales. You have been forced to awaken from the spell that you were long ago put under, the evil spell of worshipping this usurper who is no king, this false-god who is no god yet wishes to become one. He is revealed as Illuyanka, the dragon of chaos, who has risen again to destroy the sacred land of the Hatti!"

The Meshedi guardsmen, two firmly holding Suppiluliuma, the same who had been in the torture chamber, stayed silent in their places, but their widened, angry eyes and clenched jaws indicated they felt a great truth was being revealed to them.

"Yes, he is in truth Illuyanka, the very dragon-demon that has brought such catastrophe to our land. Was it not at the beginning of his reign that the Storm-God withdrew from the skies and the rain ceased? Did not the crops fail and the livestock cease producing? The plague ravaged us for five years for those reasons. Even the earth shook more often in despair. Why did the outlying territories begin to rebel against the Hatti? Why did trade with other great kingdoms dwindle away? What did this pretend Suppiluliuma do in response? He recruited more soldiers into his army then sent the warriors out to the frontiers, leaving the fields empty of workers and sacred Hattusa unprotected. And, worst of all, he attempted to send assassins to kill his own Great Queen and High Priestess of the Sun Goddess, the beloved Lieia-Hepa." The Meshedi shifted uncomfortably at the memory of their participation. "Why is he so accursed? The great gods know that these catastrophes began because he murdered his own brother, the rightful Great King, Arnuwanda, in the same way as he was about to kill your noble Gal-Meshedi!"

The Meshedi looked aghast. "We were not aware of these things, High Priestess," spoke the captain of the guardsmen, holding Suppiluliuma's right arm behind his back. No one bothered to remember both the drought and plague began during the latter years of the reign of Suppiluliuma's father, Tudhaliya, so overwhelmed were they by the hypnotic voice of the High Priestess of Shaushka-Ishtar and its shocking revelations.

"It is you, O Noble Meshedi, the most loyal servants of the Hatti gods and the great protectors of the Hatti kingdom, who must now save the Hatti people and the remnants of the Hittite Empire. You must lead the Hatti regiment that is here onward to a new city where Hittite forces will be welcomed as reinforcements for a new Great King."

Not used to being anything more than links in a hierarchy, the guardsmen were confused. "Lead, where?", "Who will lead us?", "Who will be Great King?"

"All this will be revealed to you. My healers declare that your Gal-Meshedi, General Kil-Teshub, is likely to recover so he will lead you. If he is not able, the saviour of the Great Queen, Captain Zunan-Teshub," and she indicated the Hurrian-Hittite with the black and grey short beard on his face, "will hold his place until he is ready."

"Talmi-Teshub, the noble King of Karkemish, has always been a friend of the Hatti and kept the Assyrian bull-god from our borders," Zunan spoke up like a commander. "It is there I say we go to throw ourselves at his mercy, tell him of the downfall of Suppiluliuma, and request an honoured place in his forces. It is there and other such cities in the southeast that the Hittites will continue on in kingdoms, if not as an empire."

The royal guardsmen felt relieved to be given directions. Lilitu took the lead again: "But now you must leave this sacred Temple of Ishtar. It is sacrilege for anyone but a priestess, acolyte, or initiated guest to go further. I believe Mahhuzzi the Wiseman has further explanation and refreshments to share with you back from where you came. You will pass your royal captive to Diomedes the man of Ahhiyawa, Captain Zunan, and my Hurrian sentinels."

This was done, the Great King just now beginning to come back to his senses. Bloodstained Diomedes and Zunan took up the positions for pinning the arms of Suppiluliuma, and the Meshedi, quickly assuming marching order, turned and departed. The king opened his eyes but recognized neither of those imprisoning him. "You!" he cried out when he saw Lilitu, though it was uncertain just whom he thought he was seeing. He looked around dazed but pulled himself tall and wheezed his outrage. "Who dares bind the rays of the Sun of the Hatti? Who dares to touch My Majesty?"

"Is your Majesty not ready to escape from mere human flesh?" Lilitu, said approaching near to the wild visage of Suppiluliuma and looking into his eyes.

"Escape? Yes, yes, I am ready to attain godhead, to join the rulers of Earth."

"So, before these witnesses, you hereby declare your soul's desire to willingly enter the Rite of Apotheosis, to commit yourself entirely to the hands of the High Priestess of Ishtar?"

He paused, realizing the gravity of what was being asked yet sensing the opportunity for glorification. "I so pledge," Suppiluliuma mumbled, only slightly drooling.

"And you further willingly submit to the Sun Goddess of Arinna also leading the descending procession into the labyrinth of the Underworld?" Lieia-Hepa appeared in a flowing gown of yellow-tinted sea silk, short blue cape over her shoulders, silver tiara around her head, silver moon sceptre in her hand, and her face altered by the exotically frightening face-paint of a priestess of Ishtar. Zunan saw only a disguised goddess, but still his goddess all the same. To Diomedes she seemed simultaneously repellent yet more compelling than ever, the paradox of desire.

After a shocked moment as if staring at an apparition, Suppiluliuma burst out ingratiatingly, "O Great Queen, you live!" He feigned tears, "I am so relieved to have you back with me. I have been beside myself with concern! Are you going to join in the ritual of ultimate transformation? Will you also become a god next to me?"

"I am already learning to allow Ishtar to possess me, foolish king, so I have no need of further transformation. So do you choose to die here and now in humiliation, or do you accept our predominance as we guide you across the darksome river into the woeful land of no return?"

"*No return*?"

"You will not return the same as you are now," Lieia-Hepa finished the sentence.

"Ah. I accept your ... guidance," Suppiluliuma said, but he was now torn between feeling hope and fear though the latter was the stronger. Being under the physical control of others was entirely new to him.

With that, Lilitu gave a signal and two temple guardsmen in small caps with curved, forward-pointing tips came forward to take the king, but Diomedes demurred. "He is our prisoner," he looked at Zunan who nodded agreement, "until we release him into your custody to meet his fate, of course."

"We wish to see the fabled gateway door to the Seven Trials of Descent," Zunan added. Diomedes knew of no such door but wished to learn the hidden route.

Lilitu's eyes widened with affront, but she only turned to the guards and gave instructions. To Zunan she said, "I see your time with the Hatti has not led to your forgetting the frightful tales from your Hurrian youth about the Underworld of Allani." To the guards, "Show them the way. Take this ... *king* to the holding chamber below next to the gated mouth. Give him water, feed him broth, and have him cleansed and purged. We must obtain his most resplendent royal robes for him to wear for the journey. Then chain him to the mock throne there in which humility is learned. Put on his royal robes late tomorrow afternoon. After that, we will come for him at dusk," the silver-haired High Priestess intoned. The Hurrian guards led the way as Diomedes and Zunan guided or half-dragged the once Great King of the Hatti between them. One of the guards carried the Great King's gold-entwined mitre.

The secret pathway to the empty well that emerged in the dark grove outside but still within the temple's wall was complex enough, but this time Diomedes was sure he had learned the way. They were led deeper into the centre of the dense grove where a giant elm hid the light of day. A fallen bough over stacked leaves hid the same disguised trapdoor between it and the temple foundation. Diomedes noted what appeared to be a small silver eight-pointed Star of Ishtar hidden on the inside of the golden bough. They entered down the dry well and returned back inside by a narrow, steeply descending staircase. As they went through one by one, passing Suppiluliuma down from one to the other, the warriors were soon confused as one narrow corbelled stone passageway led into another, lighted only by small oil lamps in the wall. Still, Zunan noted the fresh air wafting past him, which indicated ventilation either natural or manmade. After some time, it became clear that they were no longer in human-built passageways at all but in reconstructed caves naturally formed in the limestone long before there were temples here. The scent of water wafted through the air and a substantial hidden stream could be heard. Here the guards each took a torch from the wall and proceeded. Often, they came to "rooms" or forks or even crossroads at which unknown caves led off in other directions. The route had indeed become labyrinthine, so the warriors tried to pick out markers to remember it. The temple guards knew the way, however, and hardly paused except to check back occasionally on those who followed.

Then they entered a well-lit clearing in which several semi-sealed doorways were revealed. In the centre was an intriguing altar with carved figures from an unknown but obviously ancient peoples and with enough stonework around it for a significant fire to be built, but it was currently dark. Down a few broad steps was a huge stone arch within which was a bronze portcullis, the bottom part of which rose upward to meet the top section coming down to suggest a slightly open mouth in which were set pointed yellowish-bronze teeth. When the sections were drawn apart, the mouth and its teeth opened. The bottom section disappeared into the stone platform so those so sanctioned could walk through the gaping mouth, teeth hanging above, to the other side.

"This is the Mouth of the Hell, the portal of the Underworld?" asked Zunan, suppressing his terror.

"It is the mouth of Irkalla," replied a guard, "And this is as far as the uninitiated dare go. We'll take the prisoner now." The Hurrian guardsmen pushed open a thick door across from the mouth and used their torches to light the oil in the clay bowls and hollowed rocks within. They took the arms of the once Great King, who at last stood up straight revealing himself to be as tall as Diomedes, and led him within. He was no longer struggling but seemed ready to embrace the glorious transformation ahead.

7. Lilitu, High Priestess of Ishtar

"Sit with me, Great Queen, and share a little of our special light wine. We must attempt to foresee the future and perhaps inspire the gods to allow our destinies to unfold in accord with our wishes. A few things must be made clear or put in order." She sent a servant for honeyed wheat cakes and wine. Lieia pulled her deep blue cape about her shoulders and over her yellow silk gown and sat.

"With pleasure. That wine is excellent and in the midst of such stormy seas sitting with you would be a welcome island of calm." Lieia realized she was being chatty, so she sat down and focussed her mind when she saw the stern visage of the High Priestess. She asked seriously, "What is now to happen?"

"Everything ends and then something else begins anew. My consort, my father-son-husband, has passed into the Underworld from where there is no return. I will be needing a new consort or some sort of personal attendant."

"The gods have taken him then. Pity. So you are seeking a new consort or devoted attendant like the Babylonians call a *sukkal*?"

"Frankly, I'd prefer a sukkal like Ninshubur was for Inanna over another old consort. But I am not an immortal, so I would be content with a loyal and loving companion to someday take my place," Lilitu smiled into the hazel eyes of the younger woman, enjoying her darkly radiant pulchritude. "Lieia-Hepa, there is a crossroads before you. Since there is no going back and you cannot go forward in three directions at once, you will have to choose one. Is it to be divinity, power, or love?"

Lieia felt she grasped the gist of the choices but added anyway, "Explain."

"Great Queen, where is the empire of the Hatti?"

"The empire? Why it is right here, all around us, is it not?"

"Who is its Great King? Where is its capital and royal palace?"

"Ah, I see. The Great King Suppiluliuma has fallen as has the royal palace at Hattusa. But there are others of royal ancestry who can take his place, at least until one of his harem sons comes of age. Surely you don't expect me to step forward! Great Queens are not permitted to rule alone though Puduhepa unofficially shared the power."

"Alas, that is so. You would not be accepted by the nobles or the rabble, though you clearly have a great queen's disposition and your survival indicates your cunning. Kil-Teshub if he lives or even Mahhuzzi, both of the royal family, might be acceptable as a king or a regent, but only amongst the Hatti from Hattusa now here in Lawazantiya – hardly a kingdom. No, my dear, the Hittite Empire is no more, so you as Great Queen are no more. You are still a priestess of the Sun Goddess of Earth, but Arinna is gone. Without a temple or a city, there is no High Priestess. Here in the city of Ishtar, you are secondary to its High Priestess. I am Tawananna here." She looked meaningfully at Lieia, ignoring that she had also said that all earth goddesses are one. "So that is one road, the devotional path of serving immortal divinity. You are invited to stay here in this temple, in this still fertile valley, and be my sukkal, perhaps my intimate," she smiled invitingly, "and someday, perhaps, my replacement. You would identify your Sun Goddess of Earth with Shaushka, with Ishtar, and perhaps even with her dark sister Allani. This is the sacred path that may lead to immortality as you dissolve into divinity.

"But the way of power may not be closed because you are a woman. In fact, that could be your path to it. There are still strong Hatti or Hatti-Hurrian kingdoms nearby, any ruler of which would seize the chance to take the title of Great King. You could carry on as sub-queen by agreeing to marry one of them as another wife. But having already been

Great Queen of the Hatti and with your devastating beauty and ruthless cunning, you would soon become first wife and Great Queen once again. Does this interest you?"

"The consort to another over-inflated Hatti king, this one probably older. Not inviting. You are thinking of Halata in Tarhuntassa or Talmi-Teshub in Karkemish?"

"We have heard Halata is now land-locked since the seaport of Ura has fallen to the pirates. Other cities like Kummiya and Halab are far enough inland so the raiders on ships have not yet burned them to the ground."

"Thank you, High Priestess, but the path of service to the Great Goddess sounds much more wondrous. But what did you mean by the path of love?"

"You know very well what I mean, Lady Lieia. Diomedes. I suspect he will soon carry on with the other adventurers soon to arrive here, moving on to Alasiya or Canaan or wherever, but it is obvious you share a powerful physical or even mystical bond. But is the attraction of love enough to get the former Great Queen of the Hatti to live on ships or in tents while new cities burn under the hand of her paramour?"

"Ah, you know of us then?"

"One would have to be blind not to know. Ishtar has merged your passions like two storms meeting at sea."

"He may choose to stay, as we have invited the approaching troop to do."

"He may, but I think it most unlikely. He is a freebooter at heart though he may someday seek a home elsewhere. If he were to stay here, you are thinking you could be both a priestess of Ishtar and his loving wife? Ishtar is not a domestic goddess; she pays scant attention to marriage or childbirth. You could not be both. If you choose to become my sukkal and a priestess, you would lose claim to sole ownership of the man. Which would suit your High Priestess well, as I myself very much desire to test his limits in the erotic rites of Ishtar, and I have seen other acolytes attracted to the man, as well."

The suggestion cut like a knife. For the first time in her life, Lieia felt an uncomfortable emotion, a keen mixture of anger and hurt. Jealousy was new to her. "At this point, I only know I must be with him, whether on a ship or not. But we are not there yet. For the time being, I ask that you accept me as a full priestess on the dark journey that begins tomorrow evening. I will follow your lead unquestioningly in all things. I shall learn much and am prepared to watch or assist the cruel Suppiluliuma to dissolve into godhead. Or not."

"You are part of this, priestess. I *insist* you lead the procession with me. You may well have a destiny of your own to meet."

There was a knock on the temple portal, but not with the butt of a spear. "This must be the Wiseman," Lilitu looked up. "Let us hear how he has dealt with the two bands of warriors who were killing each other only a short time ago."

Hurrian temple guards opened the thick oak doors and Mahhuzzi came flowing in, wearing his usual long colourful robes with the high girdle, his pointed turban of silver fabric, and his curly-toed shoes. He spotted the women seated across the room and bowed low, "Your Highnesses," he said. "Things are moving quickly. I have much to report. May I approach?"

"Of course, Mahhuzzi, dear friend. Come sit with us," Lilitu spoke and both women smiled a welcome though neither rose.

He joined them but in so doing, he found his usual calm demeanour had deserted him. He was still excited from his addressing both sets of warriors, telling them what they wanted to hear, and getting them to trust and forgive each other to a degree. The barley beer helped. But now it was the sight of two such extraordinary women, a study in contrasts yet each disturbingly beautiful, that gave him pause. Except for her darkly made-up eyes and dark jewels, Lilitu shimmered in silver and white while Lieia shone in blue and black with her sea blue cape and raven-black hair.

He allowed himself a second to take in the sight, which was noted, but then he gathered himself to sit and do business.

"When I left them, the warriors who had begun by killing each other were quaffing beer, toasting to the fallen, and even managing to speak to one another. But they all listened intently to the three half-truths I told them, may Ishtar forgive my duplicity."

"Duplicity in service to Ishtar is blessed by Ishtar, have no fear," smiled Lilitu. "What did you say?"

"First, I repeated the truths they already knew – that Suppiluliuma had gone mad and had imprisoned and attempted to kill the Great Queen and that he had tortured General Kil-Teshub to the point of death. I told them the Storm-God had deserted him, and that is the reason for the long-lasting drought. But then I added that he had gone into frothing spasms, which many remember from the last plague, and that he had died. When they asked, I added that he was to receive no royal funeral procession for he was demon-haunted and no longer the Great King when he died."

"This is great cunning, my advisor. For now he will not be sought," said Lieia. "Yet it must have left both troops in a state of confusion."

"Yes, leaderless warriors are a danger to everyone, and the Hittites certainly have no reason to love Lawazantiya. So my second half-truth was that Talmi-Teshub, King of Karkemish, had invited them and the rest of the Hatti regiment to come immediately to his city so Hittite kingdoms could continue on somewhere. I did not choose Halata in Tarhuntassa for I fear he would not welcome us even though he is threatened by the peoples from the sea. We must send a swift courier to alert Talmi-Teshub to the good intentions of the Hatti soldiers, so he does not fear an attack when he sees them approach. That he will welcome the thousand Hatti from here is likely to be true."

"Yes, we will find such a courier forthwith," Lilitu said. "The third half-truth?"

"We have not yet heard from the approaching troop of unknown warriors, but I told them a horde of barbarians was on their way likely hunting down the Hittites who had escaped them at Hattusa, so they would be better off with more forces behind formidable city walls, such as those at Karkemish. They responded with a murmur of outrage, these being the fearless Meshedi, not the regular regiment, though I believe some of Diomedes' fighters looked pleased.

"To bring back their joy, I added a bonus half-truth. I told them their Gal-Meshedi, Kil-Teshub, was favoured by the gods and that he would heal enough to be able to lead them onto fabled Karkemish. The cheering could have been heard in the lower town. I'd swear I even saw some of the barbarians cheering. But this is indeed a half-truth for I fear my stubborn old colleague may only be half-alive. We can only wait to see."

"He will pull through," the High Priestess replied. "It seems he was not spiritually present during his torture, so his mind and soul are undamaged. He will live though he may be shocked at what has happened to him. Whether he is able to be moved within days is the only question. We must also check on the other wounded."

"A further question, High Priestess?" Mahhuzzi asked.

"The High Priest, my consort, is dead," she knew the question and replied without emotion. "It appears we have an entire temple dedicated to Ishtar's Tammuz with no high priest of Tammuz. Only servants, minor priests, and a few guards dwell in it."

Mahhuzzi bowed his head gravely, yet, he wondered, did he really perceive an invitation? He had intended to follow the Hittites to Karkemish, if that's where they were going, for he would surely receive a high station there. *But what if...?*

"The Rites of Inanna's descent begin tonight, my High Priestesses?"

"Yes," the priestesses answered simultaneously and looked at each other, Lieia with amusement but Lilitu less so. "If you are wondering whether you should descend with the procession, I think not," the High Priestess of Ishtar spoke. "No disrespect to you or to your sex – men who are not men will be coming, too – but only the initiated dare undertake the journey to the Underworld."

"Of course, High Priestess, I feel I am needed here on the surface in any case. There is much that needs immediate attention. Perhaps you will allow me to attend to affairs here in your name and do as you would do while you are gone?" He hoped she would take the hint that he was the best candidate to be her new consort, intact of course, not as a gallus, so he might explore her mysteries more deeply. "I must find that courier to alert Karkemish, and I must make sure the Hatti regiment spread out throughout the lower town are willing to follow the Meshedi to Karkemish. They must agree to follow either General Kil-Teshub or, if not, Zunan the Hurrian."

"Zunan-Teshub? But he has served as my personal attendant all these years and is valuable to me as the trusted bodyguard who just helped save my life."

"He is yours to command, Great Queen," Mahhuzzi replied, "but I believe he has already expressed his willingness to temporarily serve as Gal-Meshedi if called to do so."

"Besides, *Great Queen*," Lilitu used her title sarcastically, "unless we are all greatly deceived, do you not have a new protector in the man of Ahhiyawa or was that merely a night of brief pleasure?"

Lieia raised her chin to protest the open effrontery but then softened, "I do not know," she admitted. "I also feel a calling toward Ishtar as Sun Goddess of Earth, so I may never need any protector again beyond the goddess herself." The High Priestess smiled, her sharp teeth flashing.

In the pause that followed, Mahhuzzi asked about what had been troubling him. "May I ask about this forthcoming ritual, High Priestess? Though I do not doubt the gods – blessings on all those present but unseen – I wonder about certain things. If my ignorance is too shameful, please just indicate so."

"I hear you, O Wiseman. Even in your devout wisdom you wonder if the Underworld below into which we are about to descend is the true dwelling of Ishtar's dark sister, Allani and her consort Nergal-of-the-Sword. Is it really where the dead gather as speechless shades in darkness and dust, or is it just a twisting path that leads to a dark flat room in the cavernous hollows of rock below? Is it another stone temple or is it a sacred place of death and possible deification? The answer is *yes* to your question, Mahhuzzi, it is both and more. Yes it is death the end and the end of death, that is, the beginning. But, fear not, my friend, you will not see it for many years yet."

He looked at Lieia, not sure if he was seeing a liberated lover or another priestess of Ishtar. "Is the Great Queen, Lieia-Hepa, attending you on this journey into darkness?"

"I have assumed so," Lilitu intervened. "She has an important role to play, for which we are both prepared. She is the Bride of Doom. If Suppiluliuma succeeds in overcoming his humanity and attaining apotheosis, she must enter into a sacred marriage with Tammuz, the demigod he becomes."

Lieia raised her chin proudly, her hypnotic dark eyes glittering. "If it helps Suppiluliuma leave this world and any claim he has to be Great King, I am only too happy to do my part. My royal marriage will thereby be undone, and I will be free to become either the associate of the High Priestess of Ishtar or to go gallivanting across the sea with the man, Diomedes. I do not believe ritual marriage with a god will have any relevance back here on Earth. Will it, High Priestess?"

"A sacred marriage has relevance only in the realm of the sacred, O Sister. Your spiritual status back here on Earth will no longer be of concern."

With that, Leia declared she had much to do – study, pray, and dress for her central role in the ritual. Nodding goodbye, she left to join her retainers and go to her quarters. Lilitu asked for Mahhuzzi to remain. "To avoid shock later, there are some things I must share with you now in private, future husband..."

Diomedes and Zunan were guided back to the surface and into the upper Temple of Ishtar. Was it the same path? Neither of the two was sure, but each had tried their best to memorize the natural features and markers along the way, just in case. When they arrived, it was hours later, and they discovered their memories differed. They found Mahhuzzi present and alone but also ready to leave.

"We must organize the Hatti," Mahhuzzi said, "at least as best we can." The three left together. Back at the Temple of the Storm-God, they found the post-battle beer social that Mahhuzzi had organized long shut-down and each group of warriors peacefully dispersed back to its own quarters. The men found servants who brought them a bowl of warm beer that they shared through individual reed straws. Mahhuzzi sighed as they sat down, "It has been an incredible day, a day when the destiny of our kingdom has been changed, for the better I am certain. We are each on our own trajectory that has also been permanently altered yet we are far from done yet." Mahhuzzi looked down, seemingly troubled, gathering his thoughts. "I am still digesting things, secrets that the High Priestess has shared with me that tomorrow when we meet, we must discuss. For now, I need to know if you, Diomedes, have heard news from the approaching band of warriors."

Diomedes sucked up and swallowed a large draught of the raw barley beer and replied, "Kabi has not yet returned, but he has hardly had time. We should hear from him this evening at the earliest. Is that enough time?"

"We hope so," said the chief steward. "We may need his words to help convince the Hatti regiment in the city below that leaving this city is a good idea. Tomorrow morning, if you two accompany me, we will take several Meshedi, including the captain of the guard who is known and respected, and venture into the lower town to gather up the regiment of soldiers that has spread itself around. We have been told they have rather taken over certain areas of the city with the result that the populace hates them but can do nothing. Perhaps they will be more than ready to move to a new city where they will be welcome. And of course it is best if we alert Karkemish to their coming."

"Tomorrow, after you speak to them, I will address the regiment. I know many of them from years on the job and Hattusa allowed for much interaction," Zunan offered.

Diomedes gulped back more beer. "Tomorrow then?"

"Yes, gentlemen. Take your ease, clean up, dine, and rest. In the morning, gods willing, we shall meet here again and attempt to thread the needle by bringing together events in a fortuitous manner. Zunan, you are staying in your barracks?" Zunan nodded.

"I shall be in back in the great Temple of Ishtar," Diomedes smiled wiping the beer foam from his mouth and burping behind his hand. "Doing Zunan's job and protecting the Great Queen." The two warriors laughed, Zunan a bit ruefully. Mahhuzzi forced a smile.

Before proceeding back to Lieia, Diomedes arranged with a remaining Lukkan to spread the word amongst the rest of his squad of warriors who had fought earlier that day to watch for the Hittite regiment gathering in the square the next day, so they could hang around on the edges and learn what they could. Then they each dispersed.

On the morrow, the early day was breezy with drifting clouds but the sun-goddess was already raising the temperature. It began with the best news possible as Kabi rode into the city and went directly to the Temple of Ishtar where he located Diomedes, who was late to rise. "I was delayed because travelling at night is difficult. I must get back to Sarpedon and the troop to tell them what the decision of the Hittites has been. Are they leaving, are they going to try to fight us, or had they become disorganized? It will determine whether they attack or merely pause outside the city gates."

Diomedes was delighted to learn Sarpedon was leading the approaching warriors, but was saddened to hear Payava had been killed at Nerik. Kabi, in turn, was astonished to learn of the dramatic events in Lawazantiya in the short time he had been gone, but he could see things were unfolding as they had hoped. Kabi unstrapped the silvery-iron dagger in its engraved bull's hide sheath and gave it back to its owner from Henti, saying offhand that it had been a "lifesaver". Diomedes asked him about the notable bruise in the centre of his brow, but he postponed the explanation involving love and death at this point, promising he had his own significant tale to share in the future.

After Kabi quickly bathed and shared some light sustenance with the Akhaian, the two men joined Mahhuzzi, Zunan, and the four king's guardsmen, who had been present at the torture of Kil-Teshub, in the courtyard before the Temple of the Storm-God. All were wearing full battle dress armour, the Meshedi adding the distinguishing gold insignia and red capes of their position. Mahhuzzi had anticipated sending Kabi to Karkemish as messenger, but Kabi let it be known how vital it was he return as swiftly as possible to the approaching troop lest it attack the city. The chief steward understood.

Mahhuzzi had sent orderlies ahead of them to gather the thousand-man regiment into the town square. Even with advance notice, it was not an easy task. The seven men, led by Mahhuzzi, marched down the steep roads to the square without a pause. There were no longer any guardsmen patrolling the streets. Soon word spread and most of the regimental soldiers were gathered in the public square, some with women they had acquired, and others already sucking on wineskins. They had all heard of the battle in front of the Temple of the Storm-God, but beyond that was only conjecture. Some had heard Kil-Teshub had been killed protecting the Great King in an attack by strangers; others had heard the Great King had been brought down by his own Meshedi guards; there was a further rumour that the Great Queen had led the Hurrian guards to kidnap the Great King. In any case, it was only clear that there had been bloodshed and murder on Temple Hill. No one knew who the strangers were, and no one was certain who had died. In hopes of learning the truth, they gathered in such numbers they overran the town square, which was actually a circle in honour of the Great Goddess.

"Do you see what is happening in the town centre?" Shipibaal asked the messenger, his lover and companion, who had finally asked to be called Telipinu, a name he said he had picked up *along the way.* "Like the Hittite Great King or the Hatti god of agriculture?" Shipibaal had asked.

"Neither," replied the messenger, annoyed. "Agriculture? A common mistake." He added,

> "Telipinu disappears unpredictably like time or life itself, and appears again only when ready, not like the orderly change of seasons. He is the boundary-crosser."

Back in the present, they decided to go check out the gathering but stay in the background.

They stood on the elevated stone circle, eighteen unwounded, regular Meshedi spreading out on the lowest level with the four who had carried off Suppiluliuma above them. All in parade armour, they faced the regiment and banged on their shields with their golden spears to call for quiet. Mahhuzzi took the highest point and signalled for a horn blast from the sawetra to focus attention. His clarion tenor voice carried nearly far enough to be heard by all, and those who could not hear soon got the message second-hand. The grand vizier of the Hittite Empire did not identify the men with him, but the Meshedi and Zunan were well-known. The strapping warrior with the short beard wore no helmet so his chestnut-brown hair blew in the breeze, but his bronze-plated circular shield and the strange bronze armour were unknown here. He and the wiry young man in rider's leathers with a bow slung around his shoulder were simply accepted as unusual mercenary bodyguards. Mahhuzzi in his well-recognized godlike attire was known, but he began by identifying himself anyway, "You all know who I am... I have important news." Getting right to the point, he went on, "The Great King of the Hittite Empire is no more. He has caused his own death."

After the inevitable clamour died down, he again outlined the story of the demonic possession of Suppiluliuma who must have been rejected by the Storm-God for all the calamities that had befallen the kingdom since his reign began. He told them of the imprisonment of the Great Queen and the king's attempt to have her murdered. The crowd learned of the torture and mutilation of their noble general, Kil-Teshub, as witnessed by the four Meshedi guardsmen below. The crowd roared in shock and a rising tide of outrage swept through them. With that, Mahhuzzi next explained that these four Meshedi had led a revolt of the Men of the Golden Spear and saved the life of Kil-Teshub, but as they dragged him off, Suppiluliuma (he used his name instead of his title) had fallen into a fit of madness, eyes boggling and frothing at the mouth, and died as the demons abandoned him. The crowd now cheered, and Mahhuzzi the Wiseman was pleased to have swayed them to where he wanted.

But when he next informed them that if they wished to continue their lives as loyal Hittite soldiers, they would have to do so by following Kil-Teshub and Zunan south to Karkemish to serve Talmi-Teshub who would become their Great King and High Priest of Teshub, certain sectors began to protest. When Mahhuzzi further told them that it was time to move on because there were no acceptable replacements for the throne here in Lawazantiya and, furthermore, they were not wanted here by the people in Ishtar's holy city, rebellious outcries began to spread. "Who needs a Great King!" Someone with his arm draped around a local bar-girl and a wineskin in his hand bellowed, "We have all we need right here!" At first it was only a minority who protested but the shouts and complaints soon spread as they sensed there was nobody here with power over them who could tell them what to do. They had been having things their way, freely indulging themselves in a land of plenty, why should that change? Someone even shouted, "We can take over the Temple of Ishtar! We don't need a Babylonian goddess!" "We can own this city!" Now many of the men were waving their weapons and yelling defiance.

The crowd began to shove amongst themselves and shuffle forward toward their perceived oppressors.

Things were turning ugly and the few royal guardsmen were not enough to hold the crowd back. It was then Kabi noticed the dust and the flashes from the sun's rays reflecting off metal above the steep hill across the riverbed plain. Kabi alerted Diomedes who looked in the same direction. Just where the mountains abruptly began, a large troop of warriors was coming into position and setting up camp. Diomedes pointed his spear at the sight and in his best Luwian roared, "Invaders! Hunting the Hatti who escaped Hattusa!"

Mahhuzzi looked up and took a few moments to comprehend, but then he too projected his penetrating voice to announce, "Look up, O ye bewildered army of Hatti. The sea invaders have come! They're here to do to this city what they did to Ugarit!"

Even as eyes followed the pointing spear of Diomedes and word spread, the dust cloud grew and the number of reflective flashes increased. In the moment of silence as they took in the sight, some imagined they could hear the murderous barbarians gathering on the distant bluff for their final assault. All knew of the onslaught of the peoples of the sea and what had happened to Ura, Alasiya, and Ugarit, and they felt they knew who had burnt even their inland capital of Hattusa. Everything changed in moments. Suddenly being a professional soldier in Karkemish under a new Great King seemed an excellent idea. There were already a far greater number of Hittite soldiers there than here and they could join them for a significant defence. Instead of rebelling, they began a chant for General Kil-Teshub to come forth and lead them.

"To save your lives, I have a further message to deliver. The warriors on the hill are among those who destroyed Hattusa. Some have already entered this city and killed or wounded half of our royal guardsmen. Is this not so, Captain?"

The captain of the Meshedi among the four just below Mahhuzzi saluted the heavens and declared, “Such was the will of the gods!”

Now they were listening, so Mahhuzzi continued, “They are coming here tomorrow, sworn to kill every Hatti soldier in this city!” There was a collective groan of dismay; all bravado was gone. “Gather here tomorrow morning and bring all the goods or people you wish to keep with you and the journey to Karkemish will begin. I promise you will have a general to lead you, either Kil-Teshub himself or this soldier here, Zunan-Teshub. Go then, prepare for departure! Prepare to save the Kingdom of the Hatti!” He had mentioned neither the stored food supplies they had brought nor the various forms of Hattusa treasure locked away in the temple of the Storm-God.

The crowd dispersed with some grumbles but mostly in silence, many looking up anxiously on the bluff where the large army of predatory barbarians was gathering. “How many did you say there were?” Diomedes asked Kabi, obviously impressed.

“There’s two thousand at a generous count,” Kabi replied in a low voice. “The cunning Sarpedon has spread them out in a thin line on the heights to make them look like more. Wait until tonight, there will be three times the number of campfires than are needed.”

Diomedes appreciated the planning. “Tonight just as the final descent of the fallen Great King is taking place...”

“Yes, they call it the rite of ... I forget, a very ancient goddess from the distant east. Is Lieia-Hepa taking part?”

“Inanna is the very ancient goddess, Kabi, going back at least to the Akkadians, and we know no other names more ancient than that. And, yes, Lieia has a central role.”

“May the gods protect her. I mean her gods, but any will do.”

“Strange blessing from a man who doesn’t pray or sacrifice to any gods.”

“There’s just too many, and if they are all one, that one would not notice me.”

Led by the Meshedi, the four men on the hill gathered their things to move toward the road ascending toward what was known as Temple Hill, the akropolis of the city, high and rugged, but not nearly as precipitous as the akropolis over Hattusa.

"So, young Kabi," the vizier asked, "you are going up to that troop of warriors to tell them the Hittite soldiers are leaving town tomorrow or the next day, and that there's no need to destroy this fair city?"

"Yes, that is the plan."

"So we have apparently succeeded in getting our troops out," he paused. "But without the Hittite soldiers here, won't the city be defenceless, easy prey for your friends, the seaborne infantry?"

"It is so, O Wiseman," Diomedes intervened. "But they have been told of the agreement of you, me, the High Priestess, and the Great Queen that they will be feted outside the city walls, given gifts and fed, in exchange for moving on to their destination on the sea, or, for those willing to forsake the sea, make a home here as defenders of the city of Ishtar."

"A bold offer it was, Akhaian. Your suggestion, as I recall. But what makes you think such an agreement will be honoured?"

"The offer originated with Lilitu the High Priestess. Their leader and I are indeed friends, as you say, Mahhuzzi. It is he who gave me this fine sword," Diomedes added, patting the hilt of the heavy sword across his chest. "We call it *trust*. Without it, there is no honour. Even the barbaroi must have it to function. Also, it is quite likely that a significant number of them will be more than happy to become soldiers of a standing army and settle down, and I doubt if they will care which god or king they serve."

Mahhuzzi chuckled appreciatively, but added, "I hope you are correct."

"Grand Vizier, look at that man watching us," hissed Kabi. As the circular square was clearing out, Kabi had caught sight of a familiar face lingering on the edge. "Is that not the envoy from Ugarit we met just before we freed the

Great Queen? He told us you had shown him the temple that held her prisoner."

"Yes, Shipibaal, I believe he is called. He's gesturing as though speaking even though he's alone, perhaps with his personal deities. Kabi, approach him, call him over. And smile, we don't want to scare him off. Diomedes stand back and don't look so dangerous. This could be my envoy to King Talmi-Teshub."

Kabi sauntered towards the recently retired envoy, smiling and when he caught his eye ventured a wave. Shipibaal looked startled but, disarmed by the approach, held his ground. "Greetings, Shipibaal of Ugarit. You must remember me, your friend Kabi the bowman amongst the four barbarians."

"I never knew your name," Shipibaal managed as they clasped thumbs in the greeting of old friends. "But I remember how you and your friends rescued the Great Queen in a bloody melee. And of course I recognize Mahhuzzi the vizier. This is my companion," but he looked around and there was no one there. "He's gone," Shipibaal said surprised.

"No matter. Come with me. Mahhuzzi the Wiseman would speak with you now."

Shipibaal was confused by this sudden turn of events. He had hoped never to see this murderous group of warriors again, probably part of the same invaders that had pillaged his city and killed his king. The dangerous man of Ahhiyawa was up there. But it was Mahhuzzi himself calling upon him. Why did Telipinu disappear just when he could use his counsel? Kabi took his arm and led him up the centre knoll without resistance.

Mahhuzzi greeted him without his usual formlity, clasping his thumb and, finding they were the same height, touching his forehead with his own turban-wrapped forehead. "Shipibaal, dear friend, what adventures we've had together!"

"Yes, much has happened. The Great King is dead and the Great Queen is free. You did it! Is she now the ruler or are you?"

"I am here for now," replied Mahhuzzi enigmatically.

Shipibaal continued, "So glad you cleared things up with the Hatti soldiers today. They have been running amok in the lower town, stealing what they want and generally being a pain. I had heard little news that made sense, just gossip, so I thought it best to lay low and live my life with my companion."

"No one could blame you," Mahhuzzi added, "and you have wisely kept your council, discussed what you know with no one?"

"With ... no one," Shipibaal looked about to make sure his fib would not suddenly appear. "I am so glad to hear the entire Hatti regiment is leaving."

"And this is why you have been summoned, young envoy. The Hittite regiment and Meshedi will leave tomorrow and make their slow way to Karkemish. You must get there before them and prepare King Talmi-Teshub for their coming. I believe you know the fastest route there and you indicated you have had dealings with this man."

"I have in fact stood before him. He was going to send troops to support my once beloved Ugarit but time ... ran out. And, yes, I know the fastest way to get there."

"Good. He will know you as a trusted inter-kingdom diplomat. I think it likely he will not take it badly that he is gaining new forces to add to his defences and that he will be in possession of Suppiluliuma's golden-pointed crown. It will make him in essence the new Great King of the Hatti, though unlikely to be recognized as such beyond his own city. Will you undertake this vital communication?"

Shipibaal liked the reference to him being an *inter-kingdom diplomat*, so he replied, "To hear is to obey, O Chief Steward. When am I to leave?"

"You are to leave as soon as you can find a pair of good horses, one for supplies. Are you going alone?"

"I know exactly where to find such horses, but a few iron ingots, chips of gold, or silver shekels will be necessary to purchase them and for bribes along the way. And I will likely take my companion since he is a swift-footed messenger himself. I know a passage through the mountains and once through we are already on the plain of the river the Hatti call the Mala. Perhaps we can make it by two days at nightfall and, if not, soon after."

"Here, take four fast young horses, and make sure you have weapons," Mahhuzzi said, and reached into his wallet for a significant pouch of royal coin, passing it to the young envoy. "Don't tarry. Go now, and may the god of travellers watch over you." The other three men all added their blessings and Shipibaal was off, excited to have an adventure and a part to play in royal affairs. It would be his first trip with Telipinu, so it almost sounded like a holiday.

It was still early afternoon, but Kabi knew it was time for him to return to the warriors on the mountain bluff above. He was pleased he could bring what he hoped was good news to Sarpedon, but even more he longed to be with Henti again, whom he knew must be missing him as he was missing her. The three men accompanied him to the stable on the edge of Temple Hill where he had left Pirwa. The mare had proven her strength and endurance in getting here, and he had no wish to ride anything else back, but this time he took along a spare mule just in case of the unexpected. The life of this city depended on his getting up on the steep hillside with his message. He mounted Pirwa, tying the long halter of the mule to his thigh and departed. His three companions wished for the messenger god to protect him and waved him on its way.

Mahhuzzi made to separate from Diomedes and Zunan who were going to check on their wounded comrades. "Look in on General Kil-Teshub, too, my friends. See if there's any way he could safely travel by tomorrow even if he cannot ride a horse, stand in a chariot, or sit in a cart. If so, Zunan, you will have a choice to make. If not, Zunan, you will be the acting commander and Gal-Meshedi so you must lead the soldiers to Karkemish." But before he let them go Mahhuzzi looked troubled. "Later, O Warriors, at late twilight as the Sun Goddess goes into Earth, the Moon God rises in the east and Ishtar appears in the west, I invite you to return to confer with me in Teshub's temple. Bring your two friends if they are able. By then the ritual descent of Suppiluliuma will have begun, so I will not be breaking my oath by sharing a terrible truth that you both have the right to know. For now, go."

Unsettling as that was, Diomedes was so anxious to see if Saddirme and Eruthros had improved that he brushed the warning aside for the time being. He knew neither he nor Zunan would be welcome in the Temple of Ishtar until the sacred procession had departed, so they went down into the low town to bring his scattered squad of warriors together and give them an update. The squad was relieved to hear the Hittites were departing and that the large troop of invaders on the big hill above were friends as hoped. They cheered for Sarpedon but went silent with the tragic news about the brave Payava's death in Nerik. He had been well-liked. Diomedes instructed them to stay out of sight as the Hittite soldiers departed on the morrow to avoid any chance of enmity. If all went according to plan and Sarpedon kept his troop under control, he told the men they could join the feast outside the walls after the Hittites were gone, but no one was to enter the city with hostile intentions. Further, he told them, they should prepare to make a choice: either join the big troop as their march to the sea continues or make a home here, as the missing two must already have done, and be part of the city guard.

As afternoon became evening, just as Kabi predicted and Sarpedon had planned, a field of large campfires lit up the ground on the lip of the steep bluff from end to end. Only the warriors in the camp knew how thin their line was spread and how challenging it was for each campsite to keep three fires burning into the night. From Lawazantiya, it seemed a horde of ten thousand was camped above them, only waiting for morning to descend and destroy them all.

At dusk, as Ishtar shone brightly in the western sky, the high mournful chant of the temple singers began above a low contrapuntal hum. Such voices were accompanied by the steady beat from frame drums with distant flutes and other wind instruments playing traditional Hurrian dirges. Rising from somewhere in the depths of the building were the magnified notes of the *hunzinar*, known as the Ishtar Instrument, a two-metre tall giant lyre played by two musicians. Though the source of such forbidding music was unseen, the music and chants of lamentation haunted the air of the temple by being channelled through the special vents to all rooms and levels. It was the call to gather in the holy rotunda two floors down and form the sacred procession that was to descend further to the levels below until only the core members would be allowed by the gatekeeper to go through the open mouth of despair and enter the first precincts of the Underworld where the ritual Descent of Inanna begins.

Lilitu the High Priestess emerged from her quarters having been carefully attired in the garb, precious stones, and jewel-encrusted gold diadem of her status. The burnished tiara had a diamond shape in its centre and within that was the eight-pointed Star of Ishtar, which had a sparkling blue amethyst of significant size in its centre and smaller blue jewels outlining the star. Her face was made implacable and ruthless by her dark painted lines. Her gown was of a blue so deep it edged into purple. The straps left her shoulders and the swelling of her upper breasts bare, but her bosom was obscured behind the workings of an intricate lapis lazuli necklace that was so broad it was also attached over her shoulders. Her upper arms were bare of cloth but they too had bracelets of golden serpents entwined around them. Beneath her breasts her silver girdle was decorated with two winged lions also in lapis lazuli but with startling ruby eyes. Indigo shoes with toes curling back adorned her feet. She carried a silver mace, also with the eight-pointed star. She was a study in gold, deep blue, and silver, for her long silver hair twisted into ringlets poured over her back and down her shoulders. Her attendants avoided looking directly at her. Any who dared look her way were struck with fearful awe. Surely a goddess walked among them.

She was soon joined by the Great Queen, Lieia-Hepa, another High Priestess, but in this ritual designated as secondary to the Priestess of Ishtar. She too was followed by attendants and dressed in gold and jewels, but her black flowing gown indicated she was in mourning, though her husband remained alive. She wore a black cap on her head from which hung down a head covering of black gauze obscuring her features like a new widow. The gauze merged into her own long black hair, also in ringlets, that flowed out down her back and over her shoulder brooches and her breasts. Her jewels also included the sacred lapis lazuli but most were fashioned from black onyx. Her necklace was a golden-rayed sun but the sun's orb itself in the centre of her chest startled as black obsidian: it was a black sun that still shone light, just as the dark radiance of her natural beauty could not be obscured beneath her robes of mourning.

The women greeted one another, making compliments of sincere appreciation, but there was no lavish flattery on such a sacred occasion. Each was a breath-stopping High Priestess of Ishtar in one of her manifestations, so anyone who saw them felt no doubt about the reality of the goddess's presence. "How well you manifest the goddess Ishtar," Lieia said, bowing and subduing her awe. "With such a glorious array of colours, you could also be the Goddess of the Sun."

"All great goddesses are one," Lilitu smiled. "And you are stunning as the avatar of the Sun Goddess of Earth and of Ishtar's sister, the dark Allani. Great Queen, are you ready for your descent to be the Bride of Doom?"

"Yes," Lieia heard her mouth breathe out the positive answer but it felt as though the word was spoken by another.

With attendants making sure no garment dragged along the ground and with guides preparing the path, the two varied incarnations of the Great Goddess walked out the central doors into the silence, as the background music of discordant zithers, flutes, tambourines, and drums was left behind in the temple.

They walked openly out of doors into the evening air getting nervous glances from passersby. The dread occasioned by such an uncanny evening procession kept strangers away, but the Hurrian guardsmen watched the perimeters just to be sure. They entered the wooded pathways and went to the thicket behind an intricate fence of wood and copper with apotropaic symbols along its facings. They entered the hidden grove which seemed to close behind them, and the guides led them beneath the fallen golden-starred bough, through a hidden trapdoor, and into the lower floors of the Tower of Ishtar. They passed many other pathways leading away from the stone staircase, but they were ignored. On the lowest of constructed floors, the music of the giant lyre was loud, and they realized they were passing the room in which the hunzinar was being vigorously strummed by a musician on each end. The stone walls echoed back the deep plucked notes. After that the stairway walls ended and the way opened into an actual cave. Thence they continued their descent via the curving stairway through passages carved into the rock, which were first naturally penetrated by an underground river that could be heard still rushing through the cavern unseen. Wonder filled Lieia-Hepa for the incredible location but even more because she felt herself crossing into the inhuman realm of the gods, a tingling began to rise up her spine similar to what had happened at the Mountain Temple when Hepat had spoken her own wishes through her.

8. Descent into the Underworld

Suppiluliuma was thoroughly humbled but relieved when seven priests of both sexes arrived in the full armour of the Hurrian guards. They looked fearsome enough within their plumeless war helmets and sharp spears, but the males were uniformly beardless, as was their leader, a plump, bald priest accompanied by two young attendants on the edge of leaving childhood. They entered his little prison room and freed him from the chair of humility, which had held him fast. He had been held there throughout last night and this day, too, being given occasional water and sips of goose broth and only released from his bindings for supervised excretory matters. Overall, a thoroughly humiliating experience, especially for one who only days ago had commanded an empire.

Suppiluliuma did not know what to expect but was pleased to see he was being addressed as Great King of the Hatti as the middle-aged priest knelt before him lowering his forehead to the earth. The young attendants, one boy and one girl, prostrated themselves entirely prone mumbling blessings upon his name. "You may rise," he found himself saying as of old. They did so, and he noted the small eight-pointed star branded on the left shoulder of the girl and on the neck of the boy, meaning they were slaves of Ishtar, probably from very young indeed, if not from birth.

The king also observed the priest was a eunuch, to judge by his soft muscle tone and smooth face. He announced in a strained high voice that he was here in place of the High Priest of Ishtar who had met his "day of landing". He and the attendants were to prepare the Great King to become the Great King again by giving him a thorough body cleansing, including shaving off all body hair, anointing him with the finest oils, and dressing him in the most splendid robes of his office. The priest explained that the royal "divinity" beard he must keep, though it would be oiled and curled. His proud hair, reaching nearly to his waist, would be similarly coifed then thickly braided over his upper back. The first of the sacred drinks would then be given him and he would be led out through the mouth of despair to begin his final descent into the Underworld. The words confused him, but he liked the idea of being the Great King in full splendour once again, so he smiled and nodded and drank the small cup of simple, purified water he was offered. Prayers were sung in low, sweet voices by the children while he was stripped of what he was wearing. A basin of very warm water with soft linen cloths was brought in. Incense was burnt in the braziers and the cleansing commenced, the two youths continuing to sing sacred songs and invocations the whole time, even when they washed and later shaved his genitals and between his buttocks.

A small parade of retainers entered next carrying his most dignified and glorious royal attire obtained by Mahhuzzi from the Storm-God's temple. He had fresh linen undergarments wrapped around him and then his best white robe with gold ribbon on all borders. Over that was hung his royal cloak of deep purple, made heavier with variously coloured jewels around the collar and cuffs and with a stylized crest in silver thread of the royal bull's head on one side of his chest and the vastly antlered royal stag on the other. The jewelled bull-hide royal shoes with the extravagantly long tips curling backward upon themselves were put on the king, followed by the precious royal jewels and lapis lazuli hung around his neck on solid gold chains. His silver royal dagger was belted around his waist. Finally, his tallest pointed crown was carefully placed to adorn his head. This crown included the small solid gold horns of divinity and was weighed down with more royal purple in the form of carved amethyst beads. To complete his regalia, a silver mace was given to him with an eight-pointed quartzite star on its head. He did not recognize this one as his own, but, liking the look of it, accepted it gracefully.

During this elaborate dressing, first high flutes then all the instrumentation of the approaching march of priestesses reached the ears of those below, until finally the singsong chants of the chorus could be heard as well. Speech became difficult as the noisy sacred procession descended to the level of the Great King. His attire was just being completed as the guiding young priestess attendants came into view, followed by the colourful splendour of the two high priestesses themselves. Though they looked neither right nor left but only straight ahead as though spellbound, Suppiluliuma gaped in wonder at a sight so seldom seen. He had been in much larger sacred processions than this but not with such doleful music in such a dreary place, contrasted by the unsettling radiance of two high priestesses in complementary colours. He immediately recognized the glimmering silver locks of the High Priestess of Ishtar but had to surmise the High Priestess behind the black veil and apparently in mourning was his royal wife, the Great Queen. He stood in shock as a dialogue was carried on between the silver-haired High Priestess and a deep voice that emerged from somewhere beyond the gate, presumably that of the gatekeeper. Lilitu tapped on the closed sharp teeth of the bronze gate with her silver wand. Singers and musicians abruptly ceased.

"Who dares approach this gateway into the land of the dead, into the mouth of hell, while yet breathing the air of life?" The vibrating bass tones of the invisible gatekeeper asked. Lilitu the High Priestess raised both arms heavenward and replied with a threat in even more ringing tones. A chill ran through his body for surely he was hearing the commanding tones of Ishtar-Inanna herself:

> "Keeper of the dread waters, open thy gate,
> Open thy gate that I may enter.
> If thou openest not the gate that I may enter
> I will strike the door, the bolts I will shatter,
> I will strike the threshold and will pass through the doors;
> I will raise up the dead to devour the living,
> Above the living the dead shall exceed in numbers."

"It is thou, O Ishtar, sister of my mistress, Allani? I must do my duty and consult with Allani, the Queen of the Underworld." This was a ritual exchange, however, and soon the gate made of bronze teeth partially parted with a groan. The High Priestess raised her arms skyward and released a high-pitched mourning wail, joined by Lieia, one step behind like a shadow. Then, with the women still reaching skyward, Lilitu announced in a sombre voice that yet echoed around the cavern:

> "I spread like a bird my hands.
> I descend, I descend to the house of darkness, the dwelling of the god Ereshkigal:
> To the house out of which there is no exit,
> To the road from which there is no return:

To the house from whose entrance the light is taken,
The place where dust is their nourishment and their food mud.
Its chiefs also are like birds covered with feathers;
The light is never seen, in darkness they dwell ...
Over the door and bolts is scattered dust."

As the prayer ended, ancient hinges creaked and the portcullis of the great maw of hell opened completely. The lower teeth sank beneath the paving while the bronze teeth of the upper jaw rose skyward to allow passage. In this way, the solemn cortège passed silently through. But as the last of the attendants crossed over, the strange chanting and music began again, only to recede as the retinue went on.

Suppiluliuma, spellbound like a child, wanted to join the excitement without clearly understanding it. It was now quiet again all around him, as the two sprites who had helped cleanse him so intimately suddenly appeared before him with a silver goblet of murky fluid. He handed his mace to the girl and with both hands accepted the goblet and asked, "Drink?"

"All of it," said the bald priest in charge, his dark eyes stern. The Great King drank it back as ordered, though it seemed to resist passing through his throat. He had feared the dark liquid would be blood but it was instead a fluid earthy paste tasting of vegetation and fungus. It was still roiling its way down inside him when the substitute high priest signalled, the two youths began their song again, and he was led out of his room before the forbidding giant mouth to the Underworld.

The procession stopped, the children stopped singing, and the priest stepped in front to bang his shepherd's crook upon the bronze teeth of the doorway. In a thin, reedy voice the bald priest ordered, "Open the way, Gatekeeper! It is I the High Priest of Ishtar who leads a willing initiate to enter the mouth of hell."

"Who is this who chooses to disturb the dead and enter the path of no return? Make yourself known to Allani the dark goddess who rules here."

The high priest looked back and up at Suppiluliuma and whispered, "Identify yourself, O King, by name and predominant titles."

Having done so at innumerable rituals, he did not hesitate but stepped forward to his more than two-metre height with his conical crown. In a bold, booming voice he announced: "Be it known that I am Suppiluliuma, Great King of the vast lands of the Hatti, greater than my forebear also named Suppiluliuma. I am the shining Sun of the Hatti, no matter where they dwell. My Majesty is the great warrior of the Hatti, having conquered or consolidated these cities and kingdoms..." The high priest gave him a gentle nudge with his crook, so he skipped naming them. "My Majesty is the High Priest of the Storm-God, known here as Teshub the Mighty, the most powerful god in all the firmament, who is here to protect me, his most humble and loyal servant, no matter where I am. My Majesty is one of three Great Kings who rule all the world..."

"Your Majesty is recognized, O Great King," the gatekeeper interrupted, "but Allani of the Night demands that before you are permitted entry to this realm forbidden to the living, you must realize that Irkalla is hell and not part of the firmament above and that the Storm-God himself has no power here and cannot protect you. Are you willing to abandon all hope, to descend and meet your death in a new awakening among the gods?"

Suppiluliuma gulped and felt the icy fear in the pit of his belly mixing with the turmoil of his sacred drink. In all the rituals he had led, such fear had never before occurred. He turned and looked back up the twisting passageway from which he had descended and truly realized he had already entered the path of no return. He faced the gaping mouth, pulled himself to his tallest, and announced. "I wish to proceed to meet my destiny. Open the gates."

But the gatekeeper was not quite finished. "Allani speaks to me. She knows the great Suppiluliuma and the suffering he has caused. She speaks through me now." The gatekeeper's tone changed tone into an eerie, high-pitched, sinuous voice:

> "Let me weep over the strong who have left their wives,
>
> Let me weep over the handmaidens who lost the embrace of their husbands,
>
> Over the only son let me mourn, who ere his days are come is taken away...
>
> Go, keeper, open the gate to him,
>
> Bewitch him according to the ancient rules.
>
> He shall be treated like any other living who dares to come this way."

With that, the hinges of the ancient mouth creaked as the portal to the abyss was opened. Suppiluliuma placed his silver mace across his chest and walked steadfastly forward, ignoring the huge bronze teeth hanging over him while hearing the beautiful singing of the youths subside. The mouth opened and he was swallowed. He looked back to see that his entire group was following. The gallus priest walked with him, the seven priestly guards after that, with the two children singing their low prayers behind them all. Far ahead was dark, but he felt movement in the air of the vast space around him. He heard the rushing flow of a river but could not fathom its direction. His stomach churned as he stumbled dizzily to a halt, but he then realized the earth itself was trembling and grumbling.

"It is not you shaking but Irpitiga, Lord of Earth, who must be welcoming you," said his guide. The earth tremors subsided, but Suppiluliuma himself continued to feel the trembling within himself as his stomach rumbled, twisted, and glowed.

"Come, Great King, we must meet with Ishtar before you are to descend through the Seven Gates of Inanna to your final destination."

"Seven more gates?" he asked.

"It is so, Great King. With each one you will lose a little of yourself until all that is human has been taken from you. Then you will die and perhaps awaken as *other*."

Far above in the fading light, Zunan and Diomedes entered the main doors of the Temple of Ishtar. Ignoring the guards, servants, and acolytes who approached them, they walked directly to the secret passageway outside and back in and down to the lower floor healing room of Eruthros the Danaan and Saddirme the Karkisan. Diomedes knocked with his bare knuckles and they entered the room. Behind the scent of herbal candles, the room smelled like it needed more fresh air. Saddirme was sitting on the side of his matted bed, but big Eruthros was pacing about the room. Both men were dressed in white, priestly robes, and Diomedes was relieved to see no sign of seeping blood.

"Ah, my lords!" Saddirme exclaimed.

"We are rescued!" Eruthros added. "The peace and quiet in here are driving me crazy. Nobody to be killed!"

Diomedes came forward greeting them one at a time with pats on the shoulder, avoiding the wounded right shoulder of Saddirme. "Warriors," he saluted them. "I see you are mobile."

"Good to see you two again," added Zunan grinning. He was given broad smiles and greetings in return. Comradery in battle makes for fast friends.

"I will be limping for some time and the nurse lady tells me I should use a walking stick, but I can get around," Saddirme said. "My friend the Danuna bear will deny he is anything but perfectly healed, but he has been warned not to stress his punctured lung or it will open again so he can whistle happy tunes through his chest. He's also wrong about the 'peace and quiet' in here. It wasn't long ago that a great cacophony of funeral music and chants echoed through this strange temple."

Diomedes explained what the noise had been, but the men could make little sense out of the idea that Suppiluliuma had been taken from his role as Great King and chosen to die by descending to the Underworld, so he could be reborn elsewhere as a god. "Perhaps common sense has little to do with sacred rituals. The language of the sacred – myths, poems, and rites – is inspired by the gods," Diomedes ventured and succinctly summarized events since the evening they had rescued the queen up to the battle against the Meshedi before the temple of the Storm-God.

Waving off questions, Diomedes tried to explain how the Meshedi inside refused further torture of their commander and turned on the Great King. Led by Mahhuzzi the Wiseman, they brought the poor general and Suppiluliuma without his crown outside on the steps. The battle ceased and Mahhuzzi had beer brought while the king and the general were taken here to this temple.

"Considering how many royal guardsmen Diomedes had already slaughtered in the battle, the Meshedi's agreement to the sudden truce must have resulted from divine intervention," Zunan added.

The two wounded men chortled as warriors do, but Diomedes added that it was the appearance of the leaders and the oration of Mahhuzzi that made the difference. "Suppiluliuma had already been primed by Mahhuzzi, under the influence of the High Priestess of Ishtar, to believe his only escape, if it can be called such, was to die into divinity, which is the grim procession you heard earlier just before it descended."

"After what he did to his uncle, his grand general, he is lucky he has survived at all," added Zunan, who then had to outline the behind-the-scenes movements previous to their being brought all back together in this place. The wounded were astonished when they were told that the Hittite forces were leaving in the morning but greatly pleased to hear that soon after that Sarpedon from Sardis, guided by Kabi, would be leading his troop of two thousand outside of the walls to be guests of the city.

"We next must check on General Kil-Teshub for Mahhuzzi. Zunan knows him. He has had toes chopped off, been gravely twist-stabbed on both sides of his lower back, and had an eye ripped from his head. He is unlikely to be conscious, but, if he's anywhere as stubborn as our Danaan, we may speak with him and discuss whether or not he can be moved. If he is dying or immovable, Zunan must lead the Hittites to Karkemish tomorrow."

"Sounds like this general has one foot in Hades," Eruthros opined. "Many have recovered from losing an eye, but I'm told the pain can leave a man helpless. As to the twist-stabs, that's nasty. Can mess up the organs. If the liver or both kidneys are ripped, he's a dead man."

"We shall see, my friend," Diomedes continued. "I'm told he never cried out under torture. With regard to his current pain, we have already learned these Hurrians have wondrous ways to deal with it. Is that not so, Saddirme?"

Saddirme nodded and smiled, but it was Eruthros who spoke. "Over these past days, we both have been given the sacred milk of the poppy to drink along with other magical elixirs and a honeyed, dark bread made with the resin of the hemp weed."

"These healers in the Temple of Ishtar must have been taught by some god, for I have never recovered so readily. The medicines kept me in good spirits, which I would warrant speeded the healing," Saddirme grinned from ear to ear. Eruthros nodded.

"Good to know you are well enough to travel even though fighting is out. Zunan and I will return for you once we have seen the general and evaluated the situation."

The atmosphere was more sombre in General Kil-Teshub's room. He had several attendants, but the wizened old woman in green and white robes was obviously the chief healer. Kil-Teshub looked most uncomfortable, for he was lying on his stomach with his feet slightly raised to protect his wounds in feet and back, his enwrapped head turned away into flat cushions. Bandages around his head covered the vacancy where the left eye had been, but when Zunan greeted him by name he managed to twist his head enough so his sharply-lit deep brown right eye could see who had arrived.

"Zunan," he said weakly. "So you are alive. Who is...?"

"This is Diomedes, man of Ahhiyawa, who is fighting on our side. We have come to see if..."

"If I am alive?" Kil-Teshub wheezed. "I'd be much better if only my ancient healer would allow me to sit up. I have learned what my crazed nephew did to me, but in truth I recall none of it until awakening here. I knew what was coming, so, while wounded and imprisoned, I asked for the Wise Woman to bless me in the morning. She gave me a potion of various powerful herbs that so numbed me I was brought to death's dark riverside. But as you can see I did not cross over."

"That explains a great deal," Diomedes nodded to Zunan.

"Was that a funeral procession I heard? Is his Majesty —?"

Zunan responded, "General, the Great King, or, better, Suppiluliuma the former Great King from whom the Storm-God has taken his blessing..."

"Yes, yes, just answer my question."

"The king lives, O General. Even now he is descending deep below this temple in the Rite of Inanna in expectation of dying into metamorphosis. The High Priestess of the Sun Goddess of Earth, the former Great Queen, is leading the cortège as second to the High Priestess of Ishtar herself, but it is Ishtar-Allani who presides over all."

The general grunted with impatience. "Was it Mahhuzzi who was behind all this? Did he convince Suppiluliuma that I had betrayed him?"

"Not so, O General," said Diomedes in acceptable Luwian. "It was the grand vizier who led your rescue from behind the scenes. And it was he and Zunan who brought together the Hittite army in Lawazantiya to arrange their next step."

"General Kil-Teshub," Zunan spoke, "the Hatti troops in this city, both the royal bodyguard and the general regiment, are leaving this holy city tomorrow to go to Karkemish where they will offer their services to King Talmi-Teshub. Since you cannot, I must lead them." Mentioning the nearby barbarian troop seemed unnecessary.

Something arose in Kil-Teshub, an awakening of the ancient pride of being a member of the only Hittite royal family that had ruled from the beginning. Ignoring the pain, the old warrior pulled himself over and sat up on the edge of the bed. The pupil of his single brown eye blazing, he announced with startling strength, "I am the Gal-Meshedi! I am the first General of the army! No one leads but me!"

Greatly relieved, Zunan replied, "Of course, O General. It shall be as you wish."

"You are welcome to come along as my adjutant, Zunan-Teshub, but I lead the Hatti army. Karkemish on the Mala is an excellent choice, and I have had the honour of sitting in council with King Talmi-Teshub, a down-to-earth man. Get me a solid wagon big enough for me to lie within, take along these magic healers with their spider-web wound stuffing, disgusting poultices, and secret potions to tend to me, and I am ready to leave yesterday!"

Two guards led at the front; five followed behind carrying covered baskets. Between them, the king and the priest saw the first torchlit gate not far away, a mere door in a latticed bower, minor compared to the terrible mouth the small procession had just gone through. The two children danced gaily along behind the leaders.

A voice called out from the dark ahead. "Welcome, Great King. It is I, dark Ishtar, speaking through my High Priestess." It was a stronger and more malevolent voice than had ever been heard from Lilitu. She emerged bathed in a bluish light, somehow appearing suspended above where the path should be. "We will now begin the process of relieving you of the burdens of your high office, of your dignity, of your very identity, and lastly of your mortality. Have you any doubts or questions before proceeding further? For once we enter the first gate, all doubts, all thoughts, must end and you are required to ask only the ritual questions established by the ancients of the East."

The mind of Suppiluliuma, catalyzed by the strange drink, was swirling in confusion and fear for what lay ahead. Terror rose and he hung his head and wept, but he abruptly ceased. Pulling himself together, he asked the first question that came to mind. He wanted to know who was the power down here. He knew that Lawazantiya was the sacred city of Shaushka, who was also Ishtar and sometimes identified with the Sun Goddess of Earth. He had also learned that this dark Underworld was ruled by Allani, the older sister of Ishtar, whom the Babylonians call Ereshkigal. But the ritual to which he had submitted himself was sometimes called the Rite of Inanna's Descent, and Inanna is said to be the sister of Ereshkigal. He asked how there could be so many goddesses in one place. "And, finally, which goddess are you?"

Lilitu-Ishtar glared down at him a long moment then deeply inhaled, rolled her eyes back, and breathed out her answer as though in a trance. The Goddess spoke:

> "I am she that is the natural mother of all things, mistress and governess of all the elements, the initial progeny of worlds, chief of the powers divine, queen of all that are in hell, the principal of them that dwell in heaven, manifested alone and under one form of all the gods and goddesses. At my will the planets of the sky, the wholesome winds of the seas, and the lamentable silences of hell are disposed; my name, my divinity is adored throughout the world, in divers manners, in variable customs, and by many names. ... Behold I am come to take pity of thy fortune and tribulation; behold I am present to favour and aid thee; leave off thy weeping and lamentation; put away thy sorrow, for behold the reborn day that is adorned by my providence."

Lilitu-Ishtar disappeared into darkness while Suppiluliuma stood in awe as the words "behold the reborn day" echoed promisingly back and forth in his mind. With that, the placid priest indicated it was time to continue their atavistic descent. The strange guardsmen crowded closer to encourage the increasingly disoriented Suppiluliuma to approach the first gate. As they did so, the little round priest gave clear and decisive instructions upwards into the heightened ears of the former Great King. If he wanted to complete the ritual and reach godhead, he was to repeat the formulaic incantations he was now to learn at each gate. The sacred words had been established *in illo tempore*, at the origins of things, when Inanna first descended into the Underworld of death. With his heightened awareness, Suppiluliuma felt comfort in knowing the role he was to play, for he had spent much of his time as Great King reciting rituals of incantation or propitiation.

Soon they stood before an ancient shoulder-height hardwood gate hinged within a tall latticework frame. Both door and frame were intricately carved with lively, intertwined patterns of vines, leaves, and flowers. The doorframe trellis on the narrow pathway stood on its own, supported by strong beams, making it seem more like a garden gate than a gate into hell. There was no fence on either side and the paths around the gate were worn from many passing steps.

The disembodied deep voice of the gatekeeper echoed again. "You will relinquish your golden crown," and the two children suddenly appeared before him. This was unexpected, so it took a moment for his racing mind to recall his part, but he did so, going to one knee so the pretty youths could remove the emblem of his royal status.

"*Why, O Gatekeeper, didst thou take the great crown from my head*?" he asked.

"*Enter, my lord, such is the command of Allani, the Mistress of the Nether World*," the gatekeeper replied, almost kindly. A guardsman on each side of the doorway rattled a sistrum for its apotropaic jangling hiss. Suppiluliuma passed through, finding no resistance and hearing only minor creaks as he pushed through. Once on the other side, a sawetra blast announced the transition from somewhere out of sight. In the silence he again heard the flow of an invisible river.

The rest of the small procession went around the gate and joined the High Priest of the Storm-God on the other side. The children began to sing their chant again and the notes of the invisible two-man hunzinar somehow faintly echoed and reechoed through the rock chamber again. With such music in such a strange place, the uncanny nature of the ritual, and the swirling disorientation of the murky drink, Suppiluliuma felt he had entered another world, one that, in spite of his multitude of ritual experiences, was totally unknown to him. It was dark and somehow feminine, which was disturbing.

The torchlit procession continued, usually descending but sometimes abruptly ascending or even venturing into passages through the cave wall. There was no speech, only the mournful, high-pitched singing chant of the children accompanied by the steady metallic rustle of the bronze cymbals on a *galgaturi* instrument and the steady low beat of *arkammi*, handheld frame drums, instruments sacred to Ishtar. The walk took about half of a shadow-clock hour on the meandering maze-like path, but soon they came to the second gate. This one was almost a copy of the first except the luxuriant natural growth portrayed on the first gate seemed somehow diminished. Some of the branchlets were bare of leaves and some of the flowers appeared wilted.

"You will sacrifice your weapons and your mace of silver," the gatekeeper spoke nearby, seemingly from beside him. Suppiluliuma complied, passing the heavy mace to the boy, as he appeared, and the engraved leather belt that held his dagger in its jewelled hilt he gave to the girl. But by now, as the children disappeared, Suppiluliuma could no longer be sure who was the girl and who was the boy, if he ever could.

Suppiluliuma repeated his ritual question, "Why, O Gatekeeper, didst thou take my royal dagger and my silver mace?"

Again, the gatekeeper replied, "Enter the gate, my lord, such is the command of Allani, the Mistress of the Nether World." The same two guards, probably both women, jangled the zills of their sistra as Suppiluliuma went through the gate. Again, on the far side, someone blew heartily on the horn-shaped bugle to indicate the successful transition.

In spite of the importance of his mission, Kabi the scout rode first to Sarpedon's campsite, even though he knew the leader was probably in the middle at the head of the troop. But, as he had guessed, here was Henti. He dismounted in one motion and the lovers flew into one another's arms, sighing honeyed words and trembling with relief. But after long minutes of clinging bliss, Kabi recalled himself to duty and mounted his mare, leaving the mule in camp and requesting Henti make her way walking to the front to hear what he must say. He then rode through the encampment, waving back to those who recognized him, to the leaders' circle in front of the troop within sight of the steep decline. There he found the Sardinian looking out over the green plain below. Sarpedon welcomed him with pretend disinterest, "Kabi, young scout, I was certain you had high-tailed it to the fabled Land of the Nile!"

"What, and desert my noble leader?" Kabi stopped Pirwa with his heels and leapt to the ground still holding the halter.

"I don't think I'm the one you'd be loathe to desert," Sarpedon winked. The men laughed and shared a quick thumb clasp with a shoulder touch. "What's the judgment? Do we take the city and kill everyone including our friends within it, or did the Hatti grand vizier and Hurrian High Priestess somehow convince the royal ass Suppiluliuma to lead the Hittite regiment to another doomed city? Does he expect to keep his treasures? With the Hatti gone, do we burn Lawazantiya to ashes, or do some of us settle here as guardsmen while the bold among us go on to Alasiya?"

"O my leader, the Hittites will leave in the morning, but that is only the ending before the story is told." Sarpedon looked honestly surprised. "You are about to discover just how mysterious are the ways of gods and men. This short epic should be sung by a bard with a lyre, so incredible is it. I am no bard, so I will be brief as I can. Still, I suggest you get Kuprlli and anyone else you think has influence to join us on our jewelled thrones, bring out your rarest viands, ripened goat cheese, divine wine-nectar, and

I shall tell you how the last Great King of the Hatti, or the demons of chaos within him, brought about his own downfall." Sarpedon grunted with appreciation at the sarcasm.

Sour wine with floating debris mixed with river water, dry mystery meat, and no cheese at all were brought as the people gathered to sit on rocks or the ground or remain standing to hear of the events in the city below, the fate of the fleeing Great King, and perhaps to choose their own destinies. Among the first to arrive was Henti, running like a deer through the widely extended but narrow camp. She was no longer enwrapped to hide her youthful beauty, but instead was radiant with flaxen hair flowing down over her slim neck. Her light robe was gathered like a shawl around her bare shoulders and just over her breathless breasts. She was no longer afraid. Kabi rose to greet her by taking her hands and leading her to the place beside him for all to see, but he remained standing as others arrived and a semicircle formed itself around the central fire where he stood with Kuprlli of the Lukka and Sarpedon of the Sherden.

Kuprlli welcomed them and told them he knew of their suffering and of their desire for what was in the fabled city below. "Much has happened that may affect the choice of destiny you will each have to make, but the only one who knows of these events is our scout, Kabi of Canaan, who has only now arrived. He promises a lively tale. Kabi..."

Kabi rose and, to his surprise, a loud cheer spread throughout the ranks, as the barbarian warriors recalled with pleasure his previous harangue only days earlier. He had brought them the gift of choice, real choice, undetermined by kings or gods. With Klymenos gone, assumed slain by Sarpedon, they could think freely. Like before, he was surprised how invigorated he felt, not at all timid, as the troop of warriors present gave him their full attention. The men's cheers consolidated his confidence. He knew he had an extraordinary tale to tell, but it also helped to glimpse Henti staring up at him with pride shining in her periwinkle blue eyes.

He outlined the entire incredible tale, even though he had heard much of it second-hand. The scout used simple soldier language but his voice carried like a wandering prophet of Yahweh among his own people. His official goal was simply to share what happened, but his actual purpose was to convey the bravery and fighting prowess of Diomedes, Eruthros, Saddirme, and the others. In so doing, he hoped to influence the troop against destroying the beautiful city below once they learn it is about to become virtually defenceless. Such an attack might kill his friends and would certainly break the vow Diomedes had given. Further, on his return ride he had even considered the possibility that he and Henti could settle in Ishtar's city. The rousing tale of the eleven member squad of volunteers who fought the renowned Meshedi to a standstill with the loss of only three men had the crowd's full attention. But describing the number of the guardsmen were killed in return – most in the brief *aristeia* of Diomedes – brought a boisterous roar from the men. They listened in awe to learn how the Great King was brought low by his own royal bodyguard for torturing their commander. He did not let them know that Suppiluliuma was probably still alive and might remain when the other Hittites had left in the morning; instead, he implied the king had been murdered. He said it was uncertain who would lead the Hatti but that they had sworn to leave tomorrow morning. The Great Queen would likely remain and share power with the High Priestess. At that came another cheer and Kabi sat, pouring fresh water into the stale wine to share with Henti, who had translated when necessary, and to enjoy his moment.

The Sardinian rose just in time to stifle a groundswell of protest from the former followers of Klymenos. "No defenders! It's begging for us!" "We can take the city!"

"Yes, we can," his voice boomed out, "but there still will be Hurrian defenders and our own comrades there who have given their word of honour in our name. Honour! Does anyone recall that archaic idea? We can take this city but what it has within is nothing compared to what awaits us back at sea! After Alasiya, all the riches and green lands down the Canaanite coast lie ready like panting virgins, and beyond that is the richest, most fertile land in the world spread out like a garden on either side of the Nile. Why risk it, why take the time, when they have promised to fête us outside the walls and give us gifts of riches aplenty, and probably dancing girls too? And for those of you weary of war and wandering, you have the choice to stay here and live in service, peace and plenty, probably with a young wife. If Lawazantiya is taken and destroyed, so is your freedom to choose – as the gods know, a rare thing on Earth!"

It was a convincing oration. Sarpedon himself even let the idea of staying here flicker across his mind before it disappeared like a brief falling star. His own star was a wandering star, though he doubted it would lead him toward the Nile lands some called Misri. He was not surprised that later Kuprlli confided in him that if the Hatti keep their word, he would be staying. The man had a world-weariness that was palpable.

Back at the campsite, once their excitement over the meeting had subsided, Kabi and Henti considered returning to the waterfall to reenact the ecstasy they had known, but other memories appeared that dissuaded them from that adventure. After supping with Sarpedon and a few others, however, they moved their sleeping gear into a shady nook closer to the river but still in sight of the camp so their sweet reunion would not be interrupted this time.

Afterwards, wrapped around each other as the evening star appeared and seemed to outshine the ghostly moon, it was Henti who first asked, "Now what, I mean tomorrow or later?"

Kabi did not really want to consider the question, so content were they in their little nook of timelessness, but he admitted he had been thinking about it. "I have never really had a home since being taken as a slave by the Hittites so many years ago. Fate has moved me about like a stick in a meandering stream. In fact, if I comprehend the lay of the land and sea at all, it seems arriving here so near to the Great Green again means my life's journey has gone in a vast circle. I fear I have no idea what a settled life is like, but at this moment, an *uneventful* life sounds sweet to me as long as I can be with you," and he tenderly hugged the beloved head on his shoulder against his own. "However, nothing these days is likely to remain uneventful for very long."

"Yes, Kabi, being with you seems to be all I ever could want. For the first time in my life, I realize what the tales of passion and love really mean. The poets aren't liars after all!" They smiled in agreement. "But it's because I don't want to lose you, lose ... *this*, that I wonder if living a settled life as common folk, growing crops or selling goods and raising children, would still be *us*? What would happen to the *eventful* lives of Kabi and Henti in the city?" Kabi looked at the stars as they began to appear but was not sure he understood. She continued, "We are still very young though I know by our age many townsfolk are already married parents. And unlike you, my Canaanite hero, I *have* lived a settled life, but it was not by my choice. This past while dragging myself along with this band of homeless warriors has been very difficult, probably the most difficult thing I've ever done. But, Kabi, believe it when I tell you, I would not trade a day of this life for a lifetime as a harem girl. Since we found each other, all doubt has gone, and I am even more clear on the direction I wish to go."

"And that would be forward, into the unknown, following our captains, Diomedes and Sarpedon. So it shall be: your wish is my wish, my love."

The pattern continued to the third gate, the solemn procession with its eerie music taking a similar time to descend further into the dim cavern. The youths appeared with the silver goblet on a tray. "Drink," commanded the pudgy priest. Suppiluliuma drank back the thick liquid again, the taste recognition making it almost a pleasure, and the goblet was taken away. Now the gatekeeper demanded the removal of all the king's decorative jewellery. The king removed his dangling earrings, glittering necklace, multiple rings, and bracelets and gave them to one of the child attendants who had returned. The other child helped him to undo the clasps of his heavy gold and bronze chest piece and took the weight from him by putting arms around his head. As he caught the air of her or his fresh natural child scent, forgotten memories rose in him, and he became dizzy with nostalgia for such purity. The young temple slaves put the heavy items into storage baskets ferried by the rear guard. Suppiluliuma repeated the ritual question with regard to his jewelled adornments, and the gatekeeper again intoned his order to enter the gate and that it was the will of Allani he do so. On each side of the gate, a sistrum was shaken and the metal loops on the moveable crossbars jangled as he went through, and, again, as he emerged, the sawetra blared in grim triumph.

A warm glow percolating from his belly began to spread throughout him. The distraction of the loose jewellery and the weight from his heavy gold and bronze chest piece were gone just as he was relieved of the crown earlier. As the strange music began and the procession proceeded, he felt so light he could float away. This was exciting. The distant sound of a river echoing off the walls seemed to carry him along. As they descended further into the dark, Suppiluliuma enjoyed a paradoxical sense of ascension into the brightened air. He briefly wondered where he was and how he had gotten there but decided he was already being welcomed by the gods, so such questions were meaningless. He became giddy to realize how blessed he was. The gods had surely chosen him, and he was so relieved and grateful his eyes grew misty with tears.

At that moment, however, he felt himself losing his footing. Earth was not shaking, but he felt his mind swirling into an abyss. The procession musicians abruptly seemed to play a little louder and faster, and the children's voices became more shrill. But soon everything settled down again and Suppiluliuma was at the fourth gate, his head swimming with bright lights, no longer sure whether he was floating or falling, delighted or terrified.

"Thou must remove all thy armour, all metal, and everything but thy robe and shoes," the gatekeeper's voice echoed again.

The novitiate into godhead stood stupefied for a long moment, until the twin children appeared on either side picking up his hands. When he saw them he came round and dutifully took off his engraved leather pectorals and his gemmed waist girdle. Almost gratefully, he recalled his role, comforted that he had one.

"Why, O Gatekeeper, didst thou take the armour from my body?" he asked.

"Enter, my lord, such is the command of Allani, the Mistress of the Nether World," the gatekeeper replied, more severely than before. The sistra were jangled on each side and he crossed through.

As he closed the fourth gate behind him, he noted in passing that this one depicted no flowers at all and the intricate curlicues revealed fewer carved leaves. Ironically, in this dark descent white wings were now carved in relief in its upper corners while gnarly, twisted roots were in its lower. The sawetra blared his successful passage and the procession continued. Suppiluliuma had not noticed but women mourners in dark veils had somewhere begun to follow it, and now they began to lament and weep in the background as the alien music continued.

It had been good to get out into the countryside again, as Shipibaal had always felt good on his travels unless they were made harrowing by great danger or the need for exceptional speed. This was his first journey accompanied by his new companion, so despite the world moving toward chaos, he looked forward to it. The mission required a steady pace, but they were in no danger of being overtaken by the Hittite royal guard and regiment since they were not leaving until the next morning and would take a week to get through mountain passes, across rivers, and over barren plains. The two of them would need at least two overnights and likely three.

They followed the Puruma River valley down through rugged mountains until it met an incoming tributary, which they then followed upstream to the east until the town of Bubulhum came into sight as the dusk approached. There would be some steep climbing the next day, so they agreed to camp for the night in the forest. No point in putting themselves in danger by venturing into the town. That evening, some forest dwellers approached them to trade modest items, but Telipinu had gone into the woods for personal relief. Shipibaal's skill with language stood him in good stead and he was pleased to be given four eggs of some sort in exchange for information about what had happened in Lawazantiya. The strangers were not pleased to hear that a thousand Hittites would be following them, though it was unknown what route they would take.

Shipibaal and his good-natured companion spent an impassioned night in the midst of wild nature, but they managed to get *some* sleep. They arose before dawn and continued their ride as the sun rose, spending the whole day carefully navigating a less travelled rough road through the mountains. The night's rest in a thick wood by a stream was just as engaging as the previous one. Next day, they first found themselves ascending on steep narrow paths, often forced to lead their horses, but by noon they had descended to a plain so dry it was becoming desert. With goatskins full of the last mountain stream, they crossed the empty steppe until they came to a small river emerging from below the surface that took them into sight of Sukziya, another town, but this one on the banks of the giant silty Mala. It was but mid-afternoon of the third day, and they realized they could make it to the fabled city of Karkemish before nightfall though they'd be unlikely to get an audience with the king at such time.

They noted the many lookout posts and various passing patrols alert for danger watching them as they came to the edge of the broad and often swampy river valley to approach the fabled city. Karkemish was on full alert since Ugarit had fallen. At this point, a difficulty arose when his beloved companion expressed fear – or was it horror? – at entering such a crossroads of peoples and gods. *One could be stolen*, he whispered. He obstinately refused to continue and promised to await for the envoy's return at the previous night's campsite. He departed after a long embrace, galloping away before Shipibaal could muster an argument.

Left confused but with no choice, Shipibaal continued alone onto the flat river valley and approached city walls so massive they rivalled those of Hattusa, though it had far fewer temples and no palatial akropolis on its flat surface. The ancient city was next to the great Mala where the river spread out so much it became shallow enough to provide a natural ford. In this way, Karkemish prospered for many years as a meeting place of kingdoms and empires. Across the river was now Assyria but in previous eras it had been the land of Mittani. Trade from Babylon and even further east once came through here as it did from the Levant and the Nile lands to the south. But the ancient city was no longer a thriving hub of commerce since the invasions and drought had reduced trade to a trickle and brought in hungry peasants. Karkemish had become still more crowded by the refugees from destroyed cities who had found their way there.

One of the few on horseback instead of walking or pulling a cart, Shipibaal was motioned to come forward at the city gate. The envoy's copper medallion given him by Mahhuzzi made him recognized as an envoy of the Great King, and he found himself with an escort who immediately guided him through crowded streets to the marble-walled, well-guarded royal palace where he was transferred to others who brought him dust-covered to the royal throne room. Here King Talmi-Teshub had just been alerted and awaited him with his advisors and number one queen nearby.

The first meeting was brief. Shipibaal felt enhanced when the king recognized him from previous visits from Ugarit, but he had to ask for his name. Still standing, he was brought fresh water and wine and provided an outline of events. He explained that this time he had come from the sacred city of Ishtar, Lawazantiya, where he had been abandoned when Ugarit fell. Here, Talmi-Teshub interrupted to express his regrets, saying he was about to send support troops when his scouts reported he was too late, the city was utterly destroyed. Shipibaal admitted he had read a copy of the last message from Ugarit to him that had never been sent. Shipibaal asked but there had been no news about King Ammurapi himself, so "it must be assumed that Nergal took him and he has become a god", concluded King Talmi-Teshub without irony.

Shipibaal understood but decided it was time to get to the point. "As the King of Karkemish, you must know that, before the destruction of Hattusa, the royal court, high officials, the Meshedi, a regiment of a thousand soldiers, and those who had the means had made their way to Lawazantiya. There they had not been welcomed, and division rose between the king and his chief advisors – the royal steward, Mahhuzzi, and the chief general, Kil-Teshub, whom you know. Suffice it to say the royal bodyguard did the previously unthinkable and supported the Gal-Meshedi, Kil-Teshub. Clearly, the Storm-God had deserted the Great King who was brought down and taken away. Whether he lives or not I do not know. But may you know, O King of Karkemish, that the Hatti I mention have now left the city of Ishtar and are on their way here to throw themselves at your feet and offer their service to you. Not only will you have a Hatti regiment to support your defences, you will have the Meshedi themselves to serve you as an addition to your personal bodyguard."

"The Meshedi themselves will join my personal bodyguard?" A light came into Talmi-Teshub's eyes. "You are saying that in effect I will become the Great King of the Hatti, albeit in a greatly diminished empire?" A gasp and murmurs of praise ran through his attendants and his loyal first queen nearby sat up and beamed with pride. The king had little fear of betrayal for he already had enough of his own force to defeat a thousand Hittite soldiers if necessary, and he sensed these were troops that had nowhere else to go. "They will be welcomed here!"

Shipibaal was concerned about his partner and he had accomplished his mission, but he could not avoid being kept overnight to bathe, dine and share more details on events in Lawazantiya. On their return ride, they would look for the Hatti soldiers and tell them they were expected and accepted. Of course, he was still enough of a worldly envoy to be curious about how the King of Karkemish viewed the rising chaos of the world. So, after prayers and purifications, he sat on cushions with royalty to dine, drink a dark rich wine, and exchange tales well into the night.

"Before this news," Talmi-Teshub prophesied, "even if we were left without allies, even if all cities around us were overwhelmed by these ruthless invaders and their motley followers, my patron god whispered to me that this ancient kingdom would persevere. We have our walls, our water, and still some sources of food, and now we have an additional Hittite military regiment. Karkemish will not fall, though all cities around us do. The Hatti will live on into the new age in smaller kingdoms and, gods willing, someday I shall be recognized as Great King over all."

The king wanted to know what had become of the former Great Queen, Lieia-Hepa, and his response led Shipibaal into sharing all he knew. No, Queen Lieia-Hepa was not coming. The leading wife of Talmi-Teshub, no longer young but recognized as the ruling queen though she was but one among many, expressed relief at the news. "I do not think the high priestess of the dark Sun behind the day Sun would be welcomed by our Kubaba, Mother Goddess of Karkemish," she sniffed.

However, Talmi-Teshub disagreed, "Oh she would have been welcome. She is a great beauty and it has been noticed that she has lived in her own palace for many years. Indeed, we would have found a place for her." The king leered and winked openly at Shipibaal.

Without mentioning Diomedes, Shipibaal, between sips of smooth wine told all he knew of the goings on among the nobility in Lawazantiya, from the Great Queen's imprisonment to the taking down of the Great King. It was an arresting tale. His only alteration was to have himself take a more active role in the rescue of Lieia-Hepa.

"So you managed to kill a trained Meshedi bodyguard?" asked the king.

"Uh, yes," Shipibaal blushed, "but it was merely a bowshot, after all."

As the dessert trays were taken away, the king added his personal insights into his former ruler. "Suppiluliuma is mostly a puffed-up fool," he said. "He pretended to be but a humble slave of the gods, as his father Tudhaliya was to Sharruma – did you not see the image of him being dragged along under his god's armpit? – and as his grandfather Hattusili was to Shaushka-Ishtar. At least Hattusili actually found and married Ishtar-on-Earth in the person of Puduhepa, who seems to have become a power unto herself. Anyway," he sloshed his wine in the jewelled goblet, "instead of being a servant of the gods, Suppiluliuma seems to have imagined he could become one of them, perhaps even their great king. Did he not grow a godlike beard and take his own father's sacred tomb among the gods at the Mountain Temple for his own? This is dangerous presumption. He will no doubt get what he deserves."

Shipibaal was offered his choice of dancing girls or even one or two of the king's harem to comfort him that night, but he begged off, explaining he was bound to another in exclusive love. And the next morning he was off on a fresh horse to find that other whom he loved, and secondly to find the approaching Hittites.

He was deeply disappointed when he finally made his way by mid-afternoon to where they had previously camped. There were signs of camping, fresh horseshit anyway, but Telipinu was not seen. He called out and methodically at first made his way back along the trail they had come but as time went by he became more frantic. Why must the secretive messenger torture him this way? He could read a trail well, but not like a tracker, so he took a few hours to find his way into a patch of forest near a small stream where fresh horse tracks went. They had passed through here previously, but the clearing seemed changed, darker, eerie, as though haunted. No breeze blew, and no birds sang by the dried creekbed. The air was heavy and stale as a tomb. The very wood seemed to decay and fall, as the vapours wept their burthen to the ground. Shipibaal heard the soft whinny of a horse across the creek but, as he approached the dry shore, he saw a mound of the *halenzu-plant* stir beneath a quiescent but large beehive swinging from a low branch.

He realized it was Telipinu, deep asleep. After joyful relief, a sense of indignation arose in him at being made to suffer so. As he approached his handsome lover, he noticed a fat bumblebee land on his cheek. For a moment he was tempted to agitate it just enough that it would sting the smooth face and shock him awake, but something inside, some unconscious knowledge, held him in check. Instead, he brushed the fuzzy thing harmlessly away. The messenger stirred and awoke violently in any case. He stared into the air with a kind of horror. "What have I done!" he blurted out.

Shipibaal gently cradled his beloved's head in his arms and assured him he had done nothing. The eyes of Telipinu cleared, and the mysterious messenger recognized his other and immediately became his sardonic but still nervous self. "What are you doing to me on the ground, you cad!" he smirked. Shipibaal tried to explain, but Telipinu sat up and grimly intoned, "*I dreamt I was in an uncontrollable rage. A giant bee had stung me and I was out of my mind. I destroyed everything around me in all realms. I brought life to a standstill...*"

"The world is still here, O mad messenger. It was but a passing dream."

With obvious relief, Telipinu stood and grasped Shipibaal by the curls on the back of his head. "Oh gods, yes, the world is still here and so are you, beautiful boy," following this with heartfelt kiss.

"Wait," interrupted Shipibaal in frustration. "You're always disappearing. No one else even seems to see you. Who are you, *really*?"

"I am Telipinu, your lover. You summoned me so I appeared to you in the flesh. What else matters?" He smiled lewdly and pulled the envoy against him. "You smell so fresh," the messenger sighed as he leaned from the hips and pressed his turgid member into the other. Shipibaal swooned and forgot his questions, responding in kind. Soon their hands wandered freely under wrappings and over warm skin. They sensually tussled and fell together on the grass, each finding himself as the other in the suddenly verdant grove, vibrating with life. An hour later they used the fast-flowing waters of the clear brook to refresh themselves. They found Telipinu's wandering horse and left the grove, which, it seemed to Shipibaal, had again effloresced into bright fecundity with light breezes and birdsong. Even the bees were buzzing happily about.

They left together to seek out the Hittite troop of exiles coming toward them.

Moments of despair and delight flashed through Suppiluliuma as the procession continued on its sombre way to the fifth gate, but more often his own self no longer felt anything. He now understood that this was *his* funeral procession and that it was his role to die to himself. This was not something anyone or anything outside of him could do for him. He heard the mourners lamenting, the children singing, and the hypnotic music; he saw the torches light his way down into what seemed an endless abyss. There was no fear and no desire, for at this point he felt he had accepted his death and divested himself of his humanity. Even the hope of finding the light of spiritual ascension in the darkest pit of hell was forgotten. The descent was about dying and nothing else.

Despite this, a sense of achievement crept through Suppiluliuma as the moribund procession approached the fifth gate. So this was dying! It was as grim and mournful as he had expected, but he realized he had not failed in this journey. He had not fallen into panic or denial. He was dying and deep in his mind realized he was doing well at it.

"Thou wilt remove all further garments."

For the first time, Suppiluliuma was shocked. In all the rituals he conducted, he had never been required to do this before, though he was accustomed to the nudity required for his various ritual cleansings. But this was public display. Still he proceeded and the children appeared again to help him undress and gather his clothes. Everything so carefully put on him was now to be taken off. Soon his clean-shaven body stood only in the bejewelled bullhide shoes with curled back toes. Things came a standstill, but there were no further commands until the king understood the shoes must go, as well.

"Why, O Gatekeeper, didst thou take the clothes from my body and the shoes from my feet?" he asked.

"Enter, my lord, such is the command of Allani, the Mistress of the Nether World."

Shaking off his sheepishness, as the copper tambours jangled on each sistrum, the former Great King of the Hittite Empire stood to his full height, raised his head, shook his proud roils of hair and beard, and grandly walked through the gate (on which he noted for the first time the addition of an undulating serpent around its borders). The horn-shaped bugle sounded and they continued, but Suppiluliuma found the stony path painful to negotiate with bare feet in the gloom.

The melancholy music began again, but this time the group of women mourners in their black veils were immediately behind him, chanting a lament:

> "Arise then, go, hero, the road of 'No Return'—...
>
> He goeth, he goeth, to the bosom of Earth—
>
> He will cause abundance for the land of the dead...
>
> At the call of the Goddess.
>
> Go, hero, to the distant land which is unseen."

Hero? It was difficult to see himself as a hero when his feet began to suffer cuts and bruises, but the word provided some grim consolation. He wondered what lay ahead for surely the great transition was at hand. How many gates were there, six or seven? He was far from becoming a god, but then he recognized the mournful chant as referring to Tammuz, the mortal shepherd-king lover of Ishtar. So that is who he is becoming! With a chill, he recalled that in the eastern hymns of Amurru and Babylon, the shepherd-king was called *Tammuz of the Abyss*.

Now the dark women ceased their lament, and, raising their pitch, they instead chanted the ancient tale of Ishtar returning from the Underworld to find her lover, the former shepherd Tammuz, enjoying his time on the throne instead of mourning her. The chanted hymn rose in volume as they recited the wrath of Ishtar:

> "She fixed an eye on him: the eye of death! She spoke a word against him: the word of despair! She cried out against him: the cry of damnation! 'This one', she commanded the demons, 'carry him away'!"

With that, four of the armed guardians of unknown gender took the arms of the former Hatti king and half-dragged him across the broken rocks to the next gate. His feet were torn by the time they arrived. The sinking feeling in the pit of Suppiluliuma's guts only got worse when the children brought him yet another cup of the thick earthy liquid. This time some came back up and he had to spit it out beside the path. As he was firmly held, the gatekeeper's sourceless voice announced, "You are to be shorn of thy locks, beard, and brows." He was more shocked than he was when ordered to strip off his garments.

The children quickly approached, one with a keenly sharpened bronze dagger, the other with a pouch of fine tools. He was forced to sit before the gate. Without loosening the long braid of the king, one held the hair stretched and the other quickly carved through the fibres as close to the scalp as possible. Then the same procedure was done to the curls of Suppiluliuma's chest long beard until only a fingernail's length of hair remained anywhere. At last, the former Great King first choked then began to weep freely. Small, bronze hand-razors were produced by the young barbers and, helped by a vial of olive oil, eventually the king's scalp, chin, and brows were shaved smooth with almost no blood drawn.

Suppiluliuma sat on the cold stone with no clothes and less hair than he was born with and openly sobbed. But his despair was interrupted when he recalled his role:

"Why, O Gatekeeper, hast thou ordered the shaving of my head and face?"

The voice of the gatekeeper seemed distant and somewhat mournful: "Enter the gate, my lord shepherd, such is the command of Allani, the Mistress of the Nether World." Suppiluliuma was pulled to his feet by the women and eunuch soldiers and made to walk. As the sistra were shaken he went through the gate, which appeared to be a tangle of serpents and roots, merging into one another. Once through, the sawetra sounded again.

The march continued, more gloomy than ever. Suppiluliuma was humiliated – bloodied, naked, hairless, and cold. The oblivion of death began to sound inviting. He began to silently weep again, but he now became subject to visions. He imagined he saw the gods above headed by the Storm-God himself looking down upon him and cruelly laughing, mocking him. With relief, he saw his queen, Lieia-Hepa, beckoning kindly and he wanted to approach, but then she transformed into Lilitu, Ishtar's High Priestess, with a bloody garden sickle in her hands, her face demonic and twisted, still beckoning. Suppiluliuma shook his head, but when he looked again he saw snakes and other reptiles rising from the ground to crawl up his vulnerable legs. He saw his own mother, once so dear. She was smiling, reaching for him to take him to her breast. He felt great relief to be safe, but then her mouth opened wide and within were dripping serpentine fangs and a thin, hissing tongue.

Then the little priest was beside him, feeding him lines, which he heard himself repeating as though in a dream as though he were outside himself:

"Our mother,
The goddess with the mantle of snakes,
Is taking me with her
As her child.
I weep."

Then from the group of mourning women, one came forth and glided smoothly nearer to him. "Where is my lost husband?" she asked, and Suppiluliuma was sure he recognized Lieia-Hepa behind the black veil. He wanted to reach out to her, but she began a chant and he realized she had become Ishtar, looking for Tammuz, her lost shepherd-king, whom she herself had condemned:

"Oh hero, my lord, ah me! You are lost to me.

The holy one of Ishtar, in the middle of the year the fields languish ...

The shepherd, the wise one, the man of sorrows, why have they slain you?

Because of the exalted one of the nether world, death rules the fields.

The child, lord of knowledge, abides no more.

In the meadows, verily, verily, the soul of life perishes."

The mourning woman went ahead and, glancing back briefly at the lost soul who had once been her husband, she disappeared in the darkness and reappeared in the distance as she entered into an ancient stone building with candlelit windows beyond the last gate.

The Great King was lost to himself. Suppiluliuma was lost to himself. He was alone, godless and soulless. He reached forward but found nothing to hold on to. He looked around but in the dim underworld passage, no one looked back at him. He stumbled on hopelessly, bereft of shame, bereft of pride, bereft of purpose.

Then he too saw it: the seventh and final gate. It was featureless black with no carvings or colour. Beyond it was a small stone temple, lit within by torches and candles. Before the dark gate was a candlelit stone altar – a low, flat, limestone table with dark blotches stained into it. There stood the High Priestess of Ishtar, Lilitu. Her entire visage was made into a bizarre and terrifying mask by its white base beneath dark, painted lines on her forehead and around her eyes. Her lips glistened with a glossy rouge so dark it verged into black. On her head was a tall headdress that resembled a coiled serpent. She beckoned him to her with a hand whose fingers ended in talon-like nails. He struggled forward spellbound, no longer under his own power.

He came to the goddess as if in a dream, yet he noted that in the shadows behind her stood an inhumanly large presence with a horned, conical hat, long beard, vertically-fluted robe to his ankles, and the curled-back shoe tips of a deity. In his raised right hand was a gold-plated mace from which emerged two identical lion heads, and hanging in his left hand a giant bronze khopesh gleamed in the half-light. Even in his disoriented state Suppiluliuma recognized Nergal himself, the Underworld god of inflicted death. He had often seen the depiction of Nergal as the guardian god with lower limbs as lions merging into a sword plunged into the rock between the chambers of the living and the dead at the sacred Mountain Temple of the Gods just beyond Hattusa.

The High Priestess of Ishtar raised her arms, gazed upwards, and shrieked at nothing that Suppiluliuma could see, revealing sharp white teeth. How did snakes get coiled around her arms and waist? Her eyes were wild. She hissed an incantation that he could not understand. Lowering her arms, she looked directly at him as he arrived at the altar on numb, bloody feet, hairless and naked. Three of the soldiers came up and bound his wrists together before him, lowering him onto his back on the cold stone. His arms were pulled over his head and held there. Simultaneously, more leather straps pinned his ankles apart to the stone.

"O Great King no longer, this is where Suppiluliuma is to become lost forever in the Land of the No Return. The last vestige of the ungodly Suppiluliuma dies here. Ahead, beyond the ultimate gate, only Tammuz, the forlorn shepherd, the *pre-eminent steer of heaven*, can emerge. There, as Lord Tammuz, you will enter the Temple of Awakening that you see, the tomb and womb of the Great Goddess herself. Within it awaits your Bride of Doom, who, as Ishtar, will join you in a sacred marriage and accompany you out of this dark life of the flesh to dwell amongst the immortal gods.

"There is only one final divestiture. After the gatekeeper speaks, I will ask you but once if you wish to proceed through the gate cleansed of your natural humanity, or if you wish to die here on this ancient altar as yourself." Suppiluliuma had by now blankly succumbed to whatever awaited him, but the words "final divestiture" hung in the air.

The gatekeeper's deep voice was expressed loud enough to echo in the chamber even though it was in the mournful tone of a lament: "Now is the time, O man, you are to sacrifice your organs of virility."

Suppiluliuma heard the words but it took seconds to grasp their meaning. His voice croaked, "You mean to cut off all of my ... ?"

Lilitu appeared at the foot of the altar between the legs of Suppiluliuma. "Nothing so crude as that," she smiled and revealed she held a flat obsidian slate honed on one side to a razor-sharp edge. "We shall leave your appearance intact." She walked beside the altar to give the king a better view. "What we do, O *Great King*," she said coldly, "is simply to use this primeval tool," she waved the black slate, "to slice a line up each side of your scrotal sack," and while speaking she demonstrated by reaching between his legs with her other hand and running a long fingernail down the length of each side of his bare sack, "then we pop out the testicles that are within and snip off the veins and membranes that make them a part of you. You will no longer be you."

The air stood still and everything went quiet. Then, yet again, a low rumble came from deep within the stone ground beneath them, yet nobody moved during several long seconds of earth tremor. A distant harpy-like scream was heard from the temple beyond the gate, yet no one dared to look away at this moment.

"It is time to become your destiny, O King. Are you willing to be divested of the last thing that makes you who you are? Are you willing to shed your mortal flesh to transform into the holy steer, Tammuz, and go through the last gate for your sacred marriage? Do you embrace the opportunity for you and the Bride of Doom to become one and at last both transcend all bodily existence while being welcomed amongst the gods as immortal vapours?"

Long moments passed as Suppiluliuma's first waking sense was that he was about to be delivered from all the anguish and humiliation that had been wrought upon him. He even began to feebly move his fingers to indicate his submission to the rite, but deep, deep inside of him his ancestors began to stir and resist and then to grumble and howl. First their combined voices were far away, but they came closer until they seemed to surround him. He saw familiar faces in the air approach to glare at him, to challenge him, faces that he had seen in relief sculptures, carvings, paintings. It was a recession into the past of the line of Great Kings of the Hatti going back to their beginnings when the Hattian and Nesili speakers were merging in Kussar and on to his primary royal ancestor, Labarna, who founded the First Kingdom and the beginnings of the Hittite Empire. Proud, ruthless warriors every man. A soul roar of indignant rage slowly rose in the naked, hairless man but was revealed only in the sudden tension in his body and the flame that lit his eyes.

"*I think not*," he said firmly. "I will sacrifice the immortality of my spirit for the dignity of my soul."

Lilitu was surprised, but only asked in the impartial voice of the High Priestess, "You know what this means? You know what you are giving up? You know you will die right here and now forever?"

He roared: "I am the Great King of the Hatti, the son of a Great King, who was the son of a Great King before him, as all were scions of Great Kings before them going back to the beginning of our time. I am a Hatti warrior-king – and as such will I die!"

9. Katabasis of Diomedes

"I have some disturbing news that I learned from the High Priestess to share with the two of you, so it is well you have come." Mahhuzzi looked gravely at Diomedes and Zunan, who had just arrived from the Temple of Ishtar. Eruthros and Saddirme had insisted on coming too, but they understood the meeting was not called for them and so sat further back. It was early evening with the moon and the evening star both low on opposite sides of the heavens. The ceremonial descent was by now well underway. "But first, Zunan, what is the news of my dear colleague, General Kil-Teshub?"

"He lives, O vizier, and his clear mind has returned, as has his will. He is bandaged and gravely wounded, but he fully intends to lead the Hatti troops to Karkemish in the morning, even if he must ride on piles of cushions with attendants in a strong wagon."

"And you?" asked Mahhuzzi.

"General Kil-Teshub has made me second-in-command so I feel my duty is with the soldiers. Still, I would remain as the personal bodyguard of the Great Queen if she wished, but it seems she may have a new attendant," he nodded to the Akhaian beside him, "and I am uncertain of her destiny."

"This is precisely why I felt I must meet with you two again, since you both love Lieia, albeit in different ways. Lilitu the High Priestess of Ishtar divulged to me a terrible secret, but only if I swore an oath not to share it until the procession into the Underworld had begun and could no longer be stopped." He sighed and gathered himself. "I do not think that Lieia-Hepa has been truly informed of the part she will be expected to play this night in Suppiluliuma's ritual of descent into godhead. During the descent, she will be the mourning bride of the dying Great King, as Lilitu will be the avatar of Ishtar, the processional leader. Once the descent is complete, however, the High Priestess Lilitu will become Allani, ruler of the Underworld and mistress of the sacrifices who will complete the simulated killing of Suppiluliuma by gelding him. He will be expected to walk in that condition through the seventh and final gate. If he reaches the stone temple he will now be Tammuz the mortally wounded lover of Ishtar. Lieia-Hepa will await him there, but she will now have transformed into the goddess Ishtar-Inanna where she will join with Tammuz in the rite of sacred marriage."

"The *hieros gamos*!" Diomedes expostulated in the Hellenic expression. "But in our rites, this was between the goddess-queen and her new son-lover, and it is followed by physical consummation. It is said in ancient times the death of the old year-king had already taken place and his blood and body parts were spread on the fields for fertility. How can physical consummation occur with..."

"A half-dead eunuch? It cannot. Remember, she is the Bride of Doom. Instead, after the marriage is sanctified by the High Priestess as Goddess of the Dead, the two will be immediately sacrificed to the fire – burnt alive as one at the altar of Allani-Ereshkigal, after which they will awaken as gods amongst gods in the heavens – or so it is believed. For Ishtar it is but a return as the morning star, for the Sun Goddess it is but a new arising, but for Tammuz it is ascension to divinity."

Everyone was stunned, even the two veteran warriors in the background. No one had ever heard a sacred ritual rationally explained this way, a narrative unsupported by mystic myths and images from bygone eras. The ritual was undraped of its myth. Zunan looked most agonized. He was not a barbarian and what the Wiseman had just said amounted to sacrilege. It wasn't exactly *what* he said, but *how* he said it. It was like he was explaining how to plant a garden or arrange a troop of soldiers. Told without full emotional engagement, without gods speaking through myth, song, or movement, the whole process seemed unholy, stripped of meaning, a parody. For Diomedes, such direct speaking revealed the rite as brutally ludicrous. The woman he loved was going to be killed for no sensible reason at all. He rose, his body tightening for action.

"It may not be too late. I have memorized the way. I know what I must do."

"Akhaian, it is too late, and it is impossible anyway," Mahhuzzi attempted to reason.

"No, you have your duty elsewhere," he spoke sharply to Zunan, who had begun to rise so Diomedes assumed he meant to join him.

Zunan rose anyway but admitted, "My duty is what you say, Diomedes, but my destiny is with the gods, not against them. My friend, what you propose is diabolic! Are you going to disrupt the will of the gods by going against all that is sacred? You, a mere human, cannot interfere with holy ancient ritual! I was raised as a loyal Hurrian amongst these gods. I dare not enter the Underworld of No Return, for I know both my life and my very soul would be lost forever. Akhaian, what you propose is madness – you cannot succeed. Abandon all such hopes!"

"I cannot. It must be done, no matter the outcome. I mean to steal into Hades, your Underworld, or die trying." He looked around like a cornered lion, ready to tear up anyone who blocked his way. Seeing no one, he nodded brusquely to his sitting comrades, who nodded back, eyes wide, and strode from the room. As he left, an earth tremor rumbled through the ground and shook everything on it, but it abruptly ceased. Far below, at the first gate of the Underworld, the same tremor was felt by Suppiluliuma who was told it was sent by Irpitiga the earth god to welcome him.

"Gods be damned," hissed Eruthros impiously, "I'm not going to miss another adventure!" and he attempted to rise to his feet.

"Be still, old bear. You are not ready for this task," said Saddirme, pulling him back down. Wheezing and glum, Eruthros sat again.

The Akhaian wasted little time. He securely fastened his iron dagger in its sheath and around his waist, and he sent prayers in thought to Hermes Kataibates for netherworld guidance and to Athene Pronoea in hopes rational foresight might help him defy possession by the infernal gods and demons below. Reflection worked for Perseus, he recalled, but he could only wish for winged sandals and invisibility. He knew he might already be too late, but he had never felt so certain about what he must do.

He ran out the portals to the Temple of Ishtar, disdaining the main door to go into the thick brambles at its rear, which encircled and hid the sacred copse within. Ignoring the warning of demon masks not to pass, he made his way through the secret passages and finally found the entry to the holy dark grove. There was the eight-pointed star on the fallen golden bough, and without hesitation he moved the leaves and undergrowth to open the trapdoor to the nether world. He leapt in and scrambled down, relieved to find the descending hall still lit by candles or torches.

Assuming most of the Hurrian guards would be assembled lower down where the grim procession had preceded him, he recklessly ran at a steady pace down through the stone walls. Often there were halls leading away to the left or right and sometimes a fork in the passageway. He thought of the ancient hero Theseus in the labyrinth of the Minotauros, but he had no Ariadne to help and no thread to guide him back. Once he found himself down the wrong passageway, but the lack of lighting further on alerted him to his error. He returned and continued, finally passing a dimly lit room in which stood the strangest musical instrument he had ever seen. It looked like two giant lyres facing each other yet connected as one. He hurried on and soon discovered he had gone beyond human-made walls and was descending carved steps in a widening natural cave. Off to his right in the dark, an invisible river splashed along.

He saw two Hurrian soldiers walking the steep path towards the steps, so he hid himself in a dark niche between torches as the armed guards walked by, speaking in a language he did not understand. He continued on, leaving the steps and entering on the steeply descending pathway.

Soon, he saw a lighted area ahead, a flat space with a group of soldiers idling about, playing knucklebones, betting on shekel toss, or just staring into space. As before were the two rooms on either side of the space with heavy doors and windows too narrow for a man to squeeze through, but both were now empty. Beyond that, he again looked upon the sealed portcullis that was the bronze mouth of Hades itself. Here was no Cerberus but instead a sealed gate, an invisible gatekeeper and a patrol of fully armed guardsmen. He wished he had Pegasus to fly him over but he was not Bellerophon. Beyond the boulders to the left was only the vertical cave wall. To the right, however, the boulders disappeared in darkness as the cave did not end in a wall but lowered to a space above the ground less than a man's height. Listening carefully, Diomedes was sure he could hear the murmur of the underground river somewhere out there in the darkness to the right. He knew what he had to do immediately.

Despite the lack of light and the steep descent, he left the trail and made his way as quietly as he could between the rocky base and the lowering cave roof. It became very dark, and the roof seemed to close in on him. He pushed on, feeling his way, and soon could hear and smell the rushing water ahead. But before finding himself in the invisible underground river valley, he had to squeeze through a gap so narrow his broad chest and shoulders were thoroughly scraped. Beyond was no light at all – a darkness so complete it was palpable. He was blind but soon found he could stand again. He felt wind upon him so was sure the river came out somewhere. He stumbled his way forward as best he could until he felt cold water running over his sandalled feet. He reasoned the great cave was the result of the river, so if he followed its flow, it should lead him near to where the ritual was to take place, the end of the sculpted cave.

No experience he had ever had in his adventurous, long-suffering life had prepared him for this. It was so completely black all sense of direction was obliterated. He attempted to make his way through the shallow riverbank so he could follow in whatever direction the unnamed river was flowing, but blindly blundering forward over the unseen broken rocks in the dark proved frustrating. He fell, cutting his hands. The dark worldlessness seemed to close in on him and, in spite of the flow of fresh air, he felt a suffocating fear rise in him, an unfamiliar feeling. He dispelled the intrusive emotion and dealt with his predicament simply by working his way into deeper waters where the current could carry him along at a depth in which his feet could most often feel support on the broken riverbed. If he heard rapids ahead, he would move back into the shallows, but sometimes he went deeper and just allowed himself to be carried along into the void.

He proceeded this way as his other senses became sharpened by his visual blindness. At last, he thought he saw distant points of light. Suspecting an illusion, he pulled himself from the waters, but then above the river's rush, the sound of the king's netherworld procession floated to him. It was the mournful dirge of a funeral lament, accompanied by sonorous musical instrumentation and steady low drums. In the next moment, he perceived the distant dim lights of torches moving along and he knew he had nearly drawn parallel with Suppiluliuma's immortal descent through death's dream kingdom.

Now with the distant sounds and moving lights, he had some sense of orientation. He plunged back into the centre of the tumid river and, swimming to keep his head above the waves, he allowed himself to be carried around the next bend, which proved to bring him closer to the distant cortège. He struggled to shore, not without difficulty, and painfully climbed a knoll from which he could see he was now ahead of the procession. There was a gate of sorts and beyond it a stone temple in which the windows and a doorway were brightly lit. He felt an intuition that this temple was his destination, but he would have to work his way further on to approach it from behind. Up the steep incline he crawled until he could stand. He made his way to a point from where he could see the lit door to the rear entrance of the small stone temple, which faded into darkness as he lost consciousness. Collapsing, utterly exhausted, he fell into a dream.

Awakening from momentary dreams of demons and a dark goddess with talons instead of fingers, he recalled his purpose immediately. He set out for higher ground, half on the cave wall where this section ended. The ancient stone temple was not far away now and he was behind it, but he noted that beyond it was what appeared to be an archway with a black gate or door within it. Two figures awaited in the dim light before the gate, a shimmering, smaller figure with silver hair and a very large one in a pointed Hittite helmet with a great curved sword held in his left hand. Beyond that in the distance was the approaching funeral procession, still hypnotically chanting with low music and lit with torches. It was far but he could make out a tall figure – without clothes? – dragging himself along in the front with a short round man in robes carrying a walking stick beside him. He knew he had to move fast.

With a surge of energy, he kept low and made his way in the darkness to the stone walls of the small temple. Quickly approaching the lit door, he did not take the time to hide. He crossed through a primitive portico lit with one candle that contained a jug of water, hanging cloths, and a cleansing basin. Once inside, for a second the light blinded him, for within were tapered candles and, beyond, torches surrounding the sacred room.

There were two candles lit on a central altar constructed of dark lava stones. Beyond that were another few steps up to an elevated room hidden behind thick, silvery curtains, and on the steps before the curtains facing the elevated room was a kneeling woman in the dark garments and head shawl of a widow. Her arms were folded in prayer across her chest and her head was bent forward above the next step. On each side of her was a brazier with white smoke rising from some burning substance. She was rocking and murmuring a chant in cycles of repetition.

Diomedes knew in his heart who this must be, but at that moment the ground groaned and shuddered in a second tremor – the same tremor now being felt by Suppiluliuma and Lilitu – as though to confirm it. The woman remained entranced. He ran to her and in one motion lifted her shoulders, turning her to face him, and calling her name: “Lieia!” Before he could embrace her, her kohl-rimmed eyes widened in terror and she screamed like a harpy plummeting from the sky – the same scream heard by others outside before the final gate.

He held her to him, saying her name over and over, attempting to calm her. She went quiet but passive, limp against his bare chest. He lifted her chin and looked into her misty eyes but saw no recognition in them. He carried her to the portico where he splashed water on her eyes and forehead, smearing some of the kohl. "Lieia, it's me, Diomedes. You need to awaken to me. Your life is in danger. This sacred marriage is a human sacrifice, for both of you!"

"That's not possible," she murmured, her eyes clearing. "The Hatti do not practice such barbaric rituals."

"The Hatti may not, but when Ishtar was Inanna, it seems the Babylonians, Akkadians, or someone from long ago certainly did. And it is Ishtar in the guise of Lilitu who has planned this whole thing. And Lilitu may have motivations of her own. Can there be two high priestesses? It's a good way to be rid of both the king and you!"

"Diomede," she cried as she awoke to him. "My lord, what are you doing here?" She embraced him back feverishly, tears running over her eyes to further smear the kohl. "You can't be here, for ... I am promised in sacred marriage to the dying Tammuz..." Her sentence ran out. "The High Priestess told me I would play my part and guide the king to his flaming departure to become Tammuz in heaven, but she said nothing of *my* sacrifice or ... murder."

"No one is going to murder you, my love. But from the glimpse I had, either Suppiluliuma will get here barely alive or it's already too late. Do you dare to accompany me to the black seventh gate so we can see what has occurred? I believe the lost king was about to *cross over* in one way or another. In this dim light, we should be unseen."

"I will go with you, wherever you lead, Diomedes. My heart soars to see you."

"If you become a goddess, you are lost forever to me. How many tales have been told about mortal men who fall in love with goddesses? Their fate may be akin to what is happening to your king out there, though he has never loved anyone but himself."

They ventured out the same door through which Diomedes had entered. Her dark clothes and his lack of clothes helping them to merge with the darkness, they made their way around the temple and quietly approached the latticework frame of the black gate. Before they arrived, they could hear ritual chanting from an unnaturally high-pitched male voice. As they got near the gate, what they saw startled both of them. On the other side of the black gate, the High Priestess of Ishtar stood with her back to them just in front of a giant figure in a tall conical helm with the horns of divinity on either side. He leaned on a great scimitar passively surveying the proceedings.

"This must be Nergal, the god of unnatural death," she whispered to Diomedes. No one else could hear because a plump bald priest was intoning a ritual hymn of praise in honour of Ishtar. Beyond him was the tied down, spread-legged, naked and shaven figure of Suppiluliuma, once king of the Hatti. Guards stood on each end. Suppiluliuma still lived, for his eyes glittered with rage and he struggled in his bonds.

Diomedes instinctively moved to intervene, but Lieia touched his arm and whispered, "You must not. You cannot. It is over. *Listen.*"

The little priest fell to his knees before the High Priestess of Ishtar and spread his arms wide, intoning a fearful prayer of worship in the Hattian dialect:

> "Thou art the pristine spirit, the nature of which is bliss; thou art the ultimate nature and the clear light of heaven, which illuminates and breaks the self-hypnotism of the terrible round of rebirth, and now thou art the one that muffles the universe, for all time in thine own very darkness."

Lilitu nodded imperiously and stepped forward followed by the giant swordsman with the pointed helmet. She began a ritual chant and, as she continued, the two children, who had come forward to the head of the altar, began to sing a wordless accompaniment in eerie high voices while she swayed her body like a serpent uncoiling. She finished her chant by spreading her arms upward and declaring in a brazen voice, not her own:

> "And I shall destroy everything I created. Earth will again appear as primordial ocean, as endlessness as in the beginning. I then am everything that remains – after I have turned myself back into a snake that no man knows."

The Triple Goddess nodded a command and ceased her undulations. The children stopped singing, and Nergal – or whoever was the figure that had become him – stepped forward, raised his enormous broad scimitar, and with a swish and a thud cleanly lopped off the head of Suppiluliuma, the last Great King of the Hittite Empire.

The sacred marriage was back on. It was deemed necessary by the High Priestess, avatar of Ishtar-Inanna-Allani, to bring balance back to the cosmic order and new life to the earth above. Of course, Suppiluliuma the Great King was gone forever, never to rise again, but the changed situation meant a changed nuptial arrangement.

The people watching had just finished their gasping and screaming as the king's bald head, sliced from its mooring, rolled backwards from the stone platform and fell at the feet of the two children, its final blood pulse falling onto their feet. They stopped singing and looked at one another. In the silence, the boy asked innocently, "Since the king is dead, has he now become a god?" The girl, still staring at the mutilated corpse, innocently replied, "No, he's just dead." They looked about but, receiving no directions, together they picked up the large, severed head and placed it upright on the nearby straw-covered tray they had brought to carry the king's testicles, keeping the face unstained. The mouth was open and the eyes stared wide into nothingness as if surprised. As the surrounding guards began to untether the body and drag it from the bloody altar, the children, pleased with the opportunity, replaced the decapitated body with the tray holding the severed head, still oozing gore from the neck.

As the king's suddenly disembodied head fell, Diomedes stated grimly, "It is done." At the same moment, Lilitu recovered from her trance and heard his voice. She turned and in the shadows beyond the final gate saw Diomedes standing with the former Great Queen, both silently staring, the queen's mouth agape. She ordered the guards and her executioner to go around the seventh gate and capture them. The two neither ran nor resisted. Diomedes kept his iron dagger sheathed and it was not taken from him. Under Lilitu's direction, they were marched back to the stone temple, the giant swordsman who would be Nergal walking right behind Diomedes still swinging the bloody blade in his left hand.

The unknown guards took them directly into the inner sanctum, but the swordsman and Lilitu paused for a ritual cleansing in the entry alcove. They emerged and again the swordsman stood near the Akhaian. Without missing a beat, as if performing a familiar ritual, the High Priestess announced that the sacred marriage would proceed, but now it would be the marriage of King Diomedes and Lieia-Hepa, adding the old title of Diomedes seemed necessary to the rite. She explained to them that it would be up to them to determine if it was to be truly a *sacred* marriage or merely a *social* one. They wondered how there could be human choice in a ritual ordained by the gods in the time of origins, but Lilitu smiled in response, "Ishtar has already ordained your choices."

At first, to their surprise, their hearts jumped with relief and delight at the prospect of becoming married to one another, despite the bizarre circumstances. Like any about-to-be-wed couple they found each other's hand and smiled foolishly into the other's eyes. But Lilitu interrupted their hopes to tell them she would first need to have a private meeting with each of them. Final decisions needed to be made by each alone.

Under orders of the High Priestess for the previously planned sacred wedding, wine for two was brought in, served in separate goblets, one of the moon's silver for the bride and another of the sun's gold for the groom. Candles were lit, and a single lute player appeared to strum a low tune. They poured a few drops of wine on the ground in libation to Allani and all other gods present and drank the rest themselves. They were going to spontaneously change goblets and sip from each other's as is done in country ceremonies, but Lilitu waved off such action as inappropriate as they were not yet wedded. She waited until the entire goblets were quaffed.

Lilitu met first with Lieia in the matrimonial room followed by a meeting with Diomedes. When they had both emerged, looking confused, they were placed side by side back before the High Priestess. The two did not look at one another, but again grasped hands. Neither recognized this ritual. How could this become a sacred marriage without sacred ritual? Or perhaps the High Priestess was performing a marriage ritual that was so alien it was unknown to them. No one dared imagine it could have just been invented.

She chanted in a foreign tongue, first looking skyward and then down into the earth. Diomedes thought it might be the original language of Kriti or perhaps, on the other extreme, of ancient Babylon. The children arrived hand in hand bringing a large sprig of holy mistletoe. Lilitu took up the branch and began a slow dance in a circle around the couple, chanting in the same unknown language. The children joined in, skipping further out in the opposite direction. Was that a sistrum-tambourine jangling in the air, wondered Lieia. As the dance picked up its pace, Lilitu shook the mistletoe over the couple, which dropped its sharp leaves and white buds upon them. Suddenly it was silent and once again she stood before them as her flying silver hair settled around her. She smiled with glazed eyes and flicked her serpentine tongue across her dark lips.

After a silence in which the High Priestess returned to herself, she indicated the room two steps up behind the sanctum in which they stood. It had a thick crimson curtain before its entry. She announced, "You are not yet married, in either a sacred or social way, until your union is consummated on the matrimonial bed above. There is no light in there, as it was before time began. You will each find your way into the separate alcoves on either side of the bed and disrobe in there. Then you will meet to repeat the sacred dance of love that united the first couple – the brother and sister who had torn asunder the suffocating union of the primal parents and brought light into the darkness of the eternal womb of chaos."

They were willing and ready, but at that moment, Lieia's vision blurred and darkness came over her mind like a thick cloud. Diomedes saw and caught her as she fell. The High Priestess nodded to guards that approached, but Diomedes waved them off, picking up his queen and carrying her to their intended connubial room above. Lilitu looked ready to intervene, but the deadly look Diomedes pierced her with stopped her short. She waved back the Sword God. Inside, Diomedes lay Lieia on the bed, kissing her dark lips, and her eyes opened again, albeit in darkness.

"Diomedes, I have been drugged," she spoke into his ear. "The wine... but I can taste the opium, which is not usually used in poison."

"But why?"

"Why just me? Listen, I don't know what Lilitu said to you in private, but this is what she offered me." She pressed a finger to his lips to stop him from speaking. "We have but little time. She wanted to have both of us burnt alive as a sacrifice, once our union was consummated, for we would then both be immortal, or as she said, 'Ishtar and Tammuz would be as one forever.' Or I could choose only myself to die, leaving you to Lilitu. Not likely. Or, since the Goddess of Death had been deprived of the willing sacrifice of the Great King, she would accept the life of an Ahhiyawa king. If I wished, they would sacrifice only you as Tammuz, and I would return to the surface as a second High Priestess, her co-ruler and consort to live in the second temple. No Mahhuzzi. Or, finally, I could suffer the wrath of Allani and accept my mere mortality along with yours and become your social wife, which is of course what I chose."

Diomedes nodded, his mind trying to focus. "Much the same for me," he said. "No mention of both our sacrifices, however. But if I allowed you to be sacrificed, I would become the new High Priest, her husband, and the co-ruler. She even swore I'd be left intact, for now. Mahhuzzi would be out. Such would please the dark Goddess of the Underworld, but she warned me your Persephone, Allani, would take great offence and seek vengeance if I refused. Strange as it may be, we seem to find ourselves bound by love: I also chose to remain a common person in a social marriage." She smiled and unseen tears rose into her eyes, but the man asked, "So why were you drugged?" And at that moment he realized she was not the only one drugged, as his head began to swirl from delayed effects. He realized the truth. "By choosing human marriage, we may have chosen human death – neither of us is meant to leave here alive. We must escape from this accursed place immediately!"

"It's no use," she spoke weakly, succumbing again to the drugged drink. "I could never escape to the upper world with you. I must return with the others."

Recalling his descent, he knew she spoke the truth, even as the numbness crept up his spine and into his mind. Desperately, he took her face between his hands and, looking deeply into her widening pupils, he said with severe intensity. "Lieia, I don't know how this will turn out, but if we survive I will go on to the island of Kyprios – *Kyprios*, the copper isle, do you hear? In Paphos city – *Paphos*! – I will check for you daily at the Sanctuary of Ashtart, goddess of love. Look for me there, if you can. *Remember*!" But as he rose to leave, the dark cloud enveloped his mind and he felt himself falling into an abyss.

When he came round, rising slowly out of his torpor, he sensed that not much time had elapsed. He was still on his back on the bed in the dark and the woman was bestride him, hovering over him. He reached out blindly and felt her naked breasts and the snake bracelet on her arm. Even in this dangerous situation or perhaps because of it, he unexpectedly became aroused and pulled her down to him. She grasped the back of his head as their open lips joined fully. Their teeth touched and their tongues found each other in a greedy wet kiss. Immediately, he knew it was not Lieia, the feel and scent were different, but demons of desire in him provoked him into hesitating before breaking from such an alluring embrace, desire negating love. He felt her full breasts press down on him and the dark thrill of submitting to such an unnatural sin flashed through his bestial mind like lightning in the dark. But he snuffed out the lightning as one would snuff out a candle and abruptly rose to his feet, pushing Lilitu from him.

"Lieia!" he bellowed. "Where are you?"L

"She is fine, O Akhaian," whispered Lilitu soothingly from the dark. "Lieia only sleeps and will not be harmed. Now come back to me, O warrior, for I felt your lust rise. I know it is your deepest wish to submit to my power and become mine."

In a flash, Diomedes weighed his options. Killing Lilitu would surely bring the guards and the murderous swordsman down on him and likely on Lieia. Walking out calmly would just be another kind of submission, and they would deal with him quickly. *Warriors don't run*, he thought, but he believed Lilitu when she said Lieia would not be harmed. He still had on his torn sandals, his iron dagger, and the remnants of his loin cloth, so he took that as the sign from Hermes he needed. He would run. He drew his long iron dagger and burst from the red curtain, making a brutal dash straight for the giant swordsman, knocking him backward to the floor with a shoulder-crash against the chest, pausing only to slash the keen blade across his meaty throat, releasing the man's gurgling lifeblood. The others gasped and stood back in shock, making no effort to stop him as he loped out the door and into the night.

He turned in the direction from which he had come toward the invisible river. He continued running until all torchlight disappeared, so he could not see the sharp rocks before him and he stumbled and fell upon them. Trained warrior as he was, he did not drop the dagger nor harm himself with it, but rose, replaced the blade in its sheath, and, finding nothing broken, made his way forward until he found where the cave floor came closer to the cave wall. He passed through and realized he was already beyond being pursued. He advanced nearly blind toward the sound of the onrushing river, but it was not quite a perfect darkness this time. He did not understand how or why, but a dim underglow suffused the air around him and at his feet, and he took this as another sign that Hermes Kataibates was with him.

Eventually he reached the bank of the fast-flowing river and took the measure of his task. He knew that attempting to go upstream was pointless and he would soon be overwhelmed. He needed to find some sort of log or chunk of wood that he could hold on to and throw himself into the downstream current, not knowing if a waterfall cliff lay ahead or if the unnamed river would ever emerge from beneath the ground. He set out to make his way along the shadowy bank looking for driftwood in the strange diffuse glow of the air just above the dark river waters.

He stumbled along for a time, going downstream and painfully descending over a precipitous rockfall beside a small cataract he would not have seen if it were pitch black. But there at the bottom probably thrown from the river after crashing over the waterfall he found several branches and a few larger tree limbs. He took a deep breath, again intoning a prayer to Hermes for luck and to the unnamed god of this river to allow him passage and looked for the stoutest fallen bough.

He took up a heavy limb that was green enough not to be waterlogged and waded into the wild water as far as he could before being swept away by the deeper central current. He attempted to get astride the log since by simply clinging to its side he was more likely to scrape against hidden rocks. Most of the rocks and the gravel bed in this fast-flowing stream had long been worn smooth by the current, and that gave him hope. Despite this, he spent as much time under the waters as above them, so he was pulled along nearly blind, sometimes able only to distinguish between being below water or on its surface by attempting to breathe, often resulting in taking in water. His strong arms held fast to the big limb, but he soon felt himself drowning little by little. He had no aim, no control, and he had no idea what lay ahead. At the mercy of the underground river, his only hope was to stay with it wherever it took him.

He was bruised, cut, and beaten, coughing and puking up water, yet he held on for what seemed like hours. There was nothing to see and all he could hear was the onrushing roar of the river. He had lost all track of time and often forgot himself, awakening from sporadic dreams to find himself still grasping onto the log to grapple with the current. These flashing visions were mostly memories of killings or cruelties he had perpetrated, some emerging from his childhood such as when, mockingly goaded into it by older hunters, he had reluctantly killed a fawn with his arrows. He recalled his ruthless murders when, as a youthful warrior initiate in Arkadia, he was transformed into a man-wolf for a year. He came back to himself weeping, adding his tears to the river. Even though he now refused to rape or torture, he still had continued to take savage pleasure in battle kills, and now an endless parade of dying faces appeared before him. Coughing dark water, he realized he felt shame for killing so many of the old soldiers guarding the sacred temples at Arinna, and now he even felt sorrow for unleashing his wrath upon the brave Meshedi outside the Storm-God's temple somewhere behind him in Lawazantiya. Yet, through the regrets of his melting consciousness, in the outer world he remorselessly held on.

He did so until the inevitable happened. All in a moment he found himself in the air as the tree limb leapt over another escarpment. In the cascade, he pushed his life raft away, so it crashed onto sharp rocks, splitting itself apart. But the push had allowed him to splash down into deeper waters. He still hit the bottom on his side, knocking the wind from his lungs along with a spew of air bubbles as he tumbled forward into new depths. Somehow he found the surface again, saving his life by hoarking and retching out the water from his lungs. Blindly managing to swim toward a bank, he was able to touch bottom. It was dark behind and dark ahead but now he saw it was the river itself that gave off the dim glow. Though the dark river seemed intent on his destruction, in his heart he thanked it for the diffuse light. His body began to violently shake as he exposed his chest to the air, so he dove back into the central current, stolidly determined but feeling no real sense of hope. He was washed wildly downstream but managed to occasionally swim into the shallows to rest, until at last he found himself too weary to be able to swim much at all. Was this the vengeance of Allani of the Underworld?

He began to sink under the waves, each time spending longer without air, so overcome with water and fatigue that death seemed to call to him like a siren song promising sweet rest. But then something changed as he surfaced once more and looked up. Were there spots in his eyes or a gathering of fireflies? He realize with sudden joy that stars, not the cave roof, were above him. The dark river had emerged outside! It was late at night, so when he swam and crawled his way into shallower waters where he could kneel, he caught a glimpse of the silver moon crescent resting on the eastern horizon.

> Then forth he came, his both knees faltering, both his strong hands hanging down, and all with froth his cheeks and nostrils flowing, voice and breath spent to all use, and down he sank to death. The dark river had soaked his heart through.

Diomedes fell onto a flat rock, but he was not quite senseless as the rock tipped sideways and shook him off. He heard Earth groan deep within and the ground quaked more violently than either of the first two times. A resounding crack spread up the shoreline in the night but missed him. He was thrown about like a straw doll, with no strength even to brace himself. It lasted a long minute, and finally he fell into a deep swoon, released into oblivion.

The lone man awoke with rain on his face as a cloud covered the sun. He was still exhausted, bruised, and beaten, but he knew he was alive and that fact alone soon brought him round. It was already late morning. He was not sure which way to go, but once he sat up he could see he was within the mountains a ways above the Puruma River valley. Sharing its source with the Puruma, this river would have run south out of the heights of the Anti-Taurus Mountains, but then it split from the main current and dove underground before reaching Lawazantiya. He had descended below the temple next to it, but the dark river still found its way out lower yet into the valley. He could see it would soon merge back into the Puruma and continue its journey to the sea. He had been carried along in it for a long distance! Lawazantiya was far behind.

He unsteadily rose and the first thing he noticed was that miraculously he still had his sheathed dagger, and the second thing was that the dark river had considerably lessened its volume. He recalled that Poseidon's horses had been busy last night; while he slipped into unconsciousness, a significant quake had occurred. With a cold chill, he surmised the river flow had lessened because somewhere upstream the cave roof must have collapsed and now partially blocked the river's flow, at least for the time being. Did that mean the entire underground complex of Ishtar and Allani had been crushed? Did Lieia make it out? He could not be sure, but an intuitive whisper from Hermes Pompaios, the guide of gods and men, told him to continue south toward the sea, and beyond that to a gathering point on the isle of Kyprios.

If Lieia and Lilitu had made it back to the surface, his return could be the death of both his beloved and himself, for the High Priestess had planned vengeance, and she was still the most powerful person in the city of Ishtar. Of course, the arrival of Sarpedon's troop would immediately change the balance of power, though he believed Sarpedon would not interfere in city politics and would avoid the Temple of Ishtar. He decided to continue south alone, perhaps to see if Lieia would overcome trials and temptations on a quest to find him. He knew he would miss the fine bronze tapered sword given him by the Sardinian, but surely Eruthros or Kabi would bring it back to him.

Lieia was awakened mid-morning to be told she had an important visitor. It was Zunan, her former protector, come to bid her farewell before leading the caravan of Hittite soldiers to Karkemish. The actual commander, Kil-Teshub, was being carefully carried along with attendants in a sturdy four-wheeled wagon pulled by four mules.

It took her long minutes to awaken and realize where she was. She saw she was in the same room in the Tower of Ishtar where she had been placed when she arrived there after being rescued... Rescued? How long ago was that she wondered.

Late last night, she remembered, the funeral cortège had ascended back to the surface and right into the upper temple, and this time it had indeed become a mournful march for the lost soul of the king. There was no music played and the only thing heard were low, moaning laments. Usually return journeys were joyful and celebratory, for a new god had risen. Instead the naked, bruised body and head of Suppiluliuma had been unceremoniously put to the flame on a pyre next to the stone temple. Only the Great King's crown and his other royal attire were returned to the surface. Lilitu wept and the Goddess wept through her (she was sure), for neither a new god nor goddess had arisen and the ancient holy ritual had failed in its purpose. The former king chose to end his life rather than sacrifice what remained of his human pride to become a god, so he had been denied the right to a sacred interment in a small mausoleum over a shallow shaft grave. The body of the huge unknown swordsman who had incarnated Nergal was buried in the mausoleum instead. The former Great Queen had been deceived by common love and chosen life over immortality. Allani welcomed the dead either way.

As the crackling flames had risen on the pyre and consumed the oiled flesh of Suppiluliuma, there had been a final more serious quaking of the earth. The upheaval was violent and the cave wall between the netherworld temple and the dark river came crashing down. The clamour of falling rocks could be heard for minutes, yet the cave vault of the Underworld temple of Allani somehow remained intact, as did the Tower of Ishtar above. Lilitu remained grim but calm, for she had not expected the minor earth deity Irpitiga to destroy the sacred space of mighty Ishtar. After the burning and quick burial, by Hittite standards, the procession had immediately been reorganized and returned back up through all seven gates with requisite lamentations. The High Priestess of Ishtar had led the way beneath dark veils that hid her head entirely while Lieia had walked stoically upward, her unveiled head held high. The voice of the gatekeeper had remained silent.

"Zunan, you are here!" Lieia rose and wrapped herself in a robe.

"Not for long, Great Queen. The Hatti are about to leave and I am their designated leader. I have come to bid you farewell, forever grateful that you survived the ordeal below ground." He did not want to ask about his friend, Diomedes, fearful of what he may be told.

"Brave Zunan, in spite of appearances I am a prisoner once again, and I do not know how safe I am. I must escape from this place." Zunan stood up looking perplexed. She continued, "You must tell me: where is a place called Kyprios?"

"Kyprios? That's the Hellenic name for the isle of copper in the Great Green. We call it Alasiya, which of course you know."

"In a dream – it feels like a dream – Diomedes is holding my face close to his and having me repeat these words – *Kyprios* and *Paphos*."

"He lives then?"

"I do not know, Zunan. He escaped into the darkness where the subterranean cave flattens out and there is a river. But later there was that great earth upheaval..."

"You think...?"

"No, in my heart I feel he is alive. I feel his presence still."

Zunan nodded, understanding, though unable to fathom how Diomedes could have possibly returned from the Land of the Dead. “And Paphos is a city on the west coast of Alasiya.”

“Yes, a city of their Goddess of Love. I don’t know how I know this.”

“It is also one of the major staging cities for the pirates of the sea, or so I have been told.”

“Zunan, he asks me to meet him there in the main temple! How can I accomplish this? I cannot go alone!”

“Are you asking me to give up leadership of the final Hatti expedition to Karkemish? Instead, you wish me to protect you and guide you to Alasiya?”

For a second, slightly ashamed, she lowered her eyes, but then Lieia-Hepa raised her head and looked at him as only a queen could. “Dear Zunan, you have always been my protector. Yes, that is precisely what I am asking of you.”

He was silent but then replied, “I will need others. Sneaking a queen through a war zone overrun with outlaw warriors is a dangerous undertaking, so it would help to be among the outlaws. I will seek out others we can trust for this quest. My queen, such a liberation is going to take time. Right now, they will have extra guards on alert and breaking you out at the same time the barbarian troop is here would cause political problems that may threaten the peaceful agreement. Once they leave, we will come for you. ” Zunan leaned forward and took her hand between his own. “And don’t protest that I call you *my queen.* For me you could never be anything else.” He rose, gave a quick one-knee bow and left. Lieia briefly wept in gratitude then fell back into a deep sleep.

Zunan went straight out of the city to where the Hittite forces in nearly their entirety had gathered to leave. Aside from deserters, only Penti-Sharruma the chief scribe had determined to stay. Zunan went directly to the healer’s wagon and told the bedridden but fully alert Kil-Teshub that he was resigning his commission. The general had already learned from Mahhuzzi how Suppiluliuma met his end and had applauded his last-minute courage. “To die with honour as a Hatti warrior rather than be reborn as a dishonoured god is a brave choice." Mahhuzzi had not stayed long, as he had "new business to attend to". He was remaining in Ishtar's holy city as the High Priest and future consort of the High Priestess. Even Kil-Teshub could see his eyes shine in adoration as he spoke of Lilitu though she had probably not actually seduced him yet. "Guard your balls," the old soldier had grunted.

Zunan he understood. "You are staying to continue being the private honour guard of Lieia-Hepa, are you not?" Kil-Teshub asked. Zunan nodded. "Because you realize we can easily name another a second-in-command to make it to Karkemish, or ...?"

"General Kil-Teshub, I fear the Great Queen may be in danger here. Lilitu will soon see her as a rival, if she does not already. I must take her away..." Kil-Teshub nodded but saw no point in asking further questions.

Zunan left and considered as he walked that the apparently unstoppable horde of sea warriors and the even greater number of migrants behind them are likely to follow the destruction of Ugarit by that of nearby Halab, also a rich city, and Karkemish was just a march inland across a dry plain to the northeast beyond that. He glanced back and saw Kil-Teshub's heavy wagon pulled by four mules and preceded by six marching Meshedi move to the front to begin the journey of the Hatti soldiers to fabled Karkemish. They may well all be doomed, and Lawazantiya was not likely to be ignored either. Best to be among the raiders rather than beneath them, he ruefully considered.

He had already made that choice in his position as temporary Hatti leader. Lilitu had contacted him saying she would be pleased to allow the non-military Hittites to remain in her city, including those who had taken a wife or deserted their cause. But she would not permit the departing Hittite soldiers to take the grain and other edible supplies they had brought with them from Hattusa. Otherwise, her Hurrian guard would keep them engaged until the barbarians arrived to destroy them. She encouraged them to take all the valuable items that belonged to the Great King's person and even had her slaves return the golden peaked crown and all other royal garments Suppiluliuma had removed in the Underworld. No doubt the King of Karkemish would cherish such things and it would add to their welcome. But the rest of the jewels, gold, and sacred statuary were to remain.

Zunan could have opposed her, but he realized the coming warrior troop would require treasure and food supplies to keep them from destroying the city that held Lieia, so he agreed as long as such were shared with them. Lilitu understood and it was so. Zunan had spoken for the inland sea peoples but not the Hatti. His course was set.

He made his way into the city to find his rough comrades, Eruthros and Saddirme. They would surely want to join his new expedition since it involved discovering if their revered leader Diomedes still lived, and, if so, fulfilling his wishes by taking Lieia-Hepa to him. When the entire warrior troop arrived later, surely it would not be hard to bring Kabi aboard on this clandestine adventure. Perhaps the others that remained in the city from Diomedes's original squad would be willing to join, as well.

When he found them, now ensconced in the vacated temple of the Storm-God, they greeted him with hearty comradery but also with shock that he had forsaken the Hatti military. He explained the queen's request but also had to make the time to share what little he had gathered about Diomedes's *harrowing of Hades*, as Eruthros called it. Neither thought he could have survived, "but then again, this is Diomedes of whom we speak – King of Tiryns, hero of Ilios, the man who strove with gods, so expect the impossible," said Eruthros. Saddirme hung his head and repeated that, alas, he was retiring from adventure, finding a wife or two, and staying in Lawazantiya. Eruthros, however, put a beefy arm around him and laughed, "After what we've been through together? No, you are now my battlefield comrade, Saddirme, my ale-drinking crony, and besides that you make me laugh. You are not deserting us now!" Saddirme gave his gap-toothed grin and relented, glad to be appreciated.

“Our first task is a repetition of what we’ve already done,” said Zunan. “We must free Lieia-Hepa, the High Priestess of the Sun Goddess. For that, I suggest we await the arrival of the rest of your troop from the bluff later today. Then we must wait until most of them depart, thus giving your wounds more time to heal. When we get her out, we can blend in with them and no one will dare to try to force her from us. Later, we can leave on our own or stay with them until we reach Alasiya.”

“Freeing the queen should be no problem this time without the organized Meshedi guards,” Eruthros smiled, adding, “but me and Saddirme are going to miss our proud quills.” They chortled, though neither was back in fighting form, as yet.

In late afternoon, Kabi and two accompanying scouts rode into the city and sought out Diomedes. When they learned he wasn’t present, they approached the Temple of Ishtar where they found the High Priestess and her novice High Priest and future consort, Mahhuzzi. Kabi as a known insider was permitted audience. The situation was explained to him. The Hittite military had left but without its late king, its Wiseman, or the chief scribe. The former Great Queen was here but “under protection”. The whereabouts of Diomedes was unknown but the worst was feared. Was Kabi’s leader, man of the Sherden, going to honour their agreement? Once Kabi learned that, beyond the promised hospitality, storage food and Hatti treasure would also be shared, he spoke for Sarpedon and said yes.

Word spread, and Zunan found Kabi and his two companions on the temple grounds. Kabi was taken back to Eruthros and Saddirme at their new quarters in the Storm-God’s temple. Compressed stories were exchanged, and Kabi was in full agreement with joining the fight to free the queen again and the flight to the sea, except he notified them that his new life-companion, a novice warrior (now he had their attention) named Henti, would be with him. He soon departed to meet Sarpedon’s approach.

By early evening, the nearly two-thousand warriors arrived in a long, excited cavalcade led by Sarpedon and

Kuprlli with Kabi and Henti not far behind. They were greeted outside the city walls by the High Priestess and her consort-in-waiting, Mahhuzzi, in a sturdy gold-embossed chariot with a driver. Zunan drove his own chariot nearby while the usual driver stood aside. They were surrounded by a small cohort of Hurrian guards, but Sarpedon was especially pleased to see Eruthros and Saddirme, whom he knew well, appear next in a cart. Kabi came forth and greeted them too, but he then mounted Zunan's chariot to give him a public warrior's salute so the rest would recognize he was one of them. After the greetings, it was Mahhuzzi who spoke.

"I am Mahhuzzi, once the chief advisor to the late Great King of Hatti, but now the High Priest of Ishtar in this sacred city. I am but the spokesperson for my sacred lady, the High Priestess of Ishtar, who stands next to me." In a crown of beaded black onyx, silver-haired Lilitu imperiously looked straight ahead, not deigning to acknowledge such uncivilized invaders. "According to our agreement, we will bring food, wine, and entertainment to your encampment here beyond the city gates. But first, the water of our river is fresh and plentiful and useful for bathing. To this we also add treasures and extended food supplies the Hittites brought from Hattusa!" There was a great cheer. "In a few days, anyone who chooses to embrace the Great Goddess Ishtar, by whatever name you know her, is welcome to stay among us and join our corps of guardsmen. As a result of the wars, we have many widows and maidens some of whom may choose to marry and share a home with you, but, mark, this is a city ruled by the Goddess, so these women have free choice. You cannot force that choice! You can take several days to decide, but in the meantime, we offer the services of our healers for any that need them, and we invite you as our new friends to renew your equipment for we will send out all our experts plus the cloth and materials you will need for new clothes or repairs of your old garments and armour. Feasting in honour of Ishtar will begin soon after!" The troops from everywhere roared in exultation, banging their shields. No one thought of war or further plunder since all they desired was available, and for some this city would even be a home. So the agreement stood and events proceeded from there.

Far down the valley Diomedes set out near naked, alone, and bruised to make his way south to either meet the troop of Sarpedon on its way to Alasiya or to make it there on his own. He meant to go to Paphos, the staging area for westward conquest, and thence lead a squadron of warships back to the chaos of the Peloponnese where sacred Pylos still stood. After that, he would go on into the islands of the Ionian Sea to see a man about a Palladion.

Lieia remained in her room only allowed to emerge under guard. Later, she was brought forth to represent the Sun Goddess at the long marriage rites of Lilitu and Mahhuzzi, which ended with Mahhuzzi going to his hands and knees to kiss the jewelled feet of the High Priestess of Ishtar. In the meantime, Lieia prayed, exercised in ritual dances, dreamed of Diomedes, and stayed alert, waiting and hoping for her promised rescuers. Would Zunan keep his word? She doubted it not.

After three cycles of moon phases with spring beginning, the renewed warrior troop set out south again, about halved in number. When Eruthros learned from his Danaans that Sarpedon had likely killed his cousin, Klymenos, his honour was slighted and he challenged Sarpedon to a sword duel. However, Kabi with Henti intervened, and after their tale was told to him in brutal honesty and gruesome detail, Eruthros admitted that Klymenos was most often a brainless troublemaker and agreed they were all better off without him.

Kuprlli the Lukkan kept to his word and chose to stay. He married a grateful widow and was soon happily gaining weight from her accomplished Hurrian cooking skills.

Kabi and Henti gratefully joined the secret cadre to free Lieia and, hopefully, guide her back to Diomedes, if he lived. Over time, Kabi taught Henti to ride and use light weapons, and it came to pass that she was able to join him on many of his scouting missions. He gave her trusty Pirwa and found another sturdy mount for himself. Henti had already proven her mettle in battle and had few domestic skills, so in time she became a skilled, if diminutive, warrior. All they wished was to continue living their hard but free eventful lives together, trusting Sarpedon as their leader yet driven by the wild hope of bringing Lieia back together with Diomedes and from there to carry on.

Sarpedon, the Sardinian from Sardis in the Seha River Land still yearned to someday actually dwell in Sardinia. He intended to lead warriors across the seas also going west. This was against the general current of the marauding peoples of the sea to continue attacking south through Canaan and the land of the Peleset. For them, the old dream of ultimately taking the rich lands of the Nile Delta in Misri continued. Sarpedon, however, looked the other way and hoped his comrade Diomedes still lived, for he considered that they had unfinished business with the city of Pylos that had survived the first series of raids and fiery uprisings in Hellas. This time he would not let Diomedes stand in his way. He would surely want to return to the Peloponnese, for did not the Akhaian make mention of a famous king on the island of Ithaki he wanted to see again, not far north from there?

Penti-Sharruma the scribe was found dead, apparently from self-inflicted poison. He had stacked numerous tablets carefully beside him, the early ones precisely engraved in copper or even in bronze and only the newer ones still on clay. The curious tablets had been taken by Hurrian guards to the High Priestess and the High Priest Mahhuzzi, but only the latter could with some difficulty decipher the archaic Hatti hieroglyphs in which they were written. He was amazed to discover that they were an epic narrative, uncommon in Hatti lands whose written records were mostly bookkeeping, ritual formulae, or recitations of mythology – at least since the ancient tale of Mursili I destroying the now gone city of Ebla when its Amorite rulers would not release Hatti hostages. The scribe's epic concerned the life and conquests of the Great King Suppiluliuma II, whom, it was revealed, Penti-Sharruma virtually worshipped. But the final tablets on clay became a tragedy devoted to his beloved king's downfall by becoming possessed by demons sent by Illuyanka, the dragon of chaos. But Penti-Sharruma's tale also indicated the primeval dragon was encouraged by the jealousy of the Hatti Sun Goddess of Earth and Ishtar from the East. Lilitu had all tablets destroyed. The Hatti epic disappeared from earthly records just as writing itself was disappearing with the collapse of most of the great civilizations of the eastern Great Green Sea, Anatolia, and the Levant.

Shipibaal and the messenger approached the oncoming Hittite soldiers with waves and signs of peace. A pair of young Meshedi, apparently captains or commanders, came forward to meet them. They were taken to the wagon of Kil-Teshub to tell him the good news that they are gratefully welcomed to Karkemish, but the general was sound asleep, probably under medication. They were invited to stay but they chose to ride on, Shipibaal perturbed by their strange sense of humour. Twice he was asked how he managed to keep his second, riderless horse following him on the trail with no halter.

Back home in Lawazantiya, kept safe from destruction for some years yet by its new warrior guard, the lively pair of lovers, Shipibaal and Telipinu, embraced an active outdoor life and an even more active indoor union. They had found a destiny in each other, so neither worried about the sombre fate of Ishtar's sacred city. The messenger seems to have had other causes or other groups of friends, for he regularly went off on his own, sometimes for weeks at a time, but he always returned smiling, offering no explanation. "Perhaps I replenish myself in the wild woods," he once said. Shipibaal lived for the present, unobtrusively and privately, quite happy being anti-social yet always cheerfully keeping up appearances with the disappearing god.

End or Return to the Sea?
See *Diomedeia II: Return to Tiryns*
(forthcoming)

Appendix I: Glossary of Names

Dates of historical kings, destructions, etc. are all BCE *circa* approximations suitable to the context. All places and peoples are *historical*. All gods and sacred places are mythic or legendary. Individuals in the historical record have an (h) after their name. Mythic or legendary human characters have an (m) after theirs.

(The story opens, circa 1195 BCE, but the exact date is controversial.)

Non-Hittite Anatolians and Peoples of the Sea

Kabi the Canaanite-Khabiru (pre-Israelite) scout

Kaskaili (h), the two Kaska leaders

Kuprlli the Lukkan (Lykian or Lycian) leader after Payava

Leukos the Kritin or Cretan (Peleset, Philistine, or Ekwesh) from Kriti

Payava the Lukkan (Lykian or Lycian)

Poulxeria (m), mother of Payava whose ancestors came from Kriti

Saddirme, a Karkisan warrior, fluent in Luwian, Nesili, & Hellenic

Sarpedon the Sardinian (Sherden or Shardana), named after Sarpedon (m), warrior from the Lukka lands, who fought for Ilios in the larger Trojan War (Troy VI, 1275)

Shipibaal (h), envoy-spy for Ugarit King Ammurapi who is stuck in Lawazantiya

Uhhaziti the Arzawan from Mira

Uhhaziti's uncle, the Arzawan with an Akhaian helmet

Akhaians (Achaeans, Achaioi, Argives, Danaans, Hellenes, Tjekker, Ahhiyawa)

Aietes (m) = Aeëtes, founder and 1st king of Kolkhis, father of Medea

Akhilleus (m) = Achilles, Hellene from Phthia, hero of earlier Trojan War (i.e., Troy VI)

Agamemnon (m), former Great King (*Wanax*) of Akhaians (Ahhiyawa), son of Atreus, nephew of Thyestes

Alexandros (h) = Alaksandu to the Hittites, King of Ilios 80 yrs earlier (Troy VI)

Attarissiya (h) = Atreus in Hittite spelling, mentioned in the Hittite palace archives

Atreus (m) = Attarissiya, former Great King (*Wanax*) of Akhaians (Ahhiyawa), hereditary title of Argive Great Kings going back a century

Diomedes (m), former king or *lawagetas* of Tiryns, hero at Ilios, warrior nonpareil

Eruthros, former king or *lawagetas* of the Danaans (Danuna, Denyen) of Aitolia

Eurylos (m), former king or *lawagetas* of Asine

Henti, harem-girl translator between Akhaian and Luwian

Herakles (m) = Hercules in Latin spelling, from Tiryns, archetype of Hellenic heroes

Jason (m), leader of the Argonauts in quest of the Golden Fleece

Klymenos, captain amongst the Aitolian Danaans

Menelaos (m), former king or *lawagetas* of Laconia

Odysseus (m), king or *lawagetas* of Ithaki

Sthenelos (m), former king or *lawagetas* of Lerna, charioteer of Diomedes

Thyestes (m), Thyestes, former Great King (*Wanax*) of Akhaians (Ahhiyawa), uncle of Agamemnon, who murdered Atreus to become king

Wilusans (Trojans)

Aineias (m) = Aeneas (Latinized), prince of the last Ilios, terrified of Diomedes, escaped the conflagration

Alexandros (h) = Alaksandu to the Hittites, later known as Paris, Akhaian or Aeolian King of Ilios 80 yrs earlier (1275, i.e., Troy VI), Hittite ally

Kassandra (m) = Cassandra, Princess of Ilios, enslaved by Agamemnon

Hekabe (m) = Hecuba (Latinized), Queen of Ilios

Hektor (m) = Hector (Latinized), warrior Prince of Ilios under Alexandros (i.e., Troy VI)

Laomedon (m), very early Wilusan (Trojan) king

Memnon (m), a king of Aithiopia (Ethiopia) who late in the war brought his troops to aid Ilios

Priam (m), King or vassal-king of the final Ilios (Taruisa to Hittites)

Hittites and Contemporaries

Ammurapi (h), vassal-King of Ugarit (1215-1195)

Anniwiyanni (h), the first wife of Tudhaliya IV and *Tawananna* before Lieia-Hepa

Arnuwanda III (h), Great King (1209-1208) before Suppiluliuma II, son of Tudhaliya IV

Ashur-nadin-apli (h), Great King of the Assyrians (1206-1203), during the early reign of Suppiluliuma II

Eshuwara (h), high official on Alasiya (Cyprus) before Sea Peoples take the island

Halata, nephew of Kurunta, vassal-king of Tarhuntassa

Hattusili III (h), Great King (1267-1238), brother of Muwatalli II, uncle of Mursili III, father of Tudhaliya IV, grandfather of Suppiluliuma II, husband of Puduhepa

Henti, harem-girl translator between Akhaian and Luwian

Kil-Teshub, Hittite General & *Gal-Meshedi* (Meshedi Commander), uncle to Suppiluliuma

Kurunta (h), vassal-King of Tarhuntassa, brother of Urhi-Teshub

Labarna (h), the first Great King of the Hittites (Old Kingdom, flourished around 1660)

Lieia-Hepa, Great Queen, High-Priestess and *Tawananna*

Lilitu, High Priestess of Ishtar in Lawazantiya

Mahhuzzi, Great King's chief advisor ("grand vizier"), cousin to the Suppiluliuma

Mariya (h), unknown, perhaps a Hayasa-Azzi warrior chief

Meshedi (h), royal bodyguard (once called the "Men of the Golden Spears")

Mursili I (h), ancient Great King (1620-1590), sacked Babylon, Halab (Aleppo) and Ebla

Mursili III (h), short-lived Great King, son of Mursili II

Muwatalli II (h), Great King (1295-1272), moved Hittite capital to Tarhuntassa, led Hittites to victory at Kadesh

Penti-Sharruma (h), chief scribe (& secret epic poet)

Puduhepa (h), Hattusili III's Great Queen and Goddess Ishtar on Earth

Suppiluliuma I (h), Great King of the Hittites (1350-1322), who expanded the Hittite Empire to its greatest extent

Suppiluliuma II (h), Great King of the Hittites (1207-1195), 2nd son of Tudhaliya IV, patron of the Storm-God Teshub (Hurrian) also known as Tarhunta (Hattic)

Talmi-Teshub (h), King of Karkemish (1200-1181)

Telipinu, the name chosen by *the messenger*, also a god & an early Great King

Tudhaliya IV (h), Great King (1237-1209), son of Hattusili III, father of Arnuwanda III and Suppiluliuma II, patron of Sharruma

Tukulti-Ninurta (h), Assyrian Great King (1243-1207), contemporary of Tudhaliya IV

Urhi-Teshub (h), son of Muwatalli II, became Great King Mursili III (h) (1272-1267), dethroned by his uncle Hattusili III (father of Tudhaliya IV)

Zunan-Teshub, Great Queen's Hurrian bodyguard & attendant

Misriwi = **Egyptian/Egyptians** from *Misri* (Hittite-Akkadian for Egypt) = **Aigyptoi** (Hellenic)

Merneptah (h), Pharaoh (1213-1203) during the Libu (Libyan) & Sea People desert attack (1208)

Ramses II (h), Misriwi Pharaoh (1303–1213) during the Battle of Kadesh (1275)

Ramses III (h), Misriwi Pharaoh (1190-1155) during the attack of the Peoples of the Sea in ships in the Delta (1178)

Languages

Akhaian = Achaean, Achaioi, Hellenic dialect of the districts of Achaia & Argolis in "Mycenaean" Hellas (Greece)

Aitolian = Aetolian, Hellenic dialect of the Aitolia district in ancient Hellas (Greece), which I identify with Danaan

Aigyptoi or Aigyptioi = Egyptian, what the Hellenes (Greeks) called the main language & people of Egypt

Akkadian, language of the Akkadian Empire & later a cuneiform lingua franca used in written communication among Bronze Age kingdoms

Danaan, used by Homer as equivalent to Akhaian, but my use is specific to the Aitolian region

Dorian or Doric, Hellenic dialect of the arriving Dorian tribes near end of the Bronze Age, common in Lakonia (Laconia) and the region later called Makedonia (Macedonia)

English, language of this book, non-existent in the Bronze Age

Hatti, the pre-Indo-European language & people conquered by the Hittites (Nesa) who applied their name to themselves

Hellenic, no such word existed in the Bronze Age, but it would have been Indo-European (IE) proto-Greek with different dialects for each Hellenic region

Hittite, called Nesili or *Nesite* by themselves, the language of the Nesa, an IE language influenced by non-IE Hatti, the basis of Hittite cuneiform

Hurrian, non-IE language spoken by the Hurrians in the Mittani kingdom in northern Mesopotamia, second most common language in Anatolia

Kaskian, pre-IE language spoken by the Kaska

Luwian, the IE language of the Lukka Lands (later Lykia or Lycia), so widely spoken it became the *lingua franca* of

Anatolia and largely replaced Hittite by the late Bronze Age, the basis of Luwian or Anatolian hieroglyphics

Milesian, Hellenic dialect that preceded Ionic along Aegean shore of southern Anatolia (may have been related to Aeolian)

Misriwi = Egyptian

Nesite = Nesili, what the Hittites called their own language

Sassarese, language spoken by many Sardinians

Places

Adaniya = Adana, city in southern Anatolia on a river near to the Mediterranean Sea

Aia, royal city of Kolkhis

Aigyptos = Egypt, Hellenic (Greek), Hittite-Akkadian *Misri*

Aitolia = Aetolia, region in Hellas, which I mythologize as the homeland of the Danaans

Alasiya = Cyprus (Classical Gk *Kypros*, Linear B *Kyprio* or *Kyprios*), Hittite name for island state in the eastern Mediterranean Sea, major cities burnt 1194, then occupied by Sea Peoples

Amurru, kingdom north of Canaan, modern Syria & Lebanon

Apasa, former Arzawan capital, later the site of Ephesos

Argolid, region in Hellas with major Akhaian cities, including Mykenai & Tiryns, homeland of the Argives and Akhaians (also from Achaia)

Arinna, sacred city of the Sun Goddess, just north of Hattusa, probably the modern ruins of Alaca Höyük (destroyed 1195)

Arzawa, kingdom in the SW corner of Anatolia, Hittite rival, later divided by the Hittites into three provinces: Mira, the Seha River Land, and Hapalla

Assur, origin and later capital of the Assyrian Empire

Black Sea = Pontos Axeinos or Pontos Euxinos or just *Pontos*

Bosporos = Bosporus, strait of Byzantium

Bubulhum, village in the SE Taurus Mountains of Anatolia, west of the Mala (Euphrates) River

Byzantion = early Hellenic from of Byzantium

Canaan, general name for the tribal fiefdoms of the ancient Middle East, from Amurru to the Sinai peninsula

Delice River, a major tributary of the Marassantiya River, near Hattusa

Ebla, very ancient city & kingdom in the Levant, near Halab (Aleppo), finally destroyed by the Hittite king Mursili I (1600)

Enkomi, major port of Bronze Age Cyprus (Alasiya), gathering place for Peoples of the Sea

Great Green = Mediterranean (or Mesogeios) Sea

Halab = Aleppo in Syria, SW of Karkemish, NW of Ugarit, survived the Sea Peoples

Hapalla, Hittite satellite kingdom to the west

Hattusa, sacred capital of the Hittite Empire (destroyed 1195), the Turkish site is today called *Boghazköy*

Hayasa-Azzi, fragmented kingdom to the east of the Hittites on the coast of the Pontos

Hellespont = Dardanelles, long narrow strait between the Aegean Sea and the Propontis

Hermis River, on the Aegean coast of Anatolia near Smyrna

Hurna, village north of Hattusa downstream on the Marassantiya River

Ichnussa = Sardinia

Ilios = Hittite Wilusa, also Taruisa or Troy, port city destroyed (1199) by Akhaian-led Sea Peoples (Troy VIIa); also larger city destroyed earlier (1275, Troy VI)

Isuwa, the ancient Hittite name for a neighbouring Anatolian kingdom to the east

Ithaki = Ithaka or Ithaca, small island in the "Western" (what later became the Ionian) Sea, home to Odysseus

Kapperi, town downstream on the Marassantiya River, north of Hattusa

Karassuwa, non-Hatti city downstream on the Marassantiya River, north of Hattusa

Karkemish = Carchemish or Kargamish, kingdom on the north Mala/Euphrates River, subjugated by the Hatti, later a prominent neo-Hittite site

Karkisa, Hittite name for what later became Caria

Kizzuwatna, Hittite vassal kingdom south of Hattusa containing Lawazantiya

Kolkhis = Colchis, kingdom on the Black Sea in what is now Georgia

Korax River = Raven river in Hellenic, north boundary of the kingdom of Kolkhis

Kriti = Crete, Megalonisi, Caphtor, Keftiu to the Egyptians

Kummiya = Kummanni, chief city of Kizzuwatna & sacred city of Teshub the Storm-God

Kush, kingdom south of Egypt, likely identifiable with Sheba or Nubia

Kussar, the Hittite-Hatti first kingdom before the empire was established

Kyprios = Kyprio, Linear B for Kypros in classical Greek, Alasiya in Hittite texts, Cyprus now

Kyzikos = Cyzicus, kingdom in ancient Masa (Mysia) on the Asian side of the Propontis

Lawazantiya, sacred city of Ishtar (Shaushka) in Kizzuwatna

Lazpas = Lesbos

Lukka Lands = Lykia, Lycia

Maionia = later part of Lydia, kingdom that once may have included Wilusa

Mala River (Hittite) = Euphrates River (Hellenic)

Marassantiya River = Kızılırmak or Halys River, flows near Hattusa & passed Nerik to Black Sea

Megalonisi = Kriti, Crete (means “big island” in Hellenic)

Mesogeios Sea = Mediterranean Sea

Milawata = Millawanda or Miletos (Miletus) on south Aegean coast of Anatolia

Miletos = Hellenic name for Milawata (controlled by Hittites 1200, destroyed by Sea Peoples 1197)

Mira = a southern Hittite province, once part of Arzawa, later known as Caria

Misri = Egypt, as the Hittites called it in the 14th century BCE Amarna tablets (probably from Akkadian)

Mittani = Mitanni, Hanigalbat to themselves, rival kingdom of the Hittites until early 13th century BCE when it was defeated by the Hatti then crushed by the Assyrians

"Mountain-like burial chamber" & "high-domed pillar" today called the *Südberg* & *Nisantas* by archeologists, pillar ordered by Suppiluliuma II to record his deeds, & the chamber building where his father, Tudhaliya IV, was likely interred meant to represent a sacred mountain

"Mountain Temple of the Gods" = *Yazilikaya*, as it is known today in Turkey, a pair of chambers within cliffs with relief carvings of the gods near to Hattusa

Mykenai = Mycenae, major city of the Argolid plain in the Mycenaean Age, home of the Great King (Wanax) of all Hellenes (destroyed 1205)

Mysia, small kingdom on the Asian side of the Propontis, north of Wilusa (the Troad)

Nerik, Pontus city north of Hattusa long contested between the Hatti and the Kaska (disappeared 1195), likely the modern ruins of Oymaağaç Höyük

Nihriya, city near which a great battle took place in 1230 between the Hittites and the Assyrians ending in an Assyrian victory

Okeanos = ōkeanos, Hellenic, the *ocean,* originally denoting the entire body of water thought to encompass the earth's single land mass

Paphos, also known later as Kouklia or Palaepaphos (old Paphos), west coast city of Alasiya (Kyprio or Cyprus), where goddess Aphrodite is said to have been born

Peloponnese = the Peloponnesian peninsula of Hellas (Greece)

Perkote = Percote, minor city located on the Asian side of the Hellespont

Phasis River = Rioni River in today's Georgia, main river of ancient Kolkhis

Phasis, port of Kolkhis on the Phasis River

Pitassa, Hittite satellite kingdom to the west

Pontic Mountains, of northern Anatolia beyond Hattusa and next to the Pontus

Pontos = Pontus, Black Sea, or a small kingdom next to the sea in Anatolia

Pontos Axeinos = Pontos Euxinos or Black Sea, also known simply as Pontos

Propontis = Sea of Marmara, body of water between the Hellespont and the Bosporus, and between the Aegean and the Black Sea (Pontos)

Puruma River, near Lawazantiya that flows into the Mesogeios Sea

Pylos, major southern seaport in the Peloponnesos of Hellas

Rodos = Rhodes, island of

Samura River = the Pyramos or Jihun, now the Ceyhan

Sangarios River = Sakarya River in today's Turkey

Sapinuwa, town NW of Hattusa.

Sardis, minor city of the Bronze Age Seha River Land, later Iron Age capital of the kingdom of Lydia

Seha River Land = district of Maionia, later part of the kingdom of Lydia

Sestos, minor city located on the European side (Thrace) of the Hellespont

Sikelia = modern Sicily

Smyrna = modern Izmir, settled by Aeolian Hellenes in the late Bronze Age (burned 1197, rebuilt as Ionian)

Sukziya, village in the SE Taurus Mountains of Anatolia, on the Mala/Euphrates River

Tarhuntassa, city and kingdom on south Anatolian coast near Mediterranean Sea

Tarsa = Tarsos or Tarsus, port city in southern Anatolia near to the Mediterranean Sea (likely destroyed 1195 by sea invaders)

Taruisa = Troy (Troy VI destroyed 1275 & Troy VIIa 1199) or Ilios

Tatta Lake = Lake Tuz or Salt Lake in modern Turkey

Thebai = ancient Hellenic (Greek) spelling for Thebes, major city in Boiotia in Hellas

Tiryns, major city on the Argolid plain in Hellas, known for its massive walls

Ugarit, major port kingdom in north Syria near Mediterranean Sea (destroyed 1195)

Ura, port of Tarhuntassa in the Mediterranean Sea on the coast just above Alasiya (likely destroyed 1196)

Wilusa, the Hittite province in which Taruisa is located, the Troad to the Akhaians (phonetically equal to Ilios)

Zalpa = Zalpuwa, Black Sea port north of Nerik in Kaska lands

Sea Peoples & Others

Akhaian (Hellenic) = Achaean (Latinized), Bronze Age name for people of Argolis, Ahhiyawa in Hittite

Ahhiyawa (Hittite) = Akhaian

Danuna (Egyptian) = Denyen or Danaan

Ekwesh (Egyptian) = Akhaian from Kriti (Megalonisi)

Karkisa (Egyptian) = district in SW Anatolia, later Caria

Kehek (Egyptian) = Libyan Tribe, later in Lebanon

Khabiru (Akkadian) = Habiru (Aramaic) or Hebrews, pre-Israelite nomadic herders

Kushites (Egyptian) = from a kingdom within Nubia

Libu (Egyptian) = tribe of Libya, pre-Berbers

Lukka (Hittite) = later Lykians or Lycians, dwellers in Lukka Land

Maionians (Hellenic) = later Lydians

Meshwesh (Egyptian) = Libyan tribe, pre-Berbers

Nubians (Egyptian) = Kerma people just south of Egypt in the land of Kush or Sheba

Peleset (Egyptian) = Philistines, Kritins or Cretans

Shekelesh (Egyptian) = Sikeloi or Sikels from Sicily

Sherden or Shardana (Egyptian) = Sardinians

Sikeloi (Hellenic) = Sikels, Sicels, or Shekelesh from Sikelia (Sicily)

Teresh (Egyptian) = Tyrsenoi, Taruisians, Trojans

Termilai (Hellenic) = Lukka

Tjekker (Egyptian) = Kritins from Zakros

Tyrsenoi (Hellenic) = Tyrrhenians, Teresh, Etruscans

Weshesh (Egyptian) = Wilusans from the Troad

Destroyed Mykenaian (Mycenaean) Era Citadels

Argos (1205)

Miletos (Miletus, Milawata, Millawanda) (1197)

Mykenai (Mycenae) (1205)

Pylos (1193)

Thebai (Thebes) in Boeotia (1207)

Tiryns (1204)

Other small cities in the Argolid destroyed: Lerna, Asine, Mases

Gods or Mythic Places

Alalus, also Alalu, Hurrian version of the Sumerian creator God, An or Anu

Allani, Hurrian name for Ereshkigal, Goddess of the Underworld

Amitirita, Lukkan or Kriti goddess, Amphitrite to the Argives

Anu, or An, Sumero-Akkadian creator Sky God, father of all, but a *deus otiosus*

Anus, Hurro-Hittite version of Anu, in the Kumarbi myth cycle seen as son of Alalus

Aphrodite, Hellenic (Greek) Goddess of Love & Eroticism, *not* found in Bronze Age Linear B tablets.

Apulunas (Hittite), God of Gates, later replaced Drimios as Apollo in Hellas(?)

Ares, Hellenic God of War

Arinniti, Hittite Sun Goddess of Arinna

Ashima, Canaanite Goddess of fate

Ashtart, also Astarte or Attart, Semitic Goddess of love and war

Athene (Athene), Hellenic Goddess of wisdom and war

Baalshamin, also Ba'al Hadad, Storm-God, King of the Gods in Canaan (Ugarit)

Circe, minor goddess and enchantress among the Hellenes

Drimios, son Zeus in Linear B tablets, perhaps later Apollo

Enlil, Storm-God as far back as Sumer

Ereshkigal, Goddess of the Dead & the Underworld in Sumer & Babylonia, older sister of Ishtar-Inanna, known to the Hurrians as Allani

Eros, primordial Hellenic God of creation (later, the name of Aphrodite's son)

Gad, Amorite God of Fortune

Gaia = Earth, primordial Hellenic God identified with the earth

Gul Ses – Hutena & Hutellura – Goddesses of fate in Hurrian mythology

Hades, Hellenic God of death and the Underworld

Hekate, Hellenic Goddess of witchcraft and sorcery

Hepat (Hepa), Hurrian name for the Sun Goddess

Hermes, Hellenic God of border-crossing, luck, trickery, and insight

I Am, pre-Israelite Khabiru or Hebrew Storm-God, transcribed later as YHWH or Yahweh (Jehovah)

Illuyanka, dragon (the force of evil & destruction) at the Purulli New Year Festival

Inanna, ancient Goddess of Sumer, of love, beauty, sex, war, justice and power

Irkalla = Sumerian term for hell or the Underworld

Irpitiga, Hittite lord of the earth, chthonic, sometimes associated with earthquakes

Ishtar, Goddess of erotic love, beauty, & power, sister of Ereshkigal: worshipped by the Akkadians, Babylonians, and Assyrians under that name, akin to Hurrian Shaushka, Ugaritic Ashtart, & derived from Inanna, later becoming Aphrodite at Paphos and among the Hellenes

Kamrusepa, Hittite Goddess of healing magic

Khaos = Chaos (Hellenic), timeless dynamic void, pre-exists and underlies all being

Kubaba, Mother Goddess of Karkemish

Kumarbis or Kumarbi, Hurro-Hittite son of Alalus and father of Teshub, Syrian Dagan

Mneme, original Muse of Memory, later Mnemosyne

Moirai, the Three Fates, Hellenic version of the Gul Ses

Nergal, Underworld God of instigated death, consort of Ereshkigal, pictured with the body of a sword sunk into stone at Yazılıkaya (my "Mountain Temple of the Gods")

Ninshubur, sukkal (friend, advisor, administrator) to Inanna-Ishtar

Persephone, Hellenic (Greek) Goddess of the Underworld

Pirinkir, minor Hatti Goddess, similar to Shaushka in that her gender depended on her aspect (love=female, war=male)

Pirwa, ancient Hatti Goddess of horses, the name of the mare given to Kabi

Sharruma, Hurrian God of Nerik, son of Sun Goddess & the War & Storm-God of Nerik, protector of Tudhaliya IV

Shaushka, Hurrian & Hittite form of Ishtar in Lawazantiya, male as a war God, female as love goddess

Tarhunta (Hittite), Teshub (Hurrian) = Storm-God

Tartarus, primordial Hellenic God of the deepest pit of Hades or the Underworld

Telipinu, the vanishing God of the Hittites who may symbolize life's fluctuations in time

Teshub (Hurrian), Tarhunta (Hittite) = Storm-God

Uliliyassis, minor Hittite God of sexulity

Underworld = Irkalla, netherworld, land of the dead either deep into the Earth or below it

Ouranos = Uranus, primordial Hellenic God of the sky that emerged from Khaos

Zeus, Hellenic Storm-God, ruler of all Hellenic Gods

Appendix II: Citations of Ancient Sources

18, paraphrase:

> "All the lands of the Hatti are dying, so that no one prepares the sacrificial loaf and libation for you, O God. What god or demon has decreed this wasteland? Has thy son, the god Telipinu who brings vegetation, wandered off again and forgotten his duties? The ploughmen who used to work the fields of the gods have died, so that no one works or reaps the fields of the gods any longer. The miller-women who used to prepare sacrificial loaves of the gods have died, so that they no longer make the sacrificial loaves. As for the corral and the sheepfold from which one used to cull the offerings of sheep and cattle – the cowherds and shepherds have died, and the corral and sheepfold are empty. So it happens that the sacrificial loaves, libations, and animal sacrifices are cut off. And you come to us, O gods, and hold us culpable in this matter! I beseech you mighty Teshub, all-powerful Tarhunta, to relieve my land of its woes. Turn the plague, the hostility, the famine against my enemies. The crops have dried up and my people are starving. How can we worship you? *Bring us rain*!"

30, paraphrase:

> "O Mighty Storm-God and all gods, pay heed! It is I, My Majesty, who addresses you. Are we not bound together as the sky is to the earth? What have you done? Why have you allowed this wretched drought and sickness into the land? Why does the earth shake so often? O gods, whatever sin you perceive, either let the Wise Women or the diviners determine it, or let ordinary people see it in a dream! O gods, have pity on your land of the Hatti! On the one hand, it is oppressed by the plague, on the other hand it is

> oppressed by its enemies." [*continued below from another source*]

Source for both is Trevor Bryce, *Warriors of Anatolia: A Concise History of the Hittites.* Bloomsbury Academic, 2019, p. 114:

> "O gods, What is this that you have done? You have allowed a plague into Hatti, and the whole of Hatti is dying. No one prepares for you the offering bread and the libation anymore. The plowmen who used to work the fallow fields of the gods have died, so they not work or reap the fields of the gods. The grinding women who used to make the offering bread for the gods have died, so they do not make the god's offering bread any any longer. ... The cowherds and shepherds of the corrals and sheepfolds from which they used to select sacrificial cattle and sheep are dead, so that the corrals and sheepfolds are neglected. So it has come to pass that the offering bread, the libations, and the offering of animals have stopped. And you, O gods, proceed to hold the sin against us in that matter. ... O gods, whatever sin you perceive, either let a man of god come and declare it, or let the old women, the diviners, or the augurs establish it, or let ordinary persons see it in a dream. ... O gods, have pity on the land of Hatti. On the one hand it is oppressed with the plague, and on the other it is oppressed by hostility. ... Turn the plague, the hostility, the famine, and the severe fever toward Mittanni and Arzawa."

—Bryce is citing from "Mursili's Plague Prayers", in Itamar Singer, *Hittite Prayers (*edited by Harry A. Hoffner, Jr.). Brill, 2002, pp. 52-3

22, paraphrase:

> "To Ammurapi who rules Ugarit at my mercy. From My Majesty, your Lord. With My Majesty, all is well, but My Majesty is distressed that King Ammurapi did not come to his court as ordered for his required

obeisance. However, My Majesty notes we are all troubled by the drought and the unknown invaders in our lands, so My Majesty is grateful that Ammurapi has sent food and supplies to the Hittites at great privation to himself. Still, the unknown enemy advances against us in numbers beyond count. My troops are far afield and our numbers are few. I demand your military assistance. Send whatever is available. Look to it and send it to me now!"

Source is Manuel Robbins, *Collapse of the Bronze Age: The Story of Greece, Troy, Israel, Egypt, and the Peoples of the Sea*. Authors Choice Press, 2001, p. 201:

> "Among the hardened clay tablets found burnt & hardened in Ugarit: "There is an urgent message to Ammurapi, the last Ugarit king, from 'My Majesty, your lord'. From that, it is clear that the message is from the Great King of the Hittites. ... The message opens with the customary 'With the My Majesty, all is well', but Ammurapi is not even accorded the ... good wishes which custom demands, and is berated for his failure to come to the Hittite court to do his obeisance as vassal. However, the message acknowledges that Ammurapi has sent food and supplies to the Hittites at great privation to himself. Most important, the damaged text contains words about an enemy...:
>
> > "'The enemy advances against me and there is no number. ... our number is ... . send whatever is available, look to it and send it to me'."

—Robbins is citing from Tablet: RS-18.39: C. A. Schaeffer, *Mission de Ras Shamra-Tomb XI. Palas d'Ugarit*. Paris: Library Klincksieck, p. 62.

26, paraphrase:

> "May the Tabarna, the king, be dear to the gods! The land belongs to the Storm-God alone. He has made

> the Tabarna, the king, his administrator, and has given him the entire land Land of Hatti. The Tabarna shall continue to administer the entire land with his hand. May the Storm-God destroy whoever should approach the person of the Tabarna, the King, and the borders of Hatti!"

Source (with *Labarna* replacing *Tabarna* after 1st usage) found in Gary Beckman, "Goddess Worship—Ancient and Modern" (pp. 11-23). In Saul M. Olyan & Robert C. Culley (eds.), *"A Wise and Discerning Mind": Essays in Honor of Burke O. Long*. Providence: Brown Judaic Studies, 2000, p. 19. Beckman is citing from tablet IBot 1:30.

30, paraphrase:

> "Thou mighty gods above and below who see and know all, why have you allowed the gods of foreigners to enter the Land of the Hatti? Do the invading barbarians from the sea bring with them gods unknown to you? Invite their gods to feast with you, great gods, speak with them and ask what they want here. If they refuse to parley, warn them that the wrath of the Storm-God's thunderbolt will smite them all and their people too!"

Source found in Itamar Singer, "Who Were the Kaška?" Phasis 10(I), 2007, 166-181.

> "O gods of the Kaška land! We have summoned you before this assembly. Come, eat and drink! Now hear the accusations which we bring against you! The gods of the Hatti land have done nothing against you! But you, the gods of the Kaška land began war. You drove out the Hatti gods and took over their realm for yourselves. The Kaška men also began war. From the Hittites you took away their cities and drove them out of their fields and vineyards. The gods of Hatti and the Hatti people call for bloody revenge. The vengeance of the Hatti gods and the

> Hatti people will be wrought on you, the gods of the Kaška land and the Kaška people!"

—Singer is citing (ii 1-24; ANET 354 f.; E. von Schuler, 1965. *Die Kaškäer*. Berlin.: 171 ff. *and* "Hittite Prayers" (Albrecht Götze, trans.). In James B. Pritchard (ed.), *ANET: Ancient Near Eastern Texts Relating to the Old Testament with Supplements* (3rd ed). Princeton University Press, 1978, p. 399.

31, paraphrase:

> "Sun goddess of Arinna, my lady, queen of all lands! In the land of Hatti, you ordained your name to be the 'Sun goddess of Arinna', but also in the land which you have made the land of the cedar, you ordained your name to be Hepat – yet all are the Great Goddess Ishtar who arose in Babylon. As is known to all but those who hide their eyes, you, Great Goddess, ruled this land before the Hatti became the Hittites. You ruled alone yet as three, and priestess-queens carried out your will on Earth. Tarhunta the Storm-God was but your love-slave."

Source in Pritchard, 1978, p. 393. [Tablet: KUB 29.19 + 1193/u (CTH 383) i 1-13]

> "To the Sun-goddess of Arinna, my lady, the mistress of the Hatti lands, the queen of heaven and earth. Sun-goddess of Arinna, thou art queen of all countries! In the Hatti country thou bearest the name of the Sun-goddess of Arinna; but in the land which thou madest the cedar land thou bearest the name Hebat."

37, quotation with addition. Source in Bryce, 2019, pp. 121-122.:

> "I place a spindle and a distaff in the patient's hand, and he comes under the gates. When he steps forward through the gates, I take the spindle and distaff away from him. I give him a bow and arrows,

> and say to him all the while, 'I have just taken the femininity away from you and given you masculinity in return. You have cast off the sexual behaviour expected of women; you have taken to yourself the behaviour expected of men'. After this has been accomplished, the woman in him will enter the lamb, who shall be forthwith given to the gods."

—Bryce cites extract from Gabriella Frantz-Szabó (trans.) in Jack Sasson (ed.), *Civilizations of the Near East* (vol 3). New York, 1995, p. 2014. See also: Jared Miller, "Paskuwatti's Ritual: Remedy for Impotence or Antidote to Homosexulity?" *Journal of Ancient Near Eastern Religion* 10, 2010, pp. 83-9.

40, paraphrase:

> "Do you not know that among the Hatti women are treated as respected objects? You barbarians who have sex with any woman you choose do not realize the proper way of things! For the Hittites, it is not permitted that a brother sexually take his cousin or his sister, or that you look openly upon women that do not belong to you. You can build your own harem, but you are forbidden to look upon that of another man! Do you not know the story of Mariya? And for what reason did he die?" ... "Did not a lady's maid walk by and he look at her? But the father of My Majesty himself looked out of the window and caught him in the offence, saying, 'You – why did you look at her?' So he died for that reason. The man perished just for looking from afar. And now so shall you!"

Source in Adam Nicolson, *The Mighty Dead: Why Homer Matters*. Willam Collins, 2014, pp. 220-221:

> "For us the Hittites, it is an important custom that a brother does not take his sister or female cousin sexually. It is not permitted. Whoever does such a thing is put to death. Because your land is barbaric,

> it is in conflict [without law]. There a man quite regularly takes his sister or female cousin. But among the Hittites, it is not permitted. ... When you see a palace woman, jump out of the way and leave her a broad path." Did he remember the story of Mariya, ... perhaps a chieftain from Hayasa? "And for what reason did he die? Did not a lady's maid walk by and he look at her? But the father of My Majesty himself looked out of the window and caught him in his offence, saying, 'You – why did you look at her?' So he died for that reason. The man perished just for looking from afar. So you beware."

—Nicolson is citing Gary Beckman (ed.), *Hittite Diplomatic Texts* (2nd ed). SBL Writings from the Ancient World series, Society of Biblical Literature, 1999, pp. 31-32.

48, quotation. Source in Robbins, p. 184:

> "I mobilized and I, Suppiluliuma, the Great King, immediately crossed the sea. The ships of Alasiya met me in the sea three times for battle, and I smote them; and I seized the ships and set fire to them in the sea. But when I arrived on dry land, the enemy from Alasiya came in a multitude against me for battles..."

—Robbins cites H. G. Guterbock, "The Hittite Conquest of Cyprus Reconsidered". *Journal of Near Eastern Studies* 26, 1967.

145, paraphrase:

> "O Great King of the Hatti. To my bottomless regret I am unable to send you any support in grain or troops. Ships of the enemy have been seen at sea! The enemy ships have been coming and burning my cities and doing terrible things in my country. All my troops and chariots are in the land of Hatti, and all my ships are in Lukka country. My land has been left defenceless. I beg you to send military forces to help me fight back these invaders!"

Source in Robbins, p. 188:

> "May my father know that the enemy ships came. My cities were burned and evil things were done in my country. Does my father know that my troops are stationed in the Hittite land and my ships in Lukka country? Thus, the country is abandoned to itself. May my father know this. Seven ships of the enemy have come here and did us much damage. Be on the lookout for other enemy ships and send me warning."

—Robbins cites tablet tERS 20.238 in C. A. Schaeffer (J. Nougayrol et al., trans.), *Ugartica V. Mission de Ras Shamra Tome XVI*. Paris, 1968.]

146, quotation. Source is Trevor Bryce, & Adam Hook, illustrations, *Hittite Warrior*. Osprey Publishing, 2007, p. 47:

> "As for what you have written me: 'Ships of the enemy have been seen at sea!' Well, you must remain firm. Indeed for your part, where are your troops, your chariots stationed? Are they not stationed near you? No? Behind the enemy, who press upon you? Surround your towns with ramparts. Have your troops and chariots enter there, and await the enemy with great resolution!"

—Bryce cites from: C. A. Schaeffer (J. Nougayrol et al., trans), *Ugartica V. Mission de Ras Shamra Tome XVI* (Paris, 1968), pp. 85-86, No. 23.

182, paraphrase:

> "It was the people from your country and your own ships who did this! And it was the people from your country who committed these transgressions... Truly, may you know this. Be on the alert!"

Source is Robbins, p. 188:

> "Concerning the matter of the enemy, your people and your ships, and of the about face of your people, do not complain to me. Twenty enemy ships slipped away into the mountain region and were not stopped and we don't know where they have gone. I am writing to inform you. Truly, may you know this."

—Robbins cites *RS 20.18*: C. A. Schaeffer (J. Nougayrol et al., trans), *Ugartica V. Mission de Ras Shamra Tome XVI.* Paris: Library Klincksieck, 1968.

192, paraphrase:

> "From Shipibaal your servant. To the feet of my Lord seven times seven from afar I fall. Your servant in Lawazantiya fortified his position with the Great King, telling him of the attack on our ancient city from the unknown invaders from the sea. I pleaded for help. But behold, the King wept, retreated, fled, and elsewhere made prayer and sacrifices. All is lost, my Lord. You must flee."

Source is Robbins, p. 202:

> "From Shipibaal your servant. To the feet of my lord seven times seven from afar I fall. Your servant in Lawazantiya fortified his positions with the King, And behold, the King retreated, fled, and there made sacrifices..."

—Robbins cites *RS-18.40*: C. A. Schaeffer (J. Nougayrol et al., trans), *Mission de Ras Shamra-Tomb XI. Palas d'Ugarit*. Paris: Library Klincksieck, 1968, p. 63.

198, quotation — also in the *Epigraph*, p. xi.

> "When your messenger arrived promising help, the army was already humiliated and the city sacked. Our food on the threshing floors was burnt and the vineyards were also destroyed. Our city is sacked. May you know it! May you know it!"

— Source is Bernard Knapp & Sturt W. Manning, "Crisis in Context: The End of the Late Bronze Age in the Eastern

Mediterranean." *American Journal of Archaeology* 120 (1), January 2016: 99-149, p. 120. —Knapp & Sturt are citing tablet RS-19.11 in Virolleaud, 1967, 137 (14). (Dietrich et al., 1976, 2.61). Translation by Singer, 1999, p. 722.

230, paraphrase:

> "Alalus was king in heaven, but Anus became more powerful. He served as Alalus's cupbearer for nine years and then defeated him, dispatching him to under the earth. He took his seat on the throne and made Kumarbis his cupbearer. Likewise, after nine years Kumarbis rebelled. He chased Anus and bit off and swallowed his phallus, which joined the previously swallowed Storm-God within Kumarbis. However, Anus had revenge by impregnating Kumarbis via the swallowed member. The rest of Anus hid himself in heaven, from where he advised the Storm-God, Teshub, on how to exit Kumarbis, that is, via his butt hole. After causing the monster Kumarbis much pain, the Storm-God slid through the lower channel in a messy and painful birth. Together, Storm-God (after considerable ritual cleansing) and Anus plotted to destroy Kumarbis and, with other gods, apparently succeeded."

—Source is Turkish website on the Hittite creation myth:
https://www.allaboutturkey.com/hittite-gods.html

244, quotation. Source in Nicolson, p. 221: explaining a vassal-king's proper behaviour to the King of the Amurru (ca. 1250 BCE), so from Hattusili III:

> "If the King of Egypt is My Majesty's friend, he shall be your friend. But if he is My Majesty's enemy, he shall be your enemy. And the Kings who are my equals in rank are the King of Egypt, the King of Babylonia, the King of Assyria and the King of the Ahhiyawa."

—Also in Bryce, 2019, p. 236, noting the word "Ahhiyawa" had been crossed out on original tablet. Both citing from

408
Gary Beckman, Trevor Bryce, & Eric Clyne, *The Ahhiyawa Texts*. Atlanta: Society of Biblical Literature, 2012, p. 50.

307, paraphrase:

> "Telipinu disappears unpredictably like time or life itself, and appears again only when ready, not like the orderly change of seasons. He is the boundary-crosser."

Source is Mircea Eliade, *A History of Religious Ideas: Vol 1. From the Stone Age to the Eleusinian Mysteries* (W. R. Trask, trans). University of Chicago Press, 1978, p. 143:

> "Telipinus is a god who, angered, hides—that is to say, disappears from the world around him. He does not belong to the category of vegetation gods, who die and return to life periodically. ... [W]hat distinguishes Telipinus from the vegetation gods is the fact that his discovery and reanimation by the bee make the situation worse. ... The specific characteristic of Telipinus is his demonic rage, which threatened to ruin the entire country. What we have here is the capricious and irrational fury of a fertility god against his own creation, *life* in all its forms. ... The fact that the role of Telipinus was also given to gods of the storm and the sun and to certain goddesses—that is, in general, to divinities governing various sectors of *cosmic life*—proves that the myth refers to a more complex drama than that of vegetation; in fact, it illustrates the incomprehensible mystery of the destruction of the Creation by its own creators."

321, paraphrase:

> "Keeper of the dread waters, open thy gate,
> Open thy gate that I may enter.
> If thou openest not the gate that I may enter
> I will strike the door, the bolts I will shatter,

I will strike the threshold and will pass through the doors;

I will raise up the dead to devour the living,

Above the living the dead shall exceed in numbers."

Source is Donald A. Mackenzie, *Mythology of the Babylonian People*. Bracken Books, 1915, pp. 95-96, citing original texts from Babylonia:

Keeper of the waters, open thy gate,

Open thy gate that I may enter.

If thou openest not the gate that I may enter

I will strike the door, the bolts I will shatter,

I will strike the threshold and will pass through the doors;

I will raise up the dead to devour the living,

Above the living the dead shall exceed in numbers.

321, paraphrase:

"I spread like a bird my hands.

I descend, I descend to the house of darkness, the dwelling of the god Ereshkigal:

To the house out of which there is no exit,

To the road from which there is no return:

To the house from whose entrance the light is taken,

The place where dust is their nourishment and their food mud.

Its chiefs also are like birds covered with feathers;

The light is never seen, in darkness they dwell ...

Over the door and bolts is scattered dust."

Source is Mackenzie, 1915, citing original texts from Babylonia, p. 95:

I spread like a bird my hands,

I descend, I descend to the house of darkness, the dwelling of the god Irkalla [hell]:

To the house out of which there is no exit,

To the road from which there is no return:

To the house from whose entrance the light is taken,

The place where dust is their nourishment and their food mud.

Its chiefs also are like birds covered with feathers;

The light is never seen, in darkness they dwell ...

Over the door and bolts is scattered dust.

323-324, paraphrase:

"Let me weep over the strong who have left their wives,

Let me weep over the handmaidens who lost the embrace of their husbands,

Over the only son let me mourn, who ere his days are come is taken away...

Go, keeper, open the gate to him,

Bewitch him according to the ancient rules.

He shall be treated like any other living who dares to come this way."

Source is Mackenzie, 1915, citing original texts from Babylonia, p. 96:

Let me weep over the strong who have left their wives,

Let me weep over the handmaidens who lost the embrace of their husbands,

Over the only son let me mourn, who ere his days are come is taken away...

Go, keeper, open the gate to her,

Bewitch her according to the ancient rules.

330, quotation:

"I am she that is the natural mother of all things, mistress and governess of all the elements, the initial progeny of worlds, chief of the powers divine, queen of all that are in hell, the principal of them that dwell

> in heaven, manifested alone and under one form of all the gods and goddesses. At my will the planets of the sky, the wholesome winds of the seas, and the lamentable silences of hell are disposed; my name, my divinity is adored throughout the world, in divers manners, in variable customs, and by many names. ... Behold I am come to take pity of thy fortune and tribulation; behold I am present to favour and aid thee; leave off thy weeping and lamentation, put away thy sorrow, for behold the reborn day that is adorned by my providence."

—Source in Joseph Campbell, *The Masks of God: Primitive Mythology* (rev. ed.). Penguin Books, 1969, p. 56. Campbell cites Isis addressing Apuleius, ca. 150 CE: Apuleius, *The Golden Ass* (W. Adlington, trans.), Book XI.

331, paraphrase:

> "Why, O Gatekeeper, didst thou take the great crown from my head?" he asked.
>
> "Enter, my lord, such is the command of Allani, the Mistress of the Nether World."

Source is Mircea Eliade (editor & commentator), *From Primitives to Zen: A Thematic Sourcebook on the History of Religions*. Harper & Row, 1967, pp. 321-3.

> "Why O gatekeeper, didst thou take the great crown on my head?"
>
> "Enter, my lady, thus are the rules of Allani, the Mistress of the Nether World."

—Eliade cites E. A. Speiser (trans.), *Ancient Near Eastern Texts*. Princeton University Press, 1950, p. 106.

344, paraphrase

> "...he saw a mound of the *halenzu-plant* stir beneath a quiescent but large beehive swinging from a low branch"

Source is Gary Beckman, "Intrinsic and Constructed Sacred Space in Hittite Anatolia" (pp. 153-174). In Deena Ragavan (ed.), *Heaven on Earth: Temples, Ritual, and Cosmic Symbolism in the Ancient World.* University of Chicago Press – Oriental Series Seminars 9, 2013, p. 153.

> "[The deity] proceeded to disappear into the moor. The ḫalenzu-plant spread over him."

—Beckman cites *Keilschrifturkunden aus Boghazköi.* Berlin 17.10 (Emmanuel Laroche, *Catalogue des Textes Hittites*, 2nd ed. *Études et commentaires* 75. Paris: Klincksieck, 1971 324.1.A) i 5′–18′, p. 151.)

345, paraphrase:

> "Shipibaal tried to explain, but soon Telipinu was sitting up and grimly explained,'*I dreamt I was in an uncontrollable rage. A giant bee had stung me and I was out of my mind. I destroyed everything around me in all realms. I brought life to standstill...*'"

Source is the myth of the disappearing god, Telipinu, who, angry at the world disappears for hibernation under the ḫalenzu-plant. When he is found, he cannot be awakened, so a goddess causes a bee sting him. Rather than bringing him back, this incites him to be roused into a demonic frenzy of destruction.

> "[W]hat distinguishes Telipinus from the vegetation gods is the fact that his discovery and reanimation by the bee make the situation worse. ... The specific characteristic of Telipinus is his demonic rage, which threatened to ruin the entire country." (Eliade, 1978, p. 143)

347, paraphrase:

> "Arise then, go, hero, the road of 'No Return'—...
>
> He goeth, he goeth, to the bosom of Earth—
>
> He will cause abundance for the land of the dead...
>
> At the call of the Goddess.

Go, hero, to the distant land which is unseen."

Source is Joseph L. Henderson & Maud Oakes (1963), *The Wisdom of the Serpent: The Myths of Death, Rebirth & Resurrection*. Collier-MacMillan, p. 21.

"Arise then, go, hero, the road of 'No Return'—...
He goeth, he goeth, to the bosom of the earth—
He will cause abundance for the land of the dead...
At the call of the Goddess,
Go, hero to the distant land which is unseen."

—Henderson & Oakes cite T. G. Pinches, "Tammuz," *Hastings Encyclopaedia of Religion and Ethics*, Vol XII. New York: Charles Scribner's Sons, 1909, p. 189.

347, quotation: "*Tammuz of the Abyss*", in Mackenzie, 1915, p. 81.

347-348, paraphrase:

"She fixed an eye on him: the eye of death! She spoke a word against him: the word of despair! She cried out against him: the cry of damnation! 'This one', she commanded the demons, 'carry him away'."

Source in Eliade, 1978, p. 65:

"She fixed an eye on him: the eye of death! She spoke a word against him: the word of despair! She cried out against him: the cry of damnation! 'This one' (she said to the demons), 'carry him away'."

—Eliade cites Jean Bottéro (trans.), *Annuaire de l'Ecole des Hautes Etudes*, sec. 4 (1971-72), p. 85.

349, quotation:

"Our mother,
The goddess with the mantle of snakes,
Is taking me with her

As her child.

I weep."

Source is Erich Neumann, *The Great Mother: An Analysis of the Archetype* (Ralph Manheim, trans.). Bollingen Series XLVII, Princeton University Press, 1955, p. 208. (Aztec myth: Quetzalcoatl sings a lament for himself, in which he reveals the background of his downfall.)

—Neumann cites Walter Krickeberg, *Märchen der Aztek und Inkaperuaner, Maya und Muisca.* (Märchen der Weltliteratur.) Jena, 1928, p. 67.

349-350, paraphrase:

"Oh hero, my lord, ah me! You are lost to me.

The holy one of Ishtar, in the middle of the year the fields languish ...

The shepherd, the wise one, the man of sorrows, why have they slain you?

Because of the exalted one of the nether world, death rules the fields.

The child, lord of knowledge, abides no more ...

In the meadows, verily, verily, the soul of life perishes."

Source is Mackenzie, 1915, p. 86:

"Oh hero, my lord, ah me! I will say,

Food I eat not ... water I drink not ...

Because of the exalted one of the nether world, him of the radiant face, yea radiant,

Of the exalted one of the nether world, him of the dove-like voice, yea dove-like.

The holy one of Ishtar, in the middle of the year the fields languish ...

The shepherd, the wise one, the man of sorrows, why have they slain [you]?

In his temple, in his inhabited domain,

The child, lord of knowledge, abides no more ...

> In the meadows, verily, verily, the soul of life perishes."

—Mackenzie cites Langdon, *Sumerian and Babylonian Psalms*, pp. 319-321.

351, paraphrase: "Tammuz, the forlorn shepherd, the *pre-eminent steer of heaven.*"

Source in Mackenzie, 1915, p. 85:

> "Tammuz in the hymns is called the 'pre-eminent steer of heaven'."

362, quotation:

> "Thou art the pristine spirit, the nature of which is bliss; thou art the ultimate nature and the clear light of heaven, which illuminates and breaks the self-hypnotism of the terrible round of rebirth, and now thou art the one that muffles the universe, for all time in thine own very darkness."

Source Neumann, 1955, p. 334. Neumann cites Heinrich Zimmer, *The King and the Corpse*, Joseph Campbell (ed.). New York & London, 1948, p. 264.

362, quotation — also in the *Epigraph*, p. xi:

> "And I shall destroy everything I created. Earth will again appear as primordial ocean, as endlessness as in the beginning. I then am everything that remains – after I have turned myself back into a snake that no man knows."

Source, Neumann, 1955, p. 217. Neumann cites Hermann Kees, *Der Götterglaube im alten Aegypten* (*Mitteilungen der Vorderasiatisch-Ägyptischen Gesellschaft*, Vol. 45). Leipzig, 1941, p. 216. Primordial ocean as ouroboric snake returns all existence to itself.

371, paraphrase:

> "Then forth he came, his both knees faltering, both his strong hands hanging down, and all with froth

> his cheeks and nostrils flowing, voice and breath spent to all use, and down he sank to death. The dark river had soaked his heart through."

Source Chapman's translation of *The Odyssey*:

> Then forth he came, his both knees faltering, both
> His strong hands hanging down, and all with froth
> His cheeks and nostrils flowing, voice and breath
> Spent to all use, and down he sank to death.
> The sea had soaked his heart through.

—George Chapman, *George Chapman: Homer's 'Odyssey'* (edited by Gordon Kendal). Cambridge, 2016, p. 134.

Image & Map Identification & Source

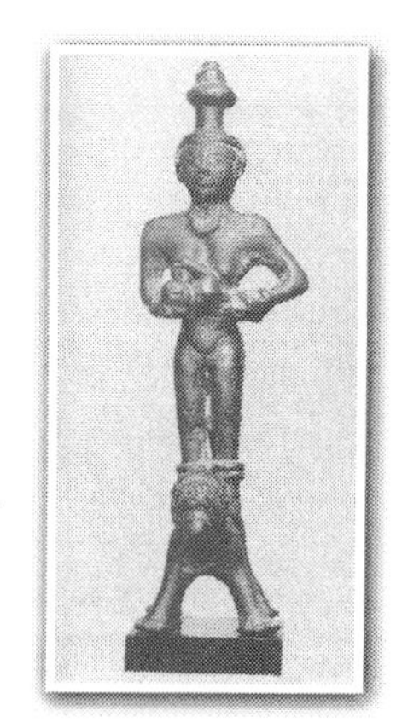

Note that in both my Ancient Sources and various images of the Goddess of the Great Round, I do not restrict myself to the time or place in which my tale is set. Since it seems to me the inspiration for all such images or quotations is archetypal or psychologically universal, they are all relevant. The teleological archetype has no form of its own but is the inspiration for the multiple cultural forms given to the Great Goddess. So one quotation about the Snake Goddess is from the Aztec myth of Quetzalcoatl, and the middle statue of the Snake Goddess on my back cover (though it may depict a dancer) is from the Dahomey Kingdom in what is now Benin, Africa, in the 19th century.

Images

— *Front cover*: head of the statue of Diomedes Stealing the Palladion, Roman copy from the 2nd-3rd century CE after a Greek original of the 5th century BCE, now in the Louvre Museum, Paris, public domain *https://salomi.tumblr.com/post/188650764521/statue-of-diomedes-roman-copy-from-the-2nd-3rd*

— *Back cover*: relief carving of Suppiluliuma II, made during his reign, part of the Hieroglyph Chamber in Hattusa, Turkey *https://pt.wikipedia.org/wiki/Supiluliuma_II* (Wikimedia Commons)

— *Back cover*: Goddesses left to right: Ishtar or Ashtart of Babylon (Parthian), Hellenistic, AD, 22cm in alabaster, gold, terracotta, & rubies, Louvre, public domain

—Snake Goddess (may be dancer), Dahomey late 19th century; copper alloy, gilt, height: 13.9cm. Brooklyn Museum, public domain

—Inanna-Ishtar or Ereshkigal – "Burney Relief" or "Queen of the Night" 49.5cm tall, baked clay. Old Babylonian, 19th - 18th BCE, British Museum, public domain (identified by some with Lilith of the Hebrew tradition)

— *Title page*: Royal Seal of Suppiluliuma II (Wikimedia Commons)

—*Epigraph*, p. iv, earth ouroboros, by Iona Miller, "Jungian Genealogy", used with permission

https://jungiangenealogy.weebly.com/alchemy.html

—*p. 27*: Charles Texier's drawing of major cliff-wall bas-relief carving at Yazılıkaya, 1862 *https://commons.wikimedia.org/wiki/File:YazilikayaTexier.jpg* (Wikimedia Commons)

—*This page* (above), Goddess Holding Child on Lion, bronze, Hittite, ca. 1500 BCE. In Neumann, *The Great Mother* (1955), p. 37 in the Plates. His source was the Eranos Archives, public domain. Preceded in wood as the Palladion?

Maps

1. Invasion & migration routes of the People of the Sea, *https://indo-european.eu/2019/07/sea-peoples-behind-philistines-were-aegeans-including-r1b-m269-lineages/*
2. Anatolia, Hittite Empire, from Manuel Robbins (2001), p. 162. Map prepared from the author's draft by MATRIX, York, Pennsylvania.
3. Hattusa, from *http://mnabievart.com/oldwebsite/old/info_mn/article_12.html*

®DokNyx Publications

Gregory Michael Nixon, Mountain Drive
Vernon, BC, Canada

websites:
linktr.ee/doknyx
https://authorgregorynixon.com/
https://www.instagram.com/doknyx86/
https://www.facebook.com/AuthorGregoryNixon/
https://www.facebook.com/profile.php?id=100089912439773
https://gregorynixon.academia.edu

Email contact welcome: *doknyx@icloud.com*

Made in the USA
Monee, IL
12 March 2024

54882098R00249